Fiona O'Brien

The Summer Visitors

HACHETTE
BOOKS
IRELAND

First published in Ireland in 2017 by
HACHETTE BOOKS IRELAND

1

Cataloguing in Publication Data is available from the British Library

ISBN 9781473647817

Typeset in Caslon by redrattledesign.com

Printed and bound in Great Britain by Clays Ltd, St Ives plc

Hachette Books Ireland policy is to use papers that are natural, renewable
and recyclable products and made from wood grown in sustainable forests. The
logging and manufacturing processes are expected to conform to the environmental
regulations of the country of origin.

Hachette Books Ireland
8 Castlecourt Centre
Castleknock
Dublin 15, Ireland

A division of Hachette UK Ltd
Carmelite House, 50 Victoria Embankment, EC4Y 0DZ

www.hachettebooksireland.ie

For Sean, with love

Author's Note

Writing *The Summer Visitors* took me back to Waterville a small village in west Kerry where I holidayed as a child and have returned to ever since. However, while Waterville inspired the writing of this book, the village of Ballyanna, its inhabitants and all the events within these pages are entirely the work of my imagination. Any resemblance to persons, living or dead, is entirely coincidental.

The idea for and details of the cable station referred to in the book are also adapted with artistic licence. In 1884 a cable was laid by *American Commercial Cable Company*. This cable came ashore in Waterville, County Kerry from Canso, Nova Scotia, and was in operation until 1962. However, the original submarine trans-Atlantic cable was laid in 1858 in Valentia Island off the coast of Kerry but it wasn't until 27 July 1866 that the Great Eastern laid what would be the successful cable between Valentia Island and Heart's Content, Newfoundland. This was operated by *The Atlantic Telegraph Company* from 1866 to 1966.

Looking out across the Atlantic Ocean, the little village of Ballyanna sits on the rugged southwest coast of Ireland. At first glance – apart from the arresting beauty of its surrounding coastline – there is not much to differentiate it from the many other seaside villages up and down the country. Around 150 years ago, however, it was a very different story indeed. Back then, Ballyanna was a vitally important location. For it was here, on this very beach, that the first transatlantic submarine cable came ashore. This ground-breaking technology meant that for the first time in history, America could connect with Europe in a matter of minutes – as opposed to news travelling by ship, which could take weeks – changing forever the way the two continents would communicate. Ballyanna and its cable station became a kind of Silicon Valley, with highly trained telegraphers relaying messages back and forth across the Atlantic via cable code, providing a communication network that would have been unthinkable just a few decades before.

But that was all a long time ago. Today, the cable station is a relic of times gone by, a low, stone ruin that looks out, rather forlornly, over the ocean its messages once traversed. The arrival of satellites in the 1960s rendered the old cable redundant. And then, as so often happens, history repeated itself. New, advanced fibre optic cables were invented and once again laid beneath the ocean from continent to continent, all around the globe.

The village of Ballyanna lost its status as a communication hub, lapsing back into its quiet, dependable rhythms. Now, though, something is disturbing those reliable patterns of village life. Something, or someone, seems determined to make themselves heard, whatever the cost, however precarious the means. And for one last time, the old cable station, for so long silent, will facilitate a vitally important communication between two very different worlds . . .

* * *

She looks around one more time, to triple check, although she knows already that everything is perfect. The small Notting Hill home she and Ed have made their own looks back at her, as if sensing her anticipation. The little house is tasteful, yet artfully flamboyant, the perfect canvas for Ed's legendary art-directing talents. Annie would never have achieved such an original effect on her own, she thinks, not in a million years. But then, everything Ed owned and worked on became beautiful, in time.

Annie straightens the dress he says he loves on her, the one he says makes her gold-flecked eyes even greener, the one, he says, with his wicked grin, that he immediately longs to take off her. Her red-gold hair is freshly washed, long and wavy, the smattering of freckles across her nose still visible through her subtle make-up. She fiddles with the silver bangle on her wrist, Ed's first gift to her and the only piece of jewellery she wears. The inscription, in small black script, reads Walk on the wild side . . . She takes a deep breath, forces herself to be still.

She has waited until tonight, their fourth anniversary. Ed is coming back after spending five days shooting a commercial in Cape Town. She has planned a special romantic dinner at home to mark the occasion.

She hears a key turning in the front door and waits. The door pushes open and there he is, handsome, irrepressible, his eyes raking over her, registering approval and pleasure. With a theatrical flourish, he produces a huge bouquet of flowers. 'Bet you thought I'd forgotten.'

'I wouldn't have cared if you had.' Annie means it. 'I'm just glad you're back. There's champagne in the fridge, and tuna steak for dinner.'

'Just let me have a hot shower first.' He drags his bags inside and grabs her in a mock weary embrace. 'Then I'll show you exactly how much I've missed you.'

Dinner is perfect, just as she hoped it would be. They drink the champagne, eat the seared tuna, talk and laugh about Ed's trip.

'Tell me about Hubble and the merger,' Ed says. 'Have you made up your mind what you're going to do?'

Annie twists the stem of her champagne flute in her fingers. Hubble is the advertising agency she set up three years ago, and she and her partners have just put the finishing touches to a lucrative merger with a global conglomerate. The payoff means she doesn't need to work again, but the board are keen for her to stay on as creative director.

'I'm not sure,' Annie says. 'Part of me would like a brand new challenge, but on the other hand, I'm not sure if I'm ready to hand over my baby to strangers just yet.'

'Are you kidding?' He grins at her. 'They'd have to prise you off the board of Hubble like a barnacle! You'll be there forever!'

After dinner, Annie makes coffee while Ed pours himself a brandy. As she sits back down, he reaches for her hand across the table, where they linger for a while.

'Happy Anniversary, babe. You're the best thing that's ever happened to me.' He kisses her wrist tenderly. It's a perfect moment. So perfect, that for weeks, months, even just days afterwards, Annie would try to remember *how* perfect. As if she could freeze-frame that one moment and erase all that came after.

'Ed, honey.' She takes a breath, her hand still in his. 'It's been over a year . . . almost two since we talked about it . . . I really want us to try for a baby . . .'

His face, even in the softness of candlelight, hardens.

'Just hear me out.' She has her pitch prepared.

'We've been through this before, Annie.'

'No we haven't! Not for ages. Not since . . . we've never even had a proper discussion about it. You just said to wait a year, and I have – more than a year.'

'I don't want a baby, Annie.'

This is a tone she hasn't heard before, weary with finality.

'But why not? What would be so terrible about having a baby of our own? You love kids. It would make everything perfect. We don't have to get married, if that's what's bothering you . . .'

'It's not, believe me.' Ed drops her hand, stands up and strides across the room until he's standing at the window, staring out into the darkness and his own reflection flickering in the candlelit glass. 'Ed, please!' Annie gets up and follows him over. 'Can't we at least just talk about this?'

'Just leave it, Annie, will you?' He turns around, wearing the look she has seen so many people shrink from in the boardroom, directed now at her. 'A baby's the last thing we need right now! Why did you have to bring this up tonight of all nights?' He runs his hands through his hair. 'I just wanted a nice quiet evening, and now it's ruined.'

'It's not ruined, Ed, *please*, just sit down.' He is scaring her now, the look on his face, the pacing, he is acting like a caged animal.

'It . . . it doesn't matter, forget I said anything, we don't have to—'

'Of course it matters!' His voice is raised now. 'Don't you think I *know* how much it matters?'

And then, just as quickly, his mood changes. He sits back down, his face in his hands, rubbing his eyes before looking at her.

'I'm so sorry, Annie. It's a complete bloody mess. I didn't want to tell you like this.'

'Tell me what?' She hears her voice, thin, unnaturally high.

And this is how she learns of Sarah, a young art director, part of a new team Ed has hired at his own agency. How he has been mentoring them, helping them with an important campaign, how Sarah has hero-worshipped him and how at first he found that amusing . . . before it turned into something different. And no, he hadn't meant for it to happen, of course not, it was just one of those things. But now . . . now he isn't so sure, and he doesn't know what to do . . . because now Sarah, who is twenty-nine, is six months pregnant.

Sean

This is it?

I didn't actually come out and say it, but that's what I was thinking. Pat was doing enough talking for both of us – he hadn't stopped, not since we'd landed at Shannon.

Shit. This was way worse than I'd expected. We were in the middle of, like, nowhere.

'Look!' Pat says, every three seconds. 'A sheep! A donkey! A bale of hay! A tractor!' Like we'd never been to the countryside before. Although the donkey, I admit, was cute.

Pat's my twin brother. We're eleven years old and identical, even Dad can't always tell us apart. We'd left the motorway about an hour ago and the roads had got narrower and twistier. We'd passed through some really strange-looking towns – nothing like home. And then, right ahead of us, beneath a cliff road, the ocean had suddenly appeared. But it was grey, like the sky – like everything here. But that was okay, it matched the way I felt inside.

'Okay back there?' Dad's eyes flicked in the rear-view mirror.

I nodded. Beside me, Pat was banging his forehead against the passenger seat.

In the mirror, Dad's eyes creased, which meant he was smiling. 'Won't be long now, we're almost there.'

Killorglin, Glenbeigh, Cahirciveen – weird names flashed by us, more twisty-turning roads, and then a church, a fork in the road, and signs that read *Ballyanna*, pointing both ways.

'Guess we'll take the scenic route,' said Dad, turning right. He always said that.

We drove by more fields, with funny stone walls in between, and came to the ocean again, turned left. There was a flash of sun just then, and for a moment everything looked bright and full of colours, but only for a moment. Then it went back to grey.

We turned in through a pair of iron gates and pulled up outside a big old house.

'This is it. Cable Lodge, that's us.'

The door opened and a woman came out. She waved. Dad got out of the car and we followed.

'Welcome.' The woman smiled, and shook hands with Dad. 'You must be the O'Connells. I'm sure you're exhausted after your journey.'

She was about the same age as Grandma, I guessed, but fatter, with chin-length brown hair that was longer at the front and shorter at the back. She had a nice smile. Her voice went up and down, like a song. Pat had already run past her, through the open door and up the stairs.

'Let me help you with your bags,' she said, bending to pick one up.

'Absolutely not.' Dad stopped her. 'I wouldn't hear of it!' He held out his hand. 'Hi, I'm Daniel. Most people call me Dan.'

'Daniel O'Connell,' she said, laughing. 'Well that's an easy name to remember around these parts. I'm Joan Coady. Welcome to Ballyanna. I'm here to let you in, see you've got everything you need.'

She was wearing cargo pants and a green t-shirt that said *Let's Swing!* in big black letters across her chest. I got the impression she was a bit hot and bothered, as Grandma would say. She looked at me then and blew a piece of hair away from her face. I decided I liked her.

'This is Sean,' said Dad.

'Hello, Sean.' She smiled down at me. 'Good to meet you.'

I nodded, but I kept my eyes on the writing on her t-shirt.

She must have noticed me looking at it because she laughed and said, 'I'm a very keen golfer – most of us are around here.'

Dad coughed. 'Take your bag inside, Sean and go choose your room. I need to talk to Joan.'

I followed after Pat, up the big old stairway that wound around and around, dragging my bag behind me. The house was warm, which was good, because the weather sure wasn't, not compared to home anyway, and it was already June. Upstairs there were some really big rooms, and the one at the front of the house had a double bed. There was a neat bathroom too, with a big old bath and lots of pipes.

I found Pat on the next floor, in a back bedroom with slanting ceilings. There were two small windows that looked out towards mountains in the distance and a big skylight above. Pat was climbing in and out of a freestanding wooden closet. There were three beds and a small, old-fashioned fireplace.

'Cool, huh?' Pat leaned in to examine the black metal shelf and coloured tiles around the grate.

I lifted my bag onto one of the beds and sat down.

'This is *my* room.' Pat said. 'I found it first. Go get your own.'

But I just kept sitting there, chewing my lip.

Pat straightened up and sighed. 'Oh, okay, we'll share it. But I get the bed by the window.'

I nodded. Easy deal. I didn't want to be on my own.

Pat went to look around and I began to unpack my clothes, putting them in the big chest of drawers that creaked when I pulled one open. Inside they were lined on the bottom with paper, the same kind that was on the walls, and someone had put in a little bag of nice-smelling stuff tied with coloured thread. It smelt of outside.

'I could hear them downstairs.' Pat came back in, and leaned against the window. 'He's telling her about how you're not talking.'

I went to stand beside him and pulled the blind up and down. It was raining now, running hard down the windowpanes.

'I heard them,' he went on. 'She said, "*the poor little fellow*".' Pat said that in a sing-song voice, just like Joan's. Pat could imitate anyone. 'It's been over a year now.' He gave me a dig in the ribs. 'Don't you think it's time you, like, said something? I mean, how long are you going to not talk for? It's really stupid.'

I knew he was right, but I just shrugged. I didn't know when I would talk again. I didn't know if I ever could.

* * *

One thing Dan O'Connell has learned in the last year – the only thing, maybe – is that life goes on. Even if you feel like you're walking through it on autopilot. Someone had stolen his, taken everything he knew, loved and lived by and turned it on its head. Some days he felt like he'd been sucked up by a twister, hurled around, and spat back down amidst the debris of a landscape he knew he should recognise but couldn't. And without familiar landmarks to navigate by, he was lost.

Husband, father, widower – those labels were supposed to tell him something about himself, but he was damned if he knew what it was. But he was still a father, even if he had no clue how to manage this new and terrifying version of parenthood. They would figure it out together. That's what he told himself anyhow.

'I think you *should* go,' Matt the bereavement counsellor had said. 'A change of scene will do you guys good, it might even be the breakthrough Sean needs. Some distance might give him a little perspective.'

'Can't do any harm,' Dr Shriver agreed when he ran the idea by her in her office. 'The question is, how will *you* handle it?' She'd looked at him through those tortoiseshell-framed glasses that made her brown eyes seem even bigger. 'You won't have the support framework you have here, Dan.'

'It's only for the summer,' he said. 'We'll be back in time for school. But at least it means I'm getting back to work. And apart from anything else, I need the money.'

'Of course you do. I understand.' As Sean's trauma specialist, Dr Shriver understood the practicalities of the situation as well as the nuances. She was a mom herself, after all. 'It could happen any time, Dan, you know that. Sean will talk when he's ready. Don't panic if it takes longer than you expect.'

'I keep telling myself that.'

'Good. You keep doing that.' She'd got up from her desk to show him out. 'I've never been to Ireland. I'd like to go. I have Irish ancestors, so does Kirk, my husband.'

'With a name like mine, I guess I must too. Maybe I'll get to look them up.' He'd smiled and turned to go.

'Dan?'

'Yes?'

'Try not to worry, try to have some fun. And remember, I'm at the other end of the phone if you need me.'

'Let's hope I don't. But thank you, Dr Shriver – for everything.'

'Any time, it's a pleasure.'

He meant it. Dr Shriver had been fabulous. In fact, everyone had been wonderful, and kept on being wonderful. Dan hadn't known so much kindness existed in the world.

It had been over a year now, since the accident, and somehow they had got through the first anniversary, but still Sean hadn't said a word – not one single word. Dan wondered if he ever would. The longer it went on, the more frightened he became. Dr Shriver said it was textbook post-traumatic stress disorder, that they had to continue as normally as possible, that Sean should go back to school, continue with his therapy and bereavement counselling and that when he was ready, then he would speak. In the meantime it was vital to keep the lines of communication open any way Dan could, to keep Sean from retreating any further.

Everyone was doing everything possible, but when it came to the crunch, Dan was still the breadwinner – whatever about not talking, they still had to eat.

The timing of this research trip couldn't have been better. He was to travel to Ireland, to a small village in the southwest called Ballyanna that was home – according to the tourist comments he'd trawled through online – to some jaw-dropping scenery, terrific trout and salmon fishing, and a world-class golf course. The irony of the project he would be researching was not lost on him. The submarine Atlantic cable had finally enabled people to communicate between continents for the first time in history. That was to be the subject of the documentary he and his crew would eventually produce. Now communication was the one thing denied him, just when they needed it most. Instead Dan had to wrestle with the silence of his son, which lay between them, as real and deep as any ocean and just as perilous to navigate.

He could do this, he knew he could. He *had* to, for the sake of his family. This was work – a return to normality of sorts, albeit in another country they'd never been to before. But maybe that was a good thing – travelling to a place without memories. That had to be an improvement, because he couldn't feel more of a stranger anywhere else than he already did in this bleak terrain his own life had become. At least in Ireland he wouldn't be surrounded by constant reminders of everything he'd lost. And maybe, just maybe, Sean might find his way to talking again. They might even find their new beginnings as a family – their way back to each other. Dan sure as hell hoped so.

* * *

It is the walking cliché bit she cannot bear, that makes her want to grind her teeth every time she thinks about it, which she can't help doing now as she takes one last look around the eerily empty house she used to call home. The contents have been divided, the furniture and paintings packed and put into storage, much like her feelings. Annie is done with feelings – look where they got her.

She drops the keys off at the estate agents, calls an Uber and heads back to Soho for a parting lunch with Theo, her co-founding partner at Hubble. It is June, and the city couldn't look prettier or more inviting. London does summer particularly well, she always thinks. It is her favourite time of year here, watching people shrug off their winter pallor along with their coats, emerging from their buttoned-up practicality and Englishness, seeming to finally unfurl in the welcome warmth. Even the statuesque architecture is softened and bathed in light. Although she is too busy these days to enjoy the typical summer pastimes of leisurely lunches in smart outdoor eateries, strolls through the parks or lazy evenings in riverside pubs, Annie enjoys knowing it is unfolding all around her. It is easier these days, she reflects, to watch other people's lives rather than to contemplate her own.

The cab drops her off at her favourite Greek restaurant in Berwick Street, where Theo is already holding court at his usual pavement table, a bottle of champagne chilling beside him.

'Celebrating already, Theo?'

'They insisted,' he says with a grin, pouring her a glass as she shakes her head and sits down. 'Although Cosmo doesn't really believe you're abandoning us, do you, Cosmo?' Theo looks to the elderly waiter for confirmation, who shakes his head and assumes an appropriately mournful expression.

'Neither can I.' Theo lifts his glass to hers. 'What will we do without you for three whole months? That's *if* you last that long. Personally I give it six weeks, max. Then you'll be climbing walls and bouncing off ceilings.'

'I thought we'd agreed that's what I'd be doing if I stayed here?'

'Ah yes.' Theo's eyes narrow. 'But that was when I thought you were going to escape to a spa on the far side of the world, or write your novel in a beach hut – not go home to Ireland . . .' He rattles their order off to Cosmo in fluent Greek then sits back in his chair to look at her. 'Are you really sure about this?'

'You know I am. And you know why.'

Theo holds her gaze and nods. 'I just, you know . . . wonder if it's the right thing . . . going home isn't always the answer.'

'Right now, it's the only one I've got. And besides, I'm needed there.'

'We need you here.'

'I'll only be an email away. We can Facetime, it'll be romantic, just as if I'm in the office, except with a different backdrop.'

'I was never good at long-distance relationships. I like my partners in the office, not another country.'

'We've been over all this,' she reminds him. 'Everything's been signed, everything's going ahead, my lawyer is on speed-dial if you need him . . .'

'I know,' Theo says, watching her carefully, 'but it won't be the same. Apart from anything else, I'm going to miss you.'

Annie smiles. 'I'll be back before you know it. When it's all over and . . . and things are back to normal.' She glances around the street, unwilling to meet his eyes.

Theo is still watching her. He sighs, takes a sip of champagne. 'Tell me about your family again, and why you have to go home to rescue everybody.'

'I'm not rescuing anybody. My dad isn't well, my sister's husband seems to have been involved in some very dubious financial dealings. Poor old mum is trying to cope with it all and could do with some help in the hotel. I need to find out what's going on and sort it. Damage limitation, Theo – not rescuing.'

'Why you?' Theo looks cross. 'You need a rest, not a family soap opera. Don't they know that?'

'You sound like my sister.'

'Why do you say that?'

'She says I'm a control freak. Too uptight for my own good and always trying to fix everyone, expecting the impossible from people, especially family.'

'And do you?' Theo raises an eyebrow.

Annie frowns. 'How can you ask me that? You know me as well as anybody.'

'I think the only person you expect the impossible from is yourself,' Theo says softly.

Annie ignores the comment. 'It's odd, I suppose, but I've never really felt I belonged with my family. I never understood all the unspoken rules the others seem to take for granted. We baffle each other at best and irritate the hell out of each other at worst. When I was younger, I couldn't wait to get away.'

'Sounds very normal to me, but then I'm Greek. You know what they say, you can choose your friends, but not your family . . . and don't forget, you have made your own family, Annie, here in London, with us.' Theo makes an expansive gesture. 'Think of all you have achieved in the last ten years. All the friends you have who care about you . . .'

'I know,' Annie sighs. 'But this is something I have to do, Theo, so no more discussions, please. I'm just going over to Ireland for twelve weeks to help out and not be here for a while, okay? Can we leave it at that?'

Theo holds up his hands in a gesture of defeat.

Lunch passes peaceably, they discuss clients, the agency and the merger. The past six months have been exhausting, since Hubble was targeted for a buyout by the multinational WHM&R. But after Ed's bombshell, Annie welcomed the chance to throw herself into work even more than usual, to the extent that her friends and colleagues began to worry about her.

That's why Theo had insisted she take a sabbatical. 'Go away, lie on a beach somewhere nobody knows you. Please, Annie, you're scaring us and it's only a matter of time before you start scaring off clients, you're radiating nervous energy. And you really don't look well.'

'I can't, Theo. I can't stop, because if I do it all comes back to me . . . work is the only escape I have.'

'I know, Annie, believe me I understand, but that's exactly why you need to stop, or you're going to make yourself ill. Is that what you want doing the rounds on the grapevine – that the inimitable Annie Sullivan has gone to pieces or had a breakdown over a failed romance . . . over a mere man?'

Annie had looked at him as if he'd slapped her across the face. The words stung, but they also achieved their intended effect, which Annie knew, deep down, was Theo's well-meaning, if blunt, attempt at forcing her to hear him and take him seriously. Reluctantly, she'd agreed. That had been six weeks ago.

People stop by the table to say hello, a television producer they work with joins them, sits down to chat for a few minutes. Theo is his usual ebullient self, but all the time he is discreetly watching her. Annie knows she is much more than a business partner to him – Theo and she are old and very dear friends, and she knows he has watched and worried about her these past three months as she has turned into someone even she doesn't recognise. Annie is far from stupid. She is fully aware people are whispering about the ridiculous hours she has been keeping at work, the weight loss, the tightness around her mouth, the uncharacteristically brittle humour and, most telling of all, the dark circles and hollows beneath her sad green eyes. But try as she might to pretend she was coping, she knew deep down she was falling apart.

Theo knew the whole story, of course, he would have anyway, even if Annie hadn't told him herself. The gossip had circulated indecently quickly.

He had listened sympathetically when she had told him. And although she was calm and matter-of-fact as she related the details, she could see from his expression that Theo felt her pain, her acute sense of betrayal and loss. He was deeply sorry for her, but not surprised. That was the hardest part, for Annie.

Theo had known Ed long before Annie had ever met him, and was well acquainted with the trail of broken hearts he'd left in his wake. So was Annie, if she was honest. She had gone in to the relationship with her eyes wide open. As womanisers go, Ed was right up there – handsome, brilliant, funny, and devastatingly charming. And the worst of it was, he was a genuinely nice guy. Theo liked him, everybody did – it was impossible not to. But as Theo's current wife, Kristina, so aptly pointed out, Ed was simply catnip to women, and he was equally enamoured of them, too. Annie had lasted longer than her predecessors. She had begun to believe they had a real future together. She tried, and failed, to hide her pleasure when people said that Ed had finally been tamed, finally found the one . . . and then the inevitable had happened.

Annie was stoic throughout the whole sorry mess that unfolded, but her close friends and colleagues knew the toll it took on her.

Eventually Theo told her he could stand it no longer and insisted she take a break. Get away, have a change of scene.

She admitted Theo was right. In certain circles – and advertising was one of them – London was as small as any village, and just as claustrophobic. It would be impossible for her to avoid Ed either in business or social situations. And given the current circumstances, that would be intolerable.

Three months will fly, Annie tells herself. She'll be back before she knows it, when all this unpleasant business is behind her and she can get back to doing what she does best.

All the same, when the waiter waves down the black cab to take her to Heathrow and Annie's suitcase is retrieved from behind the counter, she has a momentary lapse of composure. Without her artfully chic work uniform to hide behind, dressed as she is now, in just a simple t-shirt and jeans, Annie feels vulnerable and much younger than her thirty-six years.

When Theo gets up to enfold her in a bear hug, his eyes are bright.

'Stay in touch,' he instructs her. 'Call me when you have settled in, let us know how you're doing.'

Annie nods, not trusting herself to speak. It is kindness these days that is her undoing.

She clambers in to the taxi, puts on her sunglasses and closes her eyes, willing the driver not to chat. She doesn't want to be rude, but she will be curt if she has to be.

Once he has his directions, thankfully the cabbie doesn't try to engage her in cheery conversation. They manoeuvre Soho's tight corners, leaving the West End behind, then the motorway looms ahead, and for the first time, the familiar weight in Annie's chest gives way to panic. But there's no going back now, no matter what Theo might say. In her heart she knows that. So she takes a deep breath, blows her nose, and wipes the tears that leak from beneath her dark glasses. She will not cry. She will not indulge in self-pity. She is just very, very angry, and she has every right to be – at Ed, at his breathtaking betrayal and, most of all, at herself.

* * *

It is to be a perfect day on the peninsula, the local weatherman assured her on the radio this morning, but this good news has not improved Breda Sullivan's mood. Beneath the rigorously adhered-to and applied make-up regime that has sustained her for thirty years she feels sure her face is melting. This suspicion is confirmed by a trickle of sweat running down her back, stopped in its tracks only by the straining waistband of her tailored black trousers. Nonetheless she keeps a firm smile in place as she casts an eagle eye about the almost empty dining room, willing the last stragglers to get a move on so she and her staff can clear and reset the tables for the lunch service. After a lifetime spent growing up in and eventually running a small family hotel, there is precious little Breda doesn't know about handling people, and among the many talents she has cultivated is an impressive ability to persuade guests of what it is they want to do before the notion has actually dawned on them. The last diners in the room – a morose and mournful-looking couple who have been regulars of the hotel since they were honeymooners – linger over their newspapers and coffee, blissfully unaware of the seething irritation they are causing their host, who tries clattering some cutlery in their vicinity, but to no avail.

They aren't equipped for it, Breda reasons to herself, that's the problem. A normal summer is all well and good and to be hoped for, obviously, but this sudden heatwave, with temperatures soaring, is simply unnatural in Ireland. Whatever about the landscape, it doesn't suit the local temperament. Oh, the young people love it, of course, and sure why wouldn't they? They have the energy, not to mention the time and leisure, to enjoy it. She has watched the young girls strolling through the village and along the beachfront in barely-there outfits, for all the world like loose-limbed continentals. And the young lads are no better – loitering, goggle-eyed, at these newly unveiled visions of femininity and dark as gypsies themselves.

Why, to look at Ballyanna now you'd swear it was the south of France, or Italy, and not an extreme corner of southwest Ireland. Pots of colourful blossoms bloom extravagantly outside pubs and shops. Previously limp and uninspiring hanging baskets have sprung to life, trailing exotic flora, beset by bees. Outdoor tables and smart linen parasols have materialised along every available surface on Main Street, holding pride of place in courtyards of hotels, pubs, guesthouses and holiday homes, where scantily clad tourists and locals alike display deepening suntans and sip chilled white wine and designer beers. The rhododendrons and hydrangeas are preening in hitherto unheard-of inky, latticed, glory, and fuchsia abounds in a riot of scarlet along ancient low stone walls and fields.

Looking out the window of the dining room across the bay, and to the sweeping mountains beyond, Breda's heart softens. She sighs and tries to calm her racing thoughts. It's true what they say – when you get the weather, there is nowhere on earth more beautiful than Ballyanna. It's just this wretched heat she finds intolerable. It makes her feel old as well as irritable.

'All done, Mrs Carroll?' she asks brightly, whisking the heavy silver coffee pot engraved with her grandmother's initials from the table.

'What's that?' The woman looks up from her paper, confused for a moment, before rearranging her features into a mask of even greater misery.

'Oh, I suppose we are, Breda, yes.' Her tone is one of impending doom.

Her husband finally gets heavily to his feet, folding his paper under his arm.

'Your picnic will be ready at reception as usual.' Breda injects extra cheer into the exchange. 'You're certainly getting the weather to be out on the lake.' The Carrolls, like many of their regulars, are keen anglers.

As soon as they have left, Breda sets about the dining room methodically, clearing and resetting tables with unusual vigour. She thinks if she works hard and fast enough, she can keep the worries at bay, but soon realises that's just another exercise in futility. Her husband springs to mind first. She hopes to get him out from under her feet today, to play a round of golf, perhaps, although that is an increasingly rare occurrence these days. Ever since his hip replacement he's been acting like an invalid. True, it hasn't healed properly, but that's purely because Conor deliberately flouted the surgeon's explicit post-operative instructions and is now paying the price. Aren't we all, Breda thinks grimly. She checks her watch then goes quickly to the kitchen, where Conor's breakfast tray is ready and waiting to be delivered to him by Dinny, their longest-serving waiter. Dinny knows the drill – Breda will text Conor to alert him his breakfast is on the way, and if – as is often the case – Conor should still be out for the count or groggily ill-tempered, Dinny will set everything up on the table just the way Conor likes it, open the curtains, and depart quietly.

Breda knows her husband of forty years is not about to change at this stage of his life. She has learned to accept this fact, along with every other difficult situation she has encountered as a result of Conor being Conor. It is not just the easier option, she reasons, it is the only one.

Nowadays, the yearly summer flirtations are behind him and the alcohol has contributed to his deteriorating health and appalling bouts of self-pity, which means Conor no longer has the power to rip her heart apart like he used to, but he can still excel at irritating her. His state of mind is unpredictable, to say the least, these days. Although he cannot get about the place the way he used to, there is still no telling when he might show up, usually just at the most inopportune moment and clearly the worse for wear. Take, for instance, that time last month when she had been sitting in the small reading lounge with Paul Murray, their accountant, and Conor had barged in, staggered over to a chair, thrown himself into it and then proceeded to accuse Paul of defrauding them of thousands of euro and squirreling it away in an offshore bank account. Breda had been beyond mortified. Dinny and one of the sous chefs had come to the rescue, gently persuading Conor back to his quarters, and Breda had apologised profusely to Paul, who had been more than understanding about the whole incident. Then a couple of weeks later Conor had swayed into the kitchen at the busiest time of the Friday night dinner service, sporting a tea towel on his head in the manner of Marco Pierre White, and had pronounced loudly that the succulent Kerry lamb on the menu was 'tarted-up mutton' and that their new Lithuanian chef, Viktor, was a Russian spy. Fortunately, Viktor had had a sense of humour about it, thanks to his considerable experience with alcohol-soaked employers, but nonetheless, Breda had wanted the ground to swallow her up.

There is no doubt about it, her husband is a liability. But what is she to do? She will just have to keep a tighter rein on him, that's all, but so far the nice young Lithuanian and Latvian students doing their summer exchange work in the hotel were helping her out very well and doing a fine job. *Fawlty Towers* had been a wonderful television series, but she certainly doesn't need her hotel being mentioned as its Irish equivalent – as one former guest had suggested on a travel website. Although, she had to admit, bookings had increased for a short while afterwards.

Breda takes out her phone and texts Conor: *Your breakfast is on the table. Don't let it get cold.*

'Morning Breda.' She jumps, despite recognising the familiar voice, and looks up to find Declan Coady grinning at her. 'Just checking what time our girl gets in at?'

Declan is the local golf pro, a childhood friend of Breda's girls, although it is Annie, her younger daughter, that he has always had a soft spot for. When they were kids, Breda often wondered if Annie and he might end up together. But Declan's brooding good looks and roguish charm had labelled him an early heartbreaker in the village and beyond, and as a result Annie had remained immune to his advances, repeatedly assuring her mother that Declan had a far greater claim to her affections as the brother she'd never had than as the boyfriend who wouldn't last. This may, Breda correctly deduced, have had something to do with the fact that as teenagers Annie had grown weary of being the shoulder his latest ex-girlfriend would inevitably cry on. But they had remained firm friends nonetheless and now that Annie was coming home, Declan was determined to pick her up at the airport, in spite of Annie's protests that she would happily make her own way home.

'I don't have her flight details, Declan,' Breda says, 'but I remember she said she gets in at around half past three, and that she's coming from Heathrow, via Dublin.'

'That'll do.'

'Are you sure it's a good idea? She was quite definite that she'd make her own way . . . you know what she's like . . .'

'Are you kidding? I haven't heard a word from her since she ran off back to London four years ago. If locking her into a car for a couple of hours is the only chance I have to get her on her own and extract some long-withheld information, well then, a drive to Kerry Airport is a small price to pay.'

'It's good of you, Declan,' Breda says, smiling at him. 'I'm sure she'll be delighted to see you.'

'Any chance of you getting out yourself to hit a few balls, Breda? We haven't seen you up at the club for ages.'

'Are you joking? A chance would be a fine thing.'

'How's himself?' The question is casual, but Declan's eyes are kind. Conor's temperament is no secret in the hotel and beyond, and Breda knows Declan sees and hears everything. She has no doubt he is very well aware of exactly how Conor is these days.

'Ah, good and bad days, you know, he's in a lot of pain with the old hip.'

Declan nods sympathetically. 'I know it can't be easy . . . but don't work yourself to the bone, Breda. You need a break yourself, my mother was just saying that. It's good Annie's coming home, she'll be able to take some of the pressure off you.'

For a moment Breda thinks he might give her a hug, but then he steps back. She's grateful – niceness would be her undoing, she might collapse sobbing on his shoulder.

'Anyhow,' he says now, 'I'd better dash. I've got a lesson in twenty minutes. But I'll get the lovely Annie back to you one way or another. See you later.'

It had not altogether come as a surprise when Annie had announced that she was coming home – particularly given the current family circumstances – but it was the length of her proposed stay that caught Breda off-guard. She had supposed a weekend, a few days, a week at the most. Annie is unusually non-committal about how long she's staying, but Breda remembers the word 'sabbatical' featuring in the brief telephone conversation and she was so surprised she hadn't really taken in any more details after that. Annie is the career girl in the family, the success story, she doesn't do sabbaticals, and besides, the last time she was home was so fraught . . . the cups in Breda's hands rattle as she remembers . . . but no, she is determined this visit will go smoothly. It is a chance for a rapprochement between Annie and her father and quite apart from anything else, that could be a blessing in disguise. Every cloud and all that. They have agreed Annie should stay in one of the new cottages belonging to the hotel, that way no one will be on top of anyone else and Annie will have her own space. It will be alright, Breda tells herself for the umpteenth time, it'll all work out, they'll all rub along just fine . . .

Just then, Breda catches sight of her granddaughter, waving at her wildly from the kitchen in a chef's hat. Breda cannot help laughing at the sight of her. Breda's elder daughter, Dee, hasn't had the happiest marriage, but it has produced Breda's only grandchild, Gracie, who is the apple of everybody's eye. Gracie is eleven years old going on thirty-five, and she reminds Breda of her own late mother more than Gracie will ever know or Breda will ever fully admit.

It will be strange, Breda thinks as she waves back at Gracie, to have both her daughters home together. She can't remember the last time they'd been together as a family for any stretch of time, certainly not since before Dee was married.

As sisters, Breda's daughters could not be more unalike. Where Dee is impetuous, Annie is reticent. While Dee trails drama about her like a cloak, Annie is calm and sensible. Where Dee has a selfish streak, Annie is thoughtful and generous. She would have been a superb hotelier, but Annie was determined to study psychology. When she announced her decision, Breda thought it a marvellous undergraduate degree for the business they were in, although she refrained from pointing out that Annie would get as thorough a grounding in human nature and behaviour by working in the hotel as any college would provide. But neither of her girls have shown the slightest interest in taking over the hotel. This has been a huge disappointment to Breda, in the way these things often are, but one she thinks she has managed to hide admirably.

Then Dee had married John, and, well, the rest was history. She had her reservations about it at the time, but Conor had dismissed them, delighted to have a son-in-law he could take under his wing. The next best thing to having his own longed-for son, the one she had never provided. The funny thing was, Conor and John *were* very alike to look at. People who didn't know were always assuming they were father and son. Unfortunately, that wasn't where the similarities ended. In many ways, far too many ways for Breda's liking, she often thinks that Dee has married her father, in a manner of speaking. It's a thought that inevitably makes her feel guilty.

So now she will have both her girls home, but under such very different circumstances – one a successful businesswoman, the other with a marriage in meltdown. Sensitivity will be called for, tact and diplomacy will be required. It will not be easy, but it will be done. She will get through it. They all will. That's what she keeps telling herself, at any rate.

She takes over at Reception to give the girl on duty a break. She is just glancing through reservations for the week ahead when a man comes through the front hall and into the foyer. Immediately, Breda guesses he is the American who has rented Cable Lodge for the summer. Joan Coady, Declan's mother, has told her about the tenants she welcomed the other day, and this man fits the description perfectly. She watches as he walks across the lobby, towards her. He is wearing jeans and a denim shirt and one of those hoodie things, and has an easy, long-legged stride. He is good-looking, and very polite when he introduces himself, but his expression is closed and his manner rather aloof, which makes her wonder about him. He is making a documentary, he tells her, and needs access to the old cable station. Breda directs him to Battie Shannon's place, and tells him that Battie is the man to talk to, that he will find out everything he needs from him. He thanks her, enquires if there is somewhere he can get coffee and internet access, and she directs him to the front lounge.

She wonders if he's married, although he wasn't wearing a ring . . . guessing people's circumstances is part of the fun of running a hotel. And Cable Lodge is such a romantic place, it is as good a place as any for a second honeymoon – even with kids in tow. She watches him for another few moments, then shakes herself out of her idle wonderings. You're getting old, Breda, she says to herself, as she bends down to pick up her glasses and her knee twinges. She celebrated her sixty-fifth birthday six months ago, and she has far better things to be doing than speculating on visitors' romantic attachments or family situations. She looks at the clock. Almost three. Annie's plane will be touching down soon. Which reminds her, as if she needs it, that she has her own decidedly *Modern Family* dilemmas to attend to.

* * *

The small turboprop aircraft taxies to its parking slot and lurches to a halt. Annie immediately turns on her phone. There are no calls, just a couple of emails that can wait until she is settled, that's all.

On the steps of the plane she pauses to hoist her laptop bag on her shoulder, allowing the air to envelope her – the instantly familiar distillation of surf and sentiment, peat and promises almost making her dizzy.

When they were little, her father used to tell her and her sister, Dee, that Kerry air was full of magic. Part of her still believes it. They had listened to spellbinding stories of slumbering giants who masqueraded as mountains in the day, and ice-cold rivers where fish danced on the banks with mermaids at night.

'Why do the mountains come alive, Daddy?' Dee would ask.

'And why would fish want to leave the river to dance?' Annie had wondered.

'To breathe, girls, that's why! To taste this sweet Kerry air, to inhale it, to become alive . . . intoxicated with it.'

'What does intoxicated mean, Daddy?'

'It means feeling giddy and joyful and walking on air . . .'

'But fish can't walk at all, Daddy!'

'Annie!' he would exclaim, looking shocked. 'You have no imagination! What will we do with you, at all?' And his rich laughter would fill the room. 'Now off to sleep with you, my princesses, and dream wonderful dreams, and . . .' he would pause at the door to wag an admonishing finger '. . . make sure to remember them all, I'll be testing you in the morning.'

Dee took him at his word and wrote down every detail of her increasingly dramatic dreams in a copybook kept under her bed for this purpose, so she could recite them the following day. She has been competitive ever since Annie can remember, always viewing her younger sister as chief rival to both the attention and affection she demanded and, more often than not, received. Mostly, Annie didn't mind. Even way back then, she somehow understood that Dee needed it more than she did.

Bedtime was full of stories and merriment, but in the morning, if they tried to tell their father their dreams or press for a forgotten detail of a story, he was gruff and bad-tempered from behind his morning paper. Their mother would shoo them from the room and tell them to hurry up and get ready for school. Later, Annie learned to anticipate and ignore the often tense, loaded silences that greeted her on her return from school, losing herself in homework and study until the general mood had lightened and things became jovial again. Over the years it has stood to her, this ability to instantly assess and address the mood of a client, friend or boardroom, but growing up it took its toll.

Inside the small terminal, she picks up her case from the carousel and makes her way to the car hire desk, but is intercepted before she even reaches it.

'Annie Sullivan! Can that possibly be you in the flesh, or am I in the presence of an apparition?'

'Declan! What are you doing here?'

'Oh c'mon.' He spreads his hands and gives her a look of mock reproach. 'As the man said, *once is unfortunate, twice is careless.* Did you really think you could sneak back home without explaining yourself?' He scowls. 'Four long years, and not so much as a word from you.'

'Oh, don't,' she says, shaking her head and laughing. 'No recriminations. Not from you. I couldn't stand it.'

'Come here.' He pulls her into a bear hug. 'It's great to see you. Now, I'm driving you home, no arguments. Give us your case there.'

'I suppose Mum sent you?' Annie says, surrendering her case.

'No, it was my own idea entirely. I just wanted you to myself for a bit before you get swallowed up by family affairs.'

Five minutes later they are on the road. Annie could drive this route with her eyes closed and little has changed in the four years she has been away. It is just after four o'clock, and the afternoon sun is still strong. Declan chats away, bringing her up to date with things in Ballyanna since she's been away.

In the towns and villages they drive through, people sit outside pubs under umbrellas, arms tanned and faces flushed, or stroll along sea fronts, on their way to or from the novelty of a sun-soaked Irish beach, salt on their skin and sand in every crevice.

They take the sudden right-hand turn for the coast that is so easy to miss, and as Declan accelerates, Annie finds herself longing for her first glimpse of the ocean. It is still there, of course, first as a small V in the distance, between two mountains – a teaser view, as she likes to call it – and then, a couple of miles on, and around the next sweeping bend, where the cliffs drop away, a sudden spread of majestic blue stretches as far as the eye can see, ocean bleeding into sky, and it's next stop, America. It never fails to take her breath away, especially on a day like this – the kind of day when you want to believe your life could be as pretty as a picture postcard.

'How's your fellow in London? The big romance?'

She shakes her head, says nothing. The reference to Ed makes her stomach clench.

'Aw, I'm sorry, Annie,' Declan says, glancing at her. 'It took guts to call off the wedding to Philip. Any regrets?'

She has asked herself this question many times, and the answer is always the same, despite all that has happened. 'No. Philip's a wonderful guy, but it wouldn't have worked.'

Declan raises his eyebrows. 'Try telling him that. Everyone thought you were the perfect couple.'

'Dad did, for sure. He was more upset than Philip about the whole thing. That's partly why I've stayed away this long.' That is as near to the truth as she can manage.

'I heard your dad's hip operation didn't go well. I can't imagine he's an amenable patient.'

'It's been a bit of a nightmare for Mum, and that was before my brother-in-law's little caper.'

'None of us saw that coming. Well, you're home now, that's the main thing. No better girl to sort things out.'

Thankfully, Declan doesn't probe for any further details about her London romance. It's four years since she called off the wedding to her long-time boyfriend and fiancé, Philip, just two weeks before the big day, shocking even herself as she did it. But once Ed had come into her life, no one else had existed for her. Cancelling a wedding seemed a small price to pay in exchange for the life she had envisioned with Ed – although she knew only too well that Philip and her parents had been devastated.

'If I'm honest, you calling off your big wedding was great from my point of view,' Declan says. 'You took the heat off me for a good while. No one was remotely interested in my romantic escapades for months after.' He grins at her.

All the familiar names rush by her with the miles, *Glenbeigh, Cahirciveen*, the turn to the right for *Reenroe* and *Portmagee* . . . and then, finally, the church at the crossroads, where Declan takes the right fork in the road and follows the coast. And then they are driving into the village, Ballyanna basking in the rays of the slanting sun, as welcoming as ever. And as sudden as it is unexpected, Annie's eyes fill with tears.

For a while, she has managed to persuade herself that London was home – but not anymore. Right now, though, nowhere feels like home. *Give it time*, that's what everyone said. But time doesn't change anything, Annie thinks. What is it the Buddhists say? *Wherever you go, there you are.* Annie has found that out the hard way.

'How about a quick drink in the Fisherman's?' Declan pulls into the kerb without waiting for her reply. 'So you can brace yourself for the family reunion.' He grins. 'It'll be empty for a change, everyone's sitting outside in this weather.'

'Well, maybe just a quick one.'

In the dim light of the pub, Annie slips into a corner table, immediately feeling as if she has never been away. A surprised salmon looks out at her from a glass trophy case, one of several prize catches from years gone by that are dotted around the bar. Declan is right, the place is empty, except for a few old local men in flat caps at the bar, nursing pints and talking in a low burr. They might have been there for centuries.

Declan returns with the drinks and sits down. 'So, how long are you in town for?'

She shrugs. 'I don't know, really. As long as it takes, I suppose. I'm on a sabbatical from work, so I have three months off. Mum's under a lot of pressure, as you know, and I guessed she could do with an extra pair of hands. I thought I'd help her get to grips with social media, revamp the website, although that's the least of her worries just now, I'd imagine . . . How about you?'

'Still flogging houses and playing golf.'

'I can't remember the last time I played.'

'So you're single again, Annie? No man in your life?'

'That's the way I like it.'

'I find that hard to believe.'

'It's the truth.'

Declan took a long drink of his pint, watching her all the while. 'You might get away with fobbing off Londoners with that spiel, but this is your childhood buddy you're talking to . . .'

'I mean it, Declan. I've decided I'm better on my own.'

'That's bullshit. You just haven't met the right guy yet.'

'Have you met the right girl yet?'

'No, but that's—'

'Different? Can we change the subject, please?'

'Whatever you say.' Declan puts his hands up in mock defence. 'I'd forgotten how prickly you could be. There was never any point arguing with you. Maybe you're right, so, about staying single.'

She smiles, on safer ground now with their familiar bantering. 'What are you up to? Apart from tearing up the golf course . . .'

'I still give lessons, if that's what you're referring to. In fact, it's more reliable than the property business these days, but things are picking up again on that score too. Donal and I are still in business. I leave the administrative side of things to him. I prefer to do my deals on the golf course.'

'Of course you do.' She laughs.

For a moment he is serious. 'Much as we all miss you, Annie, you were right to get out of here, go to London when you did, make something of yourself. I always thought you needed a bigger stage to play on.'

'I don't know about that.' She shrugs. 'I could do with some time out while I'm home though, I know that much. I'm tired, to tell you the truth. It's been a busy few years and London can take it out of you.'

'Well I'm glad you're back, even if it's only for a short while.'

'I'll be counting on you to keep me sane while I'm here. I'll only be able to stand so much time in the hotel.'

'You mean in the bosom of your family,' Declan says, with a gleam in his eye.

'Touché!' Annie laughs and finishes her drink. 'I really have to go.'

'You won't stay for another?' He is crestfallen. 'I'm dying to hear all about your glamorous life in London. You know, *One of London's women under forty to watch . . . who creates the brands you'll buy.*' Declan is clearly impressed, quoting the recent article in the *Guardian*.

Annie shakes her head. 'Ah,' she says, 'so you saw it.'

'It was the talk of the place, sure didn't you know it would be?'

'I suppose.'

'We have the internet here and all, Annie, we're very well informed these days.'

'No kidding.'

'Seriously, we're very proud of you.'

A light breeze is blowing as they stroll back to the car, and already the air is making her drowsy. She smiles at the few people she passes along the way who say hello. She doesn't know any of them, but the warmth and ease of their greetings reminds her how long she has been away. She has forgotten how easily people interact here, how natural it is to stop to chat about nothing.

Back in the car, they drive through the village and Annie notices the new shops and cafés that have sprung up in her absence, and then smiles as she passes familiar houses, cottages and landmarks that have remained unchanged.

They head for the cliff road, the sea still and cornflower blue to her left. Her heart beats a little faster now, stirred as always by the familiar beauty of the mountains guarding the bay, the watercolour palette of purples, browns and greens, soft in the late afternoon haze, the glint of the sea below. And then, just around the bend, Ballyanna Bay Hotel rises before her, its mellow limestone glowing warm in the evening sun. Declan pulls in to the front car park, which is relatively empty, hauling Annie's suitcase from the boot and handing it to her.

'You're not coming in?' she says, suddenly apprehensive at the idea of meeting everyone again.

'Nah, I need to get back to the club. Besides, I'd hate to spoil the beautiful reunion.'

'Thank you for coming to get me, and driving me back.' She hugs him. 'It was kind of you.'

'I meant what I said,' he says, planting a kiss on her cheek, 'it's really good to have you back, Annie.'

Declan heads off and Annie takes a deep breath, picks up her bags and makes towards the hotel entrance.

It is the smell that takes her straight back to being six years old again. The minute she steps across the threshold, it hits her – the combination of polish, beeswax, smouldering turf – the unmistakable distillation of her childhood. She takes a moment to reacquaint herself with the familiar lobby, the warm panelled walls hung with landscapes, the handsome windows, the antique tables covered with books, flowers and local literature, and smiles when she sees the peat fire burning – even in summer. Breda has kept up the rigorous standards her family have always prided themselves on, not just the sense of order and unhurried hospitality, the comfortable luxury, but an air of effortless yet unobtrusive efficiency prevails, the mark of a first-rate hotelier.

Annie walks quickly to the front desk, where she introduces herself to the young girl on reception.

'I'm here to pick up the keys to my cottage.'

'Annie Sullivan, of course.' The girl looks her over with interest. 'You're in number five. We're expecting you. Let me show you the way.'

'There's no need, thank you.' Annie takes the keys. 'I know it well.'

The cottages are barely a three-minute walk away, but even before she reaches her door, her phone rings.

'Hi, Mum, I'm here, just going to get myself settled . . .'

'Oh Annie, you're here, that's marvellous! You'll come for dinner, won't you? Nothing fancy . . . you haven't seen our new apartment . . .' Her mother's voice is high with nerves.

A family dinner is the last thing Annie feels like just now, but she senses the anxiety in her mother's expectant pause and hears herself saying, 'Sure, Mum, that would be lovely.'

'Great.' Her mother's relief fairly leaps down the phone. 'Seven o'clock then, . . . and Annie . . .' her mother pauses meaningfully, '. . . your father's thrilled you're home. He'll be beside himself to see you. In fact,' she lowers her voice, 'he's quite emotional about it. All the fight's gone out of him these days, you won't recognise him, I'm telling you.'

'I'll see you at seven, Mum. Bye.'

Annie is suddenly overcome by weariness. Not from the journey, although she is pretty worn out from two flights and the drive, but the prospect of an evening with parents she has not seen together since she left so abruptly four years ago seems overwhelming. She knows they will be nervous. Her mother will fuss, and her father will be full of false cheer and heartiness, and she will play along with it all. She comes from a family well versed in pretence. She can play them at their own game. It's only dinner after all, not the Spanish Inquisition. That will come later.

She flings her bags in the bedroom, opens a window to let the air in and then checks her watch. There is time for a walk before dinner, which is a good thing because she's feeling restless. The cottage, nice though it is, is just another set of walls that taunt her – impersonal, anonymous, transient – words she identifies too easily with these days.

She borrows the keys to the hotel Jeep from Dinny, who keeps smiling and shaking his head as if he can't quite believe she has returned. Then she drives the short distance to her favourite part of the beach, just below the old manor house, Cable Lodge, parking at the distinctive set of boulders at the top of the cliff and then stepping out into the heady air.

This spot is far enough away from the hotel and village to avoid the curiosity of tourists, and most of the locals can't be bothered with the rather precarious descent involved in negotiating the long and winding wooden steps that lead to the small cove below. Some said the secluded cove once belonged to the old manor house, which overlooks it from the cliff above, but the Lodge has not been lived in for a while and no one ever bothered about trespassing or rights-of-way. It was known simply as the Cove, and it is possibly Annie's favourite place in the world.

She tries to remember the first time she came here, and can't . . . probably as a baby. She picks through the scraps of memories that surface . . . picnics with her parents and sister, surrounded by dogs, fold-out chairs, buckets and spades, lilos and armbands . . . the colourful debris of childhood summers. Later there were trysts, moonlit walks, first kisses, the young locals eager to share this secret spot with visiting teenagers, all suitably impressed with the picturesque cove, surprised, momentarily, from their studied urban nonchalance.

She kicks off her trainers, rolls up her jeans and walks at the water's edge, gasping as the incoming tide rushes over her feet. She searches for and finds the rock she used to sit on, slipping easily into its hollow, and hugs her knees to her chest, inhaling the sharp tang of ozone. The sea calms her, her breathing steadies, she allows the memories to surface and drift, dispelled by the gentle pull of the ocean.

Pat

We head for the beach, which is actually a pretty cool one. It's at the bottom of hundreds of steps that lead down from the cliff where our house, Cable Lodge, looks out over the sea. Me and Sean run ahead, Dad is slower, but eventually he gets down to the bottom too.

Sean's my twin brother. He doesn't talk anymore. I'm taller than him by half an inch. He used to be the noisy one, the talkative one – but not now. He's got PTSD, that's post-traumatic stress disorder. That's why he doesn't talk. Doesn't bother me, I can pretty much read his mind anyhow. Always could – it's a twin thing.

Coming to the beach makes me think of Mom. She used to call us the Beach Bums because any chance we had, we were always hanging out there – surfing, swimming or playing ball. And Dad called Mom his Surfer Chick when he wanted to tease her, although she said technically she was now a Surfer Hen. I miss Mom, but I'm so mad at her still that sometimes I think it's good she's not around. I'm afraid of what I might say to her. The thing is, it's her fault, all of it, she ruined everything. Dad's trying, but I know he finds it hard without her . . . and Sean . . . well, Sean's a whole other deal. Anyway, we're here now, so we have to make the best of things. The house is cool too, it's, like, really old, over a hundred years old, and started out as a hunting lodge. Dad explained that in the old days people used to stay there when they were invited to go shooting and fishing. Not shooting like we have at home, like target practice, this was shooting for birds. Then after that, the first guy who ran the very first cable station lived there, and then after that it just became a regular house. We're renting it because no one has lived there for a while, and Dad says it's atmospheric and helps him with his work. He's taking photographs with his camera now, checking out locations and stuff. The beach is quiet, there's no one but us around, I guess that's because it's six-thirty, so most people have gone home for the day.

I wanted to have my own room at the house, I mean, it's not like there aren't enough of them, but Sean wanted to share with me, and I had to let him, of course, seeing as he's still traumatised. I don't get the whole no talking thing, though. I mean, what's that about? I was there, I know what happened, so it's not like anyone's going to blame him or anything . . . anyway, it's getting really old already. I told him that, but he's still not talking.

After a while on the beach we turn around to go back. Dad says he's starving and it's time to eat . . . and that's when we see her. She's sitting on a rock, looking out to sea, and the wind's blowing her hair around her face. She reminds me of a mermaid with her long gold hair, not like Ariel or anything stupid like that, but like a real one. It's because of the way she's sitting into the rock, you can't see her legs. She can't see us, but Dad makes a sign for us to wait and be quiet, then he hunkers down and takes some shots of her, right there and then, which I think is kind of sneaky, although we're quite far away. Then we keep on walking, and when I look back, she's still there on the rock, even though it's getting pretty cold.

'Hey,' says Dad, breaking into a run. 'Last one back has to peel the potatoes.'

* * *

What kind of mother is nervous at the thought of seeing her own daughter? Breda tries to tell herself she's just excited, and she is, of course she is, but there are nerves too, definite nerves. She wants it all to be perfect for Annie, and there's so much that could go wrong. It's been four years since they have all sat down together, since Annie walked out after the row with her father when she had called off her wedding to Philip. Breda couldn't bear if they set each other off again. She never did get to the bottom of what was said in the heat of that argument, but she knew her husband well enough to imagine that when he'd heard he was about to lose a favoured prospective son-in-law, he'd probably hurled a few unsavoury accusations that were totally unfounded. It was never pretty when Conor lost his temper, and this was the first time it had happened seriously with one of his girls. Afterwards he'd refused to discuss the incident, even with Breda.

But Annie is home now. That is all that matters. All the same, she has warned Conor to be on his best behaviour and, to be fair, she knows he is nervous too. He adores both his daughters, but sometimes he just can't help himself. He is not the most tactful of men, and that is putting it nicely. That's why she has gone over it thoroughly with him: there is to be no talk of men, no references to *the wedding that never was*, no prying questions.

She wanted to add *and don't drink too much*, but that would only annoy him. She would have to keep an eye on that herself. If they can just get through this evening, that will be a good start. One day at a time, she reminds herself.

Annie and her father are too alike, she often thinks, that's the problem. Except Annie has manifested her father's shared characteristics in their positive aspect. She has inherited Conor's unusual eyes and colouring, his engaging manner with people and an eager and agile mind. But where Conor was lazy and dependent on constant attention and adulation from all around him, Annie is hardworking and independent. And so far, thank God, the only addictive tendency Breda is aware of is that her daughter is a workaholic. No, it's not Annie she has to worry about in that respect, Dee and her husband John have been flying the flag for all to see in that department, but she can't think about Dee just now ... tonight is about Annie, and this dinner has to be a success so the past can finally be laid to rest.

She checks the table one last time, and checks on Conor, who has gone to some trouble, wearing his best navy suit and a new shirt.

'Will I do?' he asks, and Breda knows he is nervous too.

'You will indeed,' she tells him. 'You look very ... handsome.'

The unexpected compliment brings a smile to his face, but it is true. He is still a handsome man, although a little worn around the edges, like herself.

'You're looking lovely yourself, Breda,' he says, reaching for his crutch.

The buzzer to their apartment goes, making them both jump.

'Will you get it?' he says tentatively.

'We both will,' she says. 'We're going to have a lovely evening and enjoy every minute of it.' She realises, with sudden clarity, she is addressing herself as firmly as her husband as together they go to answer the door and welcome their daughter home.

* * *

After she is enveloped in hugs and exclamations from both her parents, Annie barely has time to put down the gifts she has brought from London and accept the glass of champagne her father hands her before a small figure hurtles into the room and hurls herself at her.

'Gracie!' she gasps, laughing as her niece almost sends her flying with her welcome.

'She's been preparing herself all afternoon for you.' Breda laughs, and Conor tweaks Gracie's hair.

'What do you think?' Gracie stands back so Annie can have a look at her. She is wearing a blue t-shirt that says *Pink is my second favourite colour*, and stripy red-and-black leggings under a multilayered purple net skirt. Over that is the black leather biker jacket Annie sent her from London and the knee-high biker boots to match. Her hair is a wild tangle of dark curls and she looks adorable. Mad, but adorable.

'I think you look amazing,' Annie says. 'Like a real fashionista.'

'Or a Hell's Angel,' Conor says with a chuckle.

'What's a Hell's Angel?'

'A member of a motorcycle gang who rides around terrorising people.'

'Cool,' says Gracie.

'She won't be parted from the jacket or boots since you sent them,' Breda says, 'even in this heat. I have to prise them off her.'

'Mam says you have to suffer to be beautiful,' Gracie says.

'Where is Dee?' Annie asks. 'I've called her about a hundred times, but she never gets back to me.'

'She's gone away for a couple of weeks, to Portugal.' Breda's tone is light, but she will not quite meet Annie's eyes.

'She left this morning,' says Gracie. 'She said she needed to get out of here. Her head is wrecked.'

'Is that so?' Annie looks at Breda.

'The change will do her good,' Breda says, shooting Annie a meaningful look over Gracie's head. 'Sure, she'll be back before we know it . . . Now please, Gracie darling, take that beautiful jacket off you, just for dinner, pet, will you?'

'Do I have to?' She looks at Annie.

'Of course you don't, but you might spill something on it and that would be a shame.' This clinches the deal, and the jacket is hung with great care on the back of Gracie's chair.

The apartment is lovely, occupying the top floor of the wing of the hotel that has been refurbished in Annie's absence. There are three bedrooms, a spacious living and dining area and a smart new kitchen. 'We don't know ourselves in it, do we, Conor? And it's great not having any stairs to bother with.'

Dinner is a beautiful side of poached salmon that Breda immediately attributes to Viktor, the new chef. 'One of the perks of living in a hotel.'

But she has gone to great trouble, Annie knows. She has had her hair done, and is wearing her best pearls and matching earrings. She looks tired, though, Annie thinks, and more careworn since she last came to visit her in London.

'You have enough on your plate at the moment, Mum, without cooking for everyone,' Annie says. She hopes this might nudge the conversation towards the discussion that needs to be had, but that clearly is being avoided.

'Well normally I would have cooked,' she says, 'but when Viktor mentioned the salmon this morning, well, I thought I might as well ...'

'How's the hip, Dad?' Annie asks, keeping her tone neutral. Conor's colour is high and she wonders if the tremor in his hand as he tops up her glass, and then his own, generously, is due to alcohol or nerves. It is the first direct question she has asked him, and he seems relieved and pleased that it is a topic that can be safely broached.

'Tormenting me.' He shakes his head. 'That surgeon Doctor Mike referred me to above in Dublin made a complete mess of it altogether. I should sue him.'

'I'm sorry to hear that, Dad. That was bad luck.'

Annie and her mother exchange glances.

'He's in a lot of pain with it still, unfortunately,' Breda says.

'My sleep is shot to pieces, and the painkillers and sleeping tablets are useless.' He is warming to his theme. 'The only thing that gives me any relief at all is a drop of whiskey.'

'Well, that's something, I suppose.'

'Em, how long are you home for, Annie?' her father asks.

'I'm not sure. We're in the middle of a merger, it's been a very busy few months. They want me to continue as creative director, but I need to think about it. I was due a sabbatical, so I thought I'd take some time out and see how things look in a couple of months . . .'

'Well, that's lovely.' Breda beams at her. 'To have you home for a decent stretch, I mean, and not rushing off again. I mean . . .' She is flustered.

'I know what you mean,' Annie says smoothly. 'And I'm looking forward to helping out while I'm back. From what you've told me, you could do with taking things easy for a bit.'

'What have you told her?' Conor looks wary.

'Oh, just what everybody else knows . . . there's no need to go into detail just now.' Breda makes eyes to indicate Gracie, who is helping herself to more mashed potatoes. Any discussion of Dee is clearly off-limits while Gracie, her daughter, is at the table. Instead, Annie enquires about occupancy rates. Things seem quiet in the hotel and the new cottages, although lovely, are largely empty.

'Oh, things are quiet enough.' Breda gets up to bring in dessert. 'But they'll pick up soon, hopefully. Cable Lodge has been let for two months, though, maybe more.'

'Oh? Who to?'

'An American. He's making a documentary about the cable station . . . Daniel O'Connell, that's his name . . . you're bound to run into him . . . very good-looking . . .'

Swallowing down a mouthful of dessert, Conor clears his throat and says, 'Speaking of bumping into people, you'll never guess who I ran into the other day . . .' He twirls the stem of his glass, and pauses expectantly.

'Who?' Gracie asks.

'Philip . . .'

Breda glares at him. 'You never said.'

'Well I'm saying it now, aren't I? It must have slipped my mind before.'

'How is he?' Annie smiles. She has been wondering how long it would take her father to bring Philip into the conversation, but she is prepared for this.

'Oh he's grand altogether. Came down from Dublin in the helicopter, he said. He had a beautiful blonde girl with him. He was in great form, and he was asking for you, Annie. I told him you were coming home, of course, and he said he hoped to see you.' Conor looks as pleased as she has seen him this evening.

'Yes, well, we're bound to run into each other sooner or later,' she says.

'Joan Coady told me every girl between here and Dublin is chasing him, but he has time for none of them. She says all he's interested in is—'

'That's enough, Conor.' Breda's voice is sharp. 'Gracie, darling,' she says gently, 'it's past your bedtime, off you go now.'

'Will you come and say goodnight before you go?' Gracie asks Annie, slipping off her chair and pulling her leather jacket back on.

'Of course I will.'

'Oops, I nearly forgot.' Annie gets up and goes over to her bag and rummages in it. 'I brought you a little present.'

'Really?' Gracie's face lights up.

'Not another one, Annie!' Breda says, shaking her head. 'The leather jacket and boots are hardly out of their parcel! You're spoiling her!'

Gracie tears the paper off and shrieks. 'An iPad! Oh, Annie, thank you, thank you, thank you, I love it!' She flings her arms around her. 'You're the best aunt in the world!'

'Well you're the only niece I have, so I have to spoil you.' Annie laughs and promises to set Gracie up with an email address in the morning.

'There'll be no getting her to sleep now,' Breda says.

'Oh, I almost forgot!' Conor checks his watch. 'I have to meet a fellow downstairs about a sand yachting venture someone's proposing in Reenroe. It went straight out of my head.' Conor gets up from the table and limps over to the door, where he hovers awkwardly on his crutch.

'Conor!' Breda looks at him askance. 'Annie is only home . . . can you not—'

'It's okay, Mum.' Annie is not surprised that her father is making his getaway to the hotel bar. He has put on a good show over dinner and the effort was no doubt taking a toll.

'Welcome home again, Annie, love . . . I . . . I'm very glad to have you back . . . for however short or long a time it is. I'll leave you and your mother now to chat.'

'Sure, Dad, I'll see you tomorrow.'

'He knows he's in trouble,' Breda says as the door closes behind him, her mouth a thin line. 'I warned him! I absolutely forbade him to mention anything to do with Philip, and he has to go and open his big gob.'

'Relax, Mum. I'm not going to have a fit every time someone mentions Philip's name.'

'He took good care not to tell *me* he'd bumped into him . . .'

'Never mind Dad, what about you?' Annie says. 'You're looking tired.'

Breda sighs. 'I haven't been sleeping so well, and, well . . . I'm a bit distracted today, don't mind me, love.'

'Let me make some coffee and we can talk.'

Breda does not want to talk, not if talking implies what she thinks it implies. She does not want to bring Annie up-to-date on the current state of affairs, especially not on this, her first night home, but it looks as if she has no choice. She is cornered in her own kitchen.

Annie brings the coffee over and sits across from her mother. 'What's going on with Dee, really?'

Breda thinks back over what she has told Annie about John, Dee's husband, being caught out in some kind of fraud. About Dee and him probably losing their beautiful house, their marriage in tatters and how Dee has come home to the hotel with Gracie for some breathing space.

'I've tried ringing her.' Annie pours the coffee. 'She's not taking my calls.'

'She doesn't want to talk to anybody, Annie. I suppose she's just trying to cope with it all as best she can . . . with, the, um, scandal . . . I think she's a bit fragile at the moment, to be honest.'

'What about Gracie?'

Breda shifts in her seat. 'She seems alright . . . she knows her father's gone away, of course . . . to be honest, I'm not sure . . . she hasn't said anything much about it really . . .'

'Declan was filling me in. Five million euro . . .' Annie whistles. 'That was some scam.'

'I know. It didn't seem real the first time I heard it, and no matter how many times I've said it since it still won't sink in.'

'What a bastard.'

'I can't argue with that.'

'So has she left him for good? Are they over?'

'Honestly, I don't know. She's been so upset, she's not herself at the moment . . . I don't think she's thought it through properly . . . it's the shock of it all . . . and the humiliation, of course . . . I can't say I ever thought John was good for Dee, but I thought they were happy . . . and then there's poor little Gracie to think of . . .'

'Those poor people who invested with him, they'll never see a penny of it. How can he even live with himself?' Annie shakes her head in disbelief.

'That's the other thing . . .' Breda fiddles with her pearls, '. . . I mean, Dee may very well end up with nothing either. I've tried to talk to her about it, but she keeps saying she's not up to it. So I was thinking, Annie . . . maybe it's all for the best . . .'

Annie stares at her. 'How do you work that out?'

'Well, I've been thinking about nothing else lately, your father and I aren't getting any younger and, let's face it, neither Dee nor you has ever had any interest in the hotel . . . so now may be as good a time as any to wind things up. I've put away a small bit myself over the years, you know a rainy day fund . . .' Breda laughs and rolls her eyes, 'enough to retire on if we're careful . . . run a guesthouse maybe . . . something smaller . . . I think it's time to sell up, put the hotel on the market . . . then at least we'll be able to help Dee and Gracie if it comes to that . . . at least they'll have some sort of a roof over their heads . . .'

'Oh, right. I can just see you and dad in a cosy semi, renting rooms out. You'd last five minutes – although that might not necessarily be a bad thing either.'

'Annie!'

'Well, at least in the hotel you can avoid him. Look, you already know my feelings on the subject.'

'Your dad is doing his best, Annie. He's a lot weaker now since the operation, his health has suffered, I think he has a lot of regrets.'

'I'm sure he does, but whose fault is that?'

'Please, Annie, don't start, you're only just home, give him a chance. I know he regrets the row and . . . and whatever he may have said to you . . . but that's all water under the bridge now. You know what his temper is like . . . he didn't mean any of it. He was so fond of Philip, we all were. He's trying . . . and now with Dee's marriage and all . . . I just couldn't stand any more fighting.'

'Who said anything about fighting?'

'You have that look on your face. I know you, Annie, and I know how awful this state of affairs must seem to you, but what's done is done and we have to pick up the pieces as best we can and move forward. You're a businesswoman, so you of all people should understand that. Please, love, no recriminations, no rows, no I told you so's . . . we have to pull together as a family now . . . for little Gracie if for no one else . . . otherwise,' Breda lets out a shaky breath, 'well, we're finished . . .'

Annie looks at her mother for a long moment. 'Right, I see.' She gets up from her chair and then bends down to kiss Breda's cheek and give her shoulder a squeeze. 'Look, you needn't worry about any rows. I'm all out of confrontations these days. All I'm saying is don't rush into doing something you might regret, not yet, anyway. We can discuss this calmly, over the next few weeks.'

Breda looks relieved. 'Yes, yes, you're right, of course . . . it's just that time may not be on our side just now . . .'

'Don't worry, Mum, please. There's always a solution to these situations if you don't panic. Thank God *you* didn't invest with him.'

Breda nods tiredly. 'I can't say I ever trusted him, even if he was my son-in-law. There was always something about him I just never warmed to, although it wasn't for want of trying.'

'Well, it was a good performance, you fooled me.' Annie smiles and stifles a yawn. 'It's the air,' she says. 'It's knocked me out already.'

'Go on and get an early night,' Breda says. 'You must be exhausted.'

'I think I will call it a night – you should too. Get some rest, Mum, it's been a long day all round.'

'Goodnight, Annie, love – oh, I forgot, with all the talk about Dee and everything – I meant to say I was sorry to hear about your fellow in London . . .' Breda shakes her head. 'I always forget his name . . .'

'Ed.' Annie bites her lip.

'That's it, Ed . . . I'm sorry things didn't work out for you. I don't know the details of course, and I'm not asking . . .but . . . you're all right about it, aren't you, love?'

'I'm fine, Mum. It's all water under the bridge now. See you tomorrow, goodnight.'

'Goodnight, love.'

* * *

Breda is sitting up in bed when Conor comes back in from his meeting. She is halfway through her current romantic novel, but tonight she cannot concentrate. When she tried to read the words just swam before her eyes, so she gave up. But now, hearing his key in the door, she puts on her glasses and pretends to be engrossed.

'I thought you'd be asleep,' he says, his tone vaguely accusing.

'It's not that late.'

'No, but usually . . .'

'So, how did the meeting go?'

'What? Oh, it was grand, your man from the business co-op and a couple of young turks . . . well meaning, but no clue what they were about really.'

'You were a long time.'

'I ran in to a few of the old crowd after, hadn't seen them for ages . . . you know what they're like . . .'

'I do.'

Breda waits while Conor undresses and goes to the bathroom. She listens to the familiar ritual: the extracting and downing of the plethora of pills from various cupboards, the wheezing cough, and the precise swishing and swallowing of the combination of mouthwashes he insists on and that, since she has known him, have never managed to disguise the smell of whiskey on his breath. As if it matters at this stage.

'Conor . . .'

He groans as he manoeuvres himself into the bed beside her. 'What?'

'I thought dinner went well.'

'It did, certainly.'

'Apart from you making a run for it as soon as you decently could. You didn't even stay for coffee.'

'I told you, I forgot about the bloody meeting!'

'Conor, I don't know what was said at this stupid row between you and Annie, but she's home now, after four long years, and I want the air to be clear between you once and for all.'

'For the love of God . . .'

'No, Conor, listen to me. I want you to get Annie on her own tomorrow . . . call in to the cottage, the earlier the better, and talk to her. I mean *really* talk to her, tell her you're sorry for whatever you said, that you hope she can forgive you, and that you've regretted it bitterly ever since you let her go back to London that night.'

'I will do no such thing! For God's sake, Breda, you saw her with your own eyes . . . sure, she's fine about it! Wasn't she chatty? Civil? Weren't we both? What's the problem? As you so rightly point out, it was four long years ago. I can't remember what I said, and I'm sure Annie can't either. Much better to let bygones be bygones and forget about it.'

Breda stared coldly at him. 'You must think I'm awfully stupid if you think it's not as plain as the nose on your face that you're terrified of being left on your own with Annie for even five seconds, let alone five minutes. I won't have any tension or undercurrents in this family, not now we have her home.'

'What about what she said to me? Hmm? How come it's all my fault?'

'I don't care whose fault it is! You're her father . . . just tell her you're sorry.'

'She knows I'm sorry! Didn't I tell her I was glad to have her home? Now for the love of God, woman, let me go to sleep!'

Minutes later Conor is snoring loudly, while Breda lies beside him seething with anger. Her husband, so full of pills and whiskey, slips into untroubled sleep, while she will probably toss and turn into the small hours. It is not fair. But then, she reflects grimly, very little about marriage to a drinker is.

* * *

Although she is exhausted, Annie cannot sleep. She rolls over and looks at the green numbers on the digital clock on the bedside locker – 03:48 – then gets up and goes downstairs to make some peppermint tea. There is no point trying to sleep, not just now, not when it is all so fresh, so vivid.

Dinner went remarkably well, considering . . . although it was patently obvious her father was on his best behaviour. Breda would have warned him, of course, but that would not have been the only reason. If she is honest, Annie is surprised he lasted as long as he did before fleeing to the bar. Despite his talent for denial, it must have been difficult for him – even her father couldn't erase the hideousness of their last exchange, a scene that will be seared on Annie's memory for as long as she lives. At the time, four years ago now, she was psyching herself up to break the news to her father that she had met someone else and was calling off her wedding to Philip; she almost laughs at the absurdity of her worry then, given what she was about to encounter. Thinking about it, the scene plays out again, just as it has before, and will undoubtedly do again, and although she views it through the lens of as much detachment as she can muster, she still feels the disbelief, the rage, the utter bewilderment as acutely as if it were yesterday and she was bracing herself to break the news . . .

She knocks lightly, takes a deep breath and opens the door to her father's office, preparing to tell him of her decision. That she can no longer marry Philip, his ideal, imminent son-in-law. That awful though it is to do this to everybody, she has fallen deeply in love with someone else. It will be a blow. She knows this. Philip is the son of her father's old friend, heir to a hotel chain, the closest thing to a longed-for son her father could only dream of.

'Dad?' She is taken aback to find someone with him. 'I need to talk to you . . . it's important.' She hovers, as the attractive, vaguely familiar young guy turns to look at her. He is confident, curious, a half smile lifts his mouth.

Her father, on the other hand, seated behind his desk, appears agitated. 'Not now Annie.' He inclines his head towards the door abruptly, to indicate that she should leave.

'Oh, don't go on my account, please,' says the smiling stranger, who seems to find the situation amusing.

'I'm sorry,' Annie says, looking from one to the other, expecting an introduction. 'I didn't mean to interrupt.'

'I was just leaving,' he says. Looking pointedly at her father, who will not meet his eyes, or hers, but stares fixedly in front of him.

'Nice to meet you, Annie.' He shakes her hand and makes to leave.

She stands aside to let him pass. 'Have we met before?' She is intrigued. 'Your face is familiar.'

He pauses briefly, just at the door, then turns around, smiles, and says. 'That's probably because we share a father. I'm Conor, your half-brother. But I'm guessing you didn't know that.'

Then he is gone, the door closes behind him. The room is suddenly too small . . . there is not enough air . . .

Annie walks to the desk, leans her hands on it, facing him – and still he will not meet her eyes.

'Look at me!' she says, in a voice she does not recognise. 'What the hell is he talking about?'

'I'm begging you . . .' Her father is unrecognisable, a crumpled, whimpering mess. 'Imploring you . . . Annie . . . darlin'. . . don't tell your mother . . . it would break her heart.' Tears fill his eyes and roll down his suddenly shrunken cheeks. He gets up, unsteadily, walks over to the far wall, lined with hand-carved bookshelves and drawers, and pulls one open, from which he produces a bottle of Jameson. 'Here,' he says. 'Have a drink.' He fumbles with two glasses. 'You've had a shock . . . an awful shock.' Sympathy, or self-pity, she cannot decipher, flickers across his features. Before she can refuse, he has poured a stiff one for himself, and necked it, refilling his glass, instantly forgetting his consolatory offer. 'I didn't know . . . really . . . I didn't know . . . how was I to know?'

Liar.

'You can't tell her, Annie . . . you can't . . . really.' He is gaining courage now, the drink working its way into him. 'It would destroy her . . . you know it would. You must promise me . . . please . . . I'm begging you . . . not a word . . . not to your mother . . . and . . . certainly not to Dee.' He remembers his other daughter, her sister – a sudden, sobering reflection. 'Dear God, Dee would get hysterical!' He looks alarmed. 'Please, Annie . . .' he is wheedling again. 'Please . . . do this one thing for me . . . You're the strong one in this family . . . I'll never ask you anything again as long as I live . . . if not for me . . . do it for your mother . . . not for me.'

He nods, as if realising this is a surer approach. 'For your mother
...' he begins to weep, drunkenly. She cannot look at him another
minute. Instead, she says what she came to say. 'The wedding is off.
That is what I came to tell you. My engagement to Philip is over.
I have met someone else. Mum knows, I've already told her.' The
words sound hollow in her new voice.

Then she backs away, watches his features rearrange into a mask
of disbelieving comprehension as she flees the room.

When Annie runs to her room to hurl things into her backpack,
her mother follows her.

'You told him?' she asks, sounding worried, looking older.

'Yes,' Annie says tightly. 'I told him. Now I'm going back to
London.'

'But your flight isn't until tomorrow.' Breda fiddles with the
chain around her neck. 'Oh, I knew it!' She shakes her head. 'He
flew off the handle, didn't he? Don't let him upset you, Annie, he
doesn't mean it, you know, whatever he said. It's his hip, he's in
terrible pain with it these days, he's like a bull ... he needs to see a
specialist above in Dublin ... Doctor Mike is arranging it ...' She
is babbling, assuming just another outburst from her hot-headed
husband. 'I'll talk to him. I'll make him see, but he was very fond
of Philip ... we all were ... you're absolutely sure ...?'

The question hangs in the air.

Annie goes to her and takes her hands. 'I'm absolutely sure,
Mum. You have to trust me on this.'

Her mother's face softens. 'Well in that case, who am I to stand
in your way?' She smiles. 'It's all I ever wanted for you. But Annie
... be careful ... won't you? Don't rush into anything ... this is all
very sudden. You must admit that much. We'll meet him in time,
I suppose?'

'I'll be fine, Mum, now I have to go.' She hugs her. 'You take care of yourself.'

And then Annie leaves, before her mother can sense there is something else – something much bigger going on here than just a row.

'You'll stay in touch, won't you, Annie?' She calls after her, as Annie heads downstairs. 'And don't worry about your father. I'll make him see sense. He'll come around, you'll see.'

'I'll ring you, Mum, as soon as I get back. Love you.'

Then she gets in the car and drives.

Here's what Annie found out about her half-brother:

His name is Conor – *Conn* – after his – *their* – father. His mother was adamant about that. It is a name he was ambivalent about. He was thirty-one years to her thirty-two. He was the result of a summer affair her father conducted with a pretty young girl who was holidaying with her family in the hotel. She did the maths . . . it was the summer her mother was recovering from an emergency hysterectomy caused by Annie's complicated birth.

His mother went on to marry a man who loved both of them, and brought him up as his own son. He had three younger half-siblings from this, his mother's marriage –   two sisters and a brother. They were a very close family. His parents were honest with him about his birth father as soon as he was old enough to understand.

Their father, when he learned of his existence, wanted nothing to do with him. Money was offered and rejected – they had no need of it. This, apparently, was greeted with relief.

Her half-brother had no interest in developing any relationship with their father or any of his legitimate children, he merely wanted to meet him, get a look at him, tell him he needn't worry, he had no intention of upsetting his cosily constructed family life.

He knew a coward when he saw one. She gleaned all this from her father's confession and the phone call she made to Conn in the aftermath of the revelation. He was sorry, Conn told her, he did not anticipate dropping the bombshell so callously on her, but he couldn't resist the opportunity to see his father wince, to hit one back. He had not meant to hurt Annie.

'That was wrong of me,' he said. 'It's not your fault. This has nothing to do with you.'

He declined her offer to meet, just the two of them, to process things further. 'No hard feelings, you understand,' he explained. 'But I have no interest in discovering or befriending another family. I already have a wonderful one of my own. I just wanted to face him down. He deserved it, and I needed it. Now I can put it behind me, move on. I wish you all the best, Annie.' He sounded wise beyond his years, her half-brother. 'You seem like a nice girl, but when we finish this phone call, I'm going to forget all about you . . . and your family. I wish you well, Annie. I really do.' There was a beat, then he hung up.

That was the first and only time Annie ever spoke with him.

* * *

There's something about this place that's hard to define, apart from its obvious beauty. Daniel finds it peaceful in a way other places aren't – and he should know, he's travelled a lot with his work. This morning before breakfast he walked down the cliff path from the house that leads to the beach, and he had the whole place to himself, not another soul about.

Right now, though, he has to find someone called Battie Shannon, a retired fisherman who, according to Breda Sullivan at the hotel, keeps the keys to the cable station. He strolls through the village until he comes to what must be the house, which, just as she described, is more of a garage workshop. The door is wide open, the small room filled with junk, driftwood, seaweed and wood shavings. Battie's carvings, some displayed on the walls, mostly of boats, are seriously good. When he hears Daniel come in, he looks up from the back of the shop and the small black cat on his knee jumps down, fixing Dan with an intense green stare.

Battie is old, hard to tell how old, but his eyes are sharp and blue, and he gets to his feet slowly to inspect Dan.

'Welcome,' he says. It seems to be the first word out of everyone's mouth around here. He shakes his hand. 'You're the American?'

'Yes, yes, I am. Daniel O'Connell.'

'The Great Liberator.'

'So they tell me.' He has heard this before, even back home, and although he is not by any means well up on Irish history, he does know his namesake was a famous political figure from these parts, responsible for the Catholic Emancipation Act in the 1800s. 'Guess I have a lot to live up to,' he quips.

Battie seems pleased he has made the connection.

'I'm looking for—'

'The keys to the cable station . . . I have them here for you.' Battie reaches over to a wooden shelf and picks them up. 'I'll walk with you,' he says. 'I need to look in on the old place anyhow.'

The small black cat shadows them from a distance. Dan learns she was thrown from a passing car by drunken youths some years back.

'Langered, they were,' Battie says. 'It was in the middle of the night. I heard her crying and took her in. She was only a kitten, a scrap of a thing. She won't let me out of her sight ever since.'

Dan finds Battie's accent almost impossible to decipher, but manages to understand the gist of the story.

On the other side of the village, they come to a rusty gate set into the stone wall. They go through, and walk down what has become an overgrown pathway obscured by wild hydrangeas and fuchsia, on through a field that leads to a ruin of a small building overlooking the beach below.

'Well,' says Battie, 'this is it, or what's left of it at any rate.' He unlocks the old wooden door and steps back to let Dan through.

Their footsteps echo on the slate floor, and Dan has the feeling he is the first person to have entered in quite a while.

'There's not many visitors these days,' Battie confirms. 'What is it you said your interest is in the place?'

Dan hasn't said, but he tells him that his company has been hired to make a documentary about the cable station as part of a History of Communications series commissioned by an American telecoms company.

'A documentary…' Battie repeats. 'You'll want to be interviewing people then, I suppose?'

Dan says he will. This seems to please Battie.

'I'll leave you to it, so,' he says, gesturing to the door. 'You may as well hold on to the keys, there's not likely to be much demand for them.'

Dan thanks him for his help.

'No bother,' he says, his sudden smile transforming his face into a multitude of kindly creases. 'I hope you find what you're looking for.'

As he closes the door behind him, Dan feels he has undertaken and passed some important, if unspoken, test.

The building is single-storey and smaller than he expected, just a room really. From the outside it is much like many ruined cottages that remain in these parts, mostly stone walls in various states of decrepitude, remnants from lives and times past. The cable station, though, such as it is, has been restored – if not to its former working glory, then to a memorial of sorts to the work that was once its daily function. In this small room, with its plastered walls, a fireplace and its few tables, four men, or perhaps six at most, worked at sending and deciphering telegrams from continent to continent. All that remains of their labours are a few remnants of their trade: a galvanometre, inkers, relays, perforators, siphon recorders and, of course, the iconic single Morse key. There are photographs on the walls of moustached men who lived and worked here, and their wives and families who lived in the nearby houses built for them. A cricket team lined up to play the men of Valentia Island, the rival station. Books line the few shelves, and Dan finds a collection of photocopied correspondence from the first superintendent of the station, dating from 1866. There is plenty for him to get started on during the week. He is just about to leave when his phone rings. He checks the caller ID.

'Hey, Mom,' he says. 'Yeah, we're here. We're fine, a little jet-lagged, but doing fine.'

He listens, picturing his mother as she talks in California, her hand going to her throat, fiddling with the chain she always wears, her blue eyes dimmed by pain, her voice attempting cheer but leaching concern. The accident has taken its toll on her, and he knows she worries constantly.

'Really, Mom, we're fine, we'll Skype you at the weekend, we should be set up by then. The internet's not what it is back home.'

'Julie called.' His mother waits a beat. 'She's worried about you guys too, I think she and Greg are terrified of losing you and—'

'You know that's not going to happen.' Dan sighs. 'I wouldn't do that.'

'They've lost their only daughter . . . they need to know they're not going to lose you too, Daniel, you're their only link . . .'

'You think I don't know that? I'll call her in a couple of days, Mom. You can tell her that.'

'I know you will, honey.' His mother's voice cracks. 'I know it's hard, but none of it was their fault . . .'

'Nobody ever said it was.'

'I know, but as a grandparent I can appreciate how they must feel, and now with you so far away . . .'

'I have to go now, Mom. Love you.'

He doesn't feel guilty for ending the call. There's only so much reassurance he can give in any one exchange. Only so much hope he can weave into any conversation. He loves Julie and Greg, his parents-in-law, and he understands the pain they're going through, of course he does. He would never blame them, or cut them off.

He had gotten used to bending the truth when Mary was alive because sometimes it was just easier – for her parents, for his own, for the kids. He could live with that. But he isn't sure how much longer he can live with the liar the accident has turned him into. *We're fine, we're doing okay, we're coping . . .*

He could have Skyped his mother today, his computers are working just fine, but he's not up to it yet. At least on the phone it's just a conversation. Face to face, even on a computer screen, pain can spill across features as suddenly and aggressively as graffiti. He sees it in his mirror every day, and in the shifting expressions of his twin boys, Sean and Pat – Pat and Sean, one starting where the other ends, two expressions of the same soul forever.

At least he has that. Whatever else, he still has that.

Sean

Remember I said we were in the middle of nowhere? That was my first impression and it hasn't changed. Ballyanna is a tiny village right on the edge of the Atlantic, which is why we're here. So Dad can make a documentary about this place and the cable station. Dad likes to involve us in his work whenever he can, because he says you can never start learning too soon about anything. He also says that since kids these days are so glued to their smartphones, they might as well learn about how the whole system actually began. Anyway, here's what I've learned so far: after working out how to send telegrams up and down the country in the olden days, the next big problem was how to send them overseas. That's when the first undersea cable was invented and it came ashore here in Ballyanna. It was called the submarine Atlantic cable and it was a really big deal. After they set it up people could send messages of any kind between Europe and America for the first time ever. Before that, they had to wait for the mail to come in on ships, which took, like, forever.

I know all this stuff because I like to understand about Dad's work, even if it's boring sometimes. I don't talk anymore, but that doesn't mean I'm not interested. Dad says he likes having me around when he works, even if I'm not talking – maybe *especially* because I'm not talking. He's kidding, I know, when he says that, because I know that, deep down, that's what he wants more than anything right now – for me to talk again. But I can't, because that would mean I'd have to talk about what happened the day Mom died. I don't want to talk about that. So I don't say anything at all.

Pat

'I can't understand a word they say around here, can you?'

Sean shakes his head. We're upstairs in our bedroom and he's lying on his bed. Downstairs, Dad's on his computer.

'Guess it doesn't matter to you since you're not going to be talking to anyone, but I'd kind of like to make some friends.'

Sean shrugs. He's reading his book. The same one he always does. It's boring. But Dad says it might help him get back to talking again.

We've had the bereavement sessions and the therapy, so I understand all about death and stuff. It was hard for me too, losing Mom, but I'm more worried about Sean. If he doesn't get his act together soon, they're going to think he's a nut job, and that's on top of the not-talking thing. He sure knows how to mess things up, Sean. Always did, that's his problem. Without me around . . . well, I could only imagine the chaos . . .

Sean was born first, and when I came out after him, apparently I was black and blue. Not, like, because I had some weird disease or anything, it was because Sean had used me to push himself out. That means he'd been beating up on me before we were even born. But I made up for that afterwards – I can always beat him in a fight, although mostly we don't fight anymore, not since we were little kids. Sean used to talk more, but he listens to me. He knows I'm pretty much always right. So whenever we wanted to get Mom and Dad to do something, I'd tell Sean what to say and then get him to, like, present it. It mostly always worked. It still would, except now Sean can't talk, and it's just Dad on his own. We're a good team, Sean and me. We think like one person. I guess all identical twins do – it kind of comes with the territory. At least Sean and me have each other. Dad doesn't have anyone now. Sean and me are doing our best, but it's not enough to fix what happened.

Doctors and counsellors think they know everything, but they don't. They don't know how it feels to be losing someone when you don't even know why they're going. It was like that with Mom. She didn't have to say anything . . . we could feel her getting further and further away.

So it didn't really matter about the arguments or the car accident, or what Sean believes. But he doesn't understand that. He's not ready to. I'm not sure Dad is either, so I don't say anything. Sean blames himself. That's the problem. But it's not the truth.

* * *

The aroma of baking fills the room, and as she places the batch of scones by the window to cool, Jerry is struck yet again by the beauty of her view. Outside the sun has begun its steady climb, pouring a path of glittering light onto the water below. And although it is only ten o'clock, the day promises to be another hot one.

Sitting at her table in the small cottage by the lake, Jerry reads the letter again. So her brother is finally coming home. It is three years since she has last seen him, and that was when she had saved up to buy a ticket and travelled to the small, remote village in Kenya where Barry was based. She had been appalled at the poverty of his life there, the same as the people he ministered to, but she had also experienced first-hand the generosity of his flock and the overwhelming love they had for him. Barry himself, although thin and overworked, had never looked happier. She stayed for six weeks, and by the end of her visit hardly wanted to leave.

Barry had always wanted to be a missionary, but his early career had largely been determined by his superiors. The brothers had spotted his brilliance as a child and had steered him relentlessly towards the priesthood. In his days as a young priest in Rome, he had been tipped as one to watch in the Vatican, his easy grasp of languages, fine mind and natural charm almost guaranteeing a meteoric rise through the ranks. Jerry smiles at the idea. She could never have envisaged her brother as a bishop, let alone a cardinal, no matter how devout he was, and she had been proved right. What they hadn't banked on, those fellows in the Roman Boys' Club, was Barry's utter and unshakable integrity. There had been an incident, some matter involving a superior, when Barry had spoken out, refused to be silenced, refused to toe the clerical line – he had never spoken of the details, not even to Jerry, but he had put in an immediate request for transfer that was granted indecently quickly, at last finding himself on the missionary path he had longed for from the beginning.

So now he's coming home. Jerry wonders why. His letter mentions a bout of ill health, his superiors insisting on a sabbatical, a complete rest somewhere where he will be looked after and have clean air and water and decent food. Well, she can make sure of that, of course. But knowing Barry, and the love he has for his flock in Turkana, he won't be coming home lightly. She suspects there may be more to it, but she will find out in good time.

His letter says that he'd like to stay with her, if that wouldn't be an imposition, and that he is looking forward greatly to seeing her and, of course, to returning home to Ballyanna. It has been a long time since he has been home, over forty years, and he wonders if those decades have flown by as quickly for her as they have for him. The answer to that is yes, but to Jerry the past is just as tangible as the present, sometimes more so. She remembers it as if it was yesterday, wonders if he ever thinks about it too. It hadn't always been the priesthood for Barry. There had been romance too, and love – a very definite love. Hearts had been broken on both sides, she knows. It wasn't that the vocation to the priesthood had been stronger than his feelings for the girl in question, Jerry knew he had wrestled sorely with his decision. But his gift had swung the balance in making his final decision. Not the many obvious gifts he had – his brilliant mind, his facility with languages, his engaging manner with people, his genuine devotion to the faith – but the one he never spoke of, the one he dreads misusing . . . that's what had clinched the decision. And she suspects that, apart from Barry himself, she is the only person who is party to this.

She folds the letter thoughtfully and puts it in the back pocket of her dungarees. She sits for a moment, looking out at the lake, head tilted, as if listening. Then she nods to herself, picks up her phone and presses a contact number.

'I've just made a fresh batch of scones,' she says into the phone. 'Do you fancy a cuppa?'

'I'd murder one,' comes the brisk reply. 'See you in ten.'

* * *

The offer of tea couldn't have come at a more opportune moment. Conor is doing Breda's head in after his visit with the accountant, and she is feeling particularly low. Jerry is a mind-reader, but sure everyone knows that anyway. The woman is clairvoyant, everybody says so. Of course, over the years this has given rise to a certain amount of speculation and rumour-mongering. Breda has heard them all . . . hazy details handed down from mothers to daughters who were now grandmothers themselves. All of them make her laugh. Jerry had been in a convent – or was it a commune? Some said she had been Sister Jeremiah in a previous life. Some said her real name was Geraldine, but no one seemed to know for sure.

What they could say for sure was that she was an herbalist, a healer (of people and animals) and, without a shadow of a doubt, that she has the 'gift'. She wouldn't read cards or tell fortunes, she has no time for any of that 'codswallop', as she refers to it – but if someone is in trouble or grieving, she will give them a sitting, and the recipient of her ministrations always comes away peaceful, restored and more in awe of her than ever.

But Breda has known Jerry all her life . . . the real Jerry . . . the woman behind the gift, who is her dearest friend and the older sister she never had.

Breda thinks about walking to Jerry's cottage on the lake, she has been in the car for far too long already today, but walking seems overwhelming, even though she knows it would do her good to stretch her legs. She is already stretched, she thinks grimly, and in all the wrong directions. Suddenly the appeal of Jerry's calm and amusing company and her cosy, animal-filled home seems not only irresistible, but immediately necessary. Walking would take a good fifteen minutes, Breda can't wait that long.

Five minutes later she pulls up outside the open half-door of Jerry's cottage, scattering a few hens and eliciting curious stares from a goat and a small donkey, whose nose she scratches until he lifts his muzzle and grimaces at her.

Jerry appears at the door and waves her in. 'Sit yourself down, Breda, how are you?' Jerry pours the tea and pushes a scone in Breda's direction.

'Don't ask.' Breda sits down and takes a grateful gulp of tea. 'Oh, I needed that.'

'That bad?'

'No more than usual. You know yourself.'

Jerry is up-to-date on Breda's affairs, and sympathetic.

'How's Dee? Any news?'

Breda shakes her head. 'If there is, I haven't heard about it. She's gone on retreat.'

'She never struck me as the spiritual type.' Jerry seems surprised. 'But I suppose there's always a first time . . .'

'Not a retreat as we know it, Jerry. This one involves yoga, and sun . . . I think it's in the Algarve. Ah well, I suppose it'll do her good to get out of Ballyanna for a bit.'

Jerry makes reassuring noises and pats Breda's hand. 'She'll be alright, Breda, things will get better.'

'Will they, though?' Breda looks miserable. 'It doesn't look like it from where I'm sitting. She needs to consult a solicitor, find out what her situation is, but all she seems to want to do since she's come back is gad about . . . it's as if she's making herself believe the whole thing never happened. To tell you the truth, I'm at my wits' end.'

'Will she hold on to the house, do you think?'

Breda shrugs. 'I haven't a clue.'

'And little Gracie . . . how is she? What does she know?'

'It's anyone's guess. The other day she told me that before Dee left, she heard her talking on the phone and saying that her dad had buggered off and lost them all their money . . .'

'What did you say to that?'

'I said she must have misheard and not to be worrying, that her dad loves her very much, and he'll be back when all his business gets sorted out. What else could I say to the poor little pet?'

Jerry shakes her head. She has her own theories about Dee, and she's pretty sure the girl has no intention of dealing with her current marriage meltdown. Instead of being strong for her little girl and her elderly parents, who are shouldering the burden of their son-in-law's disgrace, Dee is hiding behind self-pity and denial. And she didn't pick that attitude up off the ground, Jerry thinks to herself.

'At least Annie's home now, that's good, isn't it?'

'Yes ... I suppose ... Oh, you know, Jerry, I just don't know any more.' Breda rubs her face with her hands.

'How did the dinner go?' Jerry knows Breda had been nervous about Annie's first night home.

'We got through it, anyway. Conor and she were civil, even when he had to go and say he ran into Philip, when I had warned him to keep off the subject. She seems in good enough form, although she's looking a bit worn out. But she's furious about John and if you saw her face when I said Dee had gone away ... I mean, I know everything's a disaster zone right now, but I couldn't ... I just couldn't handle Annie swooping down like an avenging angel expressing outrage and anger everywhere she goes. You know how she can be ... and you know how she and Dee can rub each other up the wrong way entirely ...'

'Don't upset yourself, Breda.' Jerry pats her hand. 'Annie will be a great help with the situation, I should think. And I'm quite sure any past squabbles and differences will be put aside to concentrate on sorting everything out. Annie will be good at that.'

Jerry speaks lightly, but behind her smile she is worried about her old friend. Breda has been under considerable strain for the last few months and neither her husband nor Dee are being any help to her as far as Jerry can see. Annie coming home is a good thing, she is sure of it. She might even have a quiet word with her herself, just to give her some perspective, fill her in on a few details, make sure she understands how much strain Breda has been under trying to cope with everything.

'I hope you're right. Things can't get much worse anyway. Oh, that reminds me, don't let me leave without some of your sleeping potion.'

'I'll get a bottle now, so you don't forget.' Jerry gets up to go into her back room where she keeps her herbs. 'I believe some Americans have taken Cable Lodge for the summer,' she calls to Breda. 'I met Joan Coady in the chemist, she was telling me that they're from California.' Jerry puts a large bottle of dark-coloured liquid in front of Breda, who promptly puts it in her handbag.

'That's right, I met the fellow actually. He's making a documentary, I think, something about the cable station, and he's come here to do his research. Imagine that. He's very handsome. Not what you'd call chatty, though. Anyway, he came in looking for the keys to the cable station, so I directed him to Battie Shannon. He had *The Irish Times* under his arm, so I told him the *Indo* was the better paper, welcomed him to Ballyanna, and told him to be sure to come into the hotel for dinner.'

'What did he say?'

'He thanked me and said he'd keep it in mind, said he'd try the *Independent* tomorrow.'

'What's his name?'

'Daniel O'Connell.'

'The Great Liberator!'

Breda smiled. 'That's what I said. He said everyone was saying that to him. That he had a lot to live up to.'

'Well that's being reasonably chatty, amusing even.'

'Then he fled.'

'Well if he's researching the cable station, we'll be seeing quite a bit of him.'

'I suppose.'

'Speaking of cables, I've had my own interesting piece of

communication.' Jerry is casual, but watchful of Breda's reaction. She doesn't want to upset her old friend in any way, particularly as she is going through such a difficult time at the moment, but Breda will have to know sooner or later, and she might even be pleased.

'Oh? What's that?'

'A letter, from Barry. He's coming home.'

'Coming home? Here? To Ballyanna?'

'Yes. It would appear so.'

'Why?' Breda is clearly taken aback. 'I mean, why now, after all these years?'

'He hasn't been well. That's all I know. I don't think he has a choice in the matter.'

'Oh, I see . . . when does he get in?'

'Next week. Wednesday. Someone's giving him a lift from Dublin.'

'He'll be staying with you, of course?'

'Yes, that's the plan.'

'That will be lovely for you, having him home for a while.'

Breda is smiling, but Jerry is not sure whether she is pleased or put out by the news; either way, she leaves shortly afterwards. At least she knows, now, Jerry thinks, she has done her duty in that respect. All the same, she can tell that the news rattled Breda, and she can't say she blames her.

People tend to assume that once you are over fifty, matters of the heart are behind you for good. In Jerry's experience, the opposite is true. The older you are, the more precious loved ones and memories of times gone by become to you. The fact that you might not have seen those loved ones for a lifetime, or that those lives have taken entirely different paths from yours, makes not one jot of difference. Once someone has found their way into your heart, then that's where they stay, as close as your own breath, however far apart life may take you.

* * *

Although Annie has been kept updated with regular accounts of the horrors involved in undertaking a new build by her best friend Barbara and her husband, Doctor Mike, she is still taken aback by how beautiful their newly finished house looks at first sight. The photographs do not do it justice, she thinks. It sits in a hollow of land, looking onto the lake, for all the world as if it has been there forever.

Barbara answers the door and pulls Annie into an enthusiastic bear hug.

'Careful,' Annie warns. 'I come bearing breakable gifts.' She disengages herself and puts the bag and bottle on the hall table. 'For the kids,' she points to the bag, 'and for us,' she indicates the bottle of rosé, Barbara's favourite.

'Oh, you shouldn't have!' Barbara says as she leads the way to the kitchen. 'But I'm not going to pretend I'm not delighted you did.'

'Where are they?' Annie looks around for Barbara's little boys.

'With Mum. She's taken them so I can enjoy a rare day off and share a bottle of wine over lunch with my dearest friend. I've missed you.'

'I've missed you too.'

'Come on, we'll eat first, then I'll give you the guided tour.'

'This wasn't part of the plan, you know.' Barbara gestures towards the table where lunch has been set out. 'That you introduce me to a man you know I will fall madly in love with, then high-tail it back to London and leave me here all alone for four whole years.'

'You know that wasn't meant to happen.'

'Of course I do, and you know I'm only joking, but still . . . never mind, you're here now.'

Barbara pours them each a glass of wine then brings over an enormous platter of seafood and plonks it on the table.

'All that's for us?' Annie's eyes widen.

'What's the matter? Forgotten your appetite? I keep telling you, you've been away too long. A few days out and about in this air and you won't know yourself. Now spill . . .'

'You first,' Annie says, after a mouthful of velvety smoked salmon and melt-in-the-mouth brown bread.

'Nothing you don't already know. Thrilled to be shot of the builders and have the house finally finished . . . run off my feet in the shop . . . got ten pounds still to lose at WeightWatchers.' Barbara pats her tummy. 'Still eternally grateful to you for introducing me to the nicest, most patient and sexiest man in the country.'

'That's all?'

'Not enough for you?'

'No more than you deserve,' Annie says with a laugh.

Annie has known Barbara since they became friends at the convent school they both attended, and they have remained close ever since. Although she was a high-powered lawyer, Barbara had been unlucky in love, lurching from one disastrous relationship to another as she travelled and worked from Paris to Brussels, LA to Dubai. Then, on a trip home for a family birthday party, Annie had introduced her to the recently widowed Doctor Mike and to everyone's surprise love had blossomed. Barbara had not only agreed to marry him, but she gave up her legal career in short order and returned to set up home in Ballyanna. Mike's daughters from his first marriage loved her, although they pretended not to at first. Then their two little boys had come along to complete their family. Barbara had opened a gift shop in the village two years ago and recently expanded her stock to include local designer jewellery and woollens, and claims she has never been happier.

'It hasn't all been roses, as you know. His girls didn't make it easy in the beginning ...'

'And now?'

'Oh, they're fine, time actually does help, I've found. They're about to spread their own wings now, so they're too busy to be bothered huffing about evil stepmother here, plus they adore the boys.'

Annie shakes her head. 'It seems like only yesterday they were little themselves. How old are they now?'

'Molly's seventeen and Nicola's nineteen, and both of them are going on forty. Now, enough about me. What about you? Has the Prodigal Daughter been welcomed back with open arms?'

Annie makes a wry expression. 'We got through dinner, just about. Dad managed to wait about half an hour before mentioning that he'd run into Philip, and Mum looked as if she wanted to throttle him. He'd obviously been warned off the topic. Then, of course, as soon as he knew he was in trouble, he escaped to the bar and Mum brought me up-to-date with things.'

'Ah.'

'Precisely ...'

'So, what's going on?'

'You probably know as much as I do.' Annie sighs. 'John was running a ponzi scheme in Cork. When investors began to look for a return on their investment ...'

'There was none?'

'Exactly. It was all gone, and now John's disappeared ... lying low somewhere, no doubt hoping it just blows over.'

'As you would. How's Dee taking it? I believe she's back in town, although I haven't seen her.'

'I wouldn't know,' Annie says dryly. 'She's off in sunny Portugal. A yoga retreat, apparently. Mum's minding Gracie on top of everything else.'

Barbara shakes her head. 'Let me guess . . .,' she breaks into a wickedly accurate imitation of Dee, *How could he do this to me? What am I going to say to all our friends? I'll never be able to hold my head up again . . . Poor me . . . Oh, I know . . . I'll run home to hide and then go on a holiday, leave Gracie with her grandparents . . . that'll reassure her . . .*' Barbara has never been a fan of Annie's older sister. 'It's Gracie I feel sorry for. How is the little pet?'

'Hard to know, really . . . she seems okay, you know, still her crazy, cheerful self, she seems to be holding up. But my bet is she's probably very scared.'

Barbara nods in agreement. 'There's something really lovely about that kid.'

'I know. I'd run away with her. We all would, but Dee . . . I don't know . . . sometimes I just don't think she gets her, you know?'

'That's mothers and daughters for you. Thank God I only have boys.'

'Now . . .' she looks at Annie, 'I know you don't want to talk about it much, but you only told me the barest outline on the phone and I want all the gory details now I've got you here. You promised you'd tell me everything.'

'I have.'

Barbara frowns. 'You look tired, and you're too thin.' She regards Annie's slight frame with disapproval. 'Much as I'm a fan of the heartbreak diet, it never actually does us the favours we imagine it does. Fill me in on you and Ed. What happened, really?'

Annie sighs. 'Just what I already told you. Exactly what everyone said would happen. What happened to the one before me, and the one before that . . .'

'Yes, I know,' Barbara says gently, 'but knowing you, you've been bottling it all up, throwing yourself into work, and just getting on with things . . .'

Annie bites her lip. 'It's not just the break-up, though . . . Barb, I feel like such a fool . . . *such* a fool . . .'

'That's just because it's a novelty for you, Miss High Achiever. I'm an old hand at foolery with men. Tell me . . . was it when you broached the baby idea again, was that it?'

'Well, yes . . . but it was more than that . . .'

As far as Barbara knew, Annie's desire for a baby had been the only point of difference between her and Ed.

'I thought it was worth one more try . . .' Annie twirls the stem of her glass. 'You know, to sit him down, unwind, romantic dinner, and it was all going beautifully until he told me he'd been having an affair for the last six months . . .'

Barbara's mouth falls open. 'The little bastard,' she breathes. 'How dare he!'

Annie shrugs, but the pain of that night is still fresh. 'That was just for openers.' Now that she's begun, Annie is relieved to talk to Barbara. It's the first time she feels able to confide in anyone, apart from Theo. 'The thing is, she was pregnant, this girl . . . six months when he told me. As you can imagine, I really didn't want to be around when the baby arrived. Couldn't face that.'

'Oh, Annie.' Barbara reaches over and puts her hand over Annie's. 'I'm so sorry.'

'I should have known.'

'How *could* you have known?' Barbara shakes her head. 'You loved him. Even if there had been signs, you wouldn't have wanted to see them. We never do. And let's face it, who would have wanted to tell you?'

'Everyone warned me, though,' Annie says miserably. 'Every woman who knew him said Ed came into your life like a whirlwind and left leaving just as much chaos. I thought we were different, that I was different.' She laughs bleakly at the idea. 'I thought he loved me.'

'I'm sure he did love you, Annie, as much as any man like Ed can love *anyone*. But I know these guys, they're self-obsessed children at heart. Yes, they're terrific fun to have around, but no help at all when it comes to cleaning up their messes. Thank God you *didn't* have a baby with him. Can you imagine?'

Annie doesn't want to even try. It's too painful. She has been stupid. Trusting and stupid. 'This Sarah girl, that's her name, she didn't wait around and ask him politely about having a baby. She just went right ahead and took her chances . . . and in the process, I've lost mine.'

'No you haven't!' Barbara is adamant. 'Listen to me, Annie, I know how terrible all this must feel now, but trust me, I've been there, one way or another, and I know, I'd stake my life on it, that Ed wasn't right for you. Ed was your . . . your . . .' Barbara searches for the right analogy, '. . . your walk on the wild side. He was an accident waiting to happen for you. Ever since I've known you, you've always done everything by the book, Annie. To be honest, I always thought everything you did was too considered, you seemed to have this duty thing going on with you, even when we were young, almost as if you were afraid to step out of line at all . . .' Barbara smiles.

'Was I really that boring?'

'Not boring! No. Wise, maybe, an old head on young shoulders. Look, the point is that you were living your whole life by erring on the side of caution . . . I mean, Philip was lovely and I know everyone thought you were the perfect match, but no one was happier than I was when you called it all off with him.'

Annie looks at her friend in surprise. 'You never said that at the time.'

'You didn't exactly give us time for a post-mortem, remember?'
Annie nods. 'No, I suppose I didn't.'

'Whatever else Ed did or didn't do for you, he was the catalyst
that allowed you to finally break out of that emotional security
thing. For once, you followed your heart, not your head. And that
was *exactly* what you needed, Annie – someone or something to
blow that safety thing apart. Let's face it, Ed was everything your
parents would have dreaded. Did they ever even meet him?'

'Mum did, once . . . it was pretty uncomfortable.' Annie remembers the strained dinner. 'And Dee met him a couple of times when
she stayed with us . . . and you met him . . .'

'Exactly. And I could see what you saw in him, believe me! He
was gorgeous, fun, clever, sexy, dangerous . . . but I had a pretty
good idea, even then, that he wasn't Your Guy.'

'You might have said something, Barb . . .'

'Really?' Barbara grins. 'You think you would have listened?
You were in the first flush of love and lust, Annie! That's a heady
combination – and one you needed to embrace. Don't regret that.
Don't beat yourself up about it. The fact that you and Ed didn't go
the distance says everything about him, not about you. Hell, you
called off a wedding for the guy! If he can still go on to cheat on
you after that, he's . . . well, I don't want to slag him off . . . but
let's face it, he's not the kind of guy any girl needs, let alone you.
And he certainly doesn't sound like my idea of a good father in the
making. No, you'll meet someone else, someone better, I know you
will. You need a real man, Annie, someone who can shoulder the
bad times as well as the good, and you'll find him . . .'

'I don't want to find him, or any of them,' Annie says vehemently.
'I'm done with it all. I'm just fine on my own.'

'Of course you are, but that would be such a waste, Annie.
What's happened to you is horrible . . . betrayal of any kind always

is . . . but don't let this colour your judgement of men, I mean, look how nice Philip was . . . and he was crazy about you.'

'Don't!' Annie puts her face in her hands. 'You think the word *karma* hasn't been reverberating in my head since all this happened?'

'Stop it! Karma has nothing to do with it. You've just had a relationship with a commitment-shy man-child. A very charming one, I'll grant you, but you've said yourself his track record wasn't good. Better you found out now, while you're still young enough to make a fresh start.'

Annie chews the inside of her mouth. 'Do you mind if we don't talk about it anymore?'

'Of course not. Consider the matter closed.'

Barbara is as good as her word and doesn't bring it up again. They linger over coffee, catching up, swapping stories, until it is time for Annie to go.

'There's a crowd of us meeting up in O'Dowd's later in the week,' Barbara says as she hugs her goodbye. 'You should come. It'd do you good, give you a chance to see a few old faces.'

'I'd like that.' Annie smiles at her. 'Thank you for lunch.'

'It's good to have you back.'

As Barbara waves her off, Annie marvels yet again at the unpredictability of life. If anyone had told them when they were schoolgirls that Barbara would be settled back in Ballyanna with a man twenty years her senior and two small children, they'd have screamed with laughter. But then, there is nothing funny about the contentment and happiness her best friend radiates. Barbara has blossomed, marriage and motherhood have softened her. Annie couldn't be happier for her.

* * *

Breda cannot sleep and has given up trying. She had wallowed in a nice bath with her favourite relaxing oils, although Conor would give out about skidding in it tomorrow, had read her favourite romance author's latest, but she is still tossing and turning hours later while Conor snores beside her. She gets up and looks in on Gracie, making sure she is out for the count, then makes herself a cup of chamomile tea and sits down on the sofa by the big floor-to-ceiling picture window that overlooks the bay. Although it is past midnight, it is not completely dark. A silken moon is high, almost full, reflecting shades of navy, purple and silver through the night sky. A light gauze of mist hovers over the bay that she knows, from experience, will be gone by dawn.

How has it come to this? Although she has to admit, bad as things are, she feels better now Annie is home, even if her daughter is clearly furious at her brother-in-law's financial deceptions and at their failure to spot what he was up to. No good telling Annie that hindsight is 20/20, her likely retort would be 'should have gone to Specsavers'. Breda can't help feeling that Annie thinks if she'd been around, she'd have sussed John out much earlier – and that she's angry at herself for not being there and at them for missing the warning signs. For not staging a rescue mission before it was too late.

But her family problems are not the only reason she is jumpy tonight, Breda acknowledges. If she is honest, she hasn't been herself since hearing that Barry is coming home. And how ridiculous is that? Barry McLaughlin – Father Barry McLaughlin, to give him his correct title – her first love, a feeling as real to her now as it was over forty years ago.

She last saw him at her wedding.

It had been her way of trying to pay him back, watching and witnessing his awkwardness on the day, while she paraded herself, radiant in her beautiful wedding gown, with her handsome bridegroom waiting for her at the top of the church. But the moment she'd slipped her hand around her father's proffered arm, before she'd even taken her first step up the aisle, she'd known it was a mistake. She wasn't fooling anyone, least of all Barry, who was not at all awkward, as she had painted him in her fond imaginings of the big day. On the contrary, he had radiated the inner tranquillity common to those secure in the knowledge they are following the path they have always known is their true calling in life. The hint of sadness in his eyes on the day was for her, Breda, because he saw exactly what she was trying to do and felt for her. He saw through the bright smile, the brittle laugh and the artificial way she posed in the photographs, looking adoringly at Conor as if he was a film star, which was no more than what many people thought and said he looked like. And she *did* love Conor then, he was handsome, funny, spontaneous and very charming. It was just that the minute she saw Barry again, when he came up to congratulate them both, she had known in her heart that she would never love any man the way she loved him.

She hadn't told Conor about her relationship with Barry, how he had been her first love. Conor would only have made a laugh about it – her first boyfriend going off to became a priest, ha, ha, ha. And joke or not, Breda wouldn't have found it a bit funny. So instead she told Conor that Barry was an old family friend – not quite a lie, just a version of the truth she felt more comfortable with.

Her mother had warned her it was not a good idea. 'I know what you think you're doing here, Breda, and it won't work. Not only that, it will backfire badly.'

'I don't know what you're talking about.' Breda had feigned innocence.

'Oh yes you do. I'm your mother and it's my duty to advise you, even if you don't want to hear it. You're still in love with Barry

McLaughlin and before you deny it, only a very foolish bride, insane even, would insist on inviting a man she had loved and lost to be at her wedding. Do you really think that Barry, seeing you looking beautiful on your wedding day, is going to regret choosing the priesthood? Really? I've never heard of anything so stupid. That's how I know you're still in love with him, only a woman madly in love would think of such a stupid undertaking. Honest to God, Breda, who do you think you are? Scarlett O'Hara pining over Ashley? This is the 1970s. Barry chose the priesthood. It was and will always be his calling and to be fair to the man, he never made you any promises, never led you up the garden path, he simply did what he knew was right in his heart. Believe me, I know it was hard, I know how much you loved him, we all did. He was, and is, a very special person. But he's not *your* special person. You know how I feel about Conor, I don't think he's the answer, but there's still time to change your mind, to call off the wedding.'

Breda had looked at her aghast, equally horrified by the suggestion and by the fact that her mother had indeed read her mind. 'I have no intention of calling off my wedding. How could you even—'

Her mother held up her hands. 'Fine, do whatever you want. But if you're going to marry Conor, at least give him a hundred percent, Breda. Don't be holding back some part of yourself on account of some nonsensical fantasy about you and a man you cannot have and who, I might point out, does not want you.'

She had been right, of course, Breda's mother, as she almost always was. But to be fair to Breda, she *had* given one hundred percent to her marriage – and she and Conor were still together forty years on. Good going by any stretch.

But on the rare occasions, such as now, when she takes down her wedding album and is transported back to that beautiful day in Ballyanna – when the sun had shone, and the sea was calm and cornflower blue, with the hotel bedecked in flowers and the marquee set up on the front lawn where she had played as a child, sunbathed as a teenager, and was now frozen in time as a beautiful bride – when she looks at those long-ago photographs, it is Barry's face she lingers on.

* * *

She was still here.

He could feel her, waiting around every corner, behind every closed door. Every footstep was a possibility, every call on his cell phone the chance of the last conversation they'd never had.

She had left him before and he had let her go, but this time it was different. This time he was angry as hell. This time, she hadn't just erased their past, she had stolen their future – and that was what he couldn't forgive.

Here in this house, this beautiful, old, rambling, decaying manor house, he kept discovering things that would both delight and infuriate her. The first glimpse of sky dissolving from deep navy to purple, then fingers of rosy pink creeping over the water as dawn broke. He watched it every morning from his bed, and each day it was different. The beautiful proportions of the reception rooms with big windows looking out onto a garden grown wild. The sweeping staircase and magnificent stained-glass window that looked down to the hall from the first return. The bath with a will of its own, generously gushing water from its old brass taps or withholding it for no reason at all in a miserly dribble. The seemingly endless succession of spiders that emerged from every nook and cranny. Those noises, most audible at night, that were the clunks and whirring of unseen, unused pipes, and the draughts that could materialise from nowhere, even on a warm summer's day.

Dan loved this house, and he knew Mary would have too.

He thought getting away, this far away, would help him to forget, but the truth was that he could see her more clearly than ever here. He still expected her to walk through the door, or to find her standing by the range at any given moment. Even though it had been over a year now. Fourteen months, two weeks and three days, to be exact.

It was the early days he thought about the most. First setting eyes on her at the production meeting, thinking how impossibly groomed and poised she was, the polished TV exec right down to her fingertips. And those legs . . . even underneath her sober business suit he could tell they went on forever. He never in a million years would have imagined someone like her would have looked at a beach bum diver like him (which was how he saw himself back then, when his production company was just getting off the ground), but then their eyes had met and he'd known he had to see her again. Had to. As it turned out, it had happened when he'd least expected it. She'd called him up, said she wanted to discuss some aspects of the documentary with him, suggested they meet over coffee. After that day, they started dating. Turned out he was wrong about her. Outside the office she was a different person, she was a hiker and swimmer too. In the water she was a natural, better even than him, which was saying something. And out of the water, well, he had been right about those legs.

He'd known early on that he was falling for her, and it had terrified him – although not as much as the thought of a life without her. His career had yet to take off and he had little or no spare cash, but he bit the bullet, bought her a modest but pretty ring, borrowed a boat from a friend and organised a picnic, champagne, candles, then called her up and asked if she would like a late supper on the ocean.

He was so nervous he forgot, briefly, where he'd hidden the ring, almost blew everything. She always swore afterwards that she had no idea of what he was planning. The important thing was that she'd said 'yes' without hesitation. They'd spent the rest of the night on the water and then watched the sun come up. Memories like that are pretty hard to forget.

They got married, Mary got pregnant, Daniel got nervous, and then came the news – twins! He didn't remember much from that moment on until they actually arrived in the world. He'd lived in a fog of terror. The thought of one helpless infant depending on him was bad enough, but two . . .

Like all new, nervous parents they'd eventually figured it out, and both sets of families had always been on hand to help. They'd called the boys Sean and Patrick after their respective grandfathers, who'd both had Irish origins. Mary had always wanted to make the trip to Ireland, it was one of the things they had planned on doing at some stage. Now here they were without her . . . Dan shook his head, as if to clear it. It was ridiculous, he knew that, but for the life of him he couldn't shake the feeling that, somehow, his beautiful late wife was right here with them.

Sean

Today we went to look around the old cable station, or what's left of it. The mess where the telegraphers used to live is gone and the office building has been sold off and turned into apartments. The room where all the telegraphers worked is pretty much an old ruin that's been restored on the inside. But you can still see where the tennis courts and cricket pitch used to be, and the water tower. And there's a plaque on the beach marking the spot where the cable was pulled ashore. Dad's explaining how it all began. He says it's really interesting because back then, like, centuries ago, the transatlantic submarine cable was the internet of its day.

'It was a game-changer,' he said, as Pat and I followed him around. I was more interested than Pat, but he could listen when he had to. If we let Dad do some exploring, he said he would take us to the beach this afternoon. 'Before the cable was laid, news could only travel as fast as people could between the old world and the new – Europe being the old world and America the new, obviously.' He stopped to show us some old photographs.

'Like we haven't heard this five hundred times already,' Pat said.

Dad ignored the comment. When he was into something, he could go on for hours . . .

'That meant it took almost two weeks for news to get to or from either continent, because that was the fastest any ship could make the crossing.'

'That's why they invented aeroplanes,' Pat mumbled. But Dad didn't hear him.

There were some maps and photographs of some really old people and buildings. The men in the photographs mostly had big moustaches, and the women wore long skirts and had their hair tied back.

'C'mon, let's go outside. We can wait for Dad there.' Pat pushed me towards the door, knocking a pile of folders from a table to the floor as he ran ahead.

'Sean!' Dad looked around, alarmed. 'Be careful, please!'

If I was talking, I could have said *it wasn't me, it was Pat.* Instead, I just bent down and picked them up and put them back. It was easier.

Outside it was warm and sunny, and the place looked really pretty. We ran over to the edge of the field, to the side of the station, and looked down to the beach below. Pat climbed down to explore and took off down the beach at a run. I was about to follow him when I heard a voice behind me. I looked around and saw a girl about our age.

'Hi,' she said.

I nodded.

'I'm Gracie.'

She was wearing a purple net skirt with stripy leggings and biker boots and a headband. Her hair was long and black, and she wound a piece of it round and round her finger.

I looked at the ground. I could tell she was studying me.

'Are you on your own?'

I shook my head and pointed to the door. But before I could go back inside, Dad came out. 'I thought I heard a voice.' He smiled at Gracie. 'Hey, there.'

'Hi, I'm Gracie. I live in the hotel. You're the Americans, aren't you?'

'That's right, we are. Good to meet you, Gracie,' Dad said. 'I'm Dan, and this is my boy, Sean. He doesn't say much right now, but he's gonna be around for a while and he'd really like to make some friends. Wouldn't you, buddy?' He looked at me encouragingly.

I wanted to kill him.

'Gracie, why don't you show Sean around the village, get yourselves an ice cream?' He handed me some money. 'I need to go through some papers here. Let's all meet in the hotel in half an hour, say? Then we can get some lunch. Maybe you'll join us, Gracie?'

'Um, I'll have to ask my Gran,' Gracie said.

'Sure, that sounds like a good idea. Off you go, guys.' He smiled widely at me.

No. Please. This cannot be happening.

Gracie looked at me hard, as if trying to decide something. For a minute she didn't say anything.

'Okay,' she said then. 'You don't have to talk. I'd talk the hind legs off a donkey, my mam says. Most of the boys around here never stop yelling, so it'll be a relief having someone quiet around.' She said it all very quickly, in the same sing-song voice they all spoke with around here. It was hard to understand, but if I listened really carefully and slowed it down in my head, I was beginning to get the hang of it.

'C'mon, let's go.' She led the way. 'I'll show what you need to know.'

Grace O'Malley was two months younger than me. She was short, fat and had wild black frizzy hair. She was named after a famous Irish pirate. She told me all this as I followed her through the village. I didn't think there were women pirates, so I didn't know if she was making that bit up. I would Google it later, I decided.

'I know I'm not pretty,' she went on, 'but that doesn't matter because I have tons of personality, and I'm a kind person.' She ran ahead of me to the ice cream van that was parked in a lay-by.

'Two double ninety-nines, Paddy,' she said to the man who looked out the window. He had white hair that went all every way and only three teeth when he smiled.

'Who's your new friend, Gracie?' he asked, handing down two cones filled with swirls of ice cream and two chocolate sticks in each.

'This is Sean, he's over from California.'

'Well isn't that grand,' Paddy said. 'And you've brought the weather with you and all.'

I didn't understand what he meant, but Grace gave me the ice cream and shooed me away when I tried to give her the money for it.

'Those are on the house, Gracie,' Paddy said. 'Sure I'll be making enough money out of you for the rest of the summer.'

Across the road we stopped at a statue of a man with a hat and a walking stick.

'Well, you must know who that is,' Gracie said.

I shook my head.

She looked amazed. 'That's Charlie Chaplin. Everyone knows who Charlie Chaplin is. And you're American!'

I shrugged, although the name, when she said it, sounded familiar.

'He's a famous actor, and a film-maker, you must have heard of him? He used to come here on his holidays with his family every year. He's dead now, of course, but some of his family still come back.'

I had the feeling that I was disappointing her. I did that a lot to people.

'C'mon,' she said. 'We'll go up to the golf club. We'll go up the cliff road and I'll show you the other beach, but we'll have to move it.' She looked at her watch. 'I know you can't talk, but you can run, can't you?'

I didn't need asking twice.

For someone with short legs, Grace O'Malley was fast. But I could still outrun her, even though I wasn't as fast since the accident. All the same, she kept up pretty well, considering. We ran all the way along the cliff by the sea and past another beach, a longer one than the one in the village, with bigger waves.

'That's the golf links beach,' Gracie panted. 'You can see seals there sometimes in the evening and early in the morning, and there's good surfing too.'

She stopped and bent over. 'Hold on a minute. I've a stitch. Let me catch my breath. We're here anyway.'

There was a restaurant on the left called The Smuggler's Inn, and across the way Grace pointed to a set of gates and a driveway. At the end of it there was a long, low stone building.

'That's the golf club. We'll go and find Declan, he's the pro. I was thinking,' she said looking at me, 'you might be able to get work caddying, there's nothing to it. The yanks are brilliant tippers, you can make a fortune. And with you not talking, they'll think you're Irish.'

I had no idea what she was talking about. We went around the back of the club, where a golf lesson was finishing up.

'That's Declan,' whispered Gracie, nodding in the direction of a tall guy with dark hair who was saying goodbye to an older woman who smiled at him a lot.

'See you next week, Doreena, make sure you practise that swing.'

'Oh, I'll be sure to. Thank you again, Declan.'

'My pleasure.' He waved her off.

'Hi, Declan!' said Gracie.

'Well, if it isn't the Pirate Queen! To what do I owe this unexpected visit?'

'This is my new friend, Sean. He's over from California for the summer. I'm showing him round. I thought you might get him a job as a caddy – you could teach him.'

'Is that so?' said Declan. 'And does Sean have any say in this idea of yours?' He held out his hand to me and I shook it.

'Sean doesn't talk.'

I looked out over the greens and sloping hills that stretched for miles.

'Very wise.' Declan was looking at me curiously, the way adults always did when they heard I didn't talk. I wanted to disappear, to be sucked into thin air. 'Talking is very overrated. Best left to you women. You do it so much better than us.'

Gracie stuck her tongue out at him, but Declan just laughed. 'C'mon inside, I have to check my schedule.'

'You'd like to get a job, wouldn't you, Sean?' Gracie said.

I really wasn't sure, but I nodded because Gracie seemed to think it was such a good idea.

'Well now, I'd be happy to help you, Sean, but I'll tell you what ... have a word ... that is, let your parents know about this idea of yours and see what they think about it first, right? Seeing as you're on holiday, they might want you to spend your time with them instead of trailing around a golf course.'

'Sean's dad is researching the cable station. Isn't that right, Sean?'

I nodded. She seemed to know everything.

'We'll ask him this evening,' she said.

Declan smiled. 'I think that would be a good idea. Now, how about a Coke?'

'I'd murder one,' said Gracie.

I preferred orange, but I didn't want to be rude.

'Kate?' Declan called across the floor to a waitress. 'Two cokes for the Pirate Queen.'

'Coming right up.' She waved at Gracie before disappearing behind the bar.

'How's your beautiful aunt?' Declan said, checking his phone as the drinks arrived.

Grace took a long gulp of her Coke and then spluttered. 'Crikey, that reminds me, she has no idea where I am. I said I'd be back at the hotel in half an hour and that's ten minutes ago – it'll take another ten, even if we run all the way.' She looked panicked.

'Relax. I'll ring her and tell her you're here. I'm finished up myself for the morning, so I'll run you both back in the car.'

'Oh, thanks, Declan, that'd be great.'

'Not at all. Any excuse to talk to the beautiful Annie.' He winked at me, and Gracie rolled her eyes.

'How much do I owe you for the drinks?' Gracie asked Kate as she passed by.

This time I was ready, and pulled a ten-euro note from my pocket. Dad had always taught us to pay our way.

'Absolutely nothing, Gracie darlin'. They're on the house.'

People said that a lot to Gracie, I would learn. I guess they just liked her. It was hard not to.

In Declan's car on the way back to the village, I watched Gracie as she talked and leaned out the window and waved to passers-by she knew. Everyone seemed to know everyone around here.

Gracie isn't fat like she said, more kind of solid. And her hair is wild and black, but it's long and curly, not frizzy. Her skin is tanned and her eyes are really blue, and she has the thickest eyelashes I've even seen. When she smiles, which is a lot, she has two big dimples and her teeth are mostly straight and white. I don't know anything much about girls, but I wonder where in the world she got the idea that she isn't pretty.

Pat

Me and Dad were waiting at the hotel when Sean came back in with Gracie. I think Dad was relieved, although he pretended to be cool about it. He had taken a chance when Gracie showed up at the cable station, getting Sean to go off on his own with her. It was kind of an experiment, I guess, part of trying to get him to communicate with people again, like Dr Shriver said. Anyway, I could always have gone after him, but Dad wanted to let Sean go on his own.

Some guy called Declan drove them back. Then Gracie ran up to a lady in the hotel called Annie, who came out from behind Reception and said, 'Oh, there you are. I was about to send out a search party.'

'It's my fault Gracie's late,' Dad tried to explain to the reception lady. 'I'm sorry if we—' then he stopped, and said, 'I think I've seen you before, on the beach?'

He was right. It was her. The girl we saw sitting on the rock.

She looked puzzled. 'Have you? Well, I'm Annie. You must be the Americans staying in Cable Lodge.'

'That's right, we are.'

I wondered how everyone knew that about us.

'Don't worry about Gracie,' she said. 'She's a free spirit, but she usually comes home when she's hungry.'

Then everyone started talking, and Declan and Annie explained they knew each other forever because he was from Ballyanna too, and he was the golf pro. Dad looked pleased about that and said he hoped to get out on the golf links as soon as he could. Then Dad said we were going to get some lunch in the hotel and would Gracie join us? Maybe Annie and Declan too?

Annie said thank you, but she was on duty, so she couldn't, but she said Gracie would love to. 'Remember your manners, Gracie!' she said, then she went back to work behind her desk.

Declan said, 'Sure, good idea.'

We decided to sit outside, in front of the hotel, under one of the umbrellas, because it was such a nice day. Declan said that we could get a bar menu there and a girl would come out to take our order. We all had sandwiches and Dad and Declan had beer. Dad and Declan talked about golf and then Dad told him about coming here for work.

Then Gracie nudged Declan and said, 'Tell Sean's dad about the caddying.'

'Not now, Gracie.'

'What's that, Gracie?' Dad looked at her.

'Oh don't mind her!' Declan said. 'Some of the kids here get work caddying during the summer,' he explained. 'Gracie just thought Sean might be interested, but as it happens we're all full up . . . maybe another time, Sean.'

Sean caught my eye and I could tell he was relieved. Anyway, there was no way Dad would allow him get a summer job. As if! Actually, I thought it might not have been a bad idea . . . we both could have done it . . . but Dad's got Sean wrapped in cotton wool right now, hardly lets him out of his sight, which means I have to look out for him too. That's a full-time job in itself.

* * *

'Can I stay with you tonight, Annie?'

Annie is working on the hotel website in the office, and Gracie has just rejoined her after a stint with the girls from housekeeping.

'I don't see why not. As long as Granny doesn't mind.'

'Oh, she won't. Ring her now.'

Annie makes the call and confirms Gracie's prediction.

'Brilliant. And can we have pizza?' Gracie hops up on a chair, trying to reach a cobweb she has spied with her feather duster.

'Good idea, it's been too long since I had pizza.'

Back at the cottage that evening, Annie runs Gracie the bubble bath she has requested and puts the large takeaway pizza in the oven to keep warm. Then she changes into a light fleece and her oldest sweatpants and sits down to check her emails.

After half an hour, she pops her head around the bathroom door, where Gracie is still submerged in bubbles, her little face puce from heat. 'I thought you'd fallen down the plughole!' Annie grins. 'Hurry up, or you'll turn into a prune.'

'They're the things Granny and Granddad eat to stay regular. Ugh, I hate them!'

'They're only dried-up plums. But that's what you'll turn into if you stay in that hot water much longer. Anyway, pizza's ready . . .'

Gracie emerges minutes later wearing one of Annie's t-shirts and a bathrobe they have borrowed from housekeeping, which trails behind her.

'Will I be pretty when I grow up, Annie?' Gracie studies her reflection in the mirror.

'You're pretty now, sweetheart. But you'll be a knockout when you grow up.'

'Mam says I look like Granddad.'

Annie sighs. 'I know it might be hard to believe, sweetie, but when he was younger, Granddad was considered very good-looking. Anyway, trust me, you're beautiful.'

Gracie doesn't seem reassured. 'I'd rather look like Mam, or you ...'

'That's only natural, Gracie. We all want to look like other people when we're younger. I wanted to look like Granny – can you imagine!'

Gracie giggles at the thought.

Snuggled up on the couch, with a large pizza between them, Gracie considers the merits of several movies while Annie flicks through channels.

'Oh wait,' she says, mid-mouthful. 'Look, there's a house makeover. I love makeovers, can we watch it?'

'Sure, if you want.'

'I think I'd like being a room co-ordinator,' Gracie says. 'D'you think Gran would give me a job in the hotel when I'm older?'

'Aren't you a little young to be deciding your career prospects just yet? Besides, I don't know if Granny and Granddad will still own the hotel when you're grown up.'

'What d'you mean?' Gracie looks up at her. 'They'll be here forever. They've *always* lived here.'

'Well ... they're not getting any younger, that's all ... and you know how people retire and take it easy when they get older? They'll want to do that too, and it might involve them selling the hotel.'

Gracie laughs. 'Don't be silly, Annie! Granny and Granddad would never sell the hotel. They'll live here until they're really old, then maybe you and me and Mam can live here and run the hotel for them.'

If only life were that simple, Annie thinks. When she was Gracie's age, she'd loved helping out in the rooms with her mum, or in the kitchen. She'd enjoyed living in a place other people thought of as an escape. She liked watching her mother's skill at looking after their guests, making sure their stay was special, seeing them leave refreshed and renewed, vowing to return.

'I love makeovers. Maybe Gran would let us do one room?' Gracie looks hopeful. 'Like a project?'

'She might . . .'

'The girls in housekeeping were saying the whole hotel could do with a makeover.'

'Were they now?'

'That was before they started teasing Karen about the German boy she met last night. She really likes him, they said he's a ride.'

'Gracie!'

'That just means he's really good-looking.'

Annie makes a mental note to warn the staff to be discreet when Gracie is about.

'Do you think Sean's dad is good-looking?'

'I hadn't really noticed.' This is not altogether true. Annie has noticed. She has noticed that Daniel O'Connell is very good-looking indeed, in a rugged, outdoor sort of way. He would not look out of place in a western, she thinks, all that was missing was the poncho and cheroot. The thought makes her smile.

'He was looking at you a lot. I saw him . . .'

'Promise me something, Gracie?' Annie looks fondly at her niece.

'What?'

'Promise me when you're older, you'll let me vet all your boyfriends.'

'What does *vet* mean?'

'Evaluate, decide if they're nice enough for you or not.'

'You mean, like, judge them? Isn't that wrong? To judge people?'

'Yes, it probably is.' Annie sighs. 'And I'd probably get it wrong anyway.'

'Are you ever going to get married, Annie?'

'I don't know, sweetie. I thought I would for a long time, but now . . . I think I'm happier on my own.'

'Me too.' Gracie nods. 'Maybe when I'm older, we can live together, and we can have our own place?'

'That sounds great.'

This seems to please Gracie, who goes back to attacking her pizza with renewed vigour.

* * *

Young Luke Nolan considers himself a priest of the new millennium. Things are changing in Ireland and whether they like it or not, the Church is going to have to get with it. Luke is determined to be part of the new evangelicalism. His particular calling, he feels, is to minister to the marginalised, the disadvantaged, the no-hopers. He understands them. He has been one of them himself, for heaven's sake, as bad on the drugs as any of them. His poor parents had given up entirely, but that was before the trip to Medjugorje, where he had been cured and returned home declaring he would be entering the priesthood. Everyone who knew him had said it was a miracle.

On leaving the seminary, he'd hoped to be posted to an inner-city parish, where he felt his skills and talents would be best served. To his great disappointment he had ended up in a corner of southwest Kerry. It wasn't exactly what he'd had in mind, but in his own way he feels he's making a difference. At least he can cook, which is a blessing in the small parochial house he shares with Father Martin. He is IT savvy too, and managed to get a pal in Dublin to donate a brand new desktop computer that will replace the ancient box that sits in the tiny room they call a study. He has just picked it up from his friend's office in the Financial Services Centre, having been on the road from Ballyanna since before seven o'clock this morning. Now he's on his way to Dublin airport, to pick up the elderly priest back from years in the missions who is coming home to recuperate after a bout of ill health. 'Two birds with one stone,' Father Martin had said, lending Luke his VW Polo to drive up to Dublin for the day to get the computer, as long as he agreed to collect this Father Barry McLaughlin from the airport and transport him safely back to Ballyanna.

Luke went through the port tunnel and arrived at Dublin airport in good time, finding a serendipitous place in short-term parking just as someone was pulling out.

In Arrivals, he holds up the written sign he made before leaving this morning, so that there would be no confusion, although he doubts he could miss a frail, elderly missionary priest walking out in the midst of the hordes of tanned and rowdy holiday-makers. With his phone in his other hand, he checks his Twitter account, delighted to see he's now up to 1,500 followers – not as much as his idol, @frpaddybarry, but definitely heading in the right direction.

'Father Luke, I presume?' The deep voice interrupting him five minutes later makes him jump.

Luke looks up blankly at the tall, handsome man in front of him. He is dressed in black, but there is no sign of a clerical collar, not that there needed to be, of course, it's just that this fellow doesn't exactly fit Luke's image of a missionary.

'Father McLaughlin?'

'Barry.' The older man holds out his hand to shake. 'And thank you for coming out of your way to pick me up. It's very good of you.'

'Not at all, my pleasure.' Luke puts his phone away quickly, smooths his hair and shakes Barry's hand. 'Can I take your case for you?' He notices Barry has an old-fashioned, battered leather case, not one on wheels.

'No thanks, I can manage, just lead the way.'

Barry chats easily on the way to the car park, although Luke has to keep sneaking sideways glances at him. This is no frail old man, as he had been led to believe, or if he was honest, had just assumed. The man walking beside him is tanned and tall, six foot three at least, and a silver-haired ringer for Paul Newman. His face is lined and creased, to be sure, but his eyes are bright, and startlingly blue. He is in good shape too, for his age – Luke can tell that there's not a spare ounce of flesh on the man. In fact, Luke's main concern, as they approach the old Polo, is how on earth he'll fit Barry into it.

'I'm afraid you'll be a bit cramped,' he says, pushing the passenger seat back as far as it can go.

'Don't worry, lad.' Barry folds his tall frame into the small car. 'I've been on three flights to get this far, a few more hours' discomfort won't make much difference.'

On the motorway, heading towards Limerick, Luke learns that Barry has not been home since the seventies. In the intervening forty-odd years, he has built three churches and one school, and organised for running water to transform the lives and livelihoods of the small farming village in Africa where he was pastor.

'You'll see a lot of changes in Ballyanna so, I'm sure.'

'I will, no doubt, but sure change is part of life, lad. We can't hold back progress, just hope to channel it in the right direction.'

Luke thinks this is a deceptively profound comment and resolves to memorise it for an appropriate occasion, even his next sermon, maybe.

'We've a long old drive ahead of us, Barry, will we start with a rosary?' Luke is keen to make a favourable impression on his enigmatic travelling companion.

'You go right ahead, lad.' Barry smiles at him. 'I'd prefer to meditate myself, if it's all the same to you.' With that he closes his eyes and leans back in his seat, leaving Luke with the distinct impression that he had been very tactfully dismissed – along with shooting himself in the foot. Now he'd have to turn off his favourite radio station and maintain a respectful silence for *at least* fifteen minutes – and that was if he said a fast rosary.

Five hours later, punctuated by a pit-stop in Adare and a reviving pot of tea, Luke and Barry are finally approaching Ballyanna.

'Well, here we are,' Luke says, 'our house is just to the right, after the church. I'll drop you off first and then pick up some groceries in the village.'

'No need. I'm staying with my sister, actually. Her house is just down on the lake, if you take the left turn just after the village.'

'Oh,' says Luke, surprised by this turn of events. 'Okay. Sure. No problem.' He turns left as instructed, after the village, and continues down the lakeshore road. It is another beautiful evening and the lake is still as glass, its depths reflecting the surrounding mountains and clouds. A pair of swans glide by, leaving barely a ripple in their wake.

'Just here, on the right up ahead.'

They come to a pretty stone cottage with a traditional thatched roof, its walls covered in climbing roses. In the garden a black-and-white collie sits watching by the open gate, starting up a volley of barking as the car pulls up. A goat tethered to the hedge looks up from the steel pail it's munching from and stares, and a small donkey scratches its neck on the wooden fence.

Luke knew this place alright, everybody did – although he's never been in it. 'But this is Jerry's house,' he blurts out, before he can stop himself.

'That's right,' Barry said. 'Jerry's my sister. Do you know her?'

'Um, no, not exactly . . . I know her to see, of course, but we haven't been introduced as such. I'm still relatively new in the parish,' he explains, feeling flustered. Was he imagining it, or did he see a gleam of amusement in Barry's eyes?

The door of the cottage opens then, and Jerry herself comes out, followed by a couple of hens, who begin to peck assiduously on the grass verge. She is wearing denim overalls tucked into wellingtons, and what looks like a man's shirt with the sleeves rolled up. Her nut-brown face is a mass of wrinkles and her long, grey hair is held back with a scarf worn headband style. Luke can't help thinking that she looks like something out of *Lord of the Rings*.

'Ah, there you are.' She comes to greet her brother, who hugs her and laughs, before holding him at arm's length. 'Welcome home, Barry. You're looking well, despite your journey.'

'This is Father Luke,' says Barry. 'He was kind enough to drive me all the way from Dublin.'

'Our new curate, of course, I've seen you about the place. You'll come in for tea, won't you, Luke?'

'Um, thanks, I'd love to . . . but I have some things to pick up in the village and—'

'Well, wait a sec,' says Jerry, darting back inside. 'Here.' She reappears. 'That's a freshly baked fruitcake for Martin and some scones, gluten-free, mind. And thank you for bringing my brother home.'

'Not at all, no bother. I'll be off now.'

'Thank you again, Luke,' Barry calls after him. 'Tell Martin I'll be happy to help out, make myself useful while I'm here.'

'I'll do that, Barry,' says Luke, getting into the car. 'And thank you Jerry for the cake and scones.' The old pair stand waving him off.

In truth, Luke would love to have gone into Jerry's cottage for tea – if the smell from the fruitcake and scones were anything to go by – but he would particularly have liked to have learned more about Barry. There is a magnetic quality about the man that Luke would very much like to cultivate. But he feels it was only fair to leave the old brother and sister alone to catch up. He couldn't get over that Barry was Jerry's brother! That had come as a shock. Father Martin hadn't said anything about that.

Everybody knew Jerry. She was legendary in these parts. That was the problem. She was an herbalist, Luke knew that, of course, and a healer, they said, but he'd heard other things too, more disturbing things that he deeply disapproved of. Apparently she held sittings and did 'readings' for people, and she was said to have the ability to connect with people in the 'spirit world'. It was all a lot of nonsense, of course, just a ruse to take money off innocent people who believed in that sort of thing. But all the same, Luke thinks it's a downright dangerous thing to be dabbling in. You wouldn't know what went on in that cottage, behind those closed doors – and chickens wandering around inside! So of course he'd declined the invitation for tea with her – and to think her brother was a priest!

Back at the house, Luke delivers the fruitcake and scones to Father Martin as instructed.

'Ah, you're back!' Martin is making a pot of tea in the kitchen. 'Just in time for a cuppa. How's Barry?'

'He's fine. You never told me he was Jerry's brother.'

'Why would I? Sure you had a long enough drive together to share any relevant information. I have enough things to be remembering without volunteering everybody's family connections. All you had to do was pick the man up from the airport.' Martin is obviously irritated by Luke's accusatory tone.

'Jerry sent you these.' Luke puts the cake and scones on the kitchen counter.

'Ah, did she now, the pet! I was hoping she might. She knows me well. Here, have a slice.' He motions to Luke to get a plate and knife. 'Her cakes are the best in the county. That reminds me, I must make an appointment with her.'

'For what?'

'My back. She's the only one who can give me any relief from it at all. And I need some more of her sleep remedy. I'm nearly out of it.'

'You go to Jerry?' Luke is incredulous.

'Doesn't everybody? Even Doctor Mike goes to her. She has the gift, everyone knows that.'

Luke decides not to enquire further, but he feels somehow let down by his superior.

'I'm looking forward to seeing Barry again, it must be ten years since I saw him last, and that was in Rome. What did you think of him?' Martin is watching him with an amused smile.

Luke has the uneasy feeling this might be a trick question. 'He seems very nice.'

'Barry McLaughlin is one of the finest human beings you will ever meet, Luke, and a gifted priest. If you've any sense, you'll get to know him and learn as much as you can from him.'

'Um, yeah, sure. He said to tell you he'd be glad to help out while he's here.'

'That's just like him. I don't think I've ever come across a more generous person. Now, c'mon inside with the tea and cake and we'll catch the news. You were great to bring Barry down all the way from Dublin, Luke. I'm sure he was glad of the lift.'

'It was no bother, sure I was going that way anyhow, and it was your car.'

'All the same, it was kind of you. Dear Lord, this cake is divine.'

Luke is relieved that he kept his thoughts to himself. Barry did seem very nice, of course he did, but if Luke is being honest, the man has had a rather unnerving effect on him. It was his eyes, Luke decides. Despite his affable manner, when Barry McLaughlin looked at you, it was as if he was looking into your very soul.

* * *

Jerry puts the finishing touches to the shepherd's pie and pops it in the oven as Barry joins her after a hot shower and change of clothes. She smiles as he ducks his tall frame under the doorway and goes to sit in the old winged chair beside the fire. His legs, stretched out in front of him, seem to reach halfway across the little room. Millie, delighted with the unexpected visitor, sits by his side adoringly, nudging his hand, and Barry obligingly strokes her head.

'How was your journey?' Jerry asks.

'Ah, it was grand. You shouldn't have gone to the bother of lighting a fire.'

'I wanted to. It can still get cool in the evenings. Besides, I knew you'd like it and I have plenty of peat left over.'

'You're right, it was the first thing that struck me when I got here, the smell of burning turf. Nothing like it.'

'How long are you back for, Barry? You never said.'

'I'm not sure to be honest, it all depends on the powers that be. Until I get a clean bill of health at any rate, I suppose.'

'Well, Doctor Mike will be the person to organise that. I'll get on to him tomorrow to make an appointment.'

'There's no rush, but yes, I'd be grateful if you would. They're insisting I need a rest. I don't, you know, but I put my back out a while ago and it's never been quite right since. If I could get that sorted, it would be a relief.'

'Well, a change of air is always good, and you've picked a good summer to come home. I can't remember the last time the weather's been so settled. What do you think of the place? Has it changed much, would you say?'

Barry smiles. 'Not really. I mean, it's looking more prosperous, of course, a lot more houses round about, but actually I was surprised at how little it's changed, at least on the drive in anyhow.'

'And what do you think of our new curate?' Jerry grins.

'He's a nice lad. He can talk, though . . .'

'He's only here for a stint, I believe, but he's very keen. Poor Martin's driving round the county like a lunatic, he seems to be on duty for about six parishes. But it's nice for him to have a bit of back-up here, even if it's only temporary.'

Barry nods. 'All part of an ageing Church. I told young Father Nolan to tell Martin I'd be happy to help out while I'm here.'

'It's changed times, alright,' Jerry says, nodding. 'The parishioners are great. Only for them, there wouldn't be a Church. They've taken on all the administrative work, and all voluntary as well. They'd say mass if they could.'

They sit at the old pine table and eat the shepherd's pie companionably, Millie staring intently at their plates.

'I told Breda you were coming home.'

'How is she?'

'Run off her feet.' Jerry is casual. 'Her two daughters are both home at the moment, one from London, and the other on a break from her marriage . . .'

'Ah.'

'The son-in-law has been found out in some kind of financial scam, they were living in Cork, he's gone to ground, and Dee, that's her name, is home with her little girl, Gracie.'

Barry shook his head. 'That must be hard . . . poor Breda.'

'Conor, her husband, hasn't been well either.'

'I remember him at the wedding. He's a fine, handsome fellow.'

Jerry pursed her lips. 'Lazy. A drinker. Now his heart is failing and his hip never healed from the replacement operation. He's very self-focused, shall we say. Poor Breda is run ragged. She'll be delighted to see you.'

'We're bound to run into each other sooner or later.'

'You won't drop into the hotel to say hello?'

'It's been forty years, Jerry!'

'I know, but she's looking forward to seeing you.'

'I'm only off the plane. Give me a few days to settle in, will you.'

'Take all the time you like.'

Jerry refuses her brother's offer to help clear the table and encourages him to go for a stroll to get some air before turning in. She watches him fondly from the window over the sink as he walks slowly down the path, Millie at his heels, and heads for the lakeshore road. She had forgotten how handsome he still is. Dressed in old jeans and a shirt, with a light sweater thrown over his shoulders, his skin darkened from years under African skies, he could pass for any one of the many continental tourists passing through on their way to tour the Ring of Kerry. You wouldn't take him for a local, Jerry thinks, smiling to herself, even though technically he is one, but then, there had never been anything ordinary about Barry.

When she has washed the dishes and thrown a couple of sods on the waning fire, she goes in to the small room she has prepared for Barry's return. There is no need for him to know it is her own room she has willingly vacated. She had easily been able to move her small single bed and few bits and pieces into the office, as she calls it, where she stores her herbs, potions and many books. Now she looks at the room with pleasure. The lack of a bed had been the main problem, but Breda had come to her rescue, giving her an old one from the hotel she insisted was being replaced. It takes up most of the room, this generous big bed, complete with crisp new linen, but Jerry is delighted to be able to provide some proper comfort for her brother, for however long he is staying. Everyone is entitled to a decent night's sleep, and Barry looks like he could do with it more than most. She straightens the small vase of wild flowers she has put on the chest of drawers, and sees that Barry has already unpacked and put away his few clothes. His prayer books are on the bedside table, and she smiles as she touches the old crucifix that hangs above the bed, belonging to their late mother, and her mother before that. Jerry has her own reasons for leaving the Church she had been baptised into a long time ago, but she wants Barry to feel comfortable and at ease here.

She makes a cup of tea and goes to sit in her rocker by the small fire, waiting for Barry to come back, while Psycho, one of her three cats, settles himself on her lap, purring loudly. She will have a word with Doctor Mike tomorrow, and in the meantime she will make up something to help Barry's back pain. She knows simply from looking at him that his back is not the problem and she suspects Barry knows this too, but now is not the time for questions. He has come back to say his goodbyes, whether or not he is aware of it. A tear rolls down Jerry's face and she brushes it away impatiently. She knows better than to cry. Everyone has their time, and Barry and she have had longer than most. But all the same, there is still a lot left to say . . .

She stays very still, listening to the whisper of sound beyond the purring cat, beyond the crackle of the flames, and nods. Just as she thought, there is more to this than Barry suspects, more than his health at stake here . . . but Barry will have to find his own way through what lies ahead. He may be home now, but Jerry suspects his most challenging journey is just beginning.

She smiles as he comes through the door, shaking his head in wonder. 'I'd forgotten the air here . . . I'm half asleep already.'

'You'll have a nightcap before turning in?'

'I thought you'd never ask.' He grins at her.

'There's a bottle of Jameson in the cupboard beside the sink. I'd get it myself only this lump of a cat has me pinned to the chair. Take the glasses from the dresser, will you.'

They sit by the fire, raise a glass to the parents they never knew, then toast each other.

'*Sláinte chuig na fir, agus go mairfidh na mná go deo!*' says Jerry, grinning. 'Health to the men, and may the women live forever!'

'*Fad saol agat, gob fliuch, agus bás in Éirinn,*' counters Barry, a gleam in his eye. 'Long life to you, a wet mouth, and death in Ireland.'

He leans back in his chair and sighs. 'It's good to be home.'

* * *

'Hey, Larry. How's it going?'

'All good, Dan, we're ticking over, how 'bout you?' Larry, his project manager, grins at him from 170 miles southeast of Galveston, Texas, courtesy of Skype.

'We're still adjusting. I'm just checking in, seeing how things are at your end.'

'Cool. I think we've got ourselves a new ROV guy.'

'Great.' There'd been a slight hiccup with their latest project, filming the investigation of a well-preserved 200-year-old shipwreck in the Gulf of Mexico, when the marine exploration company's Remotely Operated Vehicle technician had gone AWOL and taken a company Jeep with him. 'Anything interesting yet?'

'The usual . . . ceramics, bowls, liquor, medicine, a sealed bottle of ginger.'

'Still the best cure for sea-sickness I know,' Dan says.

'You an' me both, boss. Nothing much happening until they get the ROV back in the water. I'll keep you posted. Is this a good time for you?'

'Pretty much.'

'Okay. I'll check back tomorrow, same time.'

'So long, Larry.'

For a moment, Dan wished he was there. There was nothing quite like the thrill of watching and waiting for a wreck to release her secrets. And this one, lying more than three-quarters of a mile below the gulf, was too deep for divers, hence the remote-controlled undersea vehicle employed to examine the remains with its robot-like arms. So far, images had relayed the outline of an 84-foot-long, 26-foot-wide wooden hull and copper-clad sailing vessel with two masts, and its artefacts in a seemingly amazing state of preservation.

Dan never lost his sense of wonder at the mysteries of the deep. Below water, he became another man – free, unfettered, detached from the commotion and complexities of a world he didn't always like and understood less. Underwater, life was calm, straightforward, non-confrontational. Unless you came face to face with a predator, of course, but in Dan's experience you were more likely to run into those on dry land.

Growing up in a suburb of Los Angeles, Dan's parents divorced when he was six. After that first Christmas, his father left town. His mother, a serious girl and English major, whose only mistake had been marrying the wrong guy, had to work two jobs to hold on to their small home. She'd consigned her dreams of becoming a playwright to the trunk in the cellar along with her treasured journals, prom dresses and college yearbooks. A few years later she'd remarried.

He was home alone a lot as a kid, but Dan didn't mind that. They had a good and kind network of friends and neighbours and they had a TV, so Dan had all he needed. While other kids were watching *H.R. Pufnstuf*, *The Electric Company* and *Fat Albert*, Dan was glued to reruns of *Voyage to the Bottom of the Sea* and being mesmerised by Jacques Cousteau documentaries. His schoolwork suffered, sure, but his knowledge and love of the sea grew every day, and he became adept at turning off the TV just in time for it to cool down before his mother would come home and casually check its heat level on her return.

By the time he was twelve, he was running with the wrong crowd and skipping school. Then one day he found himself in Marina del Rey, watching the sports fishing boats, when a grizzly old skipper asked him what he was doing.

'Nothin'.'

'Not a good answer, kid.' He eyeballed him. 'Boys your age should be doin' somethin'.'

The skipper's name was Spence and he was an ex US Navy diver. He took Dan on as a summer deckhand for the charter trips he and his equally grizzled wife Marge ran to Catalina Island and around the Bay, where Dan had learned to bait up rods for clients, serve beers and generally help out.

He'd been working for Spence for two years before he learned that he and Marge had lost their only boy in a diving accident. That was the first and last time Spence mentioned it. But he brought Dan to his lock-up, dragged out his old scuba gear and taught him to dive. 'If you take to it, you won't ever want to come back up, and I reckon you'll take to it.'

Spence was right. When Dan just about graduated from high school, he ignored his mother's pleas to improve his grades and got work on the oilrigs off LA. By the time he was twenty-one he was one of the best divers on the west coast. When Spence died, he left Dan his boat, on the condition he sold it and got himself a college education. Marge made sure he followed through. 'It's what he wanted,' she said, steely-eyed. 'I'm not having him disappointed a second time. He may not be here, but don't think he don't know exactly what you're doin'. Spence had high hopes for you, Dan, and I do too.'

That was the conversation that changed his life. Dan got close to $100,000 for the boat and discovered a determination and natural charm he never knew he had. He secured a place in UCLA film school, where he excelled as a cameraman and discovered a talent for documentary-making. Before long, he was known as the go-to underwater cameraman for features and documentaries on the west coast.

He met Mary when she was commissioning editor at The Adventure Channel and he was pitching a thirteen-part series, *Dangerous Waters*, about demolition divers working under extreme conditions. Dan sank every penny he had into *Dangerous Waters* and the twelve-month shoot almost broke him, but it turned out to be a ratings success and his breakthrough project. Another series was commissioned and more projects ensued.

Mary left The Adventure Channel and became head of production at Dan's company, Spencer Productions, named after his old friend and benefactor.

After that, well, the commissions and money started coming in. Mary was good at what she did, and Dan had never enjoyed the negotiating side of the business. He was happier under water, or planning the technical requirements of a project. Most of the time they worked well together, although occasionally they bickered around integrity and commercialism – like taking on a feature sponsored by an oil company intent on rehabilitating its image after an oil spill, or Dan wanting to make a series about pollution of the oceans. Mostly Dan got his way, although they had to eat too, especially when the twins came along. Dan used to joke that he should have named the company *Dangerous Waters*, because that's what their marriage sailed through a lot of the time when things became heated. But that was before Mary got sick, before that sickness changed the dynamic of their little family. Before his wife became someone he had to watch, instead of just someone he loved.

Dan checked his watch; it was four-fifteen and the tide was in. A swim in this incredibly cold water would shake him out of his memories, concentrate the mind. He needed to clear his head.

Ten minutes later he was taking the steps down from the cliff road to the small section of beach below. He left his shorts and t-shirt a safe distance from the water's edge, then waded into the bracing Atlantic and dived under the waves, swimming beyond them before coming up for air and striking out to sea. He swam hard, powering through the water, testing the pull, the sway of the ocean particular to this part of the bay. Ballyanna was safe for swimming, but every ocean had its quirks, and Dan had learned long ago to treat the sea with the utmost respect. In his line of work, he had seen all too often what it could do.

He was treading water, looking around him, when he spotted the other swimmer. She was further out than him, but had turned and was headed for shore. Whoever she was, she was strong and graceful in the water. Dan swam on for a bit, then turned around and headed slowly back himself. By the time he was wading out, she was standing on the beach by a rock, towel drying her hair, her long limbs lightly tanned against the emerald green of her halter-neck swimsuit. She hadn't seen him yet, she was too busy with her hair, and for a split-second Dan felt an almost visceral longing to just stand there and watch her, unobserved. It took him by surprise, this feeling. How long was it since he had any kind of thoughts about a woman? But this one, with her long hair and gently undulating figure, alone on the shore . . . well, a guy could dream, couldn't he?

She tossed her hair back then, noticing him as she wound her hair into a knot and secured it. It was only then that he recognised her.

For a moment, she seemed as taken aback as he was, but quickly recovered herself. 'Hello. I didn't see you out there.'

'Oh, it's you! Well, you seemed pretty determined to get back to shore. I wouldn't have dared get in your way.' He walked over to her, wishing now he'd brought a towel, but at the time he'd thought he'd just go for a run to dry off. Now he was dripping with water and feeling foolish. He slicked his hair back.

'Want a towel?' She offered him hers and he took it to wipe his face.

'Thanks. It's Annie, right? From the hotel? You were working reception when we—'

'Yes, I remember.' She wrapped a towel robe around her. 'You're Dan.'

He handed her towel back. 'Well, you're a strong swimmer, Annie.'

'Oh, we were never out of the water as kids. I grew up here.'

'Lucky you, it's beautiful.'

'You might not think so in winter.'

'Well, the water couldn't be much colder. But I'll bet the place is just as beautiful in winter, just a different kind of beautiful.'

'Only an American would say that.'

'But I'm right?'

'It has its charms, I suppose.'

'You work in the hotel?'

'Yes.' A flicker of a smile.

She turned away then, making for the steps that led up to the cliff path.

'Mind if I walk with you?'

She seemed taken aback.

'I live at the top, Cable Lodge, remember? You'll pass right by it . . .' He grinned.

'Oh, sure.'

'Just let me grab my stuff.' He ran over to where he'd dropped his clothes, then hurried back to her.

'What brings you to Ballyanna, Dan?'

'Work. I'm doing some research on the old cable stations in the area for a documentary I'm making. Maybe we could have a drink sometime? You could tell me about the place . . .'

'Uh . . . I'm not sure . . . we're very busy at the moment . . .'

'You're married?'

'I didn't say that.' She threw him a look.

'Me neither.'

That look again.

'I was, though. My wife died . . . just over a year ago.'

'Oh.' She stopped in her tracks. 'I'm so sorry . . .'

'Look, I could really use some friendly locals on my side. Apart from anything else, I'd appreciate some company.' He held his hands up. 'That's all . . .'

They had reached the top of the cliff now, and Annie stopped to gaze at the house. 'It's such a beautiful old place. I always wanted to live there when I was a child.'

'I could make us some coffee, if you'd like to come in . . .?'

She shook her head. 'Thanks, but I really don't have time.'

'Maybe we could have a drink some other time?'

'Maybe.'

He didn't push it.

He watched as she got into a Jeep parked on the side of the road, and waved as she drove off. Back in the Lodge, he had a hot shower, then made some coffee and opened his laptop, feeling more invigorated than he had for a long time. Despite her reticent manner, he couldn't help remembering that, up close, Annie's eyes had been the most unusual shade of lichen green, flecked with grey and yellow, framed by thick, dark lashes . . .

Had he been too forward, asking her to meet for a drink? He just wanted to talk, have someone show him around, you know, stuff that normal people do. But Dan couldn't remember what normal felt like. Normal was another lifetime – one he had clearly forgotten how to inhabit if his recent attempt at talking to a pretty girl was anything to go by.

* * *

The cottage is gleaming. Breda had two women from housekeeping spend the previous day cleaning it from top to bottom and is now supervising the finishing touches herself. She plumps cushions, manoeuvres blinds, realigns paintings, and when she cannot genuinely think of one more single thing to do, sprays room fragrance, trailing it behind her in a gathering cloud of mist, before standing back to critically evaluate her handiwork.

'Do you think she'll like the flowers, Granny?' Gracie asks, plunging her face into the lovely vase full of hydrangeas she had cut from the garden earlier and inhaling them. 'Although you can't even smell them now with that stuff you've sprayed around.' Gracie scowls at her. 'Why did you do that?'

'She'll love them, sweetheart, and of course she'll be able to smell them. This spray only makes nasty odours go away.' Breda looks at the can in her hand for confirmation. 'See? *Eradicates household aromas from carpets and fabrics,*' she reads aloud.

'But there weren't any smells, except furniture polish and peat, and I thought they were nice smells.' Gracie looks doubtful.

'Every house needs a good spring clean every now and then, Gracie, an airing. And what better time to do it than when your mum is away, so she can come back to a lovely clean home?'

Breda marvels at the note of escalating panic in her voice and hopes her granddaughter doesn't pick up on it. It is ridiculous, she knows, it's only Dee and, technically, the cottage belongs to her parents ... but going in without permission to clean anyone's abode was a risky business at best, and Breda already feels like a cat on a hot tin roof. It isn't as if she had planned it, though. Yes, she had planned to do some shopping and make sure the essentials were there for Dee's return, but if it hadn't been for Gracie wanting a particular book she had left behind, Breda wouldn't have gone into Dee's cottage to pick it up for her. While Gracie had gone to fetch it, Breda had looked around the cottage in horror. The place wasn't just untidy . . . it was . . . filthy. Dirty dishes and plates littered the kitchen and living room, and it clearly hadn't been dusted or vacuumed in weeks. Upstairs was no better, beds were unmade and clothes and make-up were strewn all over Dee's bedroom. Gracie's room was like a bombsite, and Breda didn't know whether to applaud or be appalled at her granddaughter's ability to dig faster than a badger through the unidentifiable mountain of clothes and toys to finally unearth the bed below, where, from underneath, she produced her book. 'I knew I put it somewhere safe,' she said, grinning as she held her prize aloft.

'Gracie,' Breda said, in as light a tone as she could manage, 'how long has the house been like this?'

'Like what?'

'This . . .' Breda gestured around her.

'Oh, you mean the mess.' She thinks for a second. 'Mam's always been a bit messy, but it's got worse since Daddy went away.'

'Oh, you poor little pet, you miss him, don't you?'

Gracie shrugs. 'I don't miss them fighting, though . . . that's the worst . . . that's when I put my headphones on, but I can still hear them even then sometimes, especially at the end, when things get smashed.'

Breda's hand went to her throat. 'Wh- When what gets smashed, pet?'

'Photographs, dishes, glasses . . . Daddy's watch, one time . . . but I always pick it all up if I'm down first in the morning. I thought that would stop, you know, when he went away . . . but Mam stays up ages after I've gone to bed. I know because she plays her music then and I hear it, and even then she'll smash stuff. That's why I'm glad she's gone on holiday. Maybe she won't need to throw stuff around when she comes back.'

'Dear God . . .' Breda had to turn away to hide her expression of horror from her granddaughter. She'd had no idea such things were happening.

After she'd left Gracie safely in the hotel that day, Breda had gone back to the cottage as soon as she could, to start putting the place in order. She wasn't sure which upset her more, the dreadful unhappiness unleashed in her daughter's family or the fact that, according to Gracie's account, Dee appeared to be so . . . so . . . out of control. Surely things couldn't be that bad? But Gracie would never embellish the truth . . . which brings Breda to the only possible, troubling conclusion – that her daughter has obviously turned into someone she simply doesn't know anymore.

Breda looks around the clean, welcoming cottage and takes a deep breath to steady her nerves. She doesn't want Gracie to be tense and nervous about Dee's return. She watches as Gracie moves the vase an inch to the left, then to the right, trying to find the perfect spot. Breda reminds herself what Annie had said to her this morning – that perhaps the holiday in Portugal will have given Dee a chance to gain a new perspective on her situation. There are life coaches and therapists and all manner of experts on hand at these resorts, Annie had told her. It sounded to Breda like these places weren't holidays at all, but an opportunity to examine your life choices in a more forgiving climate – in every sense of the expression. All the same, she wishes Annie was here now, with her and Gracie, to welcome Dee home. That had been the plan, but then a group of guests had booked a trip to the Skelligs and the local man they relied on had been taken ill, so Annie had volunteered to drive them in the hotel minibus.

She wondered if Annie would ever marry. She wasn't getting

any younger and there didn't seem to be anyone on the horizon. Although, marriage wasn't always a happy outcome, as Breda well knew. She had been pleased for Dee when she'd married John, coming as he did from a wealthy, respected family, but even so Breda had known all along that it would be hard work keeping up with the fast pace, not to mention fast crowd, he ran with. When Dee would ring her, breathless between appointments, to regale her with the details of her latest social whirl, Breda had felt exhausted just listening to her. There were the fashion shows, the charity lunches, the race meetings, the parties and the holidays in chic resorts on ski slopes and yachts – and that wasn't counting the entertaining at home for business and clients, which seemed to involve armies of caterers and full home makeovers. No, marrying a man like John O'Malley was a full-time career in itself. You had a show to run, and they expected you to keep it on the road, twenty-four-seven, and that included children as well. It just wasn't possible, Breda thought, and she knew what hard work was about, that was one thing you learned in the hotel industry.

But then, just as she'd always feared, disaster had struck, and the whole house of cards had come tumbling down.

Dee needed her mother now, to rely on, to help her through this, and Breda would be there for her. She wouldn't let her down. She forced a smile, remembering reading somewhere that the human brain could not differentiate between a real smile and a forced one, so you benefited from the positive health benefits either way.

'What are you smiling at, Granny?' Gracie's voice rouses her from her thoughts.

'I'm smiling at the great work we've done, at how nice the place looks for your mother, don't you think?'

Gracie looks around and nods in agreement. 'It's beautiful. But

I don't care where we live, I just wish Mam and Dad were happy
. . .'

'Oh, sweetheart . . .' Breda is saved from commenting further
by the sound of a car pulling up outside. 'Is that a car?' Breda says,
her heart racing. 'I think that might be her.'

'Do you think she'll like my hair, Granny?' Gracie peers at her
reflection and chews a nail. 'Annie straightened it for me specially.'

'Your hair is gorgeous,' Breda assures her. 'And so are you, pet.
But it's beautiful curly as well.'

'Oh, but Mam doesn't like it curly. She says it's frizzy. She says
I have Granddad's hair.'

'Gracie, you look lovely, you'll take the eye out of her head,' Breda
says, thinking that if all Gracie inherited from her grandfather
was his hair, she'd be doing alright.

She hurries to the hall and looks out the window. 'Quick,
Gracie! It's her, she's here, the taxi's outside.'

Breda takes a deep breath and opens the front door, stepping
out to envelop her daughter in a hug. 'Dee, welcome home, darling.'
She pulls back to look at her. 'You're looking great!'

'Thanks, Mum. I'm tired out, though.'

Dee walks on in and Breda takes the suitcase in the door behind
her.

'Hi, Mam,' Gracie calls out, running to hug her mother. 'Do
you notice anything different about me?'

Breda stands back, smiling in anticipation of the reunion Dee
will surely have been counting down to, dying for the moment
when she could grab Gracie and squeeze the life out of her
little girl. But to Breda's dismay, Dee seems vague and somehow
detached.

'Well, I think you've grown again, if that's what you mean.' Dee
stands back to look at her daughter. 'How are you, sweetie? I hope
you've been good for Granny and Granddad?'

'Oh she has, the little pet,' Breda says hurriedly. 'She's been a great help to me and all the hotel staff are in love with her.'

Breda leads the way to the sitting room, and watches as Dee perches on the arm of a sofa and strokes it absentmindedly. Gracie plonks down on the seat beside her, gazing up at her mother as if she were a painting.

'I hope you don't mind me fixing the place up a bit? I just thought while you were away, you know . . .'

'Gran nearly had a conniption when she saw the mess!' Gracie giggles.

'What mess?' Dee looks around her. 'It's fine . . . don't fuss, Mum!'

'Um, you'll have a cup of tea, then? A scone? I've got fresh ones from—'

'I couldn't look at food, thanks.' Dee smiles. 'I ate on the plane. A glass of water would be nice, though.'

'I'll get it.' Gracie jumps up and runs into the kitchen.

'She's missed you,' Breda says.

'Oh, I bet she had a ball in the hotel with you.' Dee yawns. 'You spoil her rotten.'

'She's a little trouper.' Breda looks after her granddaughter fondly.

'Thank you for having her, Mum, I do appreciate it, you know.' Dee smiles at her mother and squeezes her hand. 'You're being a real rock throughout this . . . this awful business. I don't know what I'd do without you.'

'Oh not at all, Dee,' Breda murmurs, 'you know we're always here for you.'

Gracie reappears with a large glass of water and hands it to her mother.

'I've left a few things in the fridge,' Breda says. 'You know, just the basics . . .'

'That's so sweet of you. I do appreciate it, really, it's just that I'm a little tired now . . . I might have a little lie down.'

'I can bring you a cup of tea later,' Gracie says eagerly.

Dee rummages in her handbag and takes out a pack of tablets, extracts one and downs it with a gulp of water. 'My doctor said I have to take things easy . . . you know, because of the strain and everything . . .'

'Well, er, yes, yes, of course . . .' Breda looks anxiously from Dee to Gracie. 'If you're sure you're alright . . .?'

'Don't worry, Gran.' Gracie is earnest. 'I'll look after Mam.'

'I'm fine, Mum.' Dee gets up and stretches. 'Don't worry. These pills just make me a little fuzzy. I'll be fine when I lie down for a bit. Honestly. I'll call you later.' She kisses Breda on the cheek.

'Well, if you're sure, Dee . . . oh, Annie should be back by seven, she would have been here if she could, but some guests needed driving to Portmagee. She thought we might have dinner later on?'

'Oh, not tonight, Mum.' Dee is already on her way up the stairs. 'Maybe we can all meet for lunch tomorrow?'

'Right . . . well . . . whatever you think . . .'

As Breda leaves and closes the front door behind her, she tries, and fails, to ignore the feeling of foreboding that comes over her. Halfway down the path she turns around, on impulse, and looks back. At the window is a forlorn little face, waving her goodbye.

Pat

'Sean has a girlfriend, Sean has a girlfriend!'

He was ignoring me, of course, but I knew I was getting to him – had been all day. What else are twin brothers for? Right now we were watching *South Park*, but there was a vein pulsing at the side of his forehead and he was chewing his face like it was candy. He might just blow. Heck, he might even yell. He didn't, but Dad did. And just at that second, the television cut out. So did the lights.

'Goddammit!' Dad yelled from the kitchen. 'Not a power cut, not now!' He had been working since after dinner on his research, and it was past our bedtime. Guess he lost track of time. That was one of the good things about having a creative parent.

Then the lights came back on, but the television didn't. It kinda fizzed a bit, then bleeped, and wriggly lines went across the screen, like a life-support machine.

We went into the kitchen, where Dad was sitting in front of his computer shaking his head. 'Darned connection, we shouldn't be having these problems with Wi-Fi. I've never seen anything like this.'

I looked over his shoulder, and the same lines that had been on the television were criss-crossing the laptop screen. It was bleeping too. They zigzagged, and then became a series of dots and dashes, then faded to black.

'Sean, take a look at the laptop for me, would you, while I go and check the fuse box?'

Sean was the computer nerd in our house, but Dad would have asked him anyway, just to make him feel important. It was part of the therapy – inclusivity. *'Make him feel wanted, needed, talk to him just the same as you would if he were talking normally.'* That's what Dr Shriver had told us.

I know I sound jealous. I'm not, really. But sometimes, with Dad, it's like he forgets I'm even here.

It was different before the accident. Everything was, obviously. Back then, me and Dad were tight. Sean was more of a mommy's boy. That's the thing about bereavement: it's not only the dead person who dies, sometimes the living get killed off too. That's how it feels, anyway. Nobody ever tells you this, but sometimes twins really get on each other's nerves. It's natural, right? I mean, think about it. It's bad enough looking at a mirror version of yourself twenty-four-seven, never mind having it in your face all the time. We need our space too.

Sean is friends now with this local girl, Gracie. She's kind of taken him over, made him her project. That's okay. Dad thinks it's funny. Personally, I prefer hanging out with the guys. I've met a few of them and they're okay, once you learn to understand what they're saying. People talk very fast here. They play their own kind of football, called Gaelic. It's different to soccer, but they play that too. They let me hang with them, and that's cool. Like I said, Sean and I need our space.

Dad came back out from under the stairs and said the fuse box was okay, so it must have been a power cut, but none of the other lights around had gone out because we could see them. It seemed like it was just our place. The computer hadn't powered up again either. Dad couldn't understand it.

'I'll have to call the internet guy out in the morning. Nothing we can do for now, it's way too late. Speaking of which, it's past your bedtime. Hurry up, I'll lock up and then come in and say goodnight.'

Dad reached out to ruffle Sean's hair as he got up from the kitchen table, and that was when I saw it. A face. Right there on the computer screen. And I knew rightaway whose it was. There was no mistaking it. It was side-on, in grey shadow against the black of the screen. And as I watched, it turned, looked right at me, smiled, then faded to black. I stood there for a nanosecond, then hightailed it upstairs and locked myself in the bathroom. I checked in the mirror, to see if I had changed, but I looked just the same – not like a crazy person. Outside, Sean rattled the doorknob. I'd never locked it before. Guess this was just reflex.

'I'll be out in a minute,' I said, trying to sound normal.

I opened the door, and Sean walked past me, shaking his head. In the bedroom I pulled the blinds and curtains, undressed and got into bed and left the bedside light on. When Sean came back in I pretended to be asleep. Ditto when Dad came in to say goodnight and turn out the light. 'Sweet dreams,' he said. *As if.*

Sean switched the light back on and shook me by the shoulder. *What?*

'Nothing,' I said. 'Go to sleep.'

He knew I was holding out on him, but what was I gonna say – *Hey, I've just seen Mom's face looking out at me from the computer?*

One twin who can't talk and another who's hallucinating – that'd be great. Just what Dad needs.

The rational explanation, of course, was that my eyes had been playing tricks on me. The power had gone out, the laptop had crashed . . . of course, there were weird sounds and shapes coming from it. I mean, what about all those lines and squiggles? There could be a million reasons why any number of images could take shape on a fading screen that was losing power.

That's what I told myself, anyhow. Then I tossed and turned, and froze when I heard a cat yowl in the night. Sean slept soundly. I must have fallen asleep eventually, though, because I dreamt of Mom. She was right here, in our room, and she was smiling, just like she used to when she came in to say goodnight to us. She looked really beautiful. She didn't say anything, just looked down at Sean and me and kept smiling. Then she crooked her finger at us, like she wanted us to go with her, and I got out of bed to follow her. We went downstairs, just the two of us, holding hands just like we used to, and out the door, then suddenly we were somewhere else . . . beside a lake, in front of this little cottage with roses growing up the walls and a thatched roof. It had a funny door as well, made up of two halves, top and bottom, that could open separately. Mom smiled at me and said, 'Hurry, Pat, they're expecting us.' And then the door opened and a black-and-white sheepdog ran out and straight over to us and licked my hand. Then an old lady came out, with long grey hair, and she seemed to be looking for someone. 'Hello?' she called. 'Is anyone there?' And suddenly my legs grew heavy, heavier with each step, so heavy I couldn't walk. And I got scared and turned around to go home.

When I woke up the next morning, I realised it was just a dream. But all through the day, if I closed my eyes, I could still see Mom's face.

Sean

I've never seen so much stuff in one room! Although it's not really a room, more a kind of garage. It's where this guy called Battie Shannon lives, and Dad's talking to him about work. We ran into Gracie earlier at the hotel when Dad went there for coffee, and she's come with us to see this place. She says Battie's about a hundred years old and he collects stuff on the beach all day. That's what his father did too, and *his* father. Ever, like, since anyone can remember. But Battie does wood carvings as well, they're all over the place, and they're really good. Pat's looking at one now, of a boat, running his fingers over the lines and curves. He likes it here, I can tell, probably because he's way better at woodwork than I ever was.

Battie doesn't mind kids hanging out in his workshop, Gracie says, he'll even show you how to carve and make stuff, if he's not too busy. Even her mom and her aunt Annie, even her grandmother used to hang out here as kids. I think Pat's pretending to be more interested in the carving than he really is because he doesn't want to be friends with Gracie. I've had this problem before with Pat, but I've learned to ignore it. That's what Mom told me to do. He likes to choose all our friends back home, and mostly I let him ... but Gracie kind of just showed up out of nowhere that day I met her, and she's really friendly, even though I don't talk back to her . . . so I don't want to be rude to her. Besides, I like her, she's fun.

'My mam's back from her holiday, now,' she says. 'That's why I was staying with my Granny and Granddad in the hotel. But now I'm in the cottage with Mam, just the two of us . . .' She picks up Battie's little black cat, Molly, from her cushion on top of a chest of drawers and puts her on her lap, stroking her, although the cat doesn't look too happy about it. 'Black cats are lucky . . . did you know that?'

I nod. Behind her, Pat rolls his eyes.

'My dad has to go away for a while,' she goes on. 'That's why he's not here . . . there's some big problem in his job and he has to go and sort it all out, so that's why me and Mam are on our own here . . . but I don't mind . . . it means we can have pizza all the time and watch movies and have girls' nights and paint our nails and stuff . . .'

Pat sticks his fingers down his throat and silently pretends to barf, so I have to look away, in case I grin. I wonder if Mom would have liked us to have a sister, so she could do that kind of stuff with her, and that makes me feel sad again. Pat told me he dreamt about Mom last night. He said she was right here with us, while we were sleeping.

Just then, Pat knocks over the boat he's been looking at and it knocks over a whole pile of dried-up seaweed that falls straight on top of Gracie's head. The cat hisses loudly and jumps off her lap. Pat is bent double laughing, but Gracie doesn't think it's funny.

'Ow! What the heck was that?' She jumps up like she's been scalded.

I have to work hard not to laugh too. But she looks so startled, I feel sorry for her.

Dad and Battie are way down the other end of the garage, so they didn't see it happen, but Dad calls out, 'What's all the commotion back there?' Then he grins when he sees Gracie covered in seaweed and picking it out of her hair.

'Come on, let's get you pranksters home,' he says to us. Then to Battie he says, 'Thanks for your time, we'll leave you in peace now.'

Battie just smiles and says, 'No bother.'

* * *

Annie has been up early and for a long walk, partly for exercise and partly to become reacquainted with her surroundings. She has walked all the way to the old church, about two miles to the crossroads, then turned left, back towards the coast road, and has finally reached the cliff road, where she now heads back to the village. It is another clear day, as far as the eye can see, and the tide is in and the water is calm and still. Looking at the village the way a stranger might, she smiles at the brightly painted shops and houses that have jostled together on Main Street for as long as she can remember. A few more restaurants have sprung up since she left, a few new holiday homes are scattered about, but nothing mars the landscape she loves so dearly. Growing up here, she took it all for granted, but now, after years away, she understands the deep pride the locals take in Ballyanna's unique location – its oceanfront setting, the magnificent lakes to the side, the entire bay and beyond guarded by the mountains, dappled today in deep greens and purples by the summer light.

A young man jogs past her, then reverses, coming to a standstill beside her. He holds out his hand by way of introduction.

'Hi there, you must be Annie Sullivan. I'm Luke, the new curate.' He shakes her hand. 'Your mother told me you were coming home, welcome back.'

Annie can't help smiling. Luke looks about fifteen years old, and could pass for a member of a boy band. 'Thank you,' she says. 'Good to meet you.'

'It might be a bit soon to mention it, but I don't always get a second chance,' he pants. 'I've organised a prayer meeting . . . Thursday evenings, we have a room in The Bayview.' He indicates the old guesthouse. 'We're always looking for new recruits.'

Annie promises she will consider it, but her time is not always her own with hotel duties. Luke seems happy with this and says he looks forward to seeing her again and continues his run.

She passes the golf club on her left, and a little further on the Smuggler's Inn and Restaurant to her right, and then as she is coming into the village proper, she is accosted by Noreen Coffey, the village gossip.

'Annie Sullivan,' she says loudly, beaming at her. 'I heard you were home. What happened the big romance in London? Hmm?'

'It's nice to see you too, Noreen.' She pushes a strand of hair out of her face. 'Oh, it was time to go our separate ways . . . we're great friends, though . . .'

Noreen shakes her head. 'And you calling off a big wedding on account of it, and now it's come to nothing. Your poor mother was devastated, you know . . . and I believe your father's heart hasn't been good since . . . still, I hear you're a wealthy woman now. My son Lenny works in marketing above in Dublin and he's been following your career. He says—'

'I'm really very sorry, Noreen, but I haven't time to chat.' Annie extricates herself from Noreen's clutches and hurries onto Main Street, relieved to see Jerry waving at her and crossing over to meet her.

'Annie, how lovely to see you, you're looking marvellous! Welcome home!' She hugs her.

'It's good to see you, Jerry. You haven't changed a bit!' She takes in the nut-brown face wreathed in smiles, the sharp blue eyes and the long, untamed grey hair, coerced today into a long plait. Annie nods in the direction of Noreen, still covertly watching her from the street corner. 'I've just had a run-in with Noreen . . .'

'Don't mind that oul' witch.' Jerry laughs. 'It's good to have you back for a bit. I know your mother's glad of it. She's been under a bit of a strain since the whole, you know, business with your sister and all . . .'

'I can imagine,' says Annie, by chance just catching sight of Dee vanishing down a side street at that very moment. 'Speak of the devil,' she says, 'there's my sister now. I was afraid to wake her up too early this morning, I must catch up with her . . .'

'You might want to keep a bit of an eye on Dee, Annie.'

'What do you mean?'

'I suspect there's a lot going on with her just now . . . things that might not be apparent on the surface just yet. Don't be too hard on her, things will come to a head soon enough, and she's going to need you then, Annie.'

Annie is taken aback by Jerry's enigmatic words, but before she can ask her what she means, Jerry says she must dash, but tells Annie to drop in to her in the cottage any time. 'We'll have a proper chat then . . .' she calls behind her as she hurries off down the street.

Annie stares after her for a moment, but she doesn't have time to try and figure out what Jerry means right now – she just wants to catch up with her sister. She had thought about asking her to join her on her walk earlier, but when she'd passed Dee's cottage, the blinds were drawn tight and she'd reckoned Dee was sleeping.

Annie turns down the little street and looks in a couple of shops before she finally spots her.

'For someone who lives in a small village, you're a remarkably hard woman to track down.' Annie is only half joking as she catches her sister in a hug from behind.

'God almighty!' Dee jumps, before turning around from the display of candles she is contemplating in *Just The Thing*, Barbara's beautiful little shop. 'You scared the life out of me!' But she looks pleased to see Annie. 'When did you get back?'

'I might ask you the same question.'

'Yesterday, and you know full well because—'

'Mum told me, of course I know. Got time for coffee, or do I have to make an appointment?'

'Oh, go on then, although I'm not supposed to have coffee at the moment.'

'Why not?'

'It plays havoc with my anxiety levels.'

'We'll go to The Seashell, you can have all manner of exotic teas and potions there now, so I'm told.'

Annie looks around for Barbara, to say hello, but the young girl working behind the counter tells her Barbara isn't due in until after lunch.

Minutes later, seated at a window table in the pretty coffee shop, Dee orders a large cappuccino. Annie raises her eyebrows but says nothing. She knows better than to call her sister out on her fad diets. But she can't help noticing that while they are waiting for their coffees to arrive, Dee extracts a packet of pills from her handbag and washes one down with water.

'Headache?'

'What?' Dee seems distracted. 'Oh, no, these are for stress. My doctor prescribed them.' She returns the pack to her bag.

'So why didn't you return my calls? I must have tried you a million times.'

'Oh, don't start, Annie.' Dee sighs. 'I wasn't in the mood for any lecturing.'

Annie's mouth drops open. 'I was concerned about you, that's all.'

'Yes, I'm sure you were, but it would have ended up in a lecture, or well-meaning advice . . . same thing. I just wasn't up for it, and I'm not up for it now either.' Dee's fingers drum on the table. 'Look.' Her tone softens. 'I'm not being mean, but I just can't stand talking about it all, you know? I mean, everyone's going on like it's the end of the world or something, but John will sort it out, he always does . . . this is just a . . . a blip.'

'A blip?'

'Yes, Annie, a blip.'

Annie sits back in her chair and thinks carefully before saying anything. 'Right. Okay, I see.'

'I'm far more interested in hearing about you anyway. Mum says you're back on a sabbatical? What's that all about?'

'I need some time out . . . thought it would be nice to come home for a while . . .'

'What happened with your guy, Ed?'

'It didn't work out.'

Dee gives her a look. '*How* didn't it work out? You called off a wedding for him, I mean, wasn't it a match made in heaven?'

'Yes, Dee, I'm well aware that I cancelled the wedding.' Annie tries to keep her tone neutral, but Dee's attitude is pretty hurtful. 'We wanted different things from the relationship. It's for the best.'

'Was he unfaithful?'

'Would it matter if he was?'

'For you, I'm guessing, yes.' Dee's eyes narrow as she regards her sister. She blows a trail of smoke from her e-cigarette. 'You must have known . . . I mean, it was written all over him. He even flirted with me when I was staying with you. A guy like that, you've got to give them a long leash, if you want them, that is.'

Annie wonders yet again if she really is related to this person sitting opposite her. But now is clearly not the time to be confrontational. Instead, she ignores the bizarre remark.

'Well I don't. I think we've established that much.'

'Are you sure, though? He was very sexy, I'll give you that. Wicked eyes.' Dee grins.

'Are you for real?'

'You know your trouble, Annie?'

Annie heads the familiar accusation off at the pass. 'Now who's lecturing?'

Dee laughs. 'Alright. Let's not talk about men!'

'Fine, but it's your situation I'm worried about, Dee, not John. Have you seen a solicitor?'

'I don't need to.' She lowers her voice. 'There's an account in the Caymans, John set it up ages ago, in case something like this ever happened. He's not stupid, Annie, I keep telling Mum and Dad that he'll sort all this out. I know he will. It's a mistake and he'll fix it. Now, can we please talk about something else? I must tell you about Portugal. The place was amazing . . .'

Annie lets Dee rattle on. There is clearly no point in trying to talk to her here and now, she'll just have to try at another time. But as far as Annie is concerned, her sister is in deep denial of her situation, which means things must be even worse than Annie imagines.

'I ran into Declan Coady yesterday,' Dee is saying now. 'He told me there's a crowd meeting in O'Dowd's tonight, about eight. We should go. It'll be like old times.' She looks at Annie expectantly.

'Barbara said something about that, now that you mention it.'

'Good. Let's go, it'll be fun, do us both good. Mum will look after Gracie.'

'Okay.' Annie shrugs. 'Why not? It's been years since I've seen everyone.'

'Great.' Dee gets up from the table and grabs her bag.

'Let me get this,' Annie says.

'It's alright, Annie.' Dee's smile is bright. 'I can still pay my own way, you know. Buy me a drink tonight, if you want.'

'Sure. Well, thanks for coffee.'

'See you later.'

* * *

Dan has just spent a very pleasant hour or so having a bite to eat with a charming elderly couple. Mrs Ruddery's late father had been the last superintendent of the cable station prior to its closing for business in 1962, and Dan was eager to meet and talk with her. She had suggested meeting at 6.30 p.m. in the local pub, with her husband, Ron, and Dan agreed on the condition that they would allow him to buy them dinner. Peggy, as she had insisted he call her, had been well informed and a mine of information. She was sharp as a tack and remembered everything about her childhood at Cable Lodge, which was their home because it came with her father's position.

'It was originally built as a hunting lodge, you know, for the estate of Lord Lansdowne, but the Cable Company acquired it when they set up shop. It's a beautiful house, isn't it? I missed it terribly when we had to leave.'

'I can imagine,' Dan said, nodding. 'We loved it the minute we saw it.'

'The Super carried the can for everything in the old days,' Peggy said, referring to the historical correspondence she had given him from when the station first opened in 1866. 'From redesigning the equipment to dealing with misbehaviour amongst the staff. And of course the all-encompassing error count was always an issue. Ballyanna being a relay station, it meant incoming messages had to be deciphered by the Recorders, then recorded on pieces of paper for retransmission by the Senders. You can imagine the margin for error. Even one wrong letter could have disastrous consequences, especially for stockbrokers!'

'I see.' Dan was building up a picture of how the early station operated. 'And seeing as they got through about 1,000 messages a day, between six operators, that's 166 each, and if you assume a shift of eight hours, that's twenty messages per hour. Wow, that must have been a lot of hard work.'

'Some of them drank quite a lot,' Ron, Peggy's husband, whispered conspiratorially.

Dan laughed. 'Guess there's nothing new about stressful careers, just different ways of dealing with them.'

After Peggy and Ron left, Dan decided to stay on for a while and enjoy a quiet drink. Joan Coady, Declan's mother, was sitting in the Lodge for him, to let him get out on his own for a change, so he decided to make the most of it.

The pub wasn't like any he had been in before, and he found it relaxing to look over the station papers while he sipped a beer. He had become quite engrossed by the time the place filled up, and was surprised to hear a familiar voice beside him.

'Maybe now might be a good time to buy you that drink?' Annie indicates the empty glass in front of him. 'What'll it be? Same again?'

'Sure. Will you join me?'

'I've just come in with some friends, but I'll join you for one.'

She returns minutes later with two glasses and sits down opposite him.

'*Sláinte,*' she says, tipping her glass towards him and smiling.

This is a definite improvement, Dan thinks as he clinks his glass against hers. Annie seems more relaxed, cheerful, and genuinely friendly.

'So, tell me, Annie, what should I be doing while I'm here in Ballyanna?'

'Well, there's the obvious, golf and fishing,' she says.

'Uh-huh, I'm going to hit a few balls with Declan as soon as we can arrange it, and I've been meaning to organise a boat to go out on the lake, maybe take a picnic?'

'The local ghillie will be happy to set that up. I'll give you his number.'

'And besides the obvious?'

'You need to do the Skellig trip. That's a must-see.'

'The *Star Wars* location?'

She nods. 'It's unique. A real experience. You get the boat from Portmagee. It's ideal weather for it at the moment. Staigue Fort is worth a look as well, and Derrynane beach is lovely. It's further out, by Caherdaniel, maybe twenty minutes' drive from here.'

'You're not the first person to mention Derrynane to me,' Dan says. 'I'll have to go take a look.'

'I'm being very unsociable,' Annie says, inclining her head to where a group of friends are congregated at the bar. 'Come on over and meet the gang.' She gets up.

'I wouldn't want to intrude . . .' Dan says, although he's pleased at the suggestion.

'Oh, you won't be. They're a curious bunch, they enjoy seeing a new face. And Declan's there, you can talk to him about that game of golf. Come on.'

Several beers later, Dan feels well and truly included in the small gathering. He has met Barbara, Annie's best friend, who insists she's going to have him over to dinner. Her husband, Doctor Mike as everyone calls him, is quite a bit older than her, so Dan guesses it's a second marriage for him. He's an exceptionally nice man, kind and reserved, until you discovered his wry and irreverent sense of humour.

Annie, he notices, is greeted warmly at every turn by people who clearly haven't seen her for years – even the busy barman insists on welcoming her with a drink on the house. Dan suspects, judging by the way the guy looks at her, that he's harboured a long-time crush. He can understand why.

Her sister, Dee, is a totally different kettle of fish. Dan would never have guessed they were sisters, if he hadn't known. Dee is pretty, certainly, but in a kind of blonde, artificial way that does nothing for him, and Dan can see that she likes to be the centre of attention. She looks quite put out, more than once, when the person she's talking to turns to say hello to and catch up with Annie.

Dan loses track of time as he chats with everyone. But it's quite a bit later when Dee makes her way over to him. Dan is talking to Declan by then and as Dee sashays over to join them, it's obvious she's had more than enough to drink.

'Well, isn't that typical,' she says, hand on hip. 'The two best-looking men in the pub gabbing away together and I bet it's about golf. What a waste . . .'

'How'rya, Dee,' Declan says. 'Haven't seen you for a while.'

'Well you'll be seeing plenty of me now seeing as I'm persona non grata up in Cork.'

Dan has no idea what she's talking about, but Declan looks uncomfortable. 'I was sorry to hear about your, um, trouble. How's John?'

'How would I know? Sure, I'm only his wife, he doesn't tell me anything.'

'Actually,' Declan says quickly, obviously wanting to change the subject, 'I was just telling Dan about Derrynane, suggesting a trip out tomorrow . . .'

'Great idea!' Dee claps her hands enthusiastically. 'Count me and Gracie in.' She looks at Dan and tilts her head. '*You're gorgeous.*' She sways towards him. 'Are you married?' She pokes him in the chest with her forefinger.

'Uh, I was . . .'

'Divorced?'

Dan is saved from answering by Declan, who steers Dee towards another group where he has a discreet word with Barbara, who rolls her eyes and reaches out to tap Annie on the arm. Dan watches as Annie and Barbara propel Dee towards a door, possibly the restrooms.

Once or twice he has caught Annie's eye and she has smiled back at him, but he hasn't managed to talk to her on her own since that first drink at the beginning. He's intrigued by her, and decides to risk asking Declan some innocent questions about her.

'Has Annie always worked in the hotel?'

'Annie?'

'Mmhm.' Dan is eager to find out more about her, but hopes he sounds casual.

'Well, her parents own the hotel.'

'Oh, I didn't realise that. That explains it, I guess.'

'Explains what?' Declan is curious.

'Why she's working in the hotel. I mean, she doesn't seem like a regular . . .'

'Receptionist?' Declan seems amused.

'Right.'

'I think I can safely confirm that Annie is more than just the receptionist.'

'What do you mean?'

Declan grins. 'Try Googling her.'

Just then Annie and Barbara appear, supporting Dee between them. She staggers and shouts something unintelligible. Doctor Mike follows behind his wife, a phone to his ear.

'Excuse me for a minute, Dan.' Declan turns to follow them.

Dan takes in the amused glances that follow Dee being ushered out of the pub, and watches discreetly through the window as she's bundled into a car, clearly yelling abuse in Annie's face, before leaning out and throwing up neatly on the pavement. He watches Annie turn away and cover her face with her hands. Declan is with her in an instant, putting his arms around her and holding her, whispering something in her ear, before leading her around to the other side of the car as she gets in to take her sister home. The concerned and tender expression on his face tells Dan all he needs to know about Annie and Declan.

Dan decides it's a good time to call it a night. It has been a fun evening up until now, especially when he thought Annie had been warming to him a little, maybe even liking him a bit. Silly to think a girl like her would be single. No wonder she hadn't encouraged him that day on the beach. He walks home along the cliff road, listening to the waves, marvelling at the perfect night sky above, where a crescent moon hangs amidst a carpet of stars. And not for the first time, Dan despairs of his situation, the quiet loneliness he struggles with, echoing now inside him, taut and empty as a drum.

Sean

'Beauty is a curse,' Gracie said, poking her fishing net into a corner of the rock pool. 'That's what my Gran says.' She squinted up at me and grinned. 'One less thing for me to worry about.'

It was a nice day, really nice, sunny, with a clear blue sky. Not as hot as home, but it was a summer's day. We were at Derrynane beach. Declan had driven Dad and us out in his car and when we got there, Gracie and Annie were there already with some friends. We were staying for the day with a picnic, so Dad and Declan set up camp nearby, at one of the big rocks that you could shelter between, and put up the beach chairs. Gracie was pleased to see us, she said her mom couldn't make it because she had a migraine, so Annie had brought her out instead.

Me and Gracie were looking for crabs and starfish. I'd got plenty, and I was sitting on one of the rocks, watching her. I was starting to feel hungry.

She was wearing a blue swimsuit and her skin was really tanned from all the good weather. Her hair was tied up in a high ponytail and bits of it had escaped and were blowing round her face. I thought she looked really pretty.

'How come you're so pale?' she asked. 'You're white as a sheet.'

I shrugged. It was true. I'd been in hospital a lot since the accident. I couldn't remember the last time I'd been to the beach. It had probably been with Mom. Beside Gracie, I felt skinny and sickly.

'I thought everyone was tanned in California,' she said, hauling her bucket out of the water. 'You won't get any colour if you keep wearing that t-shirt. Why are you? You don't need it, you know. It's not, like, scorching . . .'

It was habit, I guess. We always wore them back home until we'd gotten used to the sun again. I didn't want to take it off, but now I felt I should. Instead I pointed to my stomach.

'I know. I'm starving too, I could eat a horse.'

I liked being with Gracie. She was real easy not to talk to. She seemed to know exactly what it was I needed to say and when I needed to say it. It didn't matter that I was silent. The rest of the time she seemed more than happy to do the talking.

'C'mon, we'll go back and get our lunch.' She almost lost her balance turning around, then jumped to another rock and down onto the sand. I followed her.

'Will we put them back?' She squatted down to peer into the bucket, where a few tiny fish fluttered around and a couple of crabs crawled around the sides.

I shrugged.

'It doesn't seem fair, that's all. I mean, it's not their fault. They didn't do anything to get captured, did they?'

I looked at her and shrugged again. It was her call.

'I'm going to put them back.' She ran out to the water's edge, waded in up to her knees and emptied the bucket back in. After a minute I did the same with mine.

'They're free now,' she said. 'Like in *Free Willy*!' She laughed.

I loved that sound. It gurgled up from somewhere deep inside and bubbled right out of her.

'C'mon, race you back. Then we'll go for a swim.'

We were at the other end of the beach and we ran all the way back. Gracie skidded to a stop and plonked down beside Annie, who was reading a magazine. She flicked her with water from the bucket.

'Gracie!' Annie yelped, as she sat up straight and the water trickled down her stomach. 'You little . . .'

'I couldn't resist it,' Gracie said, grinning. 'We're starving, but can we swim first?'

'Do you want to kill poor Sean altogether? Has he any idea how cold it is?'

'He can keep his t-shirt on to keep warm.' Gracie looked at me mischievously.

I could feel my face going red, so I turned away. Gracie had a sharp tongue, but she wasn't usually mean.

'Okay, let's go for a swim,' she said. 'If you can stand the cold. You don't feel it after a while. By the time you wade in up to your waist you're numb, then it's fine. It's the jellyfish you have to watch out for.' She shuddered. 'Sometimes there's a whole pack of them. Ugh. I hate them.'

I couldn't see any yet, but they sounded pretty tame. Back home we had to watch out for sharks. I made the hand signal for a fin, and ran alongside her.

'Sharks?' she laughed. 'Maybe miles out to sea. We get basking sharks here often, but they're harmless. I've seen some dogfish washed up, but never a shark.'

'Are you okay with going in the water, Sean?' Dad called over to me. He looked worried.

I nodded. It was too long since I'd been in the water, and anything that seemed like normal behaviour looked good to me.

'Last one in is a wuss!' Gracie ran ahead, followed by Pat. It was only twelve o'clock, and the beach was filling up. People were sunbathing, or eating, or playing ball. A lot of kids were already in the water. A couple of dogs had followed them in too, and some others just barked at the water's edge.

Gracie went in first, shrieking at the cold. Pat took off his t-shirt (he was tanned, unlike me) and followed her, running in and diving under a wave, coming up like a seal and shaking his head. He was showing off, of course. I took off my shirt and left it on the sand, along with my shorts and trainers, then I began to wade in.

It was agony. Colder than anything I had ever imagined. Pain licked up and down my legs with every ripple. Gracie was in to her waist now and squealing. Pat skimmed some water dangerously close to me and I glared at him. For an awful moment I thought he was going to splash or duck me. Then he seemed to think better of it and instead swam away in a strong front crawl. The pain was now in my chest. Gracie was right, my legs had gone numb. She ducked under finally herself and came up spluttering and hiccupping with cold. 'J-Just do it, Sean! I-I-It's the only way, I p-p-promise you.' She began a jerky breaststroke and went round in circles.

So I did. I went under. I held my breath and opened my eyes and watched my limbs turn an even ghostlier white as they floated in front of me. Cold ripped through my upper body, but it felt good. I felt as if I had come alive. I surfaced then, and looked around at sparks of sunlight bouncing off the crystal blue of the water, the other kids screaming and laughing, dogs barking, and I know it sounds corny, but suddenly I felt a part of it all again, like I had somehow reconnected.

I looked back to the shore and saw Dad waving at us from the rocks where they had pitched camp. Then he got up and walked towards the water's edge, where he patrolled up and down like a lifeguard. He looked concerned. He didn't have to be, and I wanted him to know that. Pat and I have always been excellent swimmers. I waved at him, then turned around and struck out to catch up with Pat, cutting through the water more easily than I thought. I was weaker than him still, but I had always had the edge on him in the water. It was time to remind him of that. I stopped a little farther out to tread water for a moment and look back. Gracie was jumping up and down and yelling at me. 'Sean! Wait! Come back! There are jellyfish! I saw them.'

But I just waved back and swam on. Pat was up ahead of me. I just had to catch him, then race him back to shore. That would soon scatter any jellyfish that were foolish enough to get in our way. When I reached him, Pat turned and headed back straightaway, hardly giving me time to catch my breath. He made it back ahead of me, but only just. Which proved what I suspected. I'm getting stronger every day.

When we came out, I was even hungrier than before. We dried ourselves off and then sat on the big rug to eat sandwiches and crisps and drink orange and Coca-Cola, and nobody said anything about sugar or teeth rotting, which was good. The adults sat on fold-out chairs and talked.

When we had finished, Pat got up and said he was going for a walk, to see what was at the end of the beach. I got the feeling he wanted some time on his own, so I let him go.

'Can we swim again, Annie?' Gracie asked.

'No, honey, not for an hour or so. You know you're not meant to go in right after eating. Besides, Sean looks as if he's only thawing out. Bet the water back home is a lot warmer?'

'It sure is,' said Dad, laughing.

Gracie sighed, already restless. 'Okay, then we'll go up to Abbey Island. I'll show Sean the ruins . . .'

I looked at her quickly, but she didn't catch my eye. I didn't really want to see any graveyard, but there was the ruin of an old monastery right across the beach, on the hill. Gracie had told me about it before we came out here. Said there were bones and stuff underground.

'Okay, but let me put some more sun cream on you guys first,' Annie said, reaching for the bottle. She rubbed us from head to toe, like we were heading out into the Nevada desert, but Dad just smiled. I guess she was being extra careful, and it probably reminded him of Mom. Women are better at that kind of stuff, Dad used to say.

'C'mon, Sean, I'll show you.' I followed Gracie as she walked back to the water's edge then headed right, running and jumping as she went.

We were coming to the end of this part of the beach, where it narrowed and led, through a gap in the dunes and down a stony path, onto another, smaller beach that you could only access at low tide. At the end there was a small hill and more stones, big flat ones, and there ahead was the ruin.

'There it is,' said Gracie. 'That's Abbey Island. The church was built in the sixth century by Saint Fionán.'

She climbed easily over the barred gate and hopped down the other side. I waited. Something about the place made me want to stand still for a moment. There were three interconnecting stone buildings that used to be a church, I guess, but the roof was long gone. All around there were graves – really old graves.

'What are you waiting for?' Gracie called.

I climbed over the gate and followed her up along the tiny narrow path that wound right around the cliff edge, trying not to step on graves. I had never seen so many. They were every size, some like big tombs and others so small and old that they were just like stumps of rock poking up from between the long grasses and reeds.

'The tiny unmarked graves are the really old ones. They've

totally worn away with the wind and sea,' Gracie said. 'Those are mostly the monks who used to live here.'

I tried to imagine what it must have been like back in the olden days, but I couldn't. I mean, how did people live all alone up here? Out on a cliff top, in the wilds?

The path wound around the hill and then down, leading into the interior of the church. There were stones on the ground, and three arched windows faced the sea. If you looked out the window, it felt as if you were on the edge of the world. Below was the sea, blue and clear, the beach, and those low, slanting black rocks.

'A lot of smuggling went on here in the old days,' Gracie said. 'C'mon, if you come up this way, I'll show you the bones.'

We went out and followed another stony path up onto the grass, alongside the other wall of the church. The stone walls were cold and I was glad to feel the sun warm on my back. Gracie got down on her hands and knees and peered through a hole in the ground.

'Look, Sean, it's a monk's tomb, and you can see loads of bones.'

I got down and looked through the hole, and it was true, there were lots of old bones there. It was kind of creepy.

We got up again and I followed Gracie inside the church, which had just three walls and only the sky for a roof.

'Hey,' she called. 'Look over here, this is cool.'

She was pointing to a grave, right in front of her. It was big – big enough for two people, at least. It looked like an important sort of a tomb, with a carved arch on top. There was a plaque on the side that read: *Here lies Mary O'Connell, wife of Daniel.*

'See?' said Gracie. 'It's got your dad's name on it! Daniel O'Connell!'

But I wasn't listening. Everything slowed down and went still. I didn't hear Gracie talking, or the waves, or the sound of kids playing on the beach below, or the dogs that were barking. I just felt hot, then cold, and then all the air was sucked out of me. I didn't know what was happening, but I knew I had to get out of there, so I turned and ran. I ran through the long grass and jumped over headstones, vaulted the old iron barred gate, down the stony hill and through the smaller beach, through the gap in the dunes and back onto the longer beach. I ran and I ran, up the slope to where the cars were parked, and then headed left for the harbour. I didn't know where I was going and I didn't care. I guess I heard Gracie's cries and hollers somewhere in the distance, but I had left her far behind. I didn't see Dad or Pat running after me, but Pat must have seen me first because all of a sudden he was running alongside me, pulling me up.

'Wait, Sean!' he yelled. 'Wait up!'

I stopped, not because I wanted to, but because I couldn't breathe anymore. I looked at him and tried to speak, but I couldn't. But I knew he understood.

'It's okay, Sean. I'm here. I'm with you, bro. It's okay,' he said over and over as I gulped for air.

And then Dad was there, and his arms went around me, holding me so tight I couldn't move, but it felt good. I felt safe. Bit by bit I could feel my breath coming back.

'Something freaked him out,' said Pat, standing back, watching with his arms folded from a few feet away.

'What is it, Sean? What happened?' Dad stood up and put his hands on my shoulders. He was willing me to speak, I knew, but I couldn't. 'Did someone hurt you? Scare you?'

I shook my head.

By now the others had come over. Annie had her arm around Gracie, who looked shocked and scared. I could tell she'd been crying. I hated myself. And I hated the attention I was creating.

'Gracie said they were playing on Abbey Island,' Annie said to Dad. 'They were looking at the ruins, and then Sean just ran away.'

She looked puzzled. 'She doesn't know what happened. She said there was no one else there, just the two of them, and then Sean suddenly took off.'

'What ruins?' Dad asked, looking at Annie.

'The old church and graveyard . . .' she pointed. 'Way down there, at the other end of the beach.'

'I wanted to show him the bones,' Gracie explained. 'And then . . . we saw the gravestone with your name on it . . .' her voice trailed away.

Dad sucked in his breath and got the look on his face that meant trouble. 'What are you talking about? What gravestone?'

'I didn't mean . . . I didn't know . . . it was just there . . .' Gracie stuttered. She bit her lip.

'I don't believe this.' He shook his head. 'You let a traumatised eleven-year-old kid who's lost his mom go to a graveyard?' Dad looked at Annie and Gracie as if they were mad. 'What were you *thinking?*'

Annie wrapped her arm tightly around Gracie. 'Look, Dan, I don't know what happened up there, but whatever it was, it wasn't Gracie's fault, so don't you go blaming her.'

'I'm not blaming her,' Dad almost shouted. 'I'm blaming *you.*'

'Excuse me?'

'You heard me.'

'Annie—'

'Shush, Gracie! Look, Dan, the reason I wasn't paying that much attention to where Gracie said they were going is because I was more concerned about them not going into the water after eating . . .'

'Never mind. This was a really bad idea,' Dad said, ignoring her. 'We need to go home.'

Oh shit. I caught Pat's eye. *What now?* I was thinking.

'Just act like you're fine,' Pat whispered in my ear. 'Act like nothing happened. They'll get over it. We can talk later.' He looked around and grinned. 'Poor Gracie looks like you set her hair on fire.'

That made me smile, even though I still felt really bad. But I knew he was right.

'C'mon, Sean,' Dad said to me. 'We're going home.'

I didn't want to go, but I didn't want to stay either. The day didn't seem so much fun anymore. I shrugged. Dad took Declan aside and spoke in a low voice, so I couldn't hear what they were saying, then Declan called someone on his phone. Gracie slipped away from Annie and came over to Pat and me.

'I'm really sorry, Sean, for what happened up there,' she said. 'You don't have to tell me . . . I mean, you know . . . I never meant . . . I never would have . . .' She looked as if she might start crying again.

I wanted to tell her I knew that. Of course I knew she would never mean to upset me. But I couldn't. Instead, I squeezed her hand quickly then let it go. That seemed to do the trick and she cheered up.

Pat watched and gave me a sly smile. I was going to get a hard time for that later.

'Okay, guys,' Dad said. 'We're packing up, come on, get your stuff, we're going back to the village.'

'Come on, Gracie.' Annie said. 'There's no need for us to leave, we're not going home yet.'

'But—'

'There are plenty of other kids for you to play with here. See you later, Declan.' She waved at him, but didn't look at us.

When we were in the car and heading out of the car park, Dad turned to Declan and said, 'Is it okay for us to swing by Doctor Mike's surgery?'

'Absolutely,' Declan said, nodding. 'He said he'd see you straightaway.'

I couldn't see his face, but I could tell by his voice that Dad was still really mad.

Nobody said anything after that, and Declan turned up the radio.

* * *

'Physically, he's as right as rain.' Doctor Mike looked at Dan across the desk in his small office. Declan had called the surgery before they left Derrynane, so they could go straight there on their return to the village.

Sean was seen by Doctor Mike, pronounced perfectly unharmed, and was now back in the car with the others while Dan had a word with Doctor Mike in private.

'Psychologically,' he went on, 'who can tell? But I think it's healthy he's making new friends. That's always a good sign.'

'Even if those friends bring him to look at old burial sites full of bones?' Dan has related the Derrynane debacle to Doctor Mike, and he's still upset about it.

'Wouldn't you have wanted to do that if you were their age? I know I would.' The doctor smiles at him.

'It totally freaked him!'

'But he's not retreating, Dan. He still wants to hang out with Gracie, doesn't he? He hasn't pulled back.'

'Yes, but . . .' Dan looks him in the eye and asks the question he wished he didn't have to ask. 'That's the thing. You know I said he's been spending a lot of time with Gracie? In fact, they're pretty inseparable.'

'Is that a problem?'

'I don't know. That's what I was going to ask you.' Dan chooses his words carefully. 'Gracie seems like a great kid.'

'Gracie *is* a great kid.'

'I know, but she seems to spend a lot of time with her grandparents in the hotel . . . I was just wondering . . .'

'What?'

Dan pauses, trying to find the right words. 'My boy's been through such a tough time back home, Doctor Mike. I need to know he's not going to be . . . well, I need to know he's around good, solid people. You know what I'm saying?' He runs a hand through his hair. 'Maybe I'm not putting this well, but this incident at Derrynane, well it's scared the hell out of me.'

Doctor Mike nods. 'I understand your concerns as a parent, Dan, really I do. For what it's worth, Grace O'Malley is exactly the child I would choose to befriend a vulnerable kid. I couldn't think of anyone more solid, or sensible. In fact, I'd go so far as to say she's wise beyond her years. Besides, Ballyanna is a small village. Everyone knows everyone here and looks out for everybody else, especially the kids. I don't think you have any worries on that front.'

It doesn't seem to Dan like he has a lot of choice. He thanks Doctor Mike, who assures him that he's available twenty-four-seven for Sean, if he has any concerns. 'I mean that, Dan, any time, day or night, just pick up the phone.'

Once home, Dan sent Sean off to have a nap in his room. He knew Sean wouldn't sleep, but he wanted to talk to Dr Shriver. He put in a Skype call and waited anxiously for her to reply. Finally, she appeared on his laptop screen.

'You can't wrap him in cotton wool, Dan,' she said after listening intently to the whole story about Derrynane. 'Although I know you want to, and that's perfectly understandable, but kids are much stronger than we give them credit for.'

'He was totally freaked out!'

'I don't doubt it, but he's recovering, Dan, he's getting stronger. And you say he got in the water?'

'Yes, swam out so far I thought he wasn't going to come back. I was within a hair's breadth of going in after him.'

'Well thank God you didn't. That's *huge*, Dan.' Dr Shriver smiled. 'I mean, how long has it been? Almost fifteen months, right?'

Dan nodded.

'This is good, Dan. It's all good, really. Just keep doing what you're doing, let Sean set the pace, and if he seems okay with things, then he probably is. That was a big confrontation, what he's just faced, and he got through it, despite being taken totally unawares. He's doing really well, Dan. You've got a great kid there, don't underestimate him – that would be the worst thing you could do right now. He needs to know you believe in him, that you believe in his ability to move on from the trauma.'

'If you say so . . .'

'There are no set rules, Dan, in these cases. That's the hardest part for the parents involved. But from what you tell me, Sean is coping really well. I know I sound like a broken record, but just keep doing what you're doing. If I had the slightest concern, I'd let you know immediately.'

Pat

I'm not sure coming here was a good idea. I know Dad has to do this documentary research and stuff, but he could have come on his own and left us behind in California. We could have stayed with Grandma and Grandpa Carroll. We'd have been okay. Sean freaked everyone out when he had his meltdown on the beach. It was just as well Dad and me were there. It was good that he got back in the water, though. I knew he'd be fine once he started swimming again. Gracie was the most freaked of all. That was kind of funny. She sure wasn't expecting that. I mean, what was she thinking? Bringing a kid who'd lost his mom in a car wreck up to look at graves and old bones and stuff? Jeez.

Gracie's okay, but she's not as cool as she pretends. She talks too much. That's why Sean likes her, because she doesn't make him feel like he should be talking back. I think she likes that he doesn't talk. Means he doesn't ask too many questions. I mean, why is she hanging around after him anyway? Doesn't she have friends of her own around here?

I heard Annie talking to Dad before, and she said it was nice that Gracie had a little friend she could trust, someone she could be herself with. Who else is she going to be? That's the thing about Gracie that Sean doesn't get. She's not being real. But then, neither is he. Guess that's why they get along so well. I was listening to the guys talking about Gracie's parents when we were playing football, and one of them was saying that his dad said that Gracie's dad is in trouble and might well be going to jail, and that they're probably getting divorced. That's why Gracie spends so much time with Annie and her grandparents.

Gracie thinks Sean and me are cool, that we have this great life in America. And we do, or we used to, until everything fell apart. Until the accident, when Mom died. Now she's gone forever. Sean feels guilty. I know he does, he doesn't have to say a word. But it's not his fault. I've told him that so many times. Adults do what they want to do. And there's nothing he's ever going to be able to do about that.

* * *

About last night . . .' Dee looks pale but seems fully recovered. Annie has brought Gracie straight home to her mother from Derrynane. 'I think I may have gone overboard a bit . . . I guess it's the stress getting to me . . . I know you brought me home . . . I'm sorry if I spoiled your evening . . . do I have anything else I need to, ah, apologise for . . .?'

'Apart from being completely out of it, nothing at all.' Annie is brisk. 'But never mind that now, there was a bit of an incident at the beach . . . poor Gracie got a fright.' Annie relates the Derrynane episode.

'He yelled at Gracie? What a prick!' Dee is outraged.

'Not exactly . . . it was me he was angry with, but we were together by then, so Gracie got the brunt of it too.' Annie shakes her head. 'You'd have to have been there. It was . . . well, it was baffling. He overreacted completely . . . I mean, I know Sean was upset, but it wasn't anybody's fault.'

'What's with the kid anyway?' Dee asks. 'I don't like the sound of this. I think it would be better if you made some other friends, Gracie. I don't want you spending time with Sean anymore.'

'It's wasn't Sean's fault.' Gracie looks alarmed. 'He didn't blame me for it. He couldn't help it, what happened to him, and he squeezed my hand after to show he wasn't angry with me. Do you think he won't want to be friends with me anymore, Annie?' She seems dismayed at the thought.

'I don't know, Gracie . . . maybe your mum is right . . .'

'But I don't want to make other friends. I like Sean.'

Just then Annie's phone rings. 'It's Mum,' she says, taking the call. She listens to Breda, says she'll be there in five. 'I gotta go. Mum says I'm needed at the hotel.' She looks anxiously at Gracie, who is plainly upset. 'Are you sure you're okay?' She tugs one of Gracie's curls.

Her niece nods unconvincingly.

'Have a nice hot bath, get all that sand off you, then watch a movie with your mum. You'll have forgotten all about this by tomorrow. See you later.'

'Thanks,' Dee says quietly. 'For taking care of Gracie.'

Annie looks at her sister. There are so many things she'd like to say to her, but now isn't the time. Nonetheless, she's upset and angry with Dee – for last night and for being too hungover to take her daughter to the beach this morning. Annie resolves to get Dee on her own soon and have it out with her. This situation can't be allowed to continue. Dee just has to step up and get on with things.

* * *

Annie walks quickly up to the reception desk. 'Mum's looking for me, where is she?'

The girl on duty nods in the direction of the small reading lounge across the corridor from the hotel bar.

Annie pushes open the door, and they both stand up. Her mother looks pleased, if curious.

'Well, here she is now. I'll leave you both to it. I could have some coffee sent in?' Breda suggests.

'Not on my account,' says Dan, looking uncomfortable. 'This won't take long.'

Breda slips out, closing the door behind her.

'Look, I, uh, just wanted to apologise for what happened, back at the beach . . . it must have seemed . . . well, my reaction must have seemed somewhat . . . over the top . . .'

'You could say that.' Annie is cool.

'How's Gracie?'

'She's upset, but she'll get over it.'

'Look, I can understand you're angry, but just . . . hear me out. Things have been very difficult for Sean. I had my reasons for panicking, believe me.'

'I'm sure you did. But there was still no need to yell at a little girl.'

'I wasn't yelling at her . . . well, I guess it must have seemed that way. Look, I need to talk to you about all this properly, but not now, not here. Will you meet me for a drink later this evening? Please? Let me explain . . .'

Something in his expression, the way he asks so desperately, makes her agree. Besides, she is curious now, and what has she got to lose?

'I could meet you in the Smuggler's, I suppose, opposite the golf club, after dinner, say, eight o'clock?'

'I'll be there. And thank you.'

* * *

It's a ten-minute stroll to the pub. Dan gets there first and takes a table outside, overlooking the sea. He has called on Joan Coady again to babysit, but she seems to enjoy it and he pays her generously, so it's working out well. It's good to get away on his own from time to time, there's no denying that.

Annie arrives just minutes later. She looks tired, he thinks, and still cross. She says she'll have a gin and tonic and he goes inside to order and returns with their drinks. For a few moments they chat about the usual things people do, although the real reason he is here sits like a deadweight in his chest.

He learns Annie has returned home recently, having lived for the last ten years in London.

'I thought you were the receptionist,' he confesses.

This, at least, raises a smile. 'It's one of my multiple roles at the moment.'

'Then Declan put me straight . . . or at least, he told me to Google you.' He raises his eyebrows. 'I'm impressed.'

She laughs, but her face colours just a little, enough for him to know she's not arrogant about her success, which he finds endearing.

'So, what made you decide to come home?'

'London's not where I want to settle. For a while I thought I would, but not now.' An expression Dan cannot quite decipher flickers across her face for just an instant. 'I need to take some time out, think about what I'm going to do next.'

Dan senses there is more to her story, but doesn't press for details. He understands more than most that some things are too uncomfortable to talk about until you're ready.

'My parents are going through a tough time, just now,' she goes on. 'My brother-in-law has been running a ponzi scheme in Cork. My sister's marriage is in meltdown as a result, although to listen to her she seems to be in complete denial of her situation. Last

night in the pub . . . well, she was pretty drunk . . . it's not like her
. . . I've never seen her that bad before.'

'Pressure makes people do a lot of things they don't usually do.'

She nods. 'How's Sean doing, really?' she asks.

'He's okay. As much as he can be, I guess.'

For a moment, they are silent.

'This accident,' she says finally. 'Do you want to talk about it?'

Dan doesn't. He's sick of talking about it. Sick watching his
pain reflected on other people's faces. Sick feeling their sympathy
sliding into relief that their own situation could be worse – *There
but for the grace of God* . . . That was what his mother always said
when she heard of any misfortune befalling someone they knew.
Until it was his turn, and his doorstep that tragedy showed up on.

But he has to talk, for Sean's sake. So he orders two more
drinks and begins, yet again, the story of how loss can find you,
and double the odds, even when you think you've thrown in a fair
share of the chips already.

* * *

'Ah, not a dinner party, Barbara, sure we've only just moved in and
got rid of the builders.'

'It's not a dinner party. Just a casual kitchen supper, only six or
eight of us.'

'That's Dublin-speak for a dinner party.'

'What's the point of having a new house, Mike, if we don't invite
people into it?'

'Go on then.' Mike sighed. 'Who's on the list?'

'Well, here's where I need a little help from you . . .'

Mike immediately looked wary. 'Why?'

'Because I need you to invite him.' The American fellow would be the most crucial guest to corral, and for this Barbara needed her husband's help.

Mike was doubtful. 'But I don't know him, Barbara, not that way.'

'He came to the surgery, didn't he? And didn't you see him in the pub one night?' She tried not to get exasperated, Mike could be stubborn if he felt he was being pushed. 'Didn't you tell him you'd be available to him twenty-four-seven if he needed you?'

'That's different, that's work-related.'

Barbara tried a different tack. 'What does it matter, Mike? The fellow's lonely, it's written all over him, losing his wife and all, it would be an act of kindness to invite him into our home, introduce him to some local people while he's here. Besides . . .,' she played her trump card, 'Annie's coming too.' She looked at him and smiled.

Mike looked at her over his glasses. 'Tell me you're not match-making again, Barbara.'

'Of course I am. Why wouldn't I be? I have it all worked out.' She warmed to her theme. 'Annie and the American fellow, what's his name?'

'Dan.'

'Yes, Dan, and Declan Coady, so there'll be another single man, although Declan might bring a partner, but that's alright, and then you and me. Six of us, just in the kitchen, nothing fancy . . . you have his number, don't you? Or you're bound to run into him in the village anyway.'

'I suppose . . . it would be a nice thing to do, and it's a while since we've had anyone round.'

'Exactly. Besides, it's our duty.'

'How do you work that out?'

'To pass on our good fortune, of course. We would never have met if Annie hadn't been match-making.'

'Is that what she was doing?' Mike feigned surprise.

'With a little encouragement from me, of course.'

He grinned. 'Alright. I'll give him a call this afternoon.'

Barbara got on to Declan Coady herself, who said he would be delighted to join them. Annie texted back that she was looking forward to it. Then Barbara included the Von Becks, a young Dutch couple who had bought a holiday home on the lake, and finally she invited her good friend Linda, who worked in the shop with her. Linda's husband would be going up north to visit his elderly parents, so Linda was more than happy to accept the dinner invitation when Barbara put it to her in the shop that afternoon.

'Who's coming?' she asked, as they sat at the back of the shop checking the online orders.

'Yourself, Declan Coady, Daniel O'Connell, and Annie.'

Linda's eyes grew wide. 'Do you think . . .?'

'I'm not thinking anything.' Barbara got up to get herself a cappuccino from the machine. 'I'm just throwing some people together and seeing what happens.'

'I can't wait. I'll start saving up my smart points today.' Linda was currently on a WeightWatchers drive. 'Will I come a bit early? So I can give you a bit of help, and you know me, I can talk for Ireland if things are a bit slow at the start.'

'That would be great, Linda. You're a star.'

* * *

Luke couldn't pinpoint exactly when it started. When he first began hearing of the unusual goings-on. He remembered hearing Battie Shannon talking about finding messages written in the sand, even after a retreating tide, but he hadn't paid much attention to the talk. Battie was always seeing and hearing things.

But then the few regulars who still came to confession began mentioning things. There were muttered accounts of taps turning themselves on of their own accord. Josie Mullet from the Post Office swore blind to the insurance inspector that this was how her upstairs bathroom had flooded. There was talk of lights coming on and going off in the middle of the night, televisions likewise, causing much alarm to people who assumed there was an intruder in their house, until they came downstairs and found the television blaring when they knew they had turned it off. Dogs barked at nothing at all, and cats hissed and fled the room for no apparent reason. Nellie O'Reilly from the hairdresser's said the salon was abuzz with it all.

So Luke began paying more attention to the accounts. He even mentioned the matter to Fr Martin, but Martin only gave him a look and said it was probably someone's idea of a joke to wind him up. All the same, Luke was uneasy about the whole thing. And the more he thought about it, the more he realised that all of this business had started exactly around the time Barry McLaughlin had come home. And if Martin wouldn't take the matter seriously, then it was Luke's duty to investigate. As much as he was reluctant about the notion, a visit to Jerry's cottage was clearly the place to begin.

He set out that afternoon, on foot down the lake road, and wondered how on earth he would broach the subject. He passed a goat that bleated at him, and the donkey he had seen before, which curled its lip and leered at him. Luke shuddered. He had never been comfortable around animals, even if they were God's creatures. He steeled himself to knock firmly on the door when it suddenly opened wide, leaving Luke's fist flailing in mid-air.

'I thought I saw someone coming up the path,' Jerry said, as if it was the most natural thing in the world to find Luke on her doorstep. 'Come in and have a cup of tea. I've just made a pot.'

Luke had not wanted to actually enter into the place, a few well-chosen questions at the door would have sufficed, but now he was caught on the back foot. It would be churlish to refuse the invitation.

His eyes took a moment to adjust to the dim interior of the cottage, which was really just one big room with a couple of doorways off it, presumably leading to the bedrooms. In the middle was an old pine table piled with papers, dried flowers and plants and some laundry. By the fireplace a battered winged armchair faced an old rocker. Jerry indicated the armchair. 'Sit down, and I'll bring the tea over.'

Luke did as he was told, flinching at the sight of two cats, one of them black, that sat on the windowsill. He was allergic to cats, and he hoped fervently they wouldn't bring on a fit of wheezing.

Jerry poured the tea, accompanied by a generous slice of lemon drizzle cake – by coincidence, Luke's favourite cake – placing the cup and plate on the small table beside him before sitting in the rocking chair across from him.

'Barry will be sorry he's missed you. He's gone for a walk.'

'Ah, and how is your brother, Miss, er . . .'

'Just call me Jerry, Luke, everybody else does. And Barry's fine. It's taking him a little while to get reacquainted with the place, but the air is doing him the world of good.'

'Where exactly in Africa was Barry working?'

'In Kenya, a small place called Turkana. Can I help you, or was it Barry you wanted to talk to?'

'I was just wondering . . .'

'Yes?'

'Um, that is . . . I believe you yourself have an interest in things spiritual . . .'

Jerry looked at him and smiled. 'I'm not one of your crowd, even if my brother is, but I'm always happy to help out in the parish if I can be of any service.'

'No, no.' Luke was feeling more awkward by the minute. 'I'm

not here to ask for your help in any practical sense . . . but perhaps in a more esoteric capacity . . .'

'Now you've lost me.' Jerry looked at him quizzically.

'There's only one way to say this, eh, Jerry. It has come to my attention that matters of an unusual nature have been occurring in the village.'

'What kind of unusual matters?'

'Objects being moved around, lights and taps turning on and off of their own accord, that sort of thing.' He watched her closely. 'I was wondering if you might have heard any similar accounts?'

'I can't say I have. And what is your opinion of these accounts, do you believe them?'

'The fact that these experiences have mostly been divulged in the confessional leads me to believe they are genuine.'

'Well I'm afraid I can't shed any light on that at all.'

'But you admit you, eh . . . dabble in things of that nature?' He rushed to reassure her. 'I am not here in any censorious capacity, you understand, I am merely trying to understand how and why something like this might have started up in the first place.'

Dear God, but the young fella was pompous, even if he was well-meaning, Jerry thought. Maybe he wasn't aware of it. But he'd learn, in time.

'Let me make one thing quite clear, Luke. I do not *dabble* in anything. I am, however, a psychic, clairvoyant, call it what you will. It's a family trait. I'm an herbalist and a healer by trade, you might say, but if someone needs my help and my psychic ability helps me deliver that help, then yes, I will certainly avail of it. I believe it's a God-given gift. But I do not, under any circumstances, engage in tea leaves, card readings, juju, ouija boards or any sort of ghost hunting, contrary to whatever you may or may not have heard.'

'And you haven't heard any talk about strange goings-on?'

'No, I have not.'

'I see. Well, thank you for your time, and the tea and cake, it was delicious.' Luke got to his feet. 'I won't delay you any longer.'

'I'm always happy to stop for a cup of tea. I wouldn't worry too much about things going bump in the night, Luke, these things tend to resolve themselves of their own accord in my experience.'

Luke wasn't convinced. He was certain Jerry knew something. And Barry had been out in Africa for forty years, there was no telling what he might have got involved in out there. Luke had heard of instances where that happened, where the holiest of priests could go out to these places and take up with all sorts of pagan practices. No, his gut instinct told him Jerry was hiding something from him. He would just have to keep an eye on the place and monitor the situation as best he could.

Pat

Sean was hanging out with Gracie again, even though the whole Derrynane thing was her fault. I couldn't believe it! And I didn't want to play stupid games with them anyway, so I headed out for a walk on my own.

Usually we walk on the beach, so today, for a change, I went down to explore the road by the lake. There were some pretty houses and some of them had small boats tied up outside. I walked on a bit more, around a bend in the road, and that's when I saw it. I came a bit closer, just to make sure, but there was no mistaking it. It was the cottage I had seen in my dream of Mom that night. The roof was thatched, the roses went all up the walls, and the door was painted bright green and had two halves, top and bottom. The top part was open.

Before I knew it, I was right beside it. And there was the cutest donkey I'd ever seen leaning over the fence. An old guy was trimming the hedge just beyond, and he looked over at me and smiled.

'Can I pet him?' I pointed at the donkey.

'It's a her, and you can, yes, she likes to have her nose rubbed.' He put his clippers down and came over to lean on the fence.

'What's her name?' I rubbed her nose and she twitched her mouth and then curled her lip up, that made me laugh.

'Her name's Ginny. What's yours, lad?'

'I'm Pat.'

'Pleased to meet you, Pat. I'm Barry.'

Then the black-and-white dog appeared and ran over and sat down so I had to pat her too.

'That's Millie, she loves meeting new people, but don't give her too much attention or she might follow you home.'

'Oh, I'm just visiting,' I said. I wanted to tell him I'd seen his cottage before in a dream, his dog too, but that would sound super weird.

'I didn't think I'd seen you before. Where are you from, Pat?'

'California, but we're staying here for a while. My dad has to do some work here.'

'Is that right? And where are you staying?'

'Cable Lodge.'

'Ah, a lovely old place, that.'

'It doesn't have a donkey though, or a dog. Can I bring my brother here sometime to see Ginny and Millie?'

'Surely you can, lad. Where is he?'

'He's with a friend. I'd better get back to them, they'll be wondering where I've got to.' I looked at the cottage with roses climbing all up the walls. 'Your house is real pretty.'

'Oh, it's not my house, I'm just staying here. It belongs to my sister, Jerry. She won't mind you visiting, she loves children.'

'That's good because we love animals. We were going to get a dog before the accident.'

'What accident was that?'

'A car accident. My mom died in it and my twin brother doesn't talk anymore after it.'

Barry shook his head. 'I'm very sorry to hear that, lad. That's very hard on you. You must miss her a lot.'

I nodded. 'I just want my brother to get better, though, that's more important right now.'

'Well, you and your brother, and your dad for that matter, are welcome here anytime you like.'

'Where do you live if you don't live here?' I asked him.

'I live in Africa, in a very small village called Turkana.'

'Smaller than this?'

'Much smaller.'

'How come you live in Africa?'

'It's where I work. I'm a priest. I've been living there for a long time.'

'Don't priests have to wear a uniform or something?'

'When we're working, yes. But I'm on a kind of holiday now, that's why I came home to stay with my sister.'

I wanted to talk to him some more, but it was time for me to go back.

'Well, I'd better get going. It was nice to meet you, Barry. Maybe I'll bring my brother next time.'

'Good to meet you too, lad. God Bless.'

* * *

He wanted to see this graveyard for himself, see exactly what Sean had experienced that day. So Dan got in the car and drove back out to Derrynane. It was late afternoon, and the cliff drive out was spectacular, looking out as it did over the ocean, the Skellig rock clearly etched in view, and then, coming up to Caherdaniel, the cluster of small islands and natural harbour nestled below. He turned right at the pub, following the series of winding roads, lush with vegetation and forestry, and arrived at the small parking area.

Derrynane was a popular beach with holidaymakers and Dan could understand why. The picturesque cove was sheltered, with plenty of slanting black rocks to sit against and set up camp for the day, and safe, clear, if bitingly cold, water to swim in.

Now, he parks his car and strolls down to the water's edge. At six o'clock the beach is pretty much empty, except for a few stragglers. Most people have packed up for the day and gone home. He walks to the end, and through the gap in the dunes and into the smaller cove, then up the stony path that leads to the old graveyard. The rusty red gate creaks as he opens and closes it behind him. Then he follows the narrow, well-trod path that leads around the cliff edge, pausing to study the bigger graves and, with more interest, the other, tiny, worn-away slabs of stone that mark the passage between one life and the next, and that had weathered centuries.

Despite his misgivings, he's struck by the beauty of the place. He pauses, feeling almost as if time has stood still, as if he has stepped into another world, crossed some hidden threshold. He feels a deep reverence for those intrepid souls who have lived and died here in this tiny monastery, perched on the edge of the cliffs, with nothing but their faith and a few stone walls between them, the wild Atlantic, and eternity. It settles on him now, this feeling, elusive yet familiar, and for a moment he can almost remember what it feels like to be at peace.

Inside the ruin of the small church, it doesn't take him long to spot the imposing tomb. Dan inhales sharply when he sees it. Now it all makes sense.

Here lies Mary O'Connell, wife of Daniel.

Christ, no wonder poor Sean had freaked out. He finds it pretty unsettling himself. What must it have been like for Sean to see his mother's name on a gravestone? Make that both his parents' names. Daniel couldn't begin to imagine how traumatic Sean must have found that. Must have taken him right back to that awful, awful day. He reaches out to touch the stone, tracing the names engraved on it, his and Mary's, joined forever in so many ways – marriage, parenthood. At least she had been spared this . . . this aftermath. Dan would willingly have given his own life and exchanged places with her in that car, but then what? Would Mary have managed? Could she have coped better than him? He'd never know. Either way, now he had no choice but to go on for both of them.

So much for Daniel thinking they'd be getting away from things here. It seems like there's no escape, he thinks grimly.

But then he reminds himself to be grateful that, as Dr Shriver pointed out, Sean doesn't appear to have regressed because of the shock. That would have been a cruel setback.

Daniel wants to get outside again, away from this tomb that seems to mock him. At the cliff edge, he pauses for a moment. Below him the water is cornflower blue and clear, and on the beach beyond the cove is bathed in the last rays of sun. A gentle breeze weaves through the long grasses that have sprung up around the headstones. And that's when he hears it . . . someone crying. It is a soft, insistent sound, and it seems to be coming from the direction of some of the older gravestones.

Dan walks over and looks around them. 'Hello?' he calls. 'Anybody there? Are you alright?' He listens intently, but the sound has stopped. There's no one to be seen.

He runs a hand through his hair and starts walking back down to the beach and on to his car. He shakes his head. The stress is getting to him, that's all, Dr Shriver warned him that it might.

When he reaches the end of the beach he turns back to look at Abbey Island. The ruined stone walls are washed in evening light that makes the old church look almost mythical, suspended between two worlds, touching the living and the dead.

Sean

Today we're going fishing. Gracie and her mom are coming with us. It was her mom's idea. She rang Dad and said she'd organise the whole thing and bring a picnic. I was there when Dad took the call and when he hung up he said, 'Holy Moly, I wasn't expecting that,' to nobody in particular. I was glad Gracie was coming though, not because we'd had a fight or anything, but I've been worried that since that day on Derrynane, she might think I was weird or, worse, a wimp.

It turns out I'm wrong on both counts. Gracie's just the same as ever. I think everything's okay now, I sure hope so, because I like hanging out with Gracie. She's fun, although I'm not sure Pat likes her, but that's just jealousy. He's always been possessive of me. He pretends not to be, but he is. I can always tell when he's pissed with me. He was acting up earlier and saying that maybe he wouldn't even come fishing with us, but Dad just ignored him and grinned at me and loaded the stuff in the car anyway.

We pile into Dad's car, Dee in the front with Dad, Gracie and me in the back, then, at the last minute, Pat of course comes too. I'm relieved. I wasn't sure he would. He's been acting kind of funny the last couple of days. I have the feeling I've done something to piss him off, but I can't figure out what. But either way, I'm glad he's decided to come.

The drive to Lough Currane doesn't take long, but all the way there Pat makes me laugh, making faces behind Dad and tweaking his hair, or tickling his head and ear with a fern he's picked up, so Dad keeps swatting his head and neck, talking about 'goddamned flies and midges'.

Gracie's on her iPad, so she doesn't notice, or pretends not to. But she's giggling just the same.

'What are you kids laughing about back there?' Dad smiles at us in the rear-view mirror.

'We're just having a bet about who's going to catch the biggest fish,' Gracie says, kicking me quite hard on my ankle. Pat curls his lip at her when she's not looking.

'Well, here we are,' says Dad. 'You'll find out soon enough, guys. Maybe the winner gets to cook dinner for us all!'

We meet the ghillie, a man named Sam, at the boathouse, and in the end we take two small boats instead of one. Both have oars and a small motor out back. Dad, Dee and Pat go with Sam, and Sam's son, Rory, takes Gracie and me out. That's because Dad wants to do more serious fishing, which means going to a different part of the lake. We all agree to meet on Church Island, in the middle of the lake, for a picnic lunch at one o'clock.

Rory, who's about eighteen I guess, is really nice. He rows out a little bit then starts up the engine and lets us take turns steering the boat while he hands out fishing rods and sets about making the bait for them. Then he fixes the bait on the end of each line and shows me and Gracie how to hold the rod over the side of the boat and let the line run out behind. After that, he says, all we have to do is wait.

For a while, nothing happens. Gracie talks to Rory, who asks after her family, especially her grandfather, whose name is Conor and lives in the hotel. I think it must be pretty cool to live in a hotel, but Gracie says it isn't all that great – her grandmother is always saying it will be the death of her, and now that Granddad can't get about so well any more, he's being even more of a nightmare to live with than usual. Rory laughs at this and says, 'Well, leopards don't change their spots. Not at his age.'

Listening to Gracie, Mrs Sullivan, her grandma, seems to have a lot of trouble with her husband, but they're still married, so they must get along some of the time. I mean, otherwise they'd be divorced, like most of the kids' grandparents back home. Some of them had had a few different husbands and wives by the time they got that old.

Gracie must guess what I'm thinking, because the next thing she says is, 'I asked her how come she didn't get a divorce from Granddad if he was so difficult to live with, and she said when she was younger there was no divorce in Ireland, and now that she's old, she doesn't have the energy.'

I can see Rory laughing to himself at that, but it pretty much makes sense to me, and I think it sounds honest. Divorce uses up a lot of energy with people, even with Mom and Dad, who had lots of it. But I don't want to think about that now.

Just then Gracie gets a bite, and shrieks as her line unspools. Rory tells her how to reel it in and stands beside her as she pulls in her catch, which is a fair-sized trout. Rory catches it in a net and pulls it into the boat, removing the fly from the fish's mouth.

'Are you going to take it home for supper, or do you want to release it?' Rory asks her. 'You're going to have to decide quickly.'

For a moment Gracie looks torn, and then she says, 'No, put him back, Rory, let him go.'

'We'll photograph him anyway, so you can prove you caught something,' says Rory, which pleases her.

While all this is going on I'm not paying attention to my own line, although I can hear a strange kind of clicking noise in the background. When I look around to see what it is, I notice my rod is pulled down in a steep curve. The noise I hear is the line spinning out so fast, I can hardly catch hold of the handle to stop it. I want to yell, but I can't, so I sit there, frozen, like a dork, until Rory turns around and says, 'Hey, that's a singing reel I hear. What've you got there, Sean?'

I shrug, although my heart starts to race, and I move over quickly so he can sit beside me and show me what to do. He helps me get hold of the rod and starts to reel the line back in, because very quickly we both realise this is something I can't do on my own. Rory makes sure that I'm holding the rod all the time, even though he gets behind me and puts his hands over mine and helps me to hold on.

'Crikey,' he says, sounding excited. 'This is a big one, Sean, a salmon for sure. I think you might have a fight on your hands. Hold on, now, lean back, that's it, let him run.'

Rory explains that with a big, athletic fish like this guy, you have to let them run to tire themselves out, then when they stop to catch their breath, that's when you reel them in. This goes on until one or other of you gets tired and gives up.

This one must be pretty fit, because it doesn't seem like he needs time to rest at all. Just as soon as we – I mean, I – reel him in some, he takes off again rightaway, peeling off like a rocket. Pretty soon my hands are so tired I think they might fall off, sweaty too, but I keep holding on, just like Rory showed me. This goes on for over half an hour, and I'm scared I'll lose the fight.

'You have to play him now, Sean,' Rory warns. 'A battle like this is as much about strength of mind as strength of body. Let him run some more, that's it. This one's an acrobat, he'll break your line if you try to pull him in too hard or too quickly.'

Some chance, I think. I'm fading fast, and this fish seems like he'll run and twist and duck and dive forever. I wish Pat could see me. Gracie's literally breathing down my neck, and yelling so much I can hardly concentrate on what I'm doing. The excitement is almost too much. I can't lose him now. I'll never live it down, not in front of Gracie . . .

Then, suddenly, he goes quiet. Rory reels the line in with me as fast as we can. As it comes nearer and nearer the boat, I almost feel scared. It's like pulling a monster up from the black deep. And then, as if he can read my thoughts, about twenty feet from the boat I see a flash of silver, and that fish leaps right out of the water, straight in front of me – big and bold – before diving and running again. It's just as well Rory is helping me or I'd lose him. I get such a shock, I nearly drop the rod. For a second it feels as if he's looking right at me, and I lose my nerve.

'Stay with him, Sean, stay with him,' Rory urges. 'Let him run again. Won't be long now, he's tiring, I can tell.'

He's right. This is the last run. Although I'm almost too weak to stand up, Rory and I reel him in, and Gracie's ready with the net to hand to Rory, who gets that salmon twisting and thrashing into it, lifting him out of the water and whooping before landing him on the floor of the small boat.

'Congratulations, Sean!' Even Rory is out of breath. 'I'd say you've got yourself a fifteen-pounder there! That fella's been out to sea more than once, I'll bet.' He works quickly to remove the hook from its mouth. 'This could make you eligible for catch of the week! Do you want to keep him? I would, he's a fine specimen.' Rory holds him up by the tail as the fish twists, then goes still.

I shake my head quickly.

'No? You sure? This is the biggest salmon I've seen this season.' Rory looks doubtful. The salmon's mouth is opening and closing, and it looks as if he's gasping for air. It makes me feel sick. I shake my head again.

'Quick, get a photograph,' says Gracie, grabbing the iPad. 'You and Sean hold him and I'll take it.'

Rory holds the front end and I hold the bottom, and even so it's really heavy. If I held it vertically, it would be almost as big as I am. Gracie makes sure she has a few good shots, and then we put it back in the net. We watch as Rory releases him. With a flick of his tail, and a flash of silver scales, he is gone.

Part of me feels sad. I know Pat will think I'm a loser. He would never have let a catch like that go. He would have kept it to show Dad, and then they'd have filleted it and cleaned it and we'd all have had salmon for supper. But the thought of that just makes me feel more sick, even though I know Dad will be disappointed in me. But all that struggling, and the poor fish lying gasping on the floor of the boat about to die . . . well it just reminded me of . . . of . . .

'Don't be sad, Sean,' says Gracie, pretty much reading my thoughts once again. 'You did the right thing.' She nods affirmatively. 'You set him free to go back to his family instead of killing him and eating him.'

That doesn't really make me feel any better, and I see Rory grinning and shaking his head at us.

'Speaking of eating, I'd say it's time for lunch,' he says. 'We'll head over to the island, so.'

When we get there and pull ashore, I see that Dad, Dee and Pat have got there first and are standing waiting for us. Pat is clowning around, dragging his leg and making a face like the hunchback of Notre Dame. I help Rory offload our picnic basket.

The sun is shining and it's nice and warm, so we sit down on the rugs we have spread out in front of the ruined watchtower and unpack our lunch. Sam and Rory set up a small gas cooker and put on a tin kettle to boil water for tea.

Dad and Pat have caught a few sea trout, which they're pleased about, until Gracie shows them the shot of the guy I caught.

'Is this for real?' Dad asks.

'It is, yeah,' says Rory. 'I reckon it could have been catch of the week at least. Must have been a good fifteen pounds anyway, maybe eighteen.'

'Wow,' says Dee, but she doesn't even look at the photo when Gracie tries to show her. 'That's some catch.'

Dad whistles. 'You didn't want to keep it?' he asks me.

I shake my head and look away.

'It was *ginormous*,' says Gracie, holding out her hands wide to demonstrate. 'It could have been the salmon of knowledge!' she says, laughing.

'Maybe we should have held on to it, so!' says Rory.

Dee laughs. 'Men are always short on wisdom,' she says.

'Ah now,' says Sam, smiling, 'that's not very fair. Sure don't we have to figure out what you women want.'

'As if any of you have ever figured out what we want,' Dee says, and I don't really like the way she's smiling. The whole time she says this, she's staring real hard at my dad. I think he's pretending not to notice that she's looking at him. Sam looks from her to Dad and back again and he says nothing either. There's something weird about Dee, and I think they can sense that too.

As we eat, Dad, Dee and the ghillies are busy talking fishing stories. I can see Pat walking around the other side of the watchtower, or what's left of it, then bending down to go in through the tiny entrance. I get up to follow him, bringing my sandwich with me, and Gracie comes after me, although I'd prefer if she didn't.

Inside, it's really narrow, although from the outside it seems bigger. When Pat sees Gracie come in behind me, he turns away from me and faces the wall, shoving his hands in his pockets and kicking a couple of rocks. He looks around at Gracie and scowls.

'It's small, isn't it?' she says, ignoring him, feeling the dry stone wall with her hand as she gazes up. 'What would you have done, Sean, if you'd been able to eat the salmon of knowledge and had all the wisdom in the world?'

It was a stupid question, because there *was* no salmon of knowledge, it was just an old fairy tale. I glance over at Pat and he sticks out his tongue. I just shrug. I suddenly wish that Gracie would leave us alone, but she sits down and keeps on talking. When Pat can't listen any more he crawls back out the entrance to outside, and I follow him and we go back to Dad.

I think we might have hurt her feelings, walking off like that, but I don't care. I'm feeling angry all of a sudden, and I don't know why. So I pick up some stones and start skimming them into the water to make them hop, like Dad taught us.

After a little while it's time to go back on the boats and head home. Gracie is quiet for the ride back to shore. I guess she can tell I'm not in the mood for her talking. When Dad drops her and Dee back to the hotel, I shake my head when Gracie asks if I want to play a game on the iPad with her. So she goes off to find her grandmother and we go home.

Upstairs in our room, I lie on my bed while Pat sits at the computer, and I think about what Gracie asked me.

What would I do if I had all the wisdom in the world?

That was a no-brainer. I'd turn back time, of course.

* * *

It had been a very long day and Breda's feet were aching. Two tour buses had arrived, which meant eighty people had to be welcomed, assigned rooms, fed and watered. She was delighted to get the business, of course, but she hadn't stopped running since six o'clock this morning. On top of that, Gracie had arrived up at the hotel on her own at lunchtime, telling Breda she was to spend the day with her. Apparently this was Dee's idea of 'helping out'. Breda could have strangled her for being so unthinking, but she wouldn't for a second let Gracie see it was an imposition, so she'd welcomed her with open arms and tried to keep her occupied.

It was now ten o'clock, and the guests were nearly all in the bar. A wave of noise broke out across reception every now and then, the sound of laughter and animated chatter and glasses clinking. Breda breathed a sigh of relief – it sounded like they were all having a good time.

'Mrs Sullivan, if you don't mind me saying, you're looking worn out. Why don't you go on now and I'll take care of everything. Go and put your feet up.'

Breda smiles at Joanne, her reliable, hardworking receptionist. She knows the place is in safe hands once Joanne is at her post.

'Thank you, Joanne. I am feeling a bit tired. I think I will head up to the apartment, if you're sure . . .'

She is just walking towards the stairs when one of the young bar staff comes running out, looking panicked.

'What is it, Joseph?' she asks, turning and walking briskly towards him.

'Em . . .' the boy blushes and stares at her. 'Em . . .'

'Yes?' Breda says impatiently. 'What is it?'

'It's just, like . . .'

'Oh for goodness sake, Joseph,' Breda cries. 'Just spit it out!'

He glances back towards the bar. 'It's Mr Sullivan . . .'

Breda's heart plummets. She feels bone-tired, weary at the idea of whatever problem she is about to be asked to solve. She wants to sink onto the carpet and weep. But she pulls herself together and says quietly, 'Just tell me. I'll sort it.'

'Mr Sullivan's inside in the bar and he's been drinking double whiskies for a while now and I think . . . I'd say he needs to be got out of there, like.'

Out of the corner of her eye, she can see Joanne's hand moving towards the telephone and she knows she's paging Dinny.

'There was no stopping him,' Joseph goes on. 'He got hold of a bottle of Jameson – Larry sent me out to find you. He – Mr Sullivan, that is – he's telling everyone the drinks are on the house.'

Breda takes a very deep breath. 'Thank you for letting me know, Joseph. I'll handle this, you can tell Larry.'

Dinny appears as if by magic across reception, his cheerful expression trying and failing to hide his pity, which makes Breda feel even worse. Why does her husband have to do this? When in God's name will he ever learn that he's making a fool of himself and the whole family? That nobody is fooled by his ridiculous acts of grandiosity, that they are laughing at him and not with him? And that it's disastrous for business?

'You're very good to come over, Dinny,' she says, nodding towards the bar. 'We'll go in together and get him.'

'No bother,' Dinny says stoically.

For what feels like the umpteenth time in her long marriage, Breda girds her loins and prepares to thwart her husband's efforts to bankrupt the bar. Even as she hears the loud boos and chorus of disappointment fill the room as realisation dawns on the more ebullient guests that the offer of free drinks has been exposed as a hoax.

Exhausted though she is, afterwards, Breda is not inclined to go up to the apartment – not now that Conor will be ensconced there. Even if he's out for the count, she needs some space, somewhere to breathe for a moment. She goes back to the office where she has left her handbag, and prays the keys to her car are in it. Then she heads outside to the car park, slips behind the wheel, and drives out of the hotel, through the village and onto the lakeshore road.

When she reaches a suitably secluded spot she pulls over and turns off the engine, lowering her window to let the sweet night air wash over her, and to listen to the lilt of the lapping water. Then she leans her head on the steering wheel and weeps.

* * *

Barry knew coming home would be a challenge. And young Father Luke had been right about one thing: there have been a lot of changes in Ballyanna. The village was essentially much the same, still very recognisable, but what took him by surprise was how much the past was coming alive for him. He hadn't expected that.

Out in Turkana, he had been firmly rooted in the present. There wasn't time for any other way. Life there wasn't just lived one day at a time, but sometimes from hour to hour, even minute to minute. Now, back home and with little to do, and feeling older, much older, Barry finds the intrusion of memories disconcerting.

He remembers another little cottage by the lake, smaller than this one and long gone now, where an old spinster aunt had reared himself and Jerry, with barely enough for herself, never mind the two young orphans she suddenly inherited. They didn't have much, but there was always turf for a fire, food enough from the chickens and few vegetables they grew, and neighbours were always kind. People had stuck together. And Barry thought nothing of walking five miles every day in the dark of an early morning to mass or, if he was lucky, getting a lift from an elderly neighbour who would then feel obliged to go into great detail about the excuse for *why* he or she was not going to mass, even though they were literally passing the door of the Good Lord's house. As if he, whose second religion was minding his own business, cared. But there had always been something otherworldly about Barry, people said. And no one had been in the least surprised when he had chosen the priesthood.

Now, after over forty years of service as a missionary, Barry knew pretty much all there was to know about the frailty of human nature – and none of it shocked him. In his day he had seen and heard it all. In fact, he reflected, nowadays it was rather the reverse: *he* seemed to be the one shocking people.

He knew, for instance, that he had shocked the group of Polish nuns he'd got chatting to in the village, who were driving around the Ring of Kerry, when he'd told them he hoped with all his heart that Pope Francis would shake up those boyos in the Vatican every bit as much as his namesake had done – and preferably before the Catholic Church collapsed entirely.

He had certainly caused a few eyebrows to raise in the chemist when he'd interrupted Mutty Dargan, who was in full ranting mode, sniping and speculating about a gay couple who lived outside the village. Barry had interjected to say that as far as he was concerned, whatever two people got up to in the privacy of their own home was really between themselves and God and nobody else.

And then there was that young pup Billy Joe Coffey, whose sole occupation in life appeared to be loitering on street corners with his woolly cap pulled down to his nostrils, a fag hanging from the corner of his mouth, jeans hanging off his bony arse and a group of young girls hanging on his every monosyllabic grunt. He'd shouted drunken obscenities after Barry as he was on his way home from a quiet drink in the Fisherman's Bar, the offensive words hanging in the air like acrid smoke. Barry had stopped in his tracks, turned around and walked slowly back to Billy Joe, who'd eyed him warily.

He had then proceeded to tell Billy Joe, in no uncertain terms, just what he thought of his foul-mouthed exhibition, but that he expected no more from a verbally challenged, slack-jawed gombeen like himself.

The youngsters had stared at him open-mouthed, hands over their mouths as they stifled their laughter while Barry went on to remind Billy Joe that his own father, and indeed grandfather, Jim Coffey, had served at mass regularly, along with many others, and had emerged from the experience unscathed. There was silence then for a few seconds. Unable to meet Barry's gaze or formulate a smart reply, Billy Joe had turned his face instead to spit on the path. The girls tittered nervously, nudging each other as they chewed their glossy lips and tossed their hair.

Barry knew he should have ignored him, turned the other cheek, not risen to the bait, but then, he reminded himself, even Jesus had answered back sometimes.

He was, he reflected, acquiring what he had heard referred to as 'the devastating honesty of old age'. To tell the truth, it unnerved him. These days there was no telling what would come out of his mouth once he opened it.

Despite genuinely wanting to help out in the parish and make himself useful, Barry found his offers, although graciously received, had not been taken up. Although he made all the right noises, Father Martin seemed to race around the county in his VW Polo, dealing with matters of administration that, he assured Barry, he could be of no help with. Meanwhile young Father Luke, with his convoluted hairstyle and exercise regime, said mass, ran the prayer group and zealously guarded the confessional. He had looked quite put out when Barry had offered to hear confessions. Barry wondered if the powers-that-be had a hand in it all, if perhaps his superiors had left quiet but firm instructions that he was to take things quietly. God knows it wouldn't be the first time they'd interfered in his life.

Anyhow, he had done what he had been told to do – he had gone to visit Doctor Mike and was now awaiting the results of blood tests. But Barry didn't need any blood tests to tell him what he already knew. Not regarding his health, at any rate. His time was drawing to a close, he could feel it in the labour of every breath, the seeping of energy from every cell in his body, the nights he spent asleep but more awake to the other world than ever before. He suspected Jerry knew too, but he wasn't ready to have that conversation just yet. There was something else more important unfolding here in Ballyanna, and he had to figure that out first.

* * *

'You should have seen the size of the salmon Sean caught, it was absolutely ginormous!' Gracie stretches out her arms wide. She is sitting with Annie and Declan, who are having a sandwich on the steps of the croquet lawn.

'Well, I think it was very nice of him to put it back in the water,' Annie says.

'That's what I said! I put mine back too, but mine was only a trout. Still, at least they got to go back to their families. Imagine someone not coming back ever and you never knew what happened to them?'

'I'm not sure it works quite like that with fish, Gracie.'

'Well, whales live in pods . . . loads of fish travel together for miles across oceans. I've seen it on TV. Dolphins have families, so why wouldn't salmon?'

'She's got a point,' Declan says, smiling at Annie.

'So this is where you're all hiding out!' Dee breezes out and flops into a deckchair.

'I was telling Annie and Declan about the huge fish Sean caught,' Gracie says.

'Well, we never actually got to *see* this fish.' Dee raises her eyebrows. 'I think there might be a little bit of wishful thinking going on here.'

'Everybody saw it!' Gracie is indignant. 'We took a photo on the iPad. I can get it if you don't believe me!'

'Oh relax, honey, of course I believe you. I must have missed it, that's all. You can show me later.'

'I tried to show you on the island, but you were too busy talking to Dan and drinking wine.'

'It was a picnic, Gracie. That's what people do on picnics.' Dee's voice is sharp.

'So, I believe it was a great success, the fishing?' Annie says, to break the tension between Dee and Gracie.

'Couldn't have been better,' Dee says. 'Just what we all needed, a day out on the lake. I'd forgotten how relaxing it is. Dan couldn't get over it. He's fantastic company. I'm going to have him over to dinner next. That would be fun, wouldn't it, Gracie? I'd like to get to know him better, spend some quality time together, we have so much in common.'

Gracie doesn't meet her eyes, just shrugs.

'Gracie,' Annie says lightly, 'would you mind bringing your glass and mine inside to Ciaran in the clubhouse. I'm afraid of them getting broken.'

Gracie's doesn't say anything, but she does as she's asked.

Once she's out of earshot, Annie rounds on her sister.

'Dee, for God's sake, you're still married – and to Gracie's father. You can't say stuff like that in front of her. She's not five years old anymore.'

'For heaven's sake, Annie, take the poker out, will you? I'm just having a bit of fun, that's all. Anyway, what's it to you? I thought you were off men altogether. Although I notice you got over your Derrynane dispute quickly enough to have a drink with Dan yourself.'

'That was different. That was because—'

'Oh, spare me the excuses.' Dee rolls her eyes at Declan. 'I get it, he's a grieving widower . . . but who says you get to have a monopoly on consoling him? After all, as a mother I understand what he's going through far better than you ever could.'

'Don't be ridiculous!' Annie is furious at her sister for being so silly. 'But you're right about one thing – you are Gracie's mother, do you think you could maybe put her first for just once?'

'Ah now, let's just—' Declan tries to pull them both back from the edge, but both women are glaring at each other now.

Dee swings her legs out of the deckchair and leans towards Annie. 'I was wondering how long it would take for Madam Boardroom to come out to play. Well I have news for you, Annie. Gracie is mine, not yours. So don't tell me how to take care of my own child. You don't have one, remember? So don't go handing out advice on how to parent. You haven't a clue what you're talking about.'

Annie is staring at her in disbelief. 'How could you? Of all the horrible things you've ever said to me . . .'

'Oh grow up,' Dee says bitterly. 'Just grow up and cop on, Annie. Do us all a favour.' Dee turns on her heel and walks off in the direction of the cottages.

Annie and Declan stare after her in silence.

'That was harsh,' Declan says quietly. 'Don't listen to her, Annie.' He puts his arm around her and gives her a squeeze. 'That's drink talking, or something . . . God knows, it's not the Dee I remember. I don't know what's going on with her, but that was totally uncalled for.'

* * *

'You're sure you're okay babysitting again?'

'It's hardly babysitting, Dan, and yes, of course I'm okay with it.

It's not a bother. Easy work! Go on out and have a good evening. And don't hurry back now.'

Dan thanked the heavens for Joan Coady, who loved children and seemed perfectly happy to pop over for an evening any time he asked.

The invitation had come as a surprise. When Dan had answered the phone and heard Doctor Mike's measured tones, he'd assumed the GP was ringing to check on how Sean was doing. Instead, he'd invited Dan to dinner in his home.

'Just a casual kitchen supper,' he'd said. 'Nothing fancy, just a few of us . . .' He had given him the directions and asked Dan to be there by eight.

So now Dan is showered and ready, with two bottles of Californian red he'd purchased in Cahirciveen under his arm. He isn't sure if he's too early or not, but decides to err on the side of punctuality. This isn't Spain or Italy after all, and Mike and Barbara have small children – he's pretty sure a late night isn't what they have in mind.

The house isn't hard to spot, and Dan finds it easily by following Mike's instructions. It is a beautifully designed affair of stone, brick and wood, with lots of glass. Although contemporary, it blends unobtrusively into the site from where it looks out onto the lake.

As he had feared, he is the first to arrive, but he's put quickly at ease with a warm welcome and a large drink thrust into his hand. He follows Doctor Mike down to a comfortable sitting area adjoining the spacious kitchen and separated only by a long counter, 'so whoever's cooking can still keep an eye on the food and chat to guests at the same time,' Doctor Mike's wife, Barbara, informs him.

Then a girl called Linda arrives, who Dan learns works in Barbara's shop, and shortly afterwards a lovely young Dutch couple join them. They have bought and refurbished an old house further along the lake, from which they run a small guesthouse and guided hiking business. Last to arrive are Declan and Annie. Annie seems a little taken aback to see him there, although she recovers herself quickly. She is wearing a longish, 1970s-style dress of ochres, greens and golds, with floaty sleeves and a deep V-neck, and a pair of kooky sandals that make Dan smile. He can tell he isn't the only one who thinks she looks beautiful. Declan is a lucky man.

Barbara has gone to a lot of trouble, despite her protestations, and dinner starts with a cheese fondue followed by a delicious rack of lamb and new potatoes. Everyone comments on how nice Dan's wine is, which pleases him. It feels good to share a bit of home with his new acquaintances. Dan is seated across from Doctor Mike and beside Barbara, on one side, and Linda on the other side, neither of whom is short of conversation. He can't remember when he's had a more enjoyable evening.

'Have Annie and Declan been together for long?' he asks Linda when the others are discussing politics loudly. 'I know they grew up together . . .'

'Are you kidding?' Linda puts down her glass and laughs. 'Annie and Declan? They've known each other forever, yes, but they're just old friends. I think he's basically the brother she never had.' Linda lowers her voice. 'Mind you, I'm not sure Declan would think of Annie in quite the same way, but they are certainly *not* a couple, if that's what you mean.'

'Oh, I see,' Dan says. 'I just assumed . . .'

'I can see how you would.' Linda smiles. 'If it's of any interest to you, I also have it on authority that Annie has broken up with the chap she was involved with in London. So you can take it from me, the coast is clear.' She seems happy to share the information.

'Am I that obvious?'

'You'd be a fool not to.'

The rest of dinner passes with a great flow of chat and after coffee, Declan is the first to leave, claiming an early morning meeting with a client in Killarney.

A while later, Annie thanks Barbara and Doctor Mike and gets up to leave.

'I should be getting along too.' Dan stands up from the table. 'Thank you for a wonderful evening, it's been a real pleasure.'

'Not at all, Dan, the pleasure was ours, wasn't it, Mike? It was great you could make it,' Barbara says warmly, looking not at all put out that two of her guests are leaving.

As soon as Barbara and Mike have waved them off, Dan turns to Annie and says, 'You don't mind me walking with you, I hope?'

'No, not at all.'

It's coming up to eleven o'clock, not late by any standards, but unusually late for Dan to be out. Above them, a clutch of stars seem close enough to touch, and moonlight glistens on the still water.

'I believe Sean caught a whopper of a salmon on your outing the other day,' Annie says. 'Gracie's been talking about nothing else since.'

'He sure did. I'm just sorry I wasn't there to see it, but we were in a different boat. It's true though, he has the photos to prove it.'

Annie just nods. She seems thoughtful and not inclined to talk.

Then he decides to risk it. 'Look,' he says. 'This is probably none of my business, but your sister . . .'

'Dee . . . what?'

'Look, like I said . . . it's probably not my business, except . . . I can't help thinking about what you said when we spoke last and, put it this way, I'm no stranger to problematic behaviours myself. But Dee was drinking pretty constantly that day out on the lake, and she was pretty harsh with Gracie once or twice when she tried to get her attention. I know you said she's under pressure, but I thought it was better to say something. I hope you don't find that offensive? Normally I'd mind my own business, but . . .'

Annie stops in her tracks and looks at him. A couple of seconds pass in awkward silence before she starts to walk again. When she speaks, her voice is quiet, unsure.

'No, I don't find it offensive. I've been thinking that very thing ever since Dee's come back. I just thought that maybe I was overreacting. I . . . I'm glad you said that. It means I'm not imagining it.'

'No, I don't think you're imagining it,' Dan says gently. He doesn't think it necessary to mention Dee's unsuccessful and rather drunken attempts to flirt with him.

Annie sighs. 'My father's an alcoholic, but my mother has never confronted his drinking, not to my knowledge anyhow. It's the great big elephant in the room that we all tiptoe around, you know?'

'So it would be unlikely that anyone would tackle your sister about it, then?'

'Exactly.'

'That's difficult. But when there's a young girl involved . . . Gracie . . .'

Annie nods. 'Yes, I know. I've been too reticent. That's my fault. Something will have to be said . . . I can see that now. In the meantime I'll have to keep as close an eye on Gracie as I can.'

'I hope I haven't upset you?'

'No, it's nothing I haven't been worrying about myself. It's actually reassuring to hear someone call it like it is. I appreciate that you care enough to be honest.' She smiles wanly at him. 'It's not easy, I know.'

'Well, if I can help at all, you know where to find me. Anything at all.'

They reach the gates of the hotel, and Annie turns to go up the driveway.

'Thank you, Dan. Goodnight.'

He waits until she turns the corner and disappears, swallowed up in the darkness.

* * *

'Mum?'

'Mmhm.' Breda checks her handbag for the list she wrote earlier.

'We need to talk about Dee.' Annie is behind the wheel, driving herself and Breda to Cahirciveen to pick up some shopping.

'What about her?'

'You must have noticed she's behaving oddly, even for her.'

'What do you mean?' An edge has crept into Breda's voice.

'She's drinking all the time, Mum, and popping pills like there's no tomorrow. Plus she's in complete denial of her situation. I really think she has a problem.'

Breda's mouth sets in a line. 'Annie, she's under a lot of pressure. It's all been a terrible shock, this . . . this whole business with John. Her doctor has her on the tablets, and a little wine occasionally won't do her any harm at the moment. Everything will settle down once this whole thing gets sorted out.' Breda nods to herself and looks steadfastly out the window.

'It doesn't work like that, Mum.' Annie tries to keep the mounting irritation from her voice. 'Things aren't going to improve for her until she stops self-medicating and faces up to the facts.'

'Self-medicating! Listen to you! And what *are* the facts, Annie, according to you, who's only been home five minutes, when the rest of us don't even know the full story?'

Annie is taken aback by her mother's sharpness.

'Forget it, Mum. I was just trying to help.'

The rest of the journey passes in loaded silence. Annie tries not to let it get to her. She has been here many times before. But in this instance it is little Gracie she is worried about. She can't bear her falling victim to this vicious circle that no one will talk about, or even admit exists. She had thought getting her mother alone like this for a couple of hours would be the perfect opportunity to have a heart to heart with her. But Breda shows no sign of wanting to admit to any problem with her daughter.

Why should that surprise her, Annie thinks angrily. Her family is clearly not about to change at this stage of the game.

* * *

Breda was much more worried about Dee than she let on. She wasn't going to discuss it with Annie, in fact she'd been surprised when Annie had broached it yesterday, but if she was honest, her elder daughter had become someone she hardly recognised any more. There was a visible tremor in Dee's hands when she held her cup of coffee, and she was snapping or being snide at everyone around her. More worrying still, Dee seemed less interested in her daughter every day. There was an alarming vagueness when she referred to Gracie and she seemed more than happy to delegate her little girl's needs to anyone willing to take them on. Breda understood that Dee was under a lot of pressure and she felt for her, but there were some needs only a mother could fulfil. While Gracie seemed happy enough to spend time with her grandparents or with Annie, Breda knew that she must be scared and worried.

Only the other day, Gracie had mentioned to Breda that when she had been at home in Cork, she had overheard her father talking to Granny O'Malley, his own mother, telling her that Gracie irritated Dee. Breda had been appalled when she'd told her, although Gracie had been quite matter-of-fact about it. Imagine any child hearing her father saying that about her. Breda didn't like to think what else she might have overheard. If it wasn't for this wretched financial mess John had got into . . . it was ruining everything. Dee was adamant that John's lawyers were on the case and sorting everything out, but why, then, wasn't she back in Cork with her husband, helping him through this difficult time? Breda didn't really understand what was going on with her daughter and her marriage, but she told herself that in time everything would settle down again – it always did if you kept calm and waited it out. *This too shall pass* . . . she couldn't remember who said that, some president? Or maybe it was in the Bible? Well, whoever said it knew what they were talking about.

Breda was driving back from Cill Rialaig, where she had met an artist friend for coffee, and was not yet ready to go back to the hotel. She was certainly not ready to listen to Conor and his opinions on everything from how she stacked the dishwasher to how John had hoodwinked them all. Breda wasn't up to that just now.

Instead she drove through the village and took the lake road, parking in a secluded location. She got out to walk the path along the water's edge to her favourite spot, where she sat down in the quiet hollow of an old wooden bench placed to enjoy the view. It was another warm day, but a pleasant breeze was blowing, and it was cooler here in the shade of the giant trees whose branches made a canopy overhead. Breda loved this part of the lake, she always came to walk here when she needed calm and quiet, space to think. And she got little enough of that these days.

What Annie would do from here on out she had no idea, but it wasn't her place to advise or pry. Annie would find her own way. Breda only wished she would find a nice man and settle down somewhere, have a family of her own. Anyone could see how much she adored little Gracie, and she was thirty-six now, the years were

slipping by. Being a successful businesswoman was wonderful –
Breda was as proud of Annie as she was worried about Dee –
but no matter how successful you were it wasn't much use if you
didn't have someone to share it all with, someone in your corner to
support you through thick and thin. But maybe nobody had that
all the time. She certainly couldn't remember Conor being any
particular support to her throughout the years. But he had been
there, beside her, and they had had plenty of good times, as well as
the bad, and Breda knew that deep down he loved his family, he
just wasn't very good at showing it.

But whatever about Annie, Breda certainly had never
anticipated Dee's marriage unravelling as spectacularly as it
seemed to be. God only knows what poor little Gracie must have
been party to over the past months. Marriages and family life were
hard enough, never mind when you added warring parents to the
equation. But what would happen now? What would become of
Dee and Gracie? Dee had to either sort out her marriage or make
a new life for herself and her daughter. Unfortunately, she didn't
appear to be in any shape or hurry to attempt either.

'Breda?'

She was so lost in thought, she hadn't seen or heard anyone
approaching, but the air around her became even more still as she
heard the voice she would know anywhere. She looked around
to see Barry McLaughlin walking over to her, a hesitant smile
creasing his face, looking unsure as he approached. For a moment
she sat stock still, taking in every detail of the man she had loved
and lost and thought of every day of her life. Then, as eagerly as a
schoolgirl, she scrambled to her feet and hurried to take Barry's
outstretched hands in her own.

'It's been a long time, Breda.' The smile that always made her
heart miss a beat spread across his face.

'It's good to see you, Barry. How are you?'

'I'm grand. And yourself?'

'Not bad.' That was a lie. Breda was feeling far from not bad. But it wouldn't do to tell the truth. It wouldn't do to say that seeing him was the best thing that had happened to her in forty years ... that her heart was racing so much she had trouble catching her breath. No, that would make her sound like a lunatic.

They slipped into step easily, strolling together like the two old friends they were, neither of them betraying how they had feared this meeting, or how relieved they were that no anticipated awkwardness had found its way into their reunion. It was quite the opposite.

As they walked along the familiar route they had taken as much younger and untroubled people, Breda's cares receded. Instead, she concentrated on relishing every second of reconnecting with the one person in the world she had missed and thought of every day of her life without him.

Sean

Today we're going to climb Skellig Michael. It's a big rock west of the Iveragh peninsula, which is the area our house is in. So it's right out in the ocean. It's really tall and steep and it's famous because monks used to live out there in olden times, like, over a thousand years ago. The best thing about it, though, is that it's where they filmed *The Force Awakens*, which is an awesome movie.

It's a really nice day, which is good, because if it's too windy or rough, sometimes you can't land on the rock. We were all meant to go, but Gracie's mom isn't here. She isn't feeling well. So Gracie almost wasn't able to come, but then Annie said she could work around it and take her. That's good because it wouldn't be as much fun without Gracie.

Anyway, we're all in this motorboat and Annie and Gracie have sandwiches for us to eat when we get to the top. There are other people on the boat too, not many, some are Americans, like us, and others are speaking different languages. There's a Japanese guy, or maybe he's Chinese (I wasn't sure at first), and he's videoing everything already. He keeps pointing the camera at his kids saying something that sounds like *high-cheez-oo*, and whatever it means it makes them laugh.

We have to wait a few minutes for the tide to be just right, and then we're able to land and get off the boat. There are some normal steps we have to go up that lead to the lighthouse path that goes around the south side of the island, then we come to some safety stuff that's written on a wall we pass. After that there's a bit of the walk that's covered over in case rocks fall down on us. Then when we get to where the old stone steps begin, we have to stop here for a safety talk from a guide. She talks about being careful and responsible, and how we should sit down if we're having difficulty and wait for her. She doesn't mean to scare us, she says, but some people have been killed going up here – they fell off, she tells us – so we have to pay attention.

After that, we finally start climbing up the really old steps, six hundred of them, that go up and up and all around. There's some really, really steep drops, and no rails, nothing to hold on to, only the sea crashing beneath you. I can't help thinking it would be a really easy place to push someone off. Pat grins at me and whispers, 'perfect place for the perfect murder!' I hate it when he does that. It's the worst thing about having a twin – it's like he can get inside my head and steal my thoughts.

After about twenty minutes we reach a little valley called Christ's Saddle, which is where people stop to rest or take pictures or have their packed lunches, but we keep going on up to the lower peak. On top there's the little monastery, just like they said. It's just six little beehive huts, and a later church bit and an oratory with a wall around it. I look around and it's just amazing. Like a little village on top of a bare rock out in the middle of the ocean. I wondered why on earth those monks wanted to build something so difficult and so far away from anywhere . . . The guide stops us to give us another little talk, and she says that living out here, like hermits, the monks felt closer to God. I thought about that for a minute, and I wondered if Mom was somewhere like this. People always say that people who die are with God, or that they're in your heart forever. Those things never made sense to me, but maybe it means they're somewhere like this, real but very distant. Either way, although it's awesome up here, I wouldn't like to stay, not even for a week – especially in winter.

When everyone's taken photos and looked around, we go back down to Christ's Saddle and have our sandwiches. Gracie's face is really red from the climb and probably the sun, although we all have sunblock on. Dad and Annie are just talking.

Going down we have to be even more careful, the guide says. Even us kids have to take it slow because there are some really sharp turns in the path and if you're going too fast and miss them, you'll walk right off the cliff. Anyhow, eventually we all get back down, and then back into the boat. On the crossing back to the mainland we see some dolphins, which makes everybody happy. And that's when it happens. When Dad takes Annie's hand in his like it's the most natural thing in the world. And she just looks at him and smiles. I'm not sure what to think about that, or how it makes me feel, so I just keep looking at the dolphins. Part of me wishes I could be one . . . just leaping and diving through the water . . . like I didn't have a care in the world.

Pat

I saw it too, the hand-holding. I think it kind of threw Sean, although it only lasted a moment. I think Dad would have liked it to last longer, but after, like, just a minute, Annie pulled away and bent to look around in her backpack and put some more sunscreen on Gracie. I think she might have been embarrassed. Personally, I didn't really mind. Both Sean and I have noticed that Dad's been in a better mood these past few days, guess now we know why. The thing is, I think he should have waited until they were alone. I'm not sure Sean is ready for anything like that, for, like, Dad to start being cute with anyone other than Mom. Guess he acted on impulse. Then I started wondering what Mom would think about it, but that was way too weird. I can't imagine a different life going forward, although I know we can't ever go back to our old one. We've been in a kind of holding pattern since the accident, like aircraft waiting for clearance to land, going around and around. I like Annie, Sean does too, she's cool, but Sean was a mommy's boy. So I don't know if he'd be okay about Dad being with anyone else. Either way, I wish Dad hadn't done it. Because now I've seen it, and I can't unsee it.

* * *

'Well somebody obviously had a good time!' Dee smiles as Gracie runs through the door of their cottage, jabbering ten to the dozen about the Skellig trip. She hauls off her backpack and scrolls through her iPad to find the photos she wants to show her mother, while Annie sits down beside Dee at the small kitchen table.

'Thanks for going without me.' Dee throws Annie a look. 'You might have waited.'

'You knew exactly what time we had to leave at to make the boat, Dee. And you weren't even awake . . .'

'It was my stupid phone.' Dee scowls. 'I set the alarm on it and it never went off.'

'It did go off.' Gracie looks up from her iPad. 'I heard it. You must have turned it off and gone back asleep.'

Dee ignores this. 'It would only have taken me a few minutes to jump in the shower and throw some clothes on, but I might have known you wouldn't wait.'

Annie closes her eyes and counts to three, maybe even four. She is thinking of Gracie's panicked call earlier that morning, telling Annie that her mum wouldn't get up, that she says to leave her alone when Gracie tries to wake her, that she says she has a headache. The horrible note of upset in Gracie's voice as she realises she will miss the boat and the trip to the Skellig she has been so looking forward to. Annie had made the day harder for Breda by pulling out of her shift at the hotel, but Breda had agreed that she should go and take Gracie. So Dee's headache had repercussions for lots of people, but of course Dee will never see that.

'If I had waited, we would have missed the boat, Dee, even if you had hurried,' Annie points out. 'At least this way, Gracie got to actually go on the outing.'

'And you got Mister America all to yourself, of course. Let's not leave out that little detail.' Dee's smile is humourless. 'Don't think I don't see what you're up to here, Annie. You might fool Mum and Dad with your career talk and holier-than-thou carry-on, but you're more desperate for a man than even I realised. How long is it since Ed dumped you?'

The spiteful words catch Annie unawares, but she will not allow Dee the satisfaction of hurting her or, more importantly, upsetting Gracie by hitting back, which she is very sorely tempted to do.

As it is, Gracie looks worried. 'Please don't fight, Mum.'

'Be quiet, Gracie,' Dee snaps. 'No one's fighting, for heaven's sake . . . and . . .' she turns on her daughter, 'and how on earth did your face get so red anyway?' She peers at Gracie's face, then glares at Annie. 'Didn't you make sure she was wearing sunblock?'

'Of course she has sunblock on. It was hot, Dee, we're all hot and bothered after the climb.'

'My face always gets red.' Gracie's voice is small. 'I can't help it.' She looks as if she might cry. 'Would you like to see the photos, Mum?'

'Not now, Gracie, maybe later.'

'Okay, I'm going to my room, then. See you later, Annie.' Gracie trails her bag behind her up the stairs.

'You could at least pretend to be interested, Dee, it wouldn't kill you.'

'*Don't* tell me what I should and shouldn't be doing. You have no idea, none whatsoever, of what I'm going through at the moment.'

Annie's self-control is wavering. Dee is being impossible.

'I don't care what you're going through, Dee. Not because I'm unsympathetic, but because you have a little girl who's confused and scared and doesn't know what's going on with her parents. You might spare her a thought in between glugging white wine and popping pills.'

'What did you say to me?' Dee stands up, her hands on her hips.

'You heard me.'

Annie leaves before she might say any more, before she points to the large glass of wine that sits on the table in front of her sister, probably preceded by and to be followed by several more. She leaves because she's so angry at Dee and her supercilious, drunken manner, she wants to slap her. But that wouldn't help anyone right now, least of all her niece.

* * *

It's ridiculous, that's what it is. Breda has told herself, in no uncertain terms, that she is behaving like a schoolgirl, and a very silly one at that. But she can't help herself. Since seeing Barry that day at the lake, over ten days ago now, everything has changed. She has lost weight (through no effort of her own), her skin is glowing, there is a spring in her step and a light in her eyes that have led to people remarking on how well she is looking, what good form she is in. What, more than one female acquaintance has asked, is her secret?

She seems to glide through the days, the hours passing in a happy fugue of daydreams. Nothing is too much trouble for her, guests are overcome by her thoughtfulness, staff take advantage of this new, softer proprietor, risking requests for afternoons off and flexi-time. The only person who hasn't noticed, in fact, is Conor. But that is hardly surprising seeing as he lives in a world where only he and his current whims or demands coexist. Although even he commented on her new, softer, layered hairstyle with honey and caramel highlights. That is, if you could call, 'there's something different about you, what is it?' as he focused bloodshot eyes on her, a comment.

But it isn't Conor she has to worry about, he's quite happy sitting in front of the television with his feet up, watching the racing. It is her daughters she has to watch out for. They are too observant, too inquisitive, too judgemental, too . . . everything. Breda sighs. It isn't as if she is having an affair! Although, truth be told, that's exactly what she thinks of it as – her own private affair. She has begun slipping out at different times during the day and these lovely light evenings. She is careful not to establish a pattern, not to draw any undue attention to these little departures from routine. She tells people that she has taken up walking to cope with stress and to try to exercise a little. And it is true. Walking is all she is doing. But it is Barry she is doing it with. That is the secret.

And now she is living for these snatched moments, innocent meetings where they walk and talk, filling in the gaps of their respective lives, sharing the hopes and joys they had won or lost, and the sadness of sorrows borne and shouldered. It goes so quickly, time. It might have been over forty years since she and Barry had spent time together like this . . . but in her heart it might only have been a few short years. Time passes, but feelings remain very much the same, Breda has discovered. When she looks at Barry, sees the familiar wisdom in his blue eyes, the same kindness in his smile, listens to his mellifluous voice, Breda knows nothing had changed. In truth, she loves him just as much now as she did then. Only this time, she can't let anyone know, least of all the man himself.

It is late afternoon and the hotel is quiet, everyone out and about enjoying the lovely sunshine. Breda swings by the kitchen because she knows there will be a fresh batch of Gracie's favourite rhubarb muffins ready for her. She plans to use them as an excuse to drop in to see Dee. She has been trying to keep an eye on her, especially after what Annie had said, or tried to say, but Dee is a grown woman, a mother herself, and Breda doesn't want to interfere directly. If her help isn't wanted or requested, well, there isn't a lot she can do about it. She can hardly spy on her own daughter.

She strolls down the path that leads to the cottages, thinking how pretty everything looks. There was every chance Dee would be out, in which case Breda would just leave the muffins on the doorstep. She knocks on the door, which flies open after a few moments to reveal Dee with her hair tied up, wearing rubber gloves and a harassed expression.

'What? Oh, it's you, Mum. It's not really a good time . . .'

'I just popped down with some muffins for Gracie. Where is she?' Breda peers about the room.

'I'm over here, Gran.'

Breda takes a moment to locate her granddaughter, until she sees her on all fours, scrubbing the tiled floor for all she is worth, her little face puce with effort.

'What on earth . . . what's going on, Dee?'

'The place is a mess, it needed a good clean.'

'But I could have got housekeeping. There's no need for Gracie to be doing women's work. Here, I can help, let me—'

'There's every need,' Dee snaps. 'It's good for her. She's developing an attitude and I won't have it. She's been far too indulged, living here in the hotel. She was downright rude to me yesterday.'

'But, Dee—'

'Anyway, her father will be back soon, and he won't tolerate any answering back, I can assure you.'

'You've heard from John?' Breda is taken aback by this turn of events.

'He's coming at the weekend. I told you he'd sort everything out.'

'Well, I suppose . . .'

'Like I said, Mum, this really isn't a good time.' Dee propels Breda towards the door.

'Thanks for the muffins, Gran.'

'Oh, you're welcome, love, see you later, maybe . . .'

As she walks back to the hotel, Breda's hands are shaking and Annie's words are ringing in her ears. What *was* the matter with Dee? This wasn't like her at all . . . and poor little Gracie, scrubbing the floor like a servant. And now John coming back . . . what would that mean for everyone?

Dan

an has escaped to the beach to clear his head and get some fresh air. He'd been doing some online research in the Lodge but his eyes were drawn to the view outside as if by a magnet. So he'd grabbed his camera and headed down to the cove. He's shooting from different angles, trying to best capture the play of evening sunlight on water. The light was just perfect – a soft shimmer falling on undulating waves and the whole effect was almost impressionistic. But now, scrolling back through the shots he's taken, none of them seem to do the scene justice, so he gives up and decides to sit on the sand and enjoy it instead.

He's really begun to settle into this place. The beach, the village, it has a sense of homeliness to it now that he hadn't expected to feel. After the incident on Derrynane he was pretty much ready to catch the next flight back to LA, but he's very glad that he took Dr Shriver's advice and stayed on. Sean seems relaxed – much more so than at any time over the past fifteen months. Dan knows the accident must play on his mind constantly, but for now he seems to be enjoying their trips and the beach and Gracie. Doctor Mike was right about her – she's sweet and kind and just the type of kid you'd pick as a friend for a traumatised boy.

As for her aunt, Dan smiles to himself, thinking of Annie and her green eyes. He'd have to be careful . . . that girl was getting under his skin. Since the trip to the Skellig, she'd been constantly on his mind. He loved her energy, her quiet determination, and most of all how she was struggling to help her sister and Gracie. On the return boat trip, when they'd seen the dolphins, he'd reached for her hand on impulse, simply because it had seemed like the most natural thing in the world *to* do, and the smile she flashed him had lit up her face. But we're just good friends, he reminds himself – that's what he has to remember.

He sees a movement out of the corner of his eye. But the beach is empty. He's the only person around for miles. He checks his watch – time to go make dinner. He gets to his feet and stands looking for the last time, savouring the beauty. As he turns to walk back, he notices them . . . footprints in the sand, just behind his own. Intrigued, he bends down to examine them; they are smaller than his own, but bigger than a child's. If he was hazarding a guess, he'd say they belonged to a woman . . . but that's ridiculous, he's the only soul on the beach. He gets up, perplexed, and a sense of movement plays at the periphery of his vision. He stops, turns three hundred and sixty degrees. No one. But then, as he resumes walking towards the steps, he sees . . . he's not sure actually what it is he sees. It's like a patch of vibrating air, blurry, indistinct. He stares hard at it, but it's like he can't quite see through it. Yet he's looking at thin air – it doesn't make sense. Out of nowhere, then, a sudden wind scatters the sand around him, startling him, and when he looks again, the footsteps are gone, but a familiar scent lingers in the air . . . Mary's perfume, he'd recognise it anywhere. He shakes his head as if to clear it, tells himself to get a grip. He doesn't do crazy . . .

Dan walks quickly towards the steps, wanting to get back to the Lodge. He'll ask Battie Shannon about the atmospherics at work here, the tides, the currents, the prevailing winds – there must be something to explain it, otherwise . . . well, it just doesn't make sense.

Pat

We're in an old ruin of a cottage by the lake.

Dad has gone to see Battie who lives down the road about some fishing stuff, and to talk to him about local currents or something. He said we could wait and hang out here until he was finished and he'd come back to pick us up. I'm bored already.

Gracie wants to play house. She doesn't come right out and say it, because she knows it wouldn't be cool, but she's talking about how things used to be in the old days, before the famine, when everyone lived in really small cottages like this one.

There's a few pieces of really old furniture here, a small table and rickety chair, and a couple of crates someone dumped. But the floor is just broken stones, with weeds and stuff growing up through them, and there's no glass in the windows, or even a roof. Just three walls and a bit of the front one left. Gracie's building room boundaries out of stones, saying, 'this is where the bedroom is . . . and this is where the kitchen is . . . and . . .'

She's run out of space already. There's only one room here, it must have been like a really small studio apartment, I guess, in the old days, without any modern stuff. I mean, where was the bathroom? Lucky for her Sean isn't talking, because he'd probably be saying what I'm thinking, but instead he's not paying much attention, just following her orders when she tells him to bring in more stones and stuff. It's really stupid.

Gracie's talking now, really getting into it, like she's in a play or something.

'Now, I think we'll have potatoes for the dinner,' she's saying. 'And you'll be going out on the lake so you'll bring us back a fine trout . . .' She's putting a make-believe pot on the make-believe oven, which is an upturned crate.

I wonder if she has any idea how stupid she sounds.

'There'll be no slovenliness in this house!' she says in a voice that sounds like she's trying to sound grown up. 'Only the best is good enough . . . appearances may not be everything, but they're the first thing people see about you and judge you on. So everything has to be perfect . . .'

I look over at Sean, who's sitting on the floor with the iPad, and roll my eyes in disbelief. He sniggers.

'What?' demands Gracie. 'What are you laughing at?'

Sean looks guilty. But Gracie doesn't miss a beat.

'Oh,' she says. 'I almost forgot. We must ask the neighbours to join us for dinner. I'll put more potatoes in the pot. Our new house will take the eyes out of their heads! We'll be the envy of everyone.'

This is too much. I shake my head and get up to go, leaving them to it.

Outside I sit on what's left of the old stone wall to wait for Dad. It's really sunny. A movement up ahead catches my eye. I can see a black-and-white sheepdog coming this way, there are lots of them around here, but this one is Millie, I'm sure of it. The dog I met before with Barry, the priest guy.

She runs over to me and sits looking up at me, her tongue hanging out to one side, panting.

'Millie? Is that you?' I ask. 'It is, isn't it?' And she puts a paw on my foot as I bend down to pat her head. I know I'm right then, because I see Barry coming around the corner and I wave at him. 'Hey, Barry.' I wonder if he'll remember who I am, but he smiles and comes straight over to me.

'It's yourself.' He sits down on the wall beside me. 'What are you doing here on a grand day like this? Shouldn't you be at the beach, or out on the lake?'

'My brother and his friend are playing in there.' I nod in the general direction of the old ruin. 'I'd rather be out here. They're being really silly.'

'Why do you say that?' he asks.

'It's stupid, that's why. They're playing house. That kind of stuff is for babies.'

'Don't you ever play make-believe?'

I shrug.

'Don't you have dreams?'

'I guess.'

'What do you dream about, Pat?'

'Stuff . . .'

I thought about it for a minute. Sure, I daydream, who doesn't? I dream of winning Olympic gold for freestyle, playing for the Chargers, starting a band, inventing a computer game . . . but I wasn't going to tell him that.

'Dreams are important,' he says. 'They help us get through the hard times.'

I snort, thinking of Gracie. 'Who needs to dream about making dinner? That's really stupid.' I kick my heel against the wall, repeatedly.

'Not if it's what someone needs to dream about,' he says. 'Sometimes the most ordinary dreams can seem the furthest out of reach.'

I don't understand what he's talking about, so I say nothing. I wait a beat, listening to his silence, then I just say it.

'I've been thinking about my mom.'

Barry doesn't say anything, just nods.

'You're a priest, right?'

'Yes, that's right.'

'So you know where people go when they die?'

He thinks before answering me. 'They go home, Pat. They go back to God.'

'Is that heaven?'

'Some people call it heaven. Why do you ask?'

I shrug again.

'You must miss her a lot.'

'Actually I don't.' I thought he'd look shocked at that, but he just smiles. 'It's because of her all this happened, you know.' Maybe I can make him understand. 'It's because of her that Sean can't talk. She ruined everything ...'

'You're still angry, lad, and that's only natural.'

I know he means well, but he really doesn't get it.

Just then I hear Gracie's voice. Sure enough, she comes out of the cottage, followed by Sean, and she skips right up to us.

'Hey, Barry,' she says. Gracie knows everybody.

'Hello, Gracie.'

'Barry is Jerry's brother back from the missions,' she says. 'I met you yesterday, with Annie, my aunt.'

'That's right, you did.'

Sean hangs back behind her, like usual.

'That's my brother,' I tell Barry. 'The one I was talking about.'

'This is Sean,' Gracie says. 'He doesn't talk, though.'

'Hello, Sean.' Barry shakes hands with him.

'Jerry was up at the hotel,' Gracie says. 'Talking to my gran. She was saying you're a friend of my gran's, from like, long ago – are you?'

Barry smiles. 'Yes, that's right, your grandmother and I grew up together, you might say. We were great friends. I hope we still are.' He pushes himself up slowly from the wall and stands up straight. 'Right, well I better get this dog home for her lunch. See you again, lads.'

Trust Gracie to interrupt us and mess everything up. Now Barry is going, just when I was about to tell him about Mom.

'See you, Barry,' Gracie calls after him in her stupid sing-song voice.

Sean is so dumb about people. How come she doesn't drive him nuts?

'Let's go and get ice creams,' she says now, and Sean nods, just like a puppy dog.

I walk away, in the opposite direction, because I don't want to be around them anymore. Sometimes I want to shake Sean so hard his voice will just fall out of his head. And right now I might throw something at Gracie if I hang around.

I head to the beach to find the rock I like to sit on. It's kind of under the cliff on Smuggler's Cove beach, that's the beach below our house. It's the right shape to sit in, there's a dip in the middle of it where I fit just right. And when the tide's coming in, the water swishes round it, but never more than knee-high deep. It's not far out or anything, just far enough away so I can get some space. I sit here when I want to be quiet, or think, or just watch the ocean.

Occasionally I wonder if Mom would have liked it here. It's hard to tell, because sometimes she could like something or someone a lot, and then she could change her mind and not like them at all. I'm still angry with her, but that doesn't mean I don't miss her. I miss her all the time. Mostly I try to think of the fun times, and there were lots of those. Like the time we came downstairs and found Mom had completely painted the sitting room crazy colours during the night because she couldn't sleep. I woke up first, because I heard the music – Mom always liked loud music playing when she was painting – and the furniture was piled in the middle of the room and the walls were purple, red and orange with all these crazy designs.

'What do you think, Pat, honey?' Mom jumped down from a chair.

'Wow!' I said. 'It's cool! I love it!' And Mom grabbed me and we danced around the room until we fell down laughing.

But then Dad came down, and he looked around like he'd just landed on another planet and said, 'Holy Shit.'

Then Grandma O'Connell came around, and she started crying. And Mom got mad and said, 'Well at least the boys like it.'

I'm not sure what happened after that, but I guess no one else liked it either because the next day the painters came in and while Mom was away for a few days, they painted it back just like it was before. And when she came back home, Mom didn't even seem to notice.

Then there was the road trip. That was maybe the best fun of all. Dad was away at work somewhere, and Grandma O'Connell was picking up the dry-cleaning, so Mom was leaving us to school. But on the way she said, 'Let's go on a road trip, boys.' So she rang school and said we had both come down with a bug and she was taking us to the doctor.

'Where are we going?' said Sean.

'I'm thinking Las Vegas, guys. I've always wanted to go there.'

'Yee-haw!' I said. This was way better than going to school.

'What about Dad?' Sean said.

'Daddy's away at work, we can tell him all about our adventure when we come home.'

So we hit Interstate 15 and headed north. And even though it was a long drive, it went quite quickly because we sang really loud songs in the car, like 'Viva Las Vegas' and 'Luck Be a Lady', and then we stopped off for burgers and ice cream.

We got as far as Primm, which is just outside Las Vegas. Then Mom wanted to visit one of the shopping outlets and also the Desperado Roller Coaster was there, so we stopped off and went shopping and bought lots of clothes that we put in the car, and then Mom took us on the roller coaster and let us play on some slot machines. After that Sean and I were too tired to do any more driving so Mom said, 'Okay, we'll spend the night here and go on to Vegas in the morning.'

We checked into a casino called Whiskey Joe's that had rooms. We watched movies until really late and then we must have fallen asleep, because the next thing I remember was banging on the door and someone saying, 'Open up, police.' I looked for Mom, but she wasn't there. But then I heard her voice outside the door, she was yelling, but it was definitely her. Even so, I put the chain on the door like we'd been taught and opened it a bit. Then a lady cop said, 'It's okay, honey, it's safe for you to open the door, we've got your mom here.' So I opened it and Mom said, 'Let go of me, you asshole.' And Sean started getting upset and said, 'Mom, Mom, what's wrong?' The police lady said, 'Nothing's wrong, honey, we're just going to stay here with you and your mom until someone comes to pick you up.'

'Like hell you will,' said Mom.

'But we don't need to be picked up, we have our own car,' Sean said.

'It's that, or you all come down to the station right now, lady. Your choice.'

And Mom said, 'Screw you.' But she must have been tired then because when they brought her into the room, she threw herself on the bed and fell asleep.

'Great. Out cold,' said the lady cop. 'Now, I want you boys to get dressed for me, will you do that? And don't worry, honey, your grandpa's going to be here real soon to pick you up.'

So we sat there, with the TV on, eating chips, and then Mom's parents, Grandma and Grandpa Carroll, arrived. Grandma started crying and hugging me and Sean and saying, 'Thank God, thank God,' and Grandpa said, 'Don't get hysterical, Julie, it's not going to help anyone.' He looked tired and sad, not like he was going on any holiday. 'Come on, boys, no harm done, let's take it easy, we're all going home now.'

'But what about Vegas?' Sean said. 'Mom said we're going to Vegas in the morning.'

But Grandpa just shook his head and said, 'Maybe another time, buddy.'

So we all got in the car with Grandpa, except Grandma, who got in Mom's car to drive it home behind us. Then we must have fallen asleep, because all of a sudden it was morning, and we were home. Inside, a doctor was waiting, and he gave Mom a shot of something to make her feel better. Then the paramedics arrived and took her to the hospital. Sean and me wanted to go with her, but Grandma and Grandpa said we couldn't, that we could see her in a day or two maybe, but not to worry because she had gotten sick and they would make her better in the hospital and she was in the very best place she could be.

There was a lot of talking on the phone after that. We spoke to Dad and he said he was flying in later that day. Grandpa said there was no need, that everything was under control, but he said he was coming anyway.

I was sorry Mom had got sick. That was really bad luck. I was also sorry we never made it to Vegas, but I didn't say that to anyone. Mom was in the hospital for quite a while that time. She came home eventually, but she was a lot quieter than before. She got tired a lot as well and had to sleep a lot. And then ... well ... then the rest of it played out.

I miss you, Mom, but I'm also mad as hell at you, and I don't know if I can ever let that go.

* * *

'So.' Jerry puts Barry's plate in front of him before she sits down to dinner herself. 'Are you going to tell me about it?'

'About what?'

'About what's troubling you?'

'Nothing's troubling me, I just felt like keeping to myself for a bit, a man's entitled to a bit of peace, isn't he?'

'Oh, surely.' Jerry is unperturbed at the intended rebuff. 'I was just thinking how peaceful you look these days, you have serenity written all over you, it must be all the walking ...'

'It's as good a way as any to pass the day.'

'I won't argue with that, but people are beginning to talk.'

'What about?' Barry snaps.

'You, naturally, they're worried, concerned about you.'

'Humph.'

'So, are you going to tell me what's eating you?'

Barry lets out a long sigh. 'I don't know, and that's the truth of it, Jerry. I don't bloody know. I don't know anything anymore.'

'Ah.'

'What's that supposed to mean?'

'It means you're getting somewhere, finally.'

'I don't see how that can be defined as progress, not even by your esoteric standards.'

'There's nothing esoteric about honesty, Barry. And admitting we know nothing, or next to nothing, is the beginning of wisdom in every culture.'

'But I'm a priest, for heaven's sake. I'm supposed to understand ... to have the answers ... I'm supposed to be able to make sense of it all ...'

'And?'

'Nothing makes sense anymore.' He looks stricken. 'I think my whole life has been wrong.'

'That's not true, and you know it,' Jerry says firmly.

'I can't even pray anymore.'

'Even better.'

'I knew you'd mock me.'

'Much as you might like to think so, I am not mocking you. Just because I'm not a fan of your crowd doesn't mean I don't respect your personal beliefs. And I know how terrifying it can be to look into the abyss, believe me.'

'So what am I supposed to do?' He looks at her accusingly.

'You know what to do,' she says quietly. 'Ask what you can do to help, and what it is you need to learn, then meditate, sit, and the answers will come.'

'Next you'll want me burning joss sticks and sitting cross-legged on the floor.'

'Not unless you feel the need.'

'But that's just it, I can't sit still, anywhere.'

'That's only because you're fighting it, running from it, and you can't, Barry, you've discovered that. Engage with it, Barry. It's a gift, not a trial, and a very special gift at that. Bit by bit you'll find it easier, and soon everything will begin to make sense. The peace will come eventually, I promise you.'

'You sound as if you're speaking from personal experience.'

'Would it surprise you if I was?'

'Nothing about your belief system would surprise me.'

'Anyway, it doesn't matter what I believe or don't believe. I'm not the one in difficulty, you are. Either way, you need to get quiet inside yourself, Barry. Look at it this way. Maybe God wants you to shut up and listen for a while. I know I do on occasion.'

Barry shoots her a look and scratches the back of his head, but he doesn't say anything. For a moment or two the stillness is broken only by the sound of Millie gnawing the bone at his feet, until she seems unnerved by the silence and pauses to look up at them expectantly.

'I'm sorry if I've been a bit remote lately.' He pauses. 'I have a lot on my mind, that's all.'

'You've been away for forty years Barry, I'm well used to my own company and way of doing things,' says Jerry. 'I just don't like to see you troubled. Tell me, have you run into Breda yet?'

Barry stiffens. 'I've bumped into her, once or twice.'

'You're as bad as each other.' Jerry sighs. 'She wouldn't mention it to me either. It's been a long time, Barry, but you were great friends . . . more than that.'

'What's that got to do with anything?'

'Don't fight the emotions, Barry, they're bound to be there, to want to make themselves felt, it's only natural. It doesn't mean the whole of your life has been a mistake, or hers either. Now, that's all I'm saying on the matter, so eat your dinner.'

* * *

'Mmm, these tapas are *deliciosos*.' Barbara polishes off the last of the prawns, washing it down with a swig of Rioja.

'Viktor's latest speciality. He's into Spanish cuisine at the moment, says with seven restaurants on the World's Top Fifty list, Spain is where's it's at, gastronomically speaking.'

'Really?'

'Mmhm, smoke and fire, it's all about the grill these days apparently.'

'Good old Viktor!'

They are sitting on the little patio outside Annie's cottage. A linen cloth covers the lumps and bumps of the well-worn table, and a vase of wild flowers sits prettily, if at a rather precarious tilt, in its corner.

Barbara fixes Annie with a look. 'So, Dan was very keen to leave the party when you did. Did he walk you home?'

'Well, we were going in the same direction, if that's what you mean, so yes, we walked together.' Annie is casual but feels her face pinking.

'Is that all you did together?'

Annie shakes her head in mock exasperation at her friend. 'You're relentless. And I know you're match-making. It's written all over your face.'

'But I'm so good at it.' Barbara grins, then notices the change in Annie's expression. 'What? What is it?'

'Nothing. Just something he said . . .'

'What?'

'Oh, nothing I didn't already know. It's Dee . . . he said he didn't want to cause trouble, but that she was drinking all day when they were out on Lough Currane. He thinks she might have a problem.'

'Thinks?!' Barbara laughs drily. 'Drinking is just one of Dee's problems right now.'

'I tried to talk to Mum about it afterwards, but she just keeps saying the doctor said Dee was under stress and has prescribed these pills she's taking and it'll all be fine.'

'I'm pretty sure those pills are not supposed to be washed down with copious amounts of alcohol,' Barbara says.

'You saw what she was like the night in O'Dowds.'

Barbara nods.

'And Gracie has talked about how she's impossible to wake up in the mornings. She even missed the trip to the Skellig and then blamed me for leaving without her.'

'What, she left you alone with Dan? How thoughtful of her.'

'I'm serious, Barbara. I'm worried about her. I know she's being obnoxious right now, but if she really has a problem, then Gracie's getting the brunt of it. That's just more than I can bear to think about.'

'Hmm . . .' Barbara is thoughtful. 'I don't want to add to your woes, but she was in the shop yesterday, trying on a linen dress. Dan walked past outside and the minute she caught sight of him, she was out the door like a rocket. The security tag on the dress set the bleeper off, not that that deterred her, so Linda had to go haring after her. Anyhow, she waylaid the poor guy and insisted he go for coffee with her. I think he was mortified, but resistance was futile, as they say. She had the nerve to run back into the shop, pick up her handbag and leg it, saying, "*Just put the dress on my account, Barb.*" I managed to hold on to her until I removed the security tag, then she was out the door like bloody Usain Bolt.'

'I don't know what all this flirting is about.' Annie shakes her head. 'I can only assume her self-esteem is rocky and she's trying to give herself some kind of boost.'

'Her sanity could do with one,' Barbara murmurs. 'But I know exactly what it's about. Dee is jealous of you, Annie. She always has been. You're just too nice to admit it. She's jealous because you've made your own money and your own way in the world, and now she's losing the one thing she had to her name, which is the lifestyle she married into. She'd choke at the thought of you finding a gorgeous guy like Dan. Remember when you called your wedding off and went back to London?'

'I could hardly forget.'

'Well, your parents were upset, obviously, but Dee was delighted. I'm sorry to be so blunt about it, Annie, but that's the truth of the matter. The alcohol and pills are just the tip of the iceberg. Dee needs to address her real demons.'

'Speaking of which, apparently John's coming back at the weekend, according to Mum anyway.'

'He's got some neck. There's a few people around here who invested in that scheme of his. I wouldn't like to vouch for his safety if they find out he's in town.'

'I know. It mortifies Mum no end. But hopefully it'll be good for Gracie. The thing is, though, none of us know what's going on, really.'

'What does your dad have to say about all this?'

Annie shrugs. 'I have no idea. I stay out of his way, which is relatively easy as he's trying equally hard to stay out of mine. It's Mum I feel sorry for. She's running around after everyone, trying to keep a lid on things. Dad just lets her wait on him hand and foot and makes sure he has a constant supply of whiskey to hand.' Annie sighs. 'To be honest, I can hardly look at him, never mind listen to him.'

'I thought you'd gotten over that row you had with him, isn't it all water under the bridge now?' Barbara looks at her curiously.

'Oh, don't mind me, Barbara, I'm just not used to being back in the bosom of my wonderfully dysfunctional family.' Annie smiles.

'Stay well out of it all, that's my advice.' Barbara is firm. 'Leave them all to their nonsense. But don't let it spoil your time at home. God knows we've waited long enough to have you back.'

But Annie just smiles. Home is a word that brings her little comfort – it's a nice concept, she thinks, but if it exists, she certainly hasn't found hers yet.

* * *

'Well, you're a dark horse!' Declan says, as he and Dan stroll back to the clubhouse. They have just played nine holes with a couple of English guys from a property investment fund. 'Rory McIlroy will have to watch out if that's how you play all the time.'

Dan grins. 'I wish!' He hadn't played in months, and the championship links was challenging, but for some reason he had driven like Tiger and putted like Stricker. He was as surprised as anybody.

Just then, the hotel minivan pulls into the club, driven by Annie, who is dropping off some guests on their first golf outing. She climbs out and introduces the golfers to Declan, and seems surprised to see Dan.

'Hey, Annie.'

'Hey,' she says, smiling warmly.

'I've just been out with Dan here. He was trying to show me up!' Declan leaves them to bring the four guests inside.

'I was thinking of grabbing a sandwich here before getting back to work, care to join me?'

'Good idea. A break would be nice.' She checks her watch. 'I can spare forty minutes or so.'

Upstairs in the clubhouse restaurant, they slip into a corner table and order some food.

'I haven't seen you since our Skellig trip,' Dan says. 'We really enjoyed it, and you were right, I'd never seen anything quite like it.'

'It's good you were able to make time for it,' Annie says, spearing a piece of tomato on her plate. 'So many people don't, and you have to experience it to understand.'

'It was good Gracie got to come along, given that, you know, her mom wasn't feeling too good.'

Annie nods, but says nothing.

Dan feels awkward. 'Uh, about what I was saying about Dee ...'

'It's okay,' Annie says quickly. 'You don't have to say any more.'

'No, it's just that, I had coffee with her yesterday. I didn't have much choice in the matter . . . she saw me on the street and rushed out of this shop.'

'I know.' Annie smiles. 'Ballyanna is a village in every sense.'

'That's what I was afraid of.' He looks at her. 'I don't know what's going on with your sister and, like I said, it's not my business, but she seems to . . .' He shakes his head, unable to find the right words and feeling embarrassed.

'It's okay. I get it. I know this may be hard to believe, but my sister does not normally behave like this. She's all over the place right now.'

'How is she with you?'

'It's hard to explain. I think she resents me at the moment, actually make that everyone with a pulse, because her own life's in disarray and she's lashing out, if that makes sense.'

'Totally. Sounds familiar actually.'

'How come?'

'I've been through something similar, in a manner of speaking, with my wife. I won't go into it, but I really do know what you mean.'

Annie nods thoughtfully. 'Well, after the Skellig trip, when I dropped Gracie back, Dee had a go at me. She said I deliberately went early so she would be left out.'

'I'm guessing that's not the case?'

Annie shakes her head. 'Gracie called me that morning in a panic, desperate not to miss the trip. Said her mum wouldn't wake up, that she kept turning off her alarm, saying she had a headache, that she told Gracie to shut up and leave her alone.'

Now it was Dan's turn to shake his head. 'That's really too bad.'

'I've tried talking to my mother, but she doesn't want to face up to it. She just says Dee's doctor in Cork has prescribed pills for her to deal with the stress she's under and that it'll all right itself soon.'

'And pills go really well with alcohol, right?'

Annie nods. 'It's all such a mess, but it's Gracie I'm worried about. I'm trying to keep an eye on things, but it's not easy.'

'I understand your concerns, but you can't be her keeper either.'

'I'm sorry.' Annie sighs. 'This must be really boring for you, me going on like this about family stuff.'

'It's not boring at all. I understand exactly the position you're in. Thing is, when someone's out of control, whether it's because of addiction or some other reason, well, it scares people, they don't want to face the implications of what it means, not just the practicalities, but the other stuff, the enabling, the underlying causes, it's much easier to pretend it isn't happening. It's classic denial. That's what you're up against.'

'That's exactly it,' Annie says, a sense of relief washing over her to have someone fully understand and empathise.

Dan shrugs. 'Been there, bought the t-shirt.'

'Damn, I have to get back,' Annie says, looking at her watch.

'Will you have dinner with me, Annie, some evening?'

She looks surprised. 'Uh, I don't know, Dan . . . it's just . . . with things the way they are at the moment . . .'

He smiles at her. 'Just dinner.'

'Let me think about it,' she says, returning his smile. 'And thank you – for lunch and the dinner invitation.'

Pat

'**D**o you have to learn a lot of stuff to become a priest?' I ask Barry. 'We're sitting at the water's edge, by Jerry's house, skimming stones into the lake. I thought I might find Barry here.

'Oh, you do, yes, and you have to unlearn a lot of things, too,' he says.

'What's the most important thing you've learned?'

Barry thinks for a minute, then he throws another pebble into the lake, but this time not skimming it. 'You see what happens in the water when I throw that pebble in, Pat?'

'Sure,' I say. 'It makes ripples.'

'Exactly. Well, our actions in life are like that stone. Everything you do, everything you put out there, however big or small, ripples out to affect other people, for better or for worse.'

That sounds a bit scary. 'Everything?'

'Everything, even the tiniest little thing.' He smiles at me. 'So when you do something good or kind, that will ripple out and affect lots of other people in ways you can't even imagine.'

'And if you do something mean or bad?'

'It's exactly the same. The action will ripple out to hurt or upset people in ways you can't ever imagine. The effects can last for decades, generations even.'

I nod. Thinking about it, that kind of makes sense, even to me.

'I think I understand what you mean.'

'Do you? Then you're ahead of an awful lot of people. Some people never learn it, even after a lifetime.'

I can't help thinking about Mom, then. As if I'm ever not thinking about her.

'I think,' I say to Barry, 'what my mom did was mean. She hurt Dad a lot when she left. She hurt us too.'

'But I'm sure she never stopped loving you.'

'Yeah, that's what she said, that's what adults always say, like it gets them off the hook or something. But if you love someone, you don't go around hurting them, do you?' I feel the anger rising up again. 'She ruined everything! It wasn't enough for her to just leave, then she had to go and . . . well . . . it's all her fault anyway. Now we're in this horrible mess.'

'Would you like to talk about it?' Barry looks at me, and I feel like he knows what I'm going to say already. I thought only Sean could do that. 'Sometimes it helps,' he says.

'It won't change anything. You can't change the stuff that's happened.'

'No, but sometimes you can see it differently, and that can be helpful.'

'How can you see something differently if it hasn't changed?'

'Because *you* change, Pat. So the way you look at the situation in question changes. Then you notice things, things you may have missed before, and when you realise these things, it makes you look at the situation in a different light.'

'Do you look at your life in a different light?'

'All the time, lad.' Barry grins. 'Even at my age.'

'Well, if I married someone, I wouldn't run out on them,

especially not if we had kids.' I whack a stone into the water. I just get so angry thinking of what Mom did.

'Nobody ever means to, Pat, not when they get married first, but sometimes . . . well, things get complicated. It's very hard to explain.'

'We didn't know anything was wrong,' I tell him, thinking back. 'Not at first. I knew Mom was sick sometimes, but most of the time we were just a regular family – me, Sean, Mom and Dad. Me and Sean were going to school, playing soccer, swimming, hiking, the usual stuff, and then one day, right out of the blue, Mom and Dad sat us down and said they had something to tell us. I knew what they were going to say right away. It was, like, textbook. Dad started with, "you know how much we both love you" . . . and then Mom says, "and how you're both the most important people in our life", so I knew, of course I knew what was coming, but Sean . . . I couldn't believe it. He looked at them both, like, stupidly and then he says, get this, "Are you guys having a baby? Are we going to have another brother or sister?" And his face lights up and his eyes are all wide and he's grinning from ear to ear, like it's Christmas or something.

'Well, that's when I knew *I* was right. Mom and Dad both looked like they'd been socked in the gut. It was obvious they never saw that coming and it totally threw them, I mean, *totally*. That's when I felt sorriest for Dad. He was really falling apart, but Mom kept it together and she said to us, "Daddy and I are going to be living apart for a while." That's when Sean began to get it. He looked at them, bug-eyed, and said, "You can't leave us." Then Mom starts saying all the usual stuff, like "it's for the best, Mommy and Daddy aren't making each other happy anymore and we both love you so much", yada, yada, yada. I could see Sean was about to have a meltdown so I gave it to them straight. "Look," I said, "if you're getting a divorce, just say so and get it over with.

Can't you see you're freaking him?" And I got up and walked from the room.'

'What happened then?'

'Dad followed me, and Mom stayed with Sean. Of course I was right, they *were* getting a divorce. When I asked Dad why, he just looked sad and said he didn't make Mom happy anymore and she needed to live in a different house so she could make new friends and meet new people. And I said, "What about us? Do we make her happy?"

'Dad looked shocked and said, "Of course you make her happy, you'll always make her happy, you're the most important thing in her life, in both our lives. She loves you more than anything ..."

"But you don't make her happy anymore," I said.

"That's different, Pat. It's an adult thing. Sometimes, in relationships, things happen that—"

"Bullshit!" I said. "You used to make her happy and now you don't. What happens when *we* don't make her happy? Or she marries someone else who has kids of their own? Is she going to divorce us too?"

'Then I went back into the sitting room, where Mom was sitting with her arms around Sean, who was crying like a baby, and I looked at her. "I hate you," I said. Then I looked at Dad and said, "I hate you too." Then I went upstairs and locked myself in our bedroom. I wouldn't even let Sean in when he tried. I stayed there for two whole days. Then I got tired and hungry and came out.'

'Then what happened?' Barry skimmed another stone in the water.

'All the usual stuff. Mom and Dad filed for divorce, our house was sold, Dad bought a condo, Mom rented a smaller house. Sean said he wanted to live with Mom.' I roll my eyes at this. 'But no one thought *that* was a good idea, so the judge and everyone decided we should spend alternate weeks with each parent. So that's what we did, every Sunday evening we'd swap parents and houses.' I threw another pebble in the water.

'That must have been very difficult for you,' Barry says.

'Oh man . . .' I shake my head. 'You have no idea. And older people say the stupidest things, you know? Like, "Oh, that's great, now you'll have two houses to call home instead of one, and your Mom/Dad will get you all to themselves to have even *more* quality time with you." Seriously, do they think we're dumb? But nobody tells you what it's like to see your home being packed up and sold to other people, I mean complete strangers. No one talks about what it's like to say goodbye every week to the parent you're leaving alone and watch their face while they're trying to act all happy and wave you off. Then you show up at the other parent's house where they're acting all weird and trying to make out it's, like, vacation or a birthday all the time. And no one for sure tells you what it's like to watch your twin brother fall apart.'

'Did he?'

'Oh, yeah. Sean couldn't get his head around it. He kept hoping they'd get back together, even though I told him it was never going to happen.'

'Sometimes it does, not often though, I grant you.'

'Well, the day of the accident, Dad was dropping us off at Mom's. We were earlier than usual because she had asked Dad could we come at lunchtime instead of in the evening, like we usually did. So we get there, and Dad drives away, and Mom tells us to get settled into our room and stuff and then to come downstairs when we we're ready, that she was doing a barbecue. So we come down, go outside to the backyard and, sure, there's a barbecue going, but there's this guy standing over it, acting like it's totally normal for him to be grilling our lunch. Then Mom says, "Say hi to my friend Frank, boys, he's going to be having lunch with us today." And I say, "Hi Frank", but Sean goes all quiet. I just acted like normal, because I wanted to see what happened next. That's usually the best thing to do around adults . . .'

Barry smiles at that.

'So we eat lunch, and Mom and Frank are talking and he says, "Boys, you have to come and see my house sometime. It's right by the ocean and I have a great pool and power boat," . . . yada, yada, yada . . . and Mom's saying, "Wow, yes, what a great idea, wouldn't you like that, guys?" But Sean is just sitting staring at his plate, not eating anything. So she says, "Sean, what's wrong, honey, what's the matter?" And Sean says nothing. Then Mom and Frank look at each other as if to say, *uh-oh*. Then Mom clears the plates and comes back to the table and sits down and says, "Boys, I have something to tell you . . ." And I'm thinking, well this should be fun, because we've already had the worst version of *that* conversation. So then Mom says, "You know how Daddy and I will always love you more than anything and anybody . . . but we both agreed that we can each have new friends now that we're not married anymore?" And she looks at Frank, who reaches out to hold her hand. "Well, Frank is my new friend, and he really wants to be your friend as well." I almost threw up right there and then.'

'Ah . . . I see,' Barry says. 'Go on.'

I don't think I could stop talking now even if he told me to. It's all pouring out and, honestly? It's a relief.

'After Mom said that, there was complete silence. No one said anything. I looked at Sean, who looked like someone had slapped him. His face was going all red and he was chewing his mouth the way he always does before he starts to cry. I kicked him under the table, but he just stayed like that, frozen. I think it might have even been okay at that stage, I could probably have gotten him to come upstairs and talked to him, explained stuff, reassured him, but then Frank has to go and shoot his mouth off.

"So," he says, "we'll be seeing a lot more of each other now, guys, and we're gonna have fun. I'm gonna make sure of that. And you'll have to meet my daughter, Sheryl, who's a little bit older than you, but—"

'Well, he never got any further. Sean jumps up and yells, "That's not fair. That's being really mean to Daddy and I don't think you're being fair."

"Honey." Mom reaches out a hand to him. "Daddy will understand, he'll be happy for all of us, I know he will."

'And that's when Sean lost it.

"I don't believe anything you say anymore," he yells. "You left us! You ruined everything! Now Daddy's sad all the time and you don't care. And now you're going to make it worse! I hate you, and I hate you too, Frank. I want to go back to Dad's *now!* I want my dad! I want my dad!" And he goes into a complete meltdown, yelling and screaming and crying. I thought he was going to make himself puke, it was that bad.

'Mom and Frank tried to calm him down, but that only made him worse. Frank kept talking about *the fun we're gonna have together*, and Mom said he could even have a dog at our house, which she had always said *no way* to before. I could have told her it was way too late for bribery.

'Meanwhile, Sean is screaming and working himself up so he can hardly breathe. "I want Dad! I want Dad! I don't want to be here anymore. I hate you!"

'And Mom starts looking panicked, and Frank's looking at Sean like he's some kind of alien or something. That's when I knew I had to step in. "Just call Dad and take us back, Mom," I said. "I'll talk to Sean when he's calmer."

'Frank butted in then. "I think that's a good idea," he said, looking relieved. "Maybe this is a good time to tell Dan about us. It was never going to be easy. Drop the kids back, hon, have the conversation. I'll come with you if you want?"

"No way!" Sean yells. "He's not coming with us!"

"I don't think that's a good idea," Mom and me said together.

'So Mom says, "Okay, boys, go get your things upstairs and I'll take you back to Dad's."

'Lucky for us, we hadn't really unpacked our stuff for the week, so we just had to get a few things together. Sean had stopped yelling and crying and was just hiccupping a bit, but he was looking pleased.

'Then I came back downstairs again, and when he thought no one was watching, Frank hugged Mom and said, "Be strong, hon, you can do this", which made me want to kill him. Anyway, it turned out Frank wasn't nice like she said. He was mean, but Mom and us didn't know that then. We made sure she knew it later, though.'

I can't believe I'm actually talking to someone about all this, but Barry is really listening. I mean properly listening, not in that pretend way some adults do, just so they can put their own spin on whatever it is you're telling them. Barry understands, he's not faking it, and that gives me the energy to go on. Because now I'm getting to the really hard part. The part I can't let go of . . .

'I still get flashbacks of the accident,' I say. 'Not as much as I used to, but it really messes with my head.'

'Of course it does, lad, it's bound to. Tell me what you remember, if you can, just take it slowly.'

So I take a deep breath and go on. 'It's really hot. We set off in Mom's Jeep and pull onto the Pacific Coast Highway. State Route 1. We're heading south, on the coast side, towards Malibu. Mom isn't saying much, but I can see in the rear-view mirror that she's crying. Sean keeps telling her to call Dad, like, *now*. He has the window on his side open all the way down, the air is blasting in and Mom tells him to close it, that it's messing with the air con. Then a bug flies in the car and lands right on his leg and he starts yelling again.

'Mom tells him to close the window because she can't hear on the phone with the wind and all. She's trying to talk to Dad on speakerphone, telling him she's on her way over to him with us, and that she needs to talk to him.

"Close the window, stupid!" I yell at Sean. But he just makes a face at me and shoves me. So I pick up the bug and squash it in his hair, and he starts yelling again and hitting me.

"Boys, please!" Mom shouts, looking at us in the mirror. "I'm trying to drive here!"

'I don't remember seeing the truck, it had kind of gone past us at that point, but we found out afterwards that it swerved to avoid a biker. Anyhow, the end of it flips out and catches the rear of the Jeep. It's not such a big noise or anything, more like a click, but then everything slows down. We go into a spin. There's a weird hissing noise, which I guess is the tyre being blown out, and then we're going round and round and round. I hear Mom scream. I look at Sean's face, and his mouth has gone into a complete O. Then Mom's shouting, "Oh, God! Oh, no! My boys! Oh God help us!" And then there's a sound of, like, metal ripping, and we're falling, falling . . . then everything goes black.'

Before Barry can say anything, I hear Gracie's voice. Sure enough, she appears, followed by Sean – I guess they must have been looking for me. My fists clench just at the sight of her. Barry looks down at my hands and reads my mind. 'She means well,' he says, nodding in Gracie's direction. 'You mustn't mind about her so much.'

'I don't,' I lie, looking away.

'Sean needs other companions his own age, it's good for him.'

'He has me,' I say, turning to look him right in the eye. 'He always has, and he always will.'

'That will mostly be the case, Pat, but not always.'

'What do you mean?' Suddenly I feel cold. It's the way he's looking at me, it makes me feel afraid of what he's going to say.

'I mean that your lives will grow in different directions, lad. Just as they would have anyway, even if you hadn't died.'

I don't like that word.

'I don't feel dead,' I tell him, and it's the truth. 'I'm still here, aren't I? So I'm not really dead, not the way *you* mean.' He's making me angry again now.

'But you're not exactly alive either, are you?'

'I am as long as Sean can see me.' I turn away from him and scowl. 'And that's all that matters to me.'

Just then I hear Dad calling, he has come to get us – just in time.

'I have to go now,' I say. So I jump up and leave him there. I don't even say goodbye.

I run down to the road, but there's no one there ... they're gone. Sean, Dad and Gracie have left without me. I feel like I'm going to puke. Panic rises in my throat and I start to run after Dad's car, shouting for Sean. Then I realise how stupid I must look, so I force myself to remain calm. I'll catch them up, I tell myself, I just have to keep walking.

'Wait, Pat!' It's Barry again, standing right in front of me. 'Where are you rushing off to?'

'What's it to you?'

'You can't keep following them, lad.' He reaches out to me. 'I know it's hard, believe me, but you have to let your brother go.'

I open my mouth to yell at him, but only a sob comes out.

'Come here and sit down again, lad. Come on. Let's have a little chat, you and me. I think I may be able to help you.'

I want to say, *Go away and leave me alone! I don't need your help.* But all of a sudden I'm tired, confused and scared. Lonely, too. And I'm trying really hard not to cry. So I shrug. And I sit down. And I listen as Barry begins to talk.

* * *

'What are you doing in here?' Annie joins Dee at the corner table in the hotel restaurant.

'Oh, please.' Her sister rolls her eyes. 'I just want a bit of peace. Is that so much to ask?'

'I just want to talk to you, Dee, that's all.'

'Spy on me, more like. Why do I feel a lecture coming on?'

'Where's Gracie?'

'With her new best friend. Does that meet with your approval?'

'Is it true John's coming down at the weekend?'

'Yes, not that it's any of *your* business.'

'You're my sister, Dee, we're family. I'm just looking out for you.'

'Of course you are, Annie.' Dee is sarcastic. 'How could I forget? After all, you know better than anyone else how to offer advice regarding situations you know nothing about.'

'Please, Dee. I'm serious. I'm worried about you. Mum is too, for that matter.'

'Well she is now, thanks to you and whatever you said to her. When are you going to learn to mind your own business?'

'Look, I don't want to fight, I just want to say . . . please, don't accept any offers or . . . or promises from him. He's left you hanging this long, or you wouldn't be here, would you?'

Dee's face goes white, which means she is very angry. But Annie presses on. She's banking on Dee not wanting to embarrass herself in front of a restaurant full of customers and staff. This is Annie's best chance to try to get through to her.

'If he's suddenly coming here now, there's every chance he's under even more pressure. There's no telling what hare-brained scheme he'll be trying to sell you to save his own skin.'

'Actually, he's talking about starting over again, in Dublin, which makes perfect sense to me. He has contacts there . . . investors . . . developers . . .'

'Dublin! You can't be serious? And how can you even think about trusting him? Anyway, Gracie would hate it there!'

'She's a child, Annie, she'll get used to it. Anyway, it's not all about her, there are other people to consider, you know.'

'Of course it's about her! She's your daughter! She can't rely on her father, that's patently obvious, you're the only mother she's got, she needs you Dee, and she needs you sober . . . not . . . not wallowing in a fog of alcohol and tranquilisers.' There. She had said it.

'What gives you the right to be so bloody judgemental!' Dee hisses. 'I have been trying to cope with unimaginable stress. I am under medical supervision. You know what this is? You just can't stand the fact that Mum and Dad are standing by me, looking after me, can you? Because it means Golden Girl Annie isn't the centre of their universe for five minutes.' Her voice rises with every syllable, and Annie is acutely aware of heads nearby starting to turn in their direction.

'You've always been jealous of me, Annie, ever since I can remember. And now you've wound up with nothing but your bloody boring business to keep you warm at night, so you're taking it out on me with your prissy, petty, pissed-off interfering.' Dee pushes back her chair from the table and jumps to her feet, her colour high, eyes narrowing, sending glasses and cutlery flying.

'You used to be Dad's favourite.' Dee gives a mirthless laugh. 'Now even *he* agrees you've turned into a giant pain in the arse! You might have been born with a poker up it, Annie, but that doesn't mean the rest of us have to live with it. So just feck off and leave me alone, why don't you! I'll live in Dublin or anywhere else that takes my fancy, *with* whoever takes my fancy, and neither you nor anyone else is going to stop me. You know why, Annie? Because I *can*!'

Despite her shock, Annie becomes aware of several things at once ... the kitchen staff coming out to see what the ruckus is about, the studiously uninterested barman, who tactfully turns away, the customers who stare in fascination at the volatile exchange ... But most of all she is aware of Gracie, running towards them across the restaurant, laughing about something, until she stops dead in her tracks at the row unfolding before her, her mother out of control and shouting. Annie doesn't know which is worse, Gracie's distraught little face, or the equally despairing look on Breda's as she gathers her granddaughter up and shepherds her away.

* * *

'Is that all you remember?' Barry asks me.

'I remember being in a tunnel . . . kind of lying in it, floating on my back. It was very dark, but a nice kind of dark, really quiet and peaceful. I wasn't afraid. I felt really safe there and I knew I could have kept on going, but I didn't want to. I wanted to stay with Sean, that's all I remember thinking, and as soon as I thought that, there was a kind of whooshing noise and I felt myself being sucked back, and then I was in the ambulance with Sean, right by his side, watching the paramedics working on him, giving him oxygen, but he was out of it. I remember telling him to hold on, that it would be okay, that I was right there with him.

'When we got to the hospital I ran alongside the trolley they put him on. There was a lot of shouting and people rushing around, and then I saw Dad. He burst through the doors, yelling, and he ran right past me. I was trying to tell him what happened, but he couldn't hear me. That's when I realised nobody could see or hear me anymore. No one except Sean ... and now you.' I look at Barry. 'You can see me. I'm glad you can see me, I was getting kind of lonely.

'Mom didn't make it either. I remember in the hospital . . . the room with the two trolleys side by side. I saw her lying there, just like she was asleep. And then I looked at the other trolley, and I saw it was me.'

I felt a pain in my chest just talking about it. I don't like to remember that time.

'It was lucky for Sean,' I went on, 'that he had his window open, you know, that's how he got out, like, when the water started coming in. Sean and me used to watch *MythBusters* all the time, it was one of our favourite programmes. People always think when a car is under water that you're meant to wait until the car fills up, so that the pressure has equalised, and then you can open the door or window. But waiting is wrong. People need to know this stuff. Even if you do wait, the pressure on the outside is going to be stronger than the pressure on the inside for quite a while. So while you're waiting, you'll most likely drown. I saw that on *MythBusters* and on *Top Gear*. So the best thing to do is to get out any way you can as *soon* as you can. I knew that, but in my case it was too late. I was killed on impact. They said that at the hospital. They said I had a clean C4/C5 break.' I rubbed my neck, thinking about it. 'I went into spinal shock. There was nothing anyone could have done. I guess Mom was knocked out too because she was a really good swimmer, better even than Dad. She probably would have made it out of the car otherwise.'

'I'm so very sorry, Pat,' Barry says, looking at me. 'Tell me, is your mother with you now? I haven't seen her.'

I shake my head. 'No. I think we're in different places.'

Barry nods. 'I see. And tell me . . . would you like to see her again, to be with her?'

I look at Barry, but I don't know what to say. I think I have to make a decision, but I'm not ready to choose.

Sean

We're playing this game, me and Gracie, where I write questions in the sand with a stick we've found, and she answers – talking, of course – then she asks me a question back and I write the answer in the sand. We already know most stuff about each other now, so I write: *tell me something you've never told anybody else.* She wrinkles up her nose for a minute and thinks. And then, instead of talking, she writes the answer in the sand as well.

Sometimes I wish Annie was my real mother instead of Mam.

Then she rubs it out with her hands like it was never there.

Why? I write.

She shrugs. 'She's never happy when I'm around,' she says. 'I don't think she likes me very much.'

She's your mom. She loves you. I'm pretty sure about this, because that's what moms do. Dads, too. We were told that all the time, even in school.

Gracie shakes her head. 'Annie loves me,' she says. 'She's always happy to have me around, and she talks to me properly, not just saying stuff to get me out of the way. Granny and Granddad love me, I think, but I don't think Mam does.'

What about your dad? Where is he?

'I think he's in Cork with my other grandparents . . . but he's coming to see us at the weekend.'

That's good.

'I don't know . . . they fight a lot.' She shrugs. 'I think maybe he left because of me.'

Why?

'Maybe if I make Mam sad, maybe she was sad around him too and they stopped having fun. I dunno.'

I wasn't sure what to think about that.

'Of course,' Gracie says quickly, 'it's much worse for you. I mean, your mam died, so I'm not saying it's the same as that or anything, but you asked me to tell you something I've never told anyone before, and I've never told anyone that. 'But what about you?' She looks at me. 'What have you never told anyone?'

I think for a minute, and wonder if I can trust her. But I'm pretty sure I can.

Pat's still here. We both stare at the words, and I hold my breath and wait to see if she thinks I'm crazy.

Gracie's eyes grow big. 'You mean he's here, like, as a ghost?'

I shake my head. *No, just like you. I can see him like normal. Same as I can see you.*

'Does he talk to you?'

I nod.

'Is he here now?' She looks around, wide-eyed.

I shake my head. *No, he's with Dad right now. But Dad can't see him.*

'Wow.' Gracie's staring at me. 'What does he look like?'

Just like me. We're identical, except he chipped his front tooth a while back.

Gracie thinks about this. 'That's *so* cool. That he's still with you, I mean, not that he died.' Then she says something I didn't expect.

'Shouldn't . . . I mean, um, don't you think Pat is, like, meant to be in heaven?'

I never thought about where Pat was supposed to be. We've always been together – that's just the way it is. I think about it now, but him being somewhere else doesn't make any sense to me. I write in the sand: *Identical twins are the same person when they're alive and they're still the same when one of them is dead. That never changes.*

People think you lose half of yourself when a twin dies, but they're wrong. You lose all of yourself. So which one of us died? I think we both did. It's just that one of us got left behind. I don't know how to be without Pat, so what does that make me? But I can't write all this for Gracie, because she wouldn't understand. Nobody does, not even Dr Shriver. They think I'm making it all up as a way to cope without Pat, that I'm still traumatised. But I'm not. Pat *is* still here. That's the only thing I'm really sure of.

But I feel sorry for Gracie, not knowing if her mom or dad love her. I can't imagine that. Even when Mom was mad, or sick, she always told us she loved us, every day, and so did Dad. Some days, Mom would leave little notes in our schoolbags, or tucked in our books, and they always made us laugh. And she'd always end them: *Love you to the moon and back.* I miss Mom too, but mostly I miss the way we used to be as a family. I can see why Gracie would like Annie as a mom. I think she'd make a really good one. But I guess she's stuck with the one she's got.

Then Gracie takes the stick and starts to write something else. When I read it, I feel my face get hot.

I like you.

I'm not sure what I'm supposed to do now, but I can tell she's expecting something because she's looking at me with her big blue eyes and chewing her lip. I like her too, and I'm really glad I met her. She's helped me a lot.

So I take the stick from her hand and write *I like you too*. I guess it was the right thing to do because she smiles and seems happy again.

Just then, something in the air around me changes. When I look up, Pat's standing right there. He looks mad at me, but then he just shakes his head and walks away.

I don't tell Gracie that.

* * *

'Annie?'

'Mmhm?'

'Where do people go when they die?'

'That's a rather profound question.' Annie looks up from the web designer's site she is studying on her laptop.

Across the open-plan room of Annie's cottage, Gracie is lying on the couch, engrossed in her iPad.

'What does *profound* mean?'

'Big . . . deep.'

'Like the sea?'

'Well, no . . . yes, sort of. But never mind that. Why do you want to know where people go when they die?'

'Dunno, I was just wondering.'

'About what?'

'Well, if they're still around you.'

'Who?'

'Dead people.'

Annie looks at her niece quizzically. 'I'm pretty sure they're having far too good a time up in heaven to be bothered about what's going on down here, isn't that what they teach you at school?'

'Sort of.' Gracie's finger scrolls across the screen. 'Sean says his twin brother is still here. He can see him.' She looks up at Annie. 'The one who died in the car crash.'

'Did he speak to you to tell you that?' Annie asks incredulously.

Gracie shakes her head. 'He wrote it all down for me. Said he can see him clear as day, hear him too, but nobody else can.'

'Poor kid,' Annie murmurs.

'So I was just wondering . . .'

'Gracie.' Annie gets up from the table and sits down beside her niece. 'Sean's been through an awful lot. He's been in a terrible car accident, he's lost his mum, and his twin brother. That's an awful, *awful* thing for any child to have to go through. Sometimes . . .' she pauses, searching for the right words, '. . . sometimes people have coping devices they use to . . . to get them through the shock. Their brains can't take in all at once what has happened to them, especially something as life-changing and traumatic as what happened to Sean. To help them get used to it, well, they can imagine things. In this case, Sean really believes he sees his brother, but we all know he is dead.'

'But *how* do you know?' Gracie persists.

'How do I know what?'

'How do you know his brother *isn't* really here? Couldn't he be staying with Sean just because he wants to?' Gracie looks hopeful.

Annie sighs. 'I don't know, honey. That's the truth. But I do know that Sean's dad lost his wife, Sean's mum, and Sean's twin brother in a horrible car crash and that poor Sean has been so traumatised by the whole thing, he hasn't spoken a word since. If thinking or believing he sees his twin brother—'

'Pat,' Gracie interjects.

'If believing he sees Pat helps Sean come to terms with his loss, well then, that's a good thing.'

'But *you* don't believe he can?'

'I believe that *he* believes he can, but no, honey, I don't think his brother is here. He was killed, Gracie. It's horrible and wrong and unfair, but Sean's brother is dead. There's no changing that, I'm afraid.'

Annie pushes a stray curl behind her niece's ear. 'What did you say to him when he told you all that?'

'Nothing.' Gracie shrugs. 'I just asked him questions about Pat and he told me all about him by writing it out. That's all.'

'That's good, I think,' Annie says thoughtfully, 'that he was comfortable sharing that with you.'

'He told me no one else wants to know. He tried to tell his dad about it in the beginning, but it just made his dad sad. So I told him he could talk to me about Pat any time, if he wanted.'

Annie smiles. 'That was kind of you, Gracie.'

A little while later, Annie walks Gracie back to the hotel, despite her pleas to stay the night.

'*Please*, Annie. Why can't I stay with you instead of Granny and Granddad?'

'Because I have to go out tonight. And you know Granny and Granddad love having you.'

'They're just being nice to me.' Gracie sighs. 'Really, Granddad just wants to drink his whiskey, and Granny wants to get back to her Bridge.'

'Gracie!'

'It's true. I heard Viktor telling the new girl in the kitchen that Mr Sullivan would drink the hotel dry if he was let, and I heard Granny talking to her friend on the phone saying if she didn't get out to play Bridge with the girls soon, she'd lose what little sanity she had left, but that she had a granddaughter to mind and a demanding husband to endure . . .'

'You mustn't listen to people's private conversations, Gracie. You hear things out of context and misunderstand their real meaning. Granny loves having you, I know she does, she says so all the time, she adores you. And Granddad can be difficult now he's getting on a bit and he's in a lot of pain with his hip. Granny's feeling a bit hemmed in, that's all.'

'I only like him when he's being funny, not when he's bad-tempered,' Gracie says matter-of-factly. 'And if I didn't listen to people's conversations, I'd never know what was going on. Nobody tells me anything, except Sean, and he can't even talk. Anyway, I'd much rather stay with you. You're the only one who ever talks to me properly.'

'Aren't you looking forward to seeing your dad?' Annie gives one of Gracie's curls a tug. 'I'm sure he's dying to see you.'

Gracie shrugs. 'I dunno. Even if he does come, Mum and him will probably end up fighting.'

'Gracie, I know things have been difficult and confusing lately, but they'll get better, you'll see. And you have Sean to hang out with now, don't you?'

Gracie brightens. 'That's true – and Pat.'

'What?'

'Pat, Sean's twin.'

'Gracie, honey—'

'What?'

'It might be better not to say anything about Sean being able to see his brother to your mum and dad, or to anyone really, just for a little while. Maybe keep it between you and Sean . . . you know?'

Gracie gives her aunt an *As if!* look as Annie leaves her at the lift to Breda's apartment. 'I'm not stupid, Annie. I know most people don't believe in ghosts. But I do. Don't worry, though, it's Sean's secret and I'm not going to share it.'

* * *

Annie tried to remember the last time she had been on a first date, and couldn't. She remembered meeting Ed, of course, but they had met at work, which was different. It was funny, but now that she tried to remember their first proper night out together, she found she couldn't. All she remembered of those early times was being swept off her feet in a blur of parties and nights out, giddily following wherever Ed led her.

And Philip, her ex-fiancé, just seemed like a lifetime ago, like he happened to a different woman, not to her. And she was different. She was older now, reticent, wary. None of the qualities anyone wanted in a date, she thought ruefully.

But this wasn't a *date*, of course, just a really nice evening out with someone she felt she had known for much longer. Dan had insisted on calling for her in a taxi, although she would have been happy to make her own way to the small new restaurant in Caherdaniel that was getting rave reviews. Now here they were, seated at a table for two in the corner of the newly converted and renovated barn.

'So did you try talking to Dee?' Dan asks as they sip a delicious Rioja.

'Can't you see my black eye?'

Dan laughs. 'So she didn't take it well, I'm guessing?'

Annie shrugs. 'There's not a lot to tell really. I confronted her, and she let rip. It wasn't pretty.'

'Did she . . . apologise?'

Annie grimaces. 'Not a chance. She was very angry, defensive. I haven't seen her since. She took to her bed afterwards, left us to take care of Gracie. There were tears, histrionics. Mum said she was completely overwrought. In fact, she thinks Dee is on the brink of a nervous breakdown.'

Dan looks at her, obviously weighing up his next words. 'Half the problem with alcoholics and addicts,' he says carefully, 'are the people around them who insist on protecting them.'

Annie nods. 'The thing is, John, her husband, is coming at the weekend. We're all walking on eggshells. All afraid of upsetting her further and pushing her over the edge. I know just how enabling that sounds, believe me, but no one has a clue what's going on, not really. I'm not sure Dee has either.'

'Well, I guess she's going to find out.'

'The worry, of course, is whether or not it'll go to court. Losing their house is nothing compared to what it would do to Gracie to see her father go to jail.'

'Is that likely?'

'I don't know. These things happen slowly in this country.'

'One day at a time, right?'

'Episode, more like.'

'How's Gracie about it all?'

'Stoic. Grumbling a bit. Putting on a good face. Pretending to cope. Probably very, very scared.'

'She's lucky to have you.'

'She's a character. We all adore her.'

'She and Sean are quite the pair, aren't they?'

Annie shakes her head. 'I don't know how that poor kid is coping.'

'Who says he is?' Dan's face darkens. 'I worry about him all the time. He was spending way too much time alone back home, though, that's why I'm glad he's taken to Gracie. After the accident, he didn't want to be around any of his friends. I guess it was too painful for him.'

'It must be so hard for him,' Annie says, 'losing not just his mother but his twin. That's just too much for anyone, let alone someone so young.'

Dan sighs. 'He hasn't spoken a single word since, as you know.

Sometimes I wonder if he ever will.' He stares into his glass. 'They were inseparable, my boys.'

'What about you?' Annie says softly. 'How are you coping?'

He looks up at her. 'Some days are harder than others, but I have to keep it together, not just for Sean, but for Pat too. He was a strong little guy. Sean is more sensitive. He idolised Pat, would have jumped off a tall building if he'd told him to.' Dan grins at his memories. 'And Pat exploited him as only a brother could. Ironically, it was Sean who was the more talkative of the two, but Pat held the reins, no question. I suppose I just worry that he'll retreat completely . . . go into his own little world and never resurface. I've already lost one boy.' Dan's voice cracks. 'I can't lose Sean as well. He's so fragile without Pat, and there's not a goddamn thing I can do to help him.'

'You're doing everything you can,' Annie says, her heart aching for him.

'What if that's not enough?'

'You have to believe it is. Just take it one day at a time, it's all any of us can do.'

'You're right. And I'm sorry.' Dan looks sheepish. 'I'm lousy company these days. Too wrapped up in my own problems. Let's change the subject, okay? Tell me about yourself, you grew up here, right?'

He listens as Annie describes growing up in the hotel and eventually leaving to live in London. How she was supposed to marry some guy, but then met someone else she fell in love with and called off the wedding.

'My parents took it badly,' she says. 'My dad, especially. Philip, my fiancé, well, his dad was one of *my* dad's closest friends.'

'Ouch.'

Annie makes a wry expression. 'Yep, I pretty much killed off the whole happy family vibe single-handedly. But it's in the past now. You have to let it live there in the end.'

Dan tilts his glass towards her. 'Amen to that.'

'So what about you . . . your wife?'

'Mary was incredible.' He smiles. 'But we were unlucky. After she had the boys, she suffered postpartum psychosis. Her doctors were great, they managed to get her through it, but unfortunately it became apparent there had been an underlying disorder all along, the pregnancy was just the trigger that revealed it. So then it became about managing the condition, classic bipolar stuff . . . highs, lows, mania, depression, the whole kit and caboodle.'

'That must have been so difficult,' Annie murmurs.

'You have no idea. You'd think the depression would be the worst part, but that, at least, was predictable and we knew what to do. It was the manic episodes that were terrifying, because she was out of control. She might get up in the middle of the night and repaint the sitting room crazy colours, or run up thousands on her credit card on a shopping spree, or buy drinks for a whole bar full of strangers. I mean, to a psychologist it's pretty much textbook behaviour, but that doesn't make it any easier to live with. Unfortunately, the manic episodes sometimes included other men. It wasn't her fault, I understood that. Someone else had taken over, and when it happened, she wanted to party, have fun, and she was a beautiful girl. But it got messy once or twice . . .' he trails off. Annie doesn't interrupt.

'The worst part was that, underneath it all, there was still the girl I fell in love with. It was so hard for her. She struggled with the medication and hated the way it made her feel. A drug that had worked for a while would suddenly stop working, and they would have to try and reconfigure a whole new drug combination. But most of all she hated the fact that she had to be "watched", as she referred to it. And she did. We had two little boys, we had to be careful. The whole family, hers and mine, did their best to help, to keep an eye on things, especially when I was at work, but I could see it was destroying her. She was dying inside. To cut a long and depressing story a little bit shorter, she met a guy called Frank, said she wanted to start a new life with him, and there was no talking her out of it. We all knew he probably had no idea about her illness, she could go months sometimes without an episode. Our divorce was about to come through when the accident happened.' He pauses. 'But things were friendly, we were working it out, moving on, joint parenting and so forth, and then this . . .'

'I don't know how you coped, really I don't,' Annie says. Her own problems seemed very small by comparison.

'I didn't cope. I don't know that you ever do, you just keep putting one foot in front of the other. People have been endlessly kind. And I'm grateful to have my work to focus on. And you know, coming here was the right thing to do. I think it's helping Sean for sure.'

Annie takes a deep breath, unsure of how he will take what she is about to say.

'About Sean,' she says.

'What about him?' Dan looks wary.

'It's just . . . it's just something he told Gracie. I'm not sure if you'll agree, but I think it sounds like progress, of a sort.'

'What do you mean, he *told* her something?' Dan said. He looks shocked.

'Oh no, I'm so sorry,' Annie explains quickly. 'Not talking. No, he wrote it down, in the sand on the beach. They were doing a question and answer thing.'

Dan's shoulders relax a bit. 'Right, I see. So, what did he tell her?'

Annie takes another deep breath. 'He told her his twin, Pat, is still here. With him.' She watches Dan anxiously, not sure if he will be pleased or upset by this new information.

'Really? I can't believe he's still thinking that. He used to write notes about it at the start, after the accident, but not for a long time now. He told her that?'

Annie nods. 'He wasn't upset or anything. He just told her Pat's here. Dan,' she reaches over to touch his hand, 'he confided in her. He trusted her and shared something important to him with her. Don't you think that's good?'

'I . . . I just don't know anymore,' Dan says, shaking his head. 'Maybe you're right.' He shrugs.

'I'm no therapist,' Annie says, 'but I can't help thinking that trusting Gracie and opening up to her has to be a good thing.'

Dan thinks about it, then nods slowly. 'Maybe you're right, Annie,' he says. 'I'll talk to Dr Shriver and ask her opinion, but I guess confiding, trusting, those are all positive actions. Maybe it's a step in the right direction, but I just don't want to get my hopes up too much, you know?' He smiles at her. 'But I do appreciate you telling me that.'

'I'm glad you're not angry with me,' Annie says. 'But I thought it was better you were aware of it.'

'And does Gracie think he's crazy?' Dan asks.

'Not at all. I think she's quite intrigued by the notion.'

Dan smiles. 'She's some kid.'

'She certainly is,' Annie says. 'And I really hope this is positive progress for Sean. He's being so incredibly brave. I've grown very fond of him myself.'

'Children are more resilient than we give them credit for,' Dan says. 'At least, that's what Sean's trauma therapist keeps telling me. I sure hope she's right. Either way, life goes on, with or without you.'

* * *

Breda thinks maybe … just maybe … the prayers might be paying off. She doesn't want to count her chickens, but Annie, who is helping out on reception while Breda is keeping an eye on the new drinks service in the front lounge, is looking better than she has since she arrived home. There is colour in her cheeks, she has put on a bit of weight, but, more importantly, the Annie Breda remembers of old is cropping up more often. Her ready smile and infectious laugh are seen and heard regularly, mostly in Gracie's company, but still, it's a good sign. Breda wonders if that nice young American fellow has anything to do with it, but Annie has not mentioned anything since the day he called to the hotel asking to see her, and Breda does not like to pry. Her daughter certainly seems happier at any rate, whatever the reason, and that's good enough for Breda.

The other reason she is hopeful is that John, Dee's husband, has arrived. She hasn't seen her son-in-law yet, of course, but the fact that he is here and the little family are together for a few days suggests that surely there is a chance of a rapprochement. This is what she has been praying for. She has Barry praying for it too, and even Father Luke has included her petition in the prayer meeting, although naturally she didn't go into any particular detail, just asked if he would pray for a 'special intention'.

It is Friday night, and the hotel is beginning to fill up. The locals always come in for a drink or two before dinner, and the new cocktail menu has brought in a few of the younger crowd, she is pleased to see.

She is over at reception, having a word with Annie, when a familiar voice rings out.

'Mum!'

Dee runs up to reception, all smiles. She has had her hair done and is wearing a glamorous dress with high, strappy sandals. She looks terrific. She is turning heads with her entrance and she knows it. Her husband saunters in behind her, in an expensive-looking suit, flashing smiles to everyone and nodding left and right. In their wake trails a dejected looking Gracie.

'Breda! Great to see you! You're looking well!' John embraces his mother-in-law.

'Mum.' Dee's tone is apologetic. 'I know it's short notice, but can you have Gracie tonight? John and I are having dinner, we might be late.'

Breda is surprised they aren't including Gracie in their plans and spending time as a family, but she recovers quickly. 'Of course we can have her. You know we're always delighted.'

'She can stay with me,' Annie says, without looking up from the computer.

'Can I?' Gracie looks hopeful.

'You can stay wherever you like, pet.' Breda propels her granddaughter into the office. 'Let's all have dinner together, you, me, Annie and Granddad, and then you can stay the night in Annie's. How does that sound?'

Gracie's face breaks into a smile. 'That sounds great, Granny. Thanks, Annie.'

'Annie?' John peers around the counter. 'What are you doing hiding in there? I heard you were back in town. We must catch up. In fact, we're having a barbecue tomorrow.' He looks around inclusively, ever the genial host. 'Drop in around four. It'll be fun.'

'Thanks, Mum.' Dee takes John's hand, pointedly ignoring Annie. 'We really appreciate it.'

Breda watches as her daughter and son-in-law stroll towards the bar, preening and canoodling like celebrities at a red carpet event.

'Well, I never . . .' Breda shakes her head.

'You do realise what that display is all about, don't you, Mum?' Annie gets up to stand beside her mother, looking after them.

Breda is not sure she wants to hear what is coming next. Annie has that look on her face that precedes an observation guaranteed to make Breda's heart sink.

'That's what we call a PR stunt . . . a strategic charade . . . and they're certainly pulling out all the stops.'

'Oh, Annie, don't be so negative! I know you and Dee have had a falling out, but they seem so in love again. And this is a real chance for them, they're obviously trying to work on their marriage.'

'At whose expense this time, I wonder,' Annie says.

Breda shakes her head. What is it with her daughters that neither one can seem to take pleasure in the other's happiness or good fortune? She doesn't know what that spat in the restaurant was about the other day. She couldn't get any sense out of Dee at all. But whatever Annie said to her had upset her terribly. She had cried so much and was in such a state, Breda had to put her to bed and sit with her. And when she rang Annie to find out what had happened, Annie said she didn't want to talk about it. Breda was feeling quite cross with both of them. They were as bad as each other, that was the problem. But at least Dee was in sparkling form now, and she was looking super. It just goes to show that if you give things time, they always work out for the best.

* * *

After delicious fish and chips – Gracie's favourite – she and Annie are ensconced in Conor and Breda's apartment, watching the end of a wildlife documentary while Annie finishes her coffee.

'Granddad?' Gracie is sitting cross-legged at the foot of Conor's leather armchair, passing him up crisps from a bowl they are sharing.

'Mmhm?'

'Why do people like alcohol so much?'

There is a beat of silence. Across the room, in her own favourite chair, Breda, Annie notices, makes a great study of the jumper she is knitting.

Conor clears his throat. 'Well, now, alcohol is . . . is . . . an acquired taste, yes, that's what it is . . .'

'What's *acquired* mean?'

'Well, it means you have to develop a taste for it . . . to like it . . . to appreciate it.'

'Work at it, you mean?'

'Well, yes, in a manner of speaking.'

'So . . . people don't like it when they first taste it?'

'No, eh . . . generally not.'

Gracie thinks about this. 'But then they get to *really* like it?'

'Not everyone likes it, Gracie, darling,' Breda interjects mildly. 'Some people don't ever like it, and you don't have to. There's no law that says you have to like alcohol.'

'Like broccoli? Or . . . avocados?' Gracie is hopeful.

'Yes.' Breda smiles. 'But broccoli and avocados are very good for you, so you should try to like them.'

Gracie wrinkles her nose. 'I hate them. Do you like alcohol, Gran?'

'I enjoy a nice glass of wine occasionally, but I far prefer a cup of tea.'

'What about vodka?'

'Vodka? Well, no, no, it wouldn't be a drink I'd particularly enjoy.' Breda looks up from her knitting, perplexed. 'Gracie, why the sudden interest in alcohol?'

Gracie shrugs. 'Dunno. Mum likes vodka, but she doesn't like anyone seeing her drink it, so I was just wondering.'

'What do you mean,' Conor shifts in his chair to look down at her, 'she doesn't like anyone to see her drink it?'

Annie holds her breath.

'Conor . . .' Breda's tone is light, '. . . isn't it time for the news now? Switch over, will you?'

'Wait a minute. Don't interrupt me. What do you mean, Gracie, that your mother doesn't like to be seen drinking vodka?'

'Conor.' Breda looks meaningfully at her husband. 'She's a child. She doesn't understand.'

'Well . . .' Gracie considers the question, ignoring Breda. 'She hides it . . . in the house, I mean. I know because I often clean the presses for her, and I try to tidy up like Granny showed me, when Mum's in bed. And I keep finding bottles of it everywhere. And last week, she was having lunch with a friend of hers from Cork, in Cahirciveen . . . remember, Annie? Annie was there as well, weren't you, Annie?'

'I was, and I remember it very well, Gracie.'

'And Mam got up to go to the loo and her bag fell off her lap, and a small bottle of vodka rolled out of it onto the floor. I ran to pick it up for her, and she was mad at me. Her friend just laughed, like it was some big joke, and she said, "Don't worry, Dee, your secret's safe with me." Gracie takes a breath. 'So I was just wondering . . . what's the secret?' She looks enquiringly from Conor to Breda. 'I mean, if alcohol's so great, why is she hiding it? Does everybody carry it around in their handbags?'

'What happened then?' Conor asks.

'Annie said it was time to go home, but Mam wanted to stay on with her friend, so Annie said I should stay with her that night and I did.'

'And rightly so,' beams Breda. 'Sure we're all of us always thrilled to have you to ourselves for a bit, aren't we, Conor?'

'Of course we are!' Conor tugs her hair. 'I don't know how we ever managed until you came along, Gracie.'

Gracie giggles. 'Will I top up your whiskey, Granddad?'

'Eh, no, Gracie. Not at all, thanks, pet, I'm grand. You just sit there and relax.'

'I think it's time we were leaving, don't you?' Annie looks at her mother, who will not quite meet her eyes. 'Come on, Gracie, you can pick the movie.'

'Night, Granny, Granddad.' Gracie kisses Conor and then Breda goodnight. 'See you tomorrow, and thank you for dinner.'

'You're welcome, darling.'

Annie thinks Breda's eyes are glistening as she kisses Gracie goodnight, but she can't be sure. Her mother is the queen of disguising emotions. But somehow, she reckons Gracie's questions have had an impact. One way or another.

Sean

Gracie's dad is back in town, so I haven't been spending as much time with her as usual. But this afternoon she's invited me around to their house to hang out for a while and stay for tea. I think they're having a barbecue. I don't really want to go, but Dad says I should, that it would be rude not to. Pat doesn't want to go either, but I didn't share that with Dad. He'll go if I go, he won't want to be left out. When Dad asked why I didn't want to go, I just shrugged. Truth is, there aren't many people I feel comfortable around not talking, and I don't know who's going to be there. I mean, Annie is okay, and her parents, Mr and Mrs Sullivan who run the hotel, but I've never met Gracie's dad. Not everyone understands about my not talking. It makes me feel worried. Anyway, Dad told me he had said yes when Gracie asked him if I could come, so he told me to think about it. He said if I *really* didn't want to go, he would make an excuse for me later. That was this morning. Now I have to decide.

'We need to leave in the next few minutes, buddy,' Dad says, checking his watch. 'You okay to go?'

I nod.

'Good.' Dad smiles at me. 'It's the right thing to do. Gracie and her family have been very kind to us. You'll have fun, you'll see.'

I wasn't so sure, but I knew Dad was right. Gracie would be hurt if I didn't show.

'You can bring Pat too,' she'd said. 'You know he's invited, don't you?'

I nodded. I guess she was trying to be nice, to show me she understands about Pat and me, but the thing is, he doesn't need an invitation. Pat will show up if he wants to, invited or not.

Anyway, we were pulling up at the cottage now, so there was no backing out. I had washed my face and hands, like Dad told me to, and had the box of chocolates for Gracie's mom under my arm. Dad had brought a bottle of wine.

Gracie opened the door. Her face was red and she was out of breath, like she'd been running. She looked worried, but I could tell she was relieved to see me.

'Hi, Sean. Hi, Dan. Come on in. I thought maybe you weren't coming.'

Then her mom came into the hallway.

'Hello!' She was, like, really loud.

Dad gives her the bottle of wine and I hand her the chocolates and she makes a big fuss about how we shouldn't have, but she looks pleased. Then she says, 'Come in and meet my husband, John. He's really looking forward to meeting you.'

Gracie makes a face at me, but pushes me after them. 'It's just for a minute,' she whispers. 'Then we can go out and play in the back and leave them to talk.'

We go in to the sitting room, and Gracie and me and Pat sit on one of the couches, while Dad and Gracie's parents stay standing.

'Good to meet you, Dan,' Gracie's dad says, shaking Dad's hand so hard it looks like it hurts. 'What'll you have?'

'Oh, no thanks,' Dad says. 'I have to get back. I've got some work calls to make, time difference and all that.'

'Oh, but you must have a drink,' says Gracie's mom, looking disappointed.

'Well . . . just a quick one then. Some sparkling water would be nice.'

'Come *on*,' John says. 'At least have a beer, or a glass of wine, Dan. Sure, you're on holidays! Or *on vacation*, I should say.'

'Well, technically, I'm not.' Dad laughs, but I can tell he's just doing that to be polite. He isn't pleased. 'I'll have a small beer, thanks.'

'Good man. It'll help the word flow, right? You're a writer, they tell me?'

'I make marine documentaries. I'm doing some research here.'

'Right, whatever.' John gets Dad a beer and they talk about work and stuff. Gracie is watching her parents, she seems nervous. I guess she's afraid they might embarrass her. Pat is watching them too, with his head on one side. I wish I knew what he was thinking.

'So,' says John. 'How does young Sean like it here?'

Pat nudges me. John is looking straight at me, like he's waiting for an answer. I feel Gracie squirm on the seat beside me.

'He likes it a lot.' Dad smiles. 'He's settling in well, thanks in no small part to Gracie.'

'Well, I hope she isn't driving you mad, Sean.' John grins at me. 'I hear you caught a great salmon? Did you have it for dinner?'

I shake my head.

'What? Why not?'

Dad clears his throat.

'Dad!' Gracie says. 'Stop asking Sean questions! I told you he doesn't talk.'

Now it was my face that went red. I bit my lip and stared at the floor.

'Well, he's come to the right house, so,' her dad says, rocking back on his heels. 'Sure no man gets a word in edgeways here, isn't that right, Gracie? No wonder you're such good friends with Sean! Did she tell you, Sean, about the imaginary friend she had when she was a little girl?'

'Come, on!' Gracie says to me, pulling my sleeve. 'We'll go outside.'

Pat stays behind on the couch.

'John!' I hear Gracie's mom say as we leave the room. 'Don't embarrass Gracie in front of Sean, poor girl.' She's laughing as she says it, though. But I can tell Gracie doesn't think it's funny.

A short while later, Dad comes out and tells me he's heading back to the Lodge. 'Just text me when you want me to come pick you up, buddy.' He winks at me. 'Bye, Gracie. Thank you for having Sean over. Make sure he remembers his manners. Have fun, kids.'

Gracie waves him off. We sit at the outside table and play Angry Birds on the iPad. I know Pat thinks it's lame, but Gracie likes playing it, and I don't mind. At least it means no one tries to talk to me.

After a while Gracie's dad starts up the barbecue and her mom starts putting lots of different dishes on the big table. It isn't a proper barbecue, just one of those outdoor gas grills, but it's big. He does our food first, because afterwards some friends of theirs are coming around to join them, Gracie tells me.

'Now, Sean, I hope you're hungry,' her dad says. He's wearing a stupid apron that says *Head Honcho* on it. 'I know you weren't playing football with the lads, but I'm sure it's just as easy to work up an appetite on the iPad. And Gracie always has a grand appetite, don't you, Gracie?'

There's something about Gracie's dad that's making me feel uncomfortable, although I'm not even sure why.

'Will you have a burger, Sean? Or chicken wings? Or both?'

I point to the burgers.

'A burger, right. And how would you like it done, Sean?' He looks at me. He's smiling, but I get the feeling he's not smiling underneath. I decide I definitely don't like Gracie's dad. I just have a feeling that he's mean.

'Well, Sean?'

'He likes it well done, don't you, Sean?' Gracie looks at me and I nod.

'Sean's perfectly capable of answering for himself, Gracie. He doesn't need you to be his mouthpiece.' John keeps his eye on the burgers he's turning, but I can see by his face that I'm annoying him.

'Sean doesn't talk. I told you.' Gracie is angry.

'Well he'll have to, sooner or later. But he certainly won't get around to it while you're jumping in for him, missy.'

I don't like where this is heading, so I write on the iPad for Gracie. *I'm not really hungry. I'd like to go home now.*

I know it is the wrong thing to say, but I'm being honest. She grabs the iPad from me and writes: *Please don't go, please stay for a while longer, if you go home now they'll want to know why, they'll blame me.* Looking at her face, I understand. I know that look, and it speaks to me more than words ever could. So I nod and write: *Okay, I'll stay.*

Gracie and me eat at the small table with the parasol in the middle of it, leaving the bigger table for them. Gracie's dad laughs at us and says we're very unsociable, the pair of us. He keeps on asking me questions, even though it's making Gracie really mad. I just keep nodding, shrugging, or shaking my head, until eventually he gets bored. Maybe he thought he could help me start talking, but somehow I don't think that's it. Anyway, I wasn't going to let Gracie's dad bother me. I didn't care what he thought of me. But I could tell he was really bothering *her*. When the rest of the adults arrived, me and Gracie went inside to watch TV. It was good to be away from her dad. I'd be happy never to see him again.

Pat

I wasn't going to go to the barbecue at Gracie's house, but I'm glad I did. Sean needed me there. And it was good to check out Gracie's house and family.

Here's what I discovered: Gracie's dad is a jerk. Gracie doesn't seem to like him very much, although she does seem to want him to like her. Go figure. And Gracie's mom doesn't seem to pay her much attention. Gracie's always running in to ask her stuff, or get her to watch her doing stuff, but I could tell she wasn't really interested. She only pretended to be because Sean was there.

Gracie's dad kept asking Sean questions, like Sean was suddenly going to start talking or something. I mean, what is he? Stupid? At one point Sean was going to leave and go home, but then he didn't because Gracie begged him to stay. I'm glad he didn't leave, not just because he stood his ground but because if he had left then, I would have missed the rest of the evening, which got very interesting, especially when the adults arrived. There weren't many, just two other couples, and Annie.

Gracie's mom, Dee, and Annie are sisters, but they're not alike. Annie is more like our mom was. She wears jeans and stuff and looks natural. She's fun too, and likes doing stuff outdoors, and she's nice to kids, but not in that fake way some adults are, you can tell she's interested, not just pretending to be. And she smiles a lot. I like that about her. Gracie's mom is different. Kind of more dressed up. She wears make-up and jewellery. She smiles and laughs when people are talking to her, but the rest of the time she's watching everyone else, especially Gracie's dad. Did I mention he's a jerk? Make that an asshole. I know I'm not supposed to use that word, but it's what Dad would call him, trust me.

I've learned a lot from watching people. It's pretty cool when people can't see you. When I knew Gracie's dad had left off trying to get Sean to talk, I decided to have a look around the house. First of all, I went into the kitchen, where Gracie's mom was. She was on her phone, talking to someone, and pouring herself a glass of fizzy water from the fridge.

'The American boy is here, you know,' she said. 'Gracie's friend. The little boy whose twin brother and mother were killed . . . mmm, I know.' Then she lowered her voice. 'The father's *gorgeous*.'

She went on talking, then looked out the window, to the patio and garden, where Gracie's dad was starting the barbecue. Then I saw her take a smaller bottle from one of the cupboards and pour it into her glass of water. I didn't know why, but she obviously didn't want anyone to know she was drinking it. She put the bottle back quickly, and went on talking on the phone.

'We'll meet for coffee during the week,' she said to whoever she was talking to, then rolled her eyes again and laughed. 'Absolutely,' she said. 'One day at a time, right?'

Meanwhile, Gracie's dad was making a big deal about the barbecue and boasting about how good it was and that they had brought it with them from Cork. It wasn't even a proper barbecue, just an outdoor grill. All you have to do is turn the thing on. Dad always said they were nothing like the real thing, that the whole point of a barbecue is the charcoal, right? And if you're not going to do it properly, then you shouldn't do it at all.

They all sat down to eat, and bit by bit people got louder and the guys were telling jokes and laughing. I was about to go over and join them when I heard the doorbell, and then Gracie ran out and opened the front door and I heard Dad's voice saying he had come to pick up Sean.

Dad followed Gracie through the kitchen and outside to say hello to the guests and explain that he was here to pick up Sean. Gracie's mom got up and introduced him to everyone, then said, 'Sit down and have a drink before you go, Dan.' She was holding on to his arm and he looked really awkward.

'Uh, thanks . . . but I'm in the middle of something right now. And Sean needs to keep to his routine.' She started to make a big protest, so then he said quickly, 'Okay, sure, maybe just the one.'

He was being friendly, but I could tell he didn't want to stay. Gracie's mom pulled up another chair beside her, and Dad sat down, but he was looking across the table at Annie, who was looking right back at him. She smiled at him, and he winked at her. I remembered that day on the boat.

I think Gracie's dad noticed it too because he was sitting next to Annie, and he suddenly said, 'Well, Annie, and how's the love life?'

'It's just fine, thank you, John,' she said. Then turned to the woman on her other side.

'Always the woman of mystery, Annie,' John went on. I don't think Annie wanted to talk to him, but he wasn't taking the hint. 'Whatever happened your big romance?' he said then, real loud. 'The one you called off the wedding for?' He nudged her. 'I haven't seen you since you were a blushing bride-to-be, and then you dropped the bombshell and disappeared back to London. So come on, tell us all.'

'Things didn't work out. We went our separate ways.' Annie smiled at John, but it wasn't a real smile.

'Well I can see that.' John laughed, like he'd made a joke. But all around the table it went quieter.

'John,' Gracie's mom said. She gave him a look.

'What? Sure I'm only asking your sister to remind us boring married people of the joys of the single life.'

'I don't have time for a relationship,' Annie said.

'Ah, of course, the curse of the career woman.' John grinned at everyone. 'You've done well for yourself, Annie, fair dues. How much are you worth now?' John laughed, but Annie ignored him.

John leaned in to the guy beside him and joked. 'I married the wrong sister,' he said, in a lower voice, but not low enough, because Gracie's mom heard him, and if looks could kill, he'd have been flat out on the floor. But that didn't stop him. I think he might have been a bit drunk because he said in a louder voice this time. 'My sources in London tell me Annie's in line to make *millions* out of her agency buyout. I have a couple of tasty investment opportunities lined up myself, Annie, with some property boys in Dublin, if you're interested. But you'll need to move smartly.'

Annie looked at him like she wanted to kill him too. 'Speaking of sources, John, last I heard, your investment schemes weren't doing so well.'

Nobody said anything then. John kept on smiling, but his voice changed. 'That's not all my sources tell me, Annie. Apparently your lover boy that you called off the wedding for has got some young one in his agency knocked up. That must be embarrassing.' He laughed, but nobody else did.

That's when Dad stood up and said, 'It's time we were going. I'll collect Sean on my way out. Annie, can I walk you back?' He was wearing his polite face, but I could tell he was mad.

Annie looked at Dad, then she got up and said to no one in particular, 'Thanks, guys, it's been a lovely evening.'

Gracie's mom looked surprised and cross then. I guess she

didn't want Annie to leave, but she stood up to go to the door with them, except Dad said, 'There's no need to see us out, Dee, thanks.' So she just stood there, looking kind of awkward, then sat back down again.

Just as Dad, Sean and Annie were leaving, Gracie's dad laughed again and called after them, 'I'll give you this, Annie, you're a fast worker.'

But Dad just shook his head like he thought John was really lame, and he and Annie just kept right on walking and never looked back.

Outside the gate, Annie blew out a long breath and shook her head. 'I'm so sorry you had to be party to that.'

'You okay?' Dad asked her.

'Yes, I'm fine.'

'He was *way* out of line.'

'Well, that's my brother-in-law for you.'

Sean ran up ahead, but I stuck around to hear what they were saying.

'He's some jerk.'

Annie laughed. 'Or as we say in these parts, a gobshite. I've never understood what Dee saw in him. But if I'd stayed a minute longer, I wouldn't have been responsible for what I said.'

'Back home, we'd probably call him an asshole,' Dad said with a grin. 'I was just being polite with jerk.'

I smiled. I knew that's what Dad would say about him.

'Why don't you come back with us for a drink? I have a nice bottle of Merlot begging to be opened, and it will give me a good excuse not to work.'

'Sounds good,' said Annie. 'After that I could do with some normal company.'

'No pressure then,' Dad said, and they laughed. I haven't heard him laugh hardly at all since Mom died. He sounded like the old dad for a second. 'I'm not sure about normal, but we'll do our best.'

'You'll do just fine,' Annie said, and they smiled at each other.

* * *

It was late, coming up to midnight, and Dan was working. Sean was at Annie's cottage for a sleepover with Gracie. Annie had come across some old sleeping bags during a clearout at the hotel, which had given Gracie the idea of camping out under the stars with Sean, like they did in old Western movies. Annie didn't think that was a good idea, but said she and Sean were welcome to camp in her living room for the night and watch some movies. Sean was excited about the idea, and Dan was both surprised and pleased – he thought of it as progress – and he knew Sean would be safe with Annie. Now, though, even though Sean would have been in bed fast asleep if he were here, the house felt strangely empty. So Dan made a pot of strong coffee and sat down at his desk, welcoming the distraction of work.

The house was still, save for the thrum of the refrigerator in the kitchen where he sat, and the odd clunk and rattle from the pipes.

There were many reasons why Dan preferred to work at night, and he didn't need the coffee to keep him awake. Caffeine had never bothered him, not that he drank that much. It was quiet, sure, the noise and bustle of the day had subsided. Emails had been answered, calls made and any expeditions he had to make were completed throughout the day. Also, they were six hours behind in Texas, eight in California, so he liked to be available if he was needed. But none of those were the real reasons. The real reason Dan liked to work at night was because it stopped him remembering.

It was in the quiet of the night that he relived it most clearly, that last fateful conversation. Fragments of words . . . the buzz of the highway . . . the yells of the boys . . . the garbled account from Mary about how she was driving them back to him . . . they needed to talk . . . then the crunching . . . the screams . . . metal tearing . . . then, silence, reverberating, while his own voice echoed frantically back to him as he called, 'Mary? Mary? What is it? What's happened? *Mary?*'

All of it tore through Dan's head like the storm of hideous sounds that played out, ripping and clashing in a symphony of horror before Mary's car had spun out of control and hurtled off the highway, right over the cliff, plunging into the ocean below, taking his life as he knew it with it.

That was what he had to live with, along with the loss – wondering, every single time, *why?* Why on earth had she been driving back to him? What was it she needed to talk to him about? Had she or one of the boys been sick? Had there been some urgent news? But the post-mortems had shown nothing apart from the obvious – death by drowning in Mary's case, and death from C4/C5 induced spinal shock for Pat.

He never knew how he got through those next hours, dropping everything, throwing himself in his car and racing out on the highway. Then the phone call, the sirens, the police and the escort to the hospital, where he burst through the doors like a madman. The frenetic activity in the ER, the brief, wild rush of hope – until he realised the people they were working on did not belong to him. Being led gently to the other room, where two still figures lay to be identified. He heard someone yelling, shouting, pounding the wall . . . before realising it was him.

Then later, family and friends materialising by his side, thinking, acting for him, making the phone calls he couldn't contemplate, telling her parents, his own. Feeling he was walking through a living nightmare, wanting to get out of there, into his car and drive home and find none of this was happening. Then, finally, remembering the other reason he was there, the sole reason he couldn't fall apart: Sean. When they brought him to see Sean, when he realised his beautiful, innocent boy would have to go through this nightmare too, Dan had found the strength to hold on.

He tried to focus now on the papers in front of him, but it was proving impossible. Sometimes he thought he was learning to live again, spending time here in Ballyanna was healing, and since he'd met Annie he'd been feeling stronger, hopeful even, but then, right out of nowhere, the memories would ambush him, firing him right back to his own personal ground zero. He looked out the window, at the bright moon hanging over the bay. And suddenly he needed air, he needed to get out of there . . . to walk for however long it took. So he set off into the night.

* * *

It was another calm night, apart from a bank of cloud to the west, but the moon was clear and a carpet of stars winked overhead. The tide was in, leaving a narrow stretch of strand to walk as he reached the beach. For the odd hours he is keeping these days, Barry is surprised to discover he is not alone. He looks up, curious, at the tall figure who walks, head down, in his direction. As the man approaches, Barry recognises him. He has seen him once or twice before in the village, but they have never met. Now they are almost face to face.

'Grand night,' Barry greets him.

'It certainly is.' Dan stops.

Barry extends a hand. 'Barry McLaughlin.'

'Dan O'Connell.' Dan shakes his hand, his grip firm.

'Ah yes, I think I know who you are.'

'That seems to be the way around here,' Dan says with a smile.

'And I'm very sorry for your loss.'

'Thank you, I appreciate it.'

'How's your boy doing?'

'As well as can be expected. I think the change of scene is doing him good, though. He seems to be handling it well.'

'Mind if I walk with you for a bit?'

'Be my guest.' Dan falls into step beside him.

'And you?' Barry says. 'How are you managing, Dan?'

'Work keeps me busy, focused . . .'

'But you're not sleeping? The nights can be brutal.'

'You said it.'

Barry nods, looking up at the sky. 'Sometimes it's better not to try to make sense of it all – the chaos, the pain.'

'One day at a time, right?'

'I'm a priest, Dan, but I'm not going to spout any perceived wisdom at you. Let's just say I know a thing or two about grief. And I won't presume to tell you how to handle yours because the only thing we can say about grief with any real certainty is that it's entirely personal.'

Dan smiles ruefully. 'I'm finding that out the hard way.'

'There is something I've found over the years, though, Dan, that you may or may not find helpful . . .'

'I'd be happy to hear it.'

'Well, in my experience it's not always a case of letting go of your grief, sometimes it's about forcing it to let go of you, breaking the stranglehold, so to speak – even though it's entirely natural to feel you're betraying the one you love by doing that. It doesn't do to live in grief, Dan, eventually, if you allow it, it will consume everything good in your life. Sometimes you have to work to set yourself free of it.'

Dan is quiet for a minute as they walk along.

'I hope I haven't said too much, been too blunt?' Barry is concerned.

'On the contrary, Father, what you've just said makes a lot of sense to me right now. Thank you, I appreciate your honesty.'

'Barry will do, no need for formality now we've been introduced.'

'Thank you, Barry,' Dan says. 'I hadn't looked at it that way before.'

'Well now, maybe that's why you came over here,' Barry says, smiling at him. 'To see your world from a different perspective.'

'Maybe so.'

'Well, this is where I take my leave of you, I'm heading back towards the lake. I was glad to have a bit of company on my walk and I enjoyed our little chat.'

'You and me both. So long, Barry.'

'God bless, Dan.'

Pat

I've been hanging around a bit in Gracie's house, because after the barbecue I had a feeling things might be uncomfortable there. Just as I suspected, things are not cool with Gracie's family. I'm starting to understand Gracie more now and I feel kind of sorry for her. All that stupid make-believe stuff playing house with Sean and all – well, it's beginning to make sense to me now.

The evening before last, there was a really big fight. Her mom and dad are still hardly speaking to each other. It was pretty rough.

It all started when Gracie's dad, John, didn't show for dinner. He was playing golf, and Gracie's mom tried to call him on his mobile, but it kept going to voicemail. Eventually she called Gracie to the table because the roast chicken was going to be ruined, so they had to start without him. Gracie looked worried and asked her mom if she was going to keep a warm plate for her dad in the oven so he could eat later. But Dee looked at her like she was stupid and said, 'He can starve for all I care.'

Gracie looked as if she wanted to cry, but was afraid to. So they ate the chicken, which looked really good, by the way, but Dee was all on edge and kept checking her watch and looking out the window.

'Not so much as a courtesy call,' she said. 'Not even a text.'

'Maybe he forgot his phone,' said Gracie. 'Will I run up to the golf club and see if I can find him?' She looked really anxious.

'You will do no such thing,' Dee said, in a really harsh voice. Every time her mother spoke, Gracie seemed to look a little smaller.

So they finished dinner, although Gracie didn't eat all of hers. She was chewing her nails instead, which really seemed to irritate her mom.

'Gracie!' she said. 'How many times do I have to tell you not to bite your nails?'

'Sorry,' mumbled Gracie.

'It's a filthy habit. A girl should never put her hands anywhere near her mouth, never mind *in* it. It's disgusting. I don't know where you picked it up.'

So Gracie started pulling at her hair, curling a piece of it round and round her finger, and then started to chew the ends of it. It's like she doesn't even know she's doing it.

'*Gracie!*'

Gracie jumped when her mom yelled at her, and then sat on her hands. Her face got really red and she was chewing the inside of her cheek.

'I'll help you clear the table, Mam.' I could see she was trying to make it up to her mom, and I couldn't help feeling sorry for her.

'Leave it,' her mom said.

'But we—'

'I *said*, leave it.'

Gracie got quiet and followed her mom into the sunroom, where the TV is. Dee turned it on and sat down, but Gracie didn't watch the programme because she was too busy watching her mom.

Then I heard a car pull up outside and I saw John, the asshole, get out. The car drove off and he waved after it. He looked kind of unsteady. Then, before he could get his key in the door, Gracie was up and out of her seat to run and let him in.

'Mam, Mam.' Gracie ran back into the sunroom. 'Dad's back. His phone ran down, he forgot to charge it. Wasn't that why you didn't call, Dad?'

'Yes, that was it exactly,' John said, following her into the room. He was grinning, his eyes were bright, but they weren't smiling. He looked at Gracie's mom and said, 'I don't suppose you kept any dinner for me?'

She laughed then, so I guess she thought that was funny, but she was looking at the TV, not at him, and her face was mean. 'What do you think? You don't even bother to call. Run out of excuses, have we? What was her name *this* time?'

'I met a few of the lads, after the game, it went on longer than I thought.'

'Oh, and none of them had a functioning phone?'

'I lost track of time, it's no big deal. Don't start.' He sat down. 'I'm here now. Gracie, be a pet and make daddy a nice sandwich and—'

'—and I'll bring you a beer as well,' she said, all breathless, trying to be the perfect kid. I could have told her that never works. She ran off to the kitchen and there was the sound of cutlery and plates clinking.

I stayed put in the sunroom, watching. Her parents looked like two people who hated each other, not two people who are married.

'Actually,' her dad said then, 'if you must know, I ran into Seamus Quirke at the club, which was a bit of good luck. There are some papers you need to sign, Dee, just routine stuff, company transfers. Anyway, Seamus was able to run his eye over it all and said it's grand. Here.' He put some papers down in front of her. 'You might as well do it now. Look, underneath every paragraph marked with an X, that's where your signature needs to go.'

Dee took the pen and looked at the papers. 'How is Seamus?'

'He's in great form, he was asking particularly for you . . . said he and Angela must have us over for dinner one of these days.'

'Is that right?'

'That's what he said to me.'

'At the club?'

'Yes, Dee, at the club.'

'Well, he must have the gift of bilocation so, because Seamus and Angela are in Barcelona for the weekend. I met her the day before yesterday, and she was looking forward to it. An anniversary surprise. Would you like me to ring her to confirm that? I can do it right now.' Dee held up her phone.

John didn't say anything then, but his face went bright red.

'If you think I'm stupid enough to put my name to anything you wave under my nose, you've got another thing coming. I'll get my own lawyer, thank you very much, and nothing gets signed without his say-so. Annie might lecture for Ireland, but she was right about you. She warned me you'd come back here looking for me to sign stuff. I can't believe she was right.'

'Here you are, Dad.' Gracie was back with a sandwich and a beer, but she picked up the tension in the room straightaway. 'What's wrong?' She looked at her mom, who wouldn't meet her eyes. 'Dad's back now, everything's alright, isn't it?'

'Thanks, darling,' said her dad, taking the plate and glass of beer. 'You're a good girl, Gracie.'

'What's the matter? You're not fighting, are you?'

'Your mother's just tired, Gracie. Everything's grand.'

'Oh, that's right. Blame me, why don't you?' Dee shook her head like she couldn't believe him.

'Blame you for what?' asked Gracie, looking scared.

'Nothing, nobody's blaming anyone for anything.'

'Of course they're not. It's just a strange coincidence that the fraud squad have taken a sudden interest in your father, but of course that couldn't possibly be *your* fault, could it, John?'

There's a long moment of silence, then her dad said, 'Go to your room, Gracie.'

'But—'

'Go to your room. Now. It's almost your bedtime anyway.'

'No it's not, and I don't want to—'

'Do what your father says, Gracie. We need to talk.' Her mom was real sharp.

'But what's wrong? I thought you'd fixed everything. Everything was alright yesterday.'

'For Christ's sake, girl, do what your mother tells you!'

'You're going to fight, aren't you? That's what you always do when you say you need to talk. *Please* don't fight, it's been so nice . . .'

'Dee, for God's sake . . .'

'Gracie!' her mom yelled. 'Do as you're told. *Now!*'

Gracie's face began to crumple and her mouth was wobbling so much she could hardly get the words out.

'Fine! Fight all you like! See if I care. And I know you will, because that's the only time you agree about anything – when you send me to my room!' Then she ran upstairs.

Now I was torn. Part of me wanted to go after Gracie, because I know what it's like to feel cut off from the action, believe me. Our parents used to fight too, I guess all parents do, but it wasn't ever like this. They yelled at each other, sure, and sometimes a door might get slammed, or Mom would hang up the phone on Dad, she was good at that, but their arguments were over quickly and it nearly always ended with Dad making Mom laugh. Then we'd all laugh. So part of me wanted to follow Gracie, but the other part of me wanted to stay and see what happened, because it was kind of like the quiet scene in a movie before the bad stuff happens.

'You had to bring it up, didn't you? I was wondering how long you'd wait, but you couldn't, could you? Not even until your own daughter was out of the room. You'd rather turn her against me at any cost than protect her, huh? Some mother you are.'

'You're unbelievable,' Dee said. 'You have the nerve to come in here so drunk you think I'll fall for your stupid lies and—'

'Drunk? That's rich coming from you! I've had a few drinks, sure, a few pints with the lads after a game of golf, and why not? But you! You must think I'm awful stupid, Dee, if you think I don't know you're on the sauce yourself.'

Dee's face went white. 'I'm on anti-depressants, John. I have to take them, the doctor prescribed them . . . I . . .'

'Oh, God.' John groaned. 'Spare me the nervous troubles speech and the list of medications. I've seen the bottles, Dee. You're not as fastidious about getting rid of them as you used to be, and even a contortionist would run out of hiding places sooner or later. I've seen them all, Dee, even the ones you keep in your handbag, you'd want to be careful about those.' He laughed then, but it sounded mean. 'So you might want to rethink the pills, they're making you careless, even an old pro like you.'

For a moment I thought she might hit him. But then she began to cry.

'Is it any wonder I have to drink? Well, is it?'

'Oh, no, please . . . not the self-pity speech.'

'Look what you've done to me! Look what you've done to this family! You've destroyed us! If it wasn't for my parents, we'd be out on the street. And all you can think about is playing golf!'

'What else am I supposed to do? Sit at home and watch my wife drink herself into oblivion? In case you haven't noticed, Dee, my career opportunities are a bit limited just now.'

'Oh, and whose fault is that?'

'I was set up! You know I was! And what's more, you wanted it as much as I did – more, if the truth be told. Nothing was enough for you. Bigger, better, faster, richer – excess should be your middle name.'

'You're blaming me? For your . . . your criminal activity!'

'Innocent until proven guilty, my darling wife. Isn't that what the law says? You know, I *chose* you, I married you because I stupidly thought you were different. I thought you weren't like all the other greedy, gold-digging women in the company I was keeping back in those days. You seemed like a breath of fresh air. I thought you were a sweet, smart, pretty Kerry girl with her head screwed on and a great sense of humour.' He shook his head. 'I'll give you one thing, it was a great performance, flawless. I bought it hook, line and sinker. Until bit by bit the mask slipped, and you turned out to be greedier than any of them!'

The way he was looking at her then, I'd have run from the room if I were her. I was scared something really bad was going to happen, then what would I do?

'And you have the nerve to call *me* a fraud? You know what you are, Dee? You're lazy, and grasping, and when that doesn't work for you, you're cowardly and self-pitying. You're your father's daughter through and through. How I didn't spot it before quite frankly astounds me.'

'You cheap, lousy bas—'

'And before you ram it down my throat again about how good your parents are to loan us this cottage, don't think they're doing it for you, Dee, for their poor, deceived, put upon, long-suffering daughter. No, they're doing it for Gracie, your daughter, when you remember you have one.'

'What did you say?'

'You heard me, and you know perfectly well what I mean, so does most of the village by all accounts. It's well known Gracie would prefer to stay with her aunt or grandparents than with her own mother. Can't say I blame her either.'

'That's a vile thing to say!'

'But it's true, isn't it?'

'You wouldn't know what's true if it hit you in the face! You're nothing but a liar and a thief. A cheap, common thief. Why does that not surprise me? And you wonder why I drink?'

John came closer to Dee, until he was right in her face, his hands clenched in fists by his sides.

'Go on, hit me!' she said. 'That's about the only thing that'll make you feel like the big, self-important financier you want to be instead of the cheap loser you are.'

'Oh, you'd like that, wouldn't you?' he said. 'Give you a chance to run crying to Mummy and Daddy and anyone who'll listen, call the guards, *poor me, poor me, my husband hits me, my husband makes me drink*. Lie all you like, Dee, I don't care if you drink. I don't care *why* you drink. You can drink yourself to death for all I care. You make me *sick*!'

I'd heard enough. I didn't understand what they were fighting about, but it was mean and nasty and they were taking things to a whole other level.

I decided to go up to check on Gracie, so I left her parents still yelling at each other. Gracie wasn't in her room, though. She was sitting at the bottom of the next flight of stairs, hidden from below. And she was crying really hard, hiccupping so she could hardly catch her breath. She had heard every word.

Just then a door slammed, and Gracie ran into her room. I followed her. She jumped into bed, pulling the covers over her head. I heard footsteps come up the stairs, but whoever it was didn't stop to check on Gracie, they just kept on going and then another door slammed. I sat with Gracie for a while then. I felt really bad for her. There wasn't anything I could do, but I stayed anyway.

Sean

I'm in the cable station with Dad while he's working. I'm looking at one of the books all about the laying of the first cable, called *Thread Across The Ocean*, which I think is a really nice name.

I'm pretending to read it, but really I'm watching Dad. I like looking at him when he's on his own, when things are quiet. I like noticing things about him I've forgotten, and new things I haven't seen before. Like the new lines around his eyes, and the way his face is thinner now since the accident. His face still creases the same way when he smiles, though, and his mouth lifts up more on one side than the other. Me and Pat have that, too. Mom used to call it *the O'Connell killer smile*. She said it gave us an unfair advantage before we ever even opened our mouths to ask for something.

I guess he feels my eyes on him, because he looks up suddenly and smiles. 'You okay there, buddy?'

I nod.

'Listen to this,' he says. 'Thirty-five billion pieces of content are shared on Facebook every month . . . more than ninety-five million tweets are tweeted every day . . . and more than seven trillion – a trillion is a thousand billion, Sean – text messages are sent per year. That's forty thousand messages sent every second of every day. Can you believe that?'

I shrug.

'It's mind-blowing when you think about it. Every two days, we now create as much information as we did in the previous twenty thousand years.' He shakes his head. 'If people only knew how incredible that is, and it all started with the telegraph.'

I guess they will know soon, whether they want to or not, because that's what Dad's documentary is all about, the history of communications. That's why he's doing the bit about the underwater cable here. Dad goes back to his reading so I can watch him again. It's weird that it's just him and me now. I guess Pat doesn't really count if Dad doesn't want to know about him. Sometimes I wish Pat had lived instead of me, because he and Dad were really tight. I think that might have been easier for Dad.

I hope Dad knows how much I love him. I can't tell him anymore, but he's a great dad – the best. But there's stuff he doesn't know. Stuff I've never told him, or anyone, stuff I can't ever say. That's why Dad doesn't know the whole story of what happened the day Mom and Pat died. It's like this horrible secret I have to keep all to myself.

After I made the scene that day at the barbecue with Frank, and Mom decided to take us back to Dad's house, like Pat suggested, I was really pleased. I just wanted to go home, to Dad, and get out of that place with Frank hanging around. I mean, it was *weird*. Anyway, I finally went upstairs to get my stuff. Pat had packed already, so he went outside to hang with a neighbour's kid we knew from school. Mom was downstairs, clearing the table and putting plates in the dishwasher with Frank. Or so I thought. I was just grabbing stuff and shoving it into my backpack when the door opened softly. I thought it was Pat, or Mom, coming up to see if I was okay, but it wasn't. It was Frank. He closed the door behind him and walked over to the window and looked out. Then he turned around to face me.

'Sean,' he said, 'we need to have a little talk, you and me.'

I was rooted to the spot and trapped. And even though I was in Mom's house and Pat was around, I was scared. There was something about the way he was looking at me, the way that he smiled but his eyes didn't, and his voice was different, slower, kind of like when our school principal, Mr Labrowski, is mad about something and comes into our classroom, then talks very slowly, like he wants you to really listen to every word.

'Sit down, Sean. I need you to listen to me.'

I sank onto the bottom bunk and looked up at him.

'I know it's hard for you and Pat to have your parents divorce, nobody enjoys that. But it happens, unfortunately, and when it does, people have to move on. By moving on, I mean moms and dads make new lives, and those lives include other people, new friends, and sometimes they even get married to those new friends and make new families.'

I swallowed, hard.

'Now here's the thing. I really love your mom, I mean *really*. I have done for quite some time. She's exactly the woman I have always wanted and I've invested a lot of time and work in getting our friendship to this stage. So you see, Sean, I am not about to let *anyone*, least of all a spoilt little mommy's boy, mess it all up for me. I am a decent, hardworking man. I will be a good husband, in time, to your mother, and I will be a firm, but generous, stepfather to you and Pat. But if you ever again – and I mean *ever* – pull a stunt like you just did downstairs, then I won't be responsible for what I will do to you. Do you understand me?'

I nodded, even though I didn't want to, even though I could feel my mouth going dry and my bottom lip starting to wobble.

'When I was your age, I was already holding down two summer

jobs. My daughter, Sheryl, who's only a few years older than you, is already learning how to invest in stocks on the internet. I'm a totally self-made man, and a rich one, and I'm very proud of that. But what I say goes, you got that, kiddo?'

I nodded again, although I hated myself for it. What else could I do?

'Good. Your brother Pat seems like a sensible kid, you should try to be more like him.'

Direct hit. But the best was yet to come . . .

'Oh, and by the way, if you tell your mother anything about this conversation, I will deny every word of it. I will tell her you're lying because you don't want her to be happy with me. And you know what, Sean? She'll believe *me*, not you.

'So if I were you, Sean, I would remember what I have told you, but forget this conversation ever took place, hmm? It'll be our little secret, a man-to-man chat. We can be friends now. And we'll all get along just fine now the air has been cleared. I know you're a good boy, Sean, I know you want your mom to be happy, don't you? Because only a really mean kid would stand in the way of his mom's happiness.'

He stood looking at me for a few moments, then went out the door and closed it as quietly as he had come in.

I don't know how long I sat there, on the bottom bunk, not moving. I think I was in shock. But I wasn't scared anymore. I probably should have been, but I wasn't. Because somewhere inside, I knew I was right about not liking Frank, and this just proved it. But there was something else going on, too. My breathing was getting faster again, and my heart was pumping. It felt like I should be scared, but I was . . . angry. I was beyond angry, and he, Frank, was wrong. He was wrong about everything! Well, except one thing, that I was a mommy's boy. I was, and I didn't care who knew it! I loved Mom probably more than anyone in the whole world. I know you're not supposed to prefer one parent over another, and I don't, or didn't . . . not really . . . but Mom and I were really close. It makes me cry just thinking about that now. And she *did* love me, I mean us, Pat and me, more than anything in the world. Even Dad said that, and Dad *never* lies. And because of that, I knew I could trust her.

So when Mom came upstairs to see if we were ready to go and found Pat with his bag packed but me still sitting on the bed, she wanted to know what was wrong. I told her. And if Frank thought what happened at the table was 'pulling a stunt', then he didn't know much about Pat and me, or about kids in general. I mean, what? Did he think I was stupid?

'What's going on? Why aren't you packed, Sean?' And she's looking from me to Pat, while I start to cry so hard I can hardly breathe.

'Sean, honey, what is it?' She's by my side in an instant, sitting on the bed, her arms around me, rocking me, stroking my hair, kissing my head. 'It's okay, baby, we're going back to Daddy's now. I promised you, and we're going right now, honey.'

She looks at Pat, who knows all about what happened, because I've already told him.

'Frank threatened him, Mom,' he said.

'What?' She looks confused, like she's heard him wrong.

I cry even harder. 'He s-s-said h-he'd k-k-kill me if I t-t-told y-you, uh-uh-or P-Pat.'

'What?' Now she looks like we told her aliens just landed in the backyard.

'It's true,' said Pat. 'He told Sean if he ever pulled a stunt like he did downstairs again, that he'd do something terrible to him. And that if he told you or anyone what he'd said, he'd deny it, and that no one would believe Sean over him. It's true, Mom.'

I watched Mom's face carefully, while she looked at Pat and he looked directly back at her. I felt her arms tighten just a little bit more around me. Her face got kind of tight, and she opened her mouth as if she was going to say something and then just took a breath, and another one, then she let me go and rubbed her hands over her face. She shook her head and then got up and turned to look at me.

'Is this true, Sean? Was Frank mean to you? You need to be really, *really* honest with me, boys. No tricks, no funny stuff, this is really, *really* important.'

I stopped crying for a moment, and looked at her. 'He was really mean to me, Mom.' And that was all it took.

'Okay, okay.' She ran her hands through her hair and paced over to the window, then she turned around and rubbed her mouth. 'Pat, honey,' she said. 'Go downstairs and tell Frank we'll be down in a few minutes, that I'm just getting your things ready.'

'Okay, Mom.' And Pat went downstairs.

Mom knelt down beside me. 'Sean, honey, you know you can tell me anything? Anything at all in the world, don't you?'

'Sure, Mom.'

'Good, that's good.' She looked relieved. 'I'm going to ask you something really important and I want you to be absolutely honest.'

I nodded.

'Would you like it if we could all go back and live with Daddy?'

For a moment I thought I'd heard wrong. *Go back and live with Daddy . . .?*

'All of us?' I said. 'You as well?'

'Yes, baby, all of us, together again, just like it was before.'

'What about Frank?'

She bit her lip. 'I made a mistake, Sean. A really, big, stupid mistake.' She looked as if she was going to cry. 'I know that now. I've been wondering about it for a while, but today just confirmed it. I miss Daddy. I've missed him from the very beginning, but I was too stubborn and ... and ... stupid to admit it. I miss how we were as a family. And I'm really, *really* sorry I messed up, honey, but if Daddy will talk to me, listen to me, maybe he'll understand, and maybe he'll forgive me, and we can start over again, all of us.' She wiped her nose with her sleeve.

'Of course he'll listen to you, Mom,' I told her. 'He always listens to you. He loves you.'

'I know, baby. I know that now.'

Then I felt bad because now she was crying. 'Don't cry, Mom. I didn't mean to make you cry.'

'Oh, you didn't, sweetie.' She sniffs again, and rubs her hands over her face. 'I did it all by myself.'

'Mary?' Frank's voice calls from down below, and then we hear his footsteps coming up the stairs.

I looked towards the door. 'Mom?'

'It's alright, baby, don't worry.' Then she called back to him, 'We'll be with you in a moment, Frank, just give us a second.'

But he didn't. The footsteps kept coming and then the door opened, and Frank stuck his head around.'

'Hey, buddy,' he said, looking at me all innocent and smiling. Then to Mom he said, 'Everything okay? I thought you'd be ready by now.'

'We are,' Mom said. 'Can you just give us a minute?' She looked at him.

'Honey?' he said, coming in through the door now. 'You're upset. What's the matter? Have you been crying?'

'Nothing. I just need a minute with Sean, we'll be down in just a moment ... please?' She sounded impatient.

'Hey.' He came over and got down on his hunkers beside us, acting all concerned. 'I don't like to see my best girl unhappy, or you little guy.' He ruffled my hair and I pulled back and pressed back into Mom.

'Please, Frank. Can you just give us a minute?' Now she was getting mad.

So he stood up, and looked at her, and then at me, then held up his hands. 'Okay, sure thing. I'll be waiting downstairs. I just hate seeing you upset, baby.' He shook his head like he had no clue what was going on.

When he was gone and the door was closed again, Mom put her finger to her lips, in case he was listening outside, I guess.

'Not a word,' she whispered. 'Okay?'

I nodded.

'Not until we get to Dad's.'

I nodded again, then jumped, we both did, as the door opened again, but this time it was just Pat. 'I'm sorry, Mom,' he said. 'I told him you were coming down, that he didn't have to go up to you, but he wouldn't listen.'

He looked at me. 'You okay?'

'Sure,' I said happily. He looked at me and shook his head like I was crazy.

Boy, was he in for a surprise . . . but I couldn't say anything now. Not yet.

We never made it to Dad's, of course, and Mom never got to tell him she'd made a mistake, that she missed him, that she wanted us all back together again as a family. And it's all *my* fault. Now Mom and Pat are dead. Dad doesn't know anything, and I can't tell him. I can't tell him because when I go to talk and open my mouth, the words won't come. I know, I've tried lots of times. I tried to write it down too, but that was even worse. None of the words looked right.

I mean, how do you try to explain that you ruined perfect? That's what I did. If I hadn't had my meltdown that day, we would never have got in the car, and Mom would have had the chance to tell Dad she'd made a mistake, that she still loved him, that she wanted us to be back together again as a family. How do I say that it's my fault she and Pat died? How do I tell Dad that for fifteen months I haven't told him that she did love him, right to the end?

Dad thinks everything was broken, because of the divorce and all. And I ruined the only chance we had to fix it, the chance to be the family we always were. The truth is, I ruined perfect. There are no right words to say that.

* * *

Annie wakes to birdsong, and an unaccustomed feeling of content. Listening for the voice of common sense to begin its litany of caution, she finds it obligingly silent, and instead sifts through the details of her evening with Dan, much as if she were examining the contents of a long-forgotten trunk of memories, reliving each one with delight . . . and not a little surprise.

She gets up, pulls on her robe, goes to the window to look out − and that is when her reverie is rudely interrupted. Across the way, where Dee's cottage sits on the horseshoe curve of the development, she sees John marching to and from his car, grimly loading it up, while Gracie, clearly distraught, trails behind him, pleading with him not to go.

Without a second thought, Annie runs out her door, and across to the unfolding scene. 'What's going on?'

'Please, Annie,' Gracie says, clutching at her arm. 'Tell him not to go. *Please,* Dad. Mam doesn't have to get a lawyer, she didn't mean it. Please don't go . . . *please* . . . just come back inside . . .'

Annie is upset by Gracie's distress, she's never seen her like this before. 'Gracie, where's your mum?'

'Inside.' She sobs, making a grab for one of her father's bags, trying to pull it back out of the boot.

Annie takes her by the shoulders, bends down to look her in the eye. 'Listen sweetheart, you go in and put on the kettle and we'll all have a cup of tea and sort this out.'

Gracie throws a tear-stained glance in her father's direction, then looks back at Annie, wondering if she can trust this new proposition. Reluctantly, she goes back inside the cottage.

Annie steps in front of John. 'What the hell is going on?'

'Why don't you ask your lush of a sister?'

'I'm asking you, you moron. Can't you see Gracie's distraught?'

'Here we go, Wonder Woman Annie to the rescue.' He glares at her. 'Well you're too late on this account. And you're as much to blame as anyone. Telling your sister not to sign anything was the worst advice you could have given her, but you'll all find that out the hard way. I'm out of here. Good riddance to the lot of you and your crazy excuse of a family.'

'What is wrong with you both?' Annie says, anger coursing through her veins. 'I won't have you harming Gracie.'

'Don't bother your head about that, Annie. I'll be coming back for Gracie. Your sister's an unfit mother, and my parents will be only delighted to look after Gracie.' With that, he gets into the car, slams the door, and screeches off in a spray of gravel.

Annie follows Gracie into the cottage, where Dee is sitting at the kitchen table filling a tumbler glass with wine. She is fully dressed, but dishevelled, and Annie takes a moment to work out she has not been to bed. Dee stares into space, does not react to Annie coming in, or to Gracie, who plucks her mother by the sleeve repeatedly and says, 'Mammy, tell Daddy to come back. Ring him. Here's your phone. Mammy, please, say something . . . you're scaring me.'

'It's okay, sweetheart.' Annie goes to her, and gently breaks

Gracie's grip on Dee. 'Don't worry. Mummy's not well, but we're going to get her help. Now I want you to listen to me, Gracie. You need to trust me. I want you to go to Sean's house for a while, okay?' The little girl is crying now, but she nods. Annie dials Dan's number, and he picks up on the first ring.

'Hi Dan, it's me.' Annie speaks quietly, so Gracie won't hear. 'I'm at Dee's. There's been some trouble. Can you come to the cottage and take Gracie?'

Dan tells her he's on his way, then Annie rings her mother. 'I'm in Dee's. You need to get over here, Mum. Now.'

Annie takes a deep breath and turns back to her niece.

'Gracie, honey, how long has Mum been sitting like this?'

'They were fighting last night, quite late, then when I woke up this morning I heard doors slamming, and I ran down and Daddy was packing his stuff in the car, and Mam was just sitting here ... like this.'

Dan arrives first. 'Hey, guys.' He takes in the situation and acts as if it's completely normal to walk in and see a catatonic woman drinking alcohol at eight-thirty in the morning. He hunkers down in front of Gracie. 'Sean's out in the car, Gracie. He'd really like if you would come to our house for a while and hang out with him. Would that be okay?'

Gracie looks at Annie, and then at her mother. 'What's going to happen with Mam?'

'We're going to call Doctor Mike to come see her and he'll make sure she gets better. Sweetheart, I promise you, we'll take care of her. Now I think you should go to Sean's house, just for a while, okay? And I'll come and collect you later on.'

Gracie nods, but she doesn't look convinced. She raises pleading eyes to Annie. 'Promise you'll come and get me?'

'You know I will. Cross my heart and hope to die.'

'Okay.'

Dan throws Annie a sympathetic look. 'I'll talk to you later,' he says. 'Take as long as you need.' Then he takes Gracie's hand and walks her out to the car.

Once Gracie is gone, Annie sits down beside her sister. 'Dee, look at me. What happened? *Dee*! What happened?'

Dee takes another swig of wine. 'What time is it?' She looks around her, then at Annie, and drawls, 'You're too late. You missed the show. You would have loved it.'

Annie slaps her sister's face, hard. 'Dee! You have to talk to me!'

Dee's hand goes to her face, she shakes her head and looks at Annie, bemused. 'There's no need for violence, Annie.' Her voice is thick, slurred.

'What have you taken?'

'What does it matter? I don't remember.'

'Oh, God!'

'You were right, by the way.' Dee raises her eyebrows. 'He wanted me to sign stuff.'

'Did you?'

'No. I don't think so. Even I'm not that stupid. And your wise words were ringing in my ears. John didn't take it well, as you can imagine. Where's Gracie?' She looks puzzled. 'She was here.'

'She's with Dan and Sean. She's fine.'

'What time is it?'

'About nine o'clock . . . never mind . . . Dee, what did you take . . . try and remember.'

'Wine, mostly . . . a few Xanax . . . maybe . . . I need to lie down.'

'No. You're not going anywhere. Here, drink some water.'

* * *

Breda's first thought when she rushes in through the open door of the cottage is that there has been an accident.

'What is it?' she cries. 'What's happened?' Her heart is in her throat.

She is followed by Conor, who thinks to shut the door behind him, and looks around the room.

'Where is he?' he shouts. 'Where is the fecker?'

'He's gone,' Dee says flatly.

'Where's Gracie?' Breda pales. 'He never . . . he didn't take her . . . did he?'

'Gracie's at Sean's house,' Annie says.

'Oh, thank God for that. Did she stay over? She didn't . . . she didn't see . . . she wasn't here for . . .' Breda looks from Dee to Annie, as the words turn to dust on her tongue.

'Of course she did.' Annie is scathing. 'She was here for all of it. Went to bed with them fighting, and came down to find her mother like this.'

'What's happened to her?' Conor peers at Dee. 'What's the matter with her?'

'What do you think?' Annie says. 'Pills . . . booze . . . sound familiar?'

'But her face?' Conor says, pointing at Dee. 'It's all red on one side . . . those marks . . . by God, if he hit her, if he laid a hand on her, I'll—'

'I hit her. I slapped her. She was out of it.'

Conor looks at Annie, confused. 'What are you doing in your dressing gown?'

'This has been going on all night. I woke up to see John packing up the car and Gracie distraught, begging him not to go. I came over straightaway.'

'And you hit your sister?' Conor looks at Annie as if she has sprouted horns. 'What did you do that for? She needs to sleep it off, that's all. Come on, we need to get her up to bed. C'mon, Dee, just get your legs under you, sweetheart.'

'She's not going anywhere, least of all to bed. If she passes out now, she may never wake up.'

'Annie's right.' Breda marvels that her voice is steady. 'We need to call Doctor Mike.'

'Relax, will you!' Conor says impatiently. 'Stop fussing, the pair of you! She's grand! We don't need any doctor in this house. She's just a bit worse for wear. She'll sleep it off and she'll be grand.'

At the mention of sleep, Dee collapses on the table, head on her forearms.

'Stop it!' Annie's voice is steel.

'Stop what?' Conor says, sounding indignant.

'Denying what's right in front of your eyes. Stop lying! I won't listen to it anymore. Look at her! *Look* at her! Dee is an addict! She is stoned out of her mind on booze and pills. She's been drinking for months . . . years, probably. She needs help, expert help, not putting to bed!'

'That bloody conman! It's all his fault! Is it any wonder she's been driven to this? It's abuse, that's what it is! Mental abuse!'

'No it's not! It's *your* fault!' Annie rounds on her father. 'You've been lying all your life and you've encouraged her to lie. You're pathetic! And now your stupid, selfish lies are destroying Gracie.'

'Annie.' Breda takes a step towards her. 'Please.'

'What? Don't say it? Protect him? Enable him? Like you do?' Annie is way beyond holding back the torrent she has kept inside for so long.

'You're an alcoholic, Dad. A destructive, selfish, deceitful alcoholic. You and your lies are destroying this family . . . just look around you!'

There is a split second of astonished silence as the words find their target – then pierce and splinter.

'How dare you!' Conor staggers backwards as if he's been hit.

'How *dare* you speak to me like that! Breda! Are you going to let her—'

'For once in your bloody life . . .' Annie's eyes narrow, '. . . tell the truth.'

'What are you talking about?' Conor's voice is shaking now, in the face of his daughter's rage.

'Tell them! Now! Or I will!'

'Annie, darling, calm down,' Breda pleads.

'What time is it?' Dee rouses herself from the tabletop and looks around, confused. 'What are you all doing here?'

'Hush, love, it's all right,' Breda soothes her.

'He has a son,' Annie says.

'Who's had a son?' Dee hiccups.

'Him! That man there, our father, has a son outside this family. I've seen him with my own eyes. Lie your way out of that one, Dad, why don't you?'

Breda thinks she might faint, but she forces herself to go on breathing, in and out, until she finds her voice.

'Annie, stop this now, love, please!'

'I'm sorry, Mum, I'm so sorry, but I can't stand these lies any longer. And you needed to know . . .' Tears are running down Annie's face.

Breda watches her daughter watching her for a reaction. She understands that Annie is expecting shock, histrionics, accusations. When that doesn't happen, Annie looks at her in confusion.

'Oh, my God . . .' She turns to look at Breda in slow-motion horror as understanding dawns. '*You knew.*'

'Yes, Annie,' Breda says quietly. 'I've always known.' She cannot look away from Annie's face, even as she is aware of her husband's equal astonishment. And that is how she sees, quite clearly, with the utterance of those five little words, the exact moment she loses her daughter.

'Why are you all here?' Dee wails. 'Why are you shouting?' She begins to cry softly. But Breda has underestimated her husband. Or perhaps overestimated him. Conor rallies in one last desperate attempt.

'She's lying! She's taken leave of her senses, Breda. Don't listen to her! It's not Dee who needs medical help, it's her!'

But Breda is tired now, the exhaustion of years weighing down upon her.

'Stop it, Conor. I know all about him. I always have. Don't humiliate yourself any more.'

'I ... I ... but *how?*' he stutters.

'Never mind that now.' Breda ignores Conor and goes to Dee, who is clearly unravelling.

'I don't know what's happening,' Dee says, wringing her hands and looking about her in panic. 'Annie, Mum, what's happening, where's Gracie? Help me, please ... oh God ... somebody *help me!*'

'Annie, I need you to call Doctor Mike. Now.'

In a daze, Annie picks up Dee's phone and scrolls through for the number and presses Call. She can't stop staring at her mother.

'It's alright, Dee, everything's going to be alright, love, I'm here. Mum's here with you, you're alright.'

When Doctor Mike arrives, Breda remembers, and discovers for herself, why everyone in the village and beyond says he is the kindest man – never mind doctor – on the planet. He asks a few pertinent questions, takes a quick look at Dee, takes her pulse, listens to her heart, then offers to drive her to the local hospital himself. She will need accompanying, of course, and Annie immediately insists she will travel in the car with her. Breda wants to go with them, but Annie throws her such a disdainful look when she suggests it, she almost recoils.

'I think you've managed quite enough for one morning,' she says, in clipped, tight tones.

And Dee, who is now quietly sobbing, is asking for her sister, not her mother. They seem so vulnerable to Breda then, her daughters, as she looks at them together in the back seat of the car – one crying, the other comforting her, yet radiating resentment and anger. They remind her suddenly of how they had been as little girls, confused and miserable after some imagined spat or argument, so easily remedied with a hug from their mother and the promise and procuring of some favourite bag of sweets or toy. Everything made better in an instant. But there would be no such easy remedy for the blow that has just torn apart her family. As she watches the car pull away, one question reverberates in her mind: how on earth did Annie find out?

Conor looks up as she comes back into the room that moments earlier was so charged, and now feels as if all the air has been sucked out of it.

'How did you know?' His voice is hoarse, he is slumped in a chair, his crutch beside him, head in his hands. He looks frail, and older now, much older.

Breda sits at the kitchen table and folds her hands in front of her. She wants to remain calm, in control, but her fingers are digging into her knuckles like knives.

'She wrote to me, the girl, all those years ago. She felt I had a right to know.'

'You never said.'

'No, I didn't. And that is a choice that I have regretted many times since. I ignored her letter. I hoped it would go away. And in a way it did. She telephoned me then, a couple of years later, to tell me she had met a man who loved her and her little boy and that he would be a far better father to her son than you had proved to be.'

'I offered—'

'I know what you offered. Money, no more.'

Conor is quiet, defeated.

'And after that, I never heard from her again. And God forgive me, I was grateful. I prayed every day that this dreadful situation would never come back and hurt my girls the way it had hurt me.' She laughs softly. 'Ridiculous, isn't it?'

'So . . . you're not angry?'

'No, Conor, I'm not angry. I'm too tired and numb to be angry.' She closes eyes that sting like nettles and rubs her face. 'What I want to know, though, is how Annie found out.'

'He came to see me, the boy. I didn't know it was him. He confronted me. Conor takes a shuddering breath. 'I had to take him somewhere private, where we wouldn't be disturbed, so I took him to my office. That was the . . . the weekend Annie, eh, called off her wedding. She came into the office . . . it was very unfortunate timing . . . she walked in on us . . . and before I had a chance to say anything, he told her who he was. It was cruel and heartless of him, but that's what he did. He just came out and told Annie he was her half-brother.'

Breda shakes her head. 'My poor, poor Annie.'

'She gave me no chance to talk to her . . . to explain . . . she was out the door and gone back to London before I could go after her. I thought she might have told you then.'

Breda winces. 'No. She never said a word. Only that you'd had a row. I assumed it was because of the wedding.'

'Well, that's how she found out. It was low of him to do that, I thought.'

'People lash out in all sorts of ways when they've been hurt.'

'So what are we going to do now?'

'I don't know what *you* are going to do, Conor. But I am going to do something I should have done years ago. I'm leaving you.'

Her husband's jaw sags. 'But you said you weren't—'

'I'm not angry, not anymore. But I am weary, heartsore and . . . and I'm deeply ashamed of myself. I'm ashamed of what I've condoned, of what I've allowed to happen in this marriage, and to our beautiful girls. And now to Gracie. That's just unforgivable.'

'Wh-where are you going?'

'I'm not going anywhere, Conor. Not just yet anyhow. But you are going to pack a bag and stay with your sister in Dublin, if she'll have you. Then we can sort things out properly, bit by bit . . . sell the hotel . . . divvy things up.'

Conor is visibly shocked. 'You can't be serious? You're not thinking straight, Breda. We've managed for over forty years, haven't we? And you knew all about it all along. So why this now?'

She gives a humourless laugh. 'Because I'm tired of *managing*, as you so rightly put it. I don't *want* to manage, I never did. I wanted to love, and be loved, and be part of a family that lived that love and went on to give it in turn to their own families. Instead of which I have raised one daughter unable to commit to any man and another who married her father, with the same disastrous consequences. But there is still Gracie. Annie is right about that. And I'm damned if this bloody awful mess is going to affect Gracie for one more minute.'

'But . . . but I *do* love you, Breda. I've always loved you, you know that. I would never have left you. The flings, the silly romances, they never meant anything. Sure, women were always chasing me, throwing themselves at me, but you were the only one. I always stayed, I always came back to you.'

'Only because I was foolish enough to take you back. Because you knew I'd always stand by you, look after you, turn a blind eye. Not anymore. I thought I was protecting my girls, instead I was . . . well, what does it matter now?'

Breda gets up heavily from the table.

'Where are you going?' Conor says, as if he's afraid she'll disappear into thin air.

'I'm going out. And I meant what I said, Conor. I want you gone when I come back. I don't care where you go. If you can't manage packing a few clothes together, get Dinny to help you. You have plenty of time to catch a flight to Dublin, or there's always the train. But tonight, I am sleeping in my bed on my own. And I'd like you to be as far away as possible for the foreseeable future.'

'But the girls ... Annie ... Dee ... I have to explain.'

'You should have thought of that a long time ago, Conor. Send them a letter, ring them, if you want. I'll talk to them, I'll explain, if they'll listen.' She moves towards the door. 'Goodbye, Conor.' Then she steps outside, into a strange new day.

* * *

She has been expecting an episode, but all the same, the banging on the door takes Jerry by surprise. She collects herself and opens it.

'Can I come in?'

'As if you need to ask! What is it, Breda? You look terrible.'

There is only one place Breda can think of going to, one place where she can tell all that has happened, be listened to and not judged. And she needs to talk. If she doesn't, she will go mad. She is running the scenes over and over in her head and each time they are more upsetting. She does not know if she will make sense and she doesn't care.

She sits down at Jerry's table and the tears come. Jerry says nothing, just holds her hand and lets her cry.

There is a movement at the door, and Barry comes into the room.

'Breda, what is it?' he says, his voice full of concern. He looks to Jerry, who just shakes her head. 'Will I go and leave you?'

'No.' Breda looks up through her tears. 'No, stay. I have a confession to make. You might as well hear what I have to say. My family is torn asunder, and it's all my fault.'

'What on earth are you talking about, Breda?' Jerry asks.

So she tells them. She spares no detail, does not attempt to exonerate herself in any way. Jerry and Barry listen, comfort her, and although she cannot hate herself any more than she does at that present moment, she finds, enveloped in the love and understanding of her two dear friends, some little kernel of faith to hold on to, a shred of belief that maybe, just maybe, what has happened is not the end of her world.

'So, I married and lived with an alcoholic . . . enabled his deceit, his destructive behaviour . . . refused to see what it was doing to my girls . . . and now Dee has repeated the pattern. She as good as married another version of her father in John. And Annie . . . oh, Jerry, if you'd seen the way she looked at me.' Breda shudders. 'And that poor boy, his . . . his son. I could have made Conor face up to it, insisted he be a father to him, included him in our family . . . instead . . .'

'Let's leave Conor's son out of it for a moment, Breda.' Barry is calm, his voice tender. 'From what you say, he's had a happy, secure upbringing and he had his mother, he didn't lose both parents, nor was he given away, abandoned. The man who brought him up loved and cherished him as if he were his own son. His parents were honest with him, he wasn't lied to, or duped. That makes an enormous difference in these situations.'

Breda sniffs, looks up at him.

'Annie, on the other hand, has been carrying a secret, just as you have, in order to protect you, and her father. She has been doing for you what you have been doing for your girls – staying silent out of love. That was the intention here, not deceit. It was protection. That's a heavy load for anyone to carry, Breda. It eats away at you. You know that better than anyone.'

Jerry agrees. 'Now it's all come out in the wash and it feels as if your whole world has been blown apart, but this is the beginning of healing, trust me.'

'What if my girls want nothing to do with me? I couldn't–'

'That won't happen, Breda, I promise,' Jerry says. 'But you do need to talk to Annie.'

'I don't know if she'll–'

'She will. She's had a shock now, a big one, but when she's had time to think she's going to want to talk to you, even if it's only to reproach you, or to find out the whole story. That will be your chance to put things straight, to be honest with her and tell her everything you've shared with us. It might take a bit of time, but when she's had a chance to digest it all, I know she'll understand things from your point of view. Annie's a kind girl, Breda, and she's strong, like her mother. She'll weather the storm, you all will, and you'll be stronger because of it.'

'What about poor Dee? I don't even know if she understood what was happening.'

'Dee will get the help she needs, Breda. Isn't that what you'd want for her? Then, when she's stronger, she can make the decisions she has to make. In the meantime, little Gracie has you and Annie.'

Breda is grateful for their words, but she is still in turmoil. Barry reaches over and puts his hand over hers.

'You're a good woman, Breda,' he says. 'A good mother. Possibly an overly understanding wife.'

She smiles at that.

'You did your best. Your girls will see that. You did what you did out of love. And that's what's going to matter in the end.'

* * *

Annie listens to the sounds around her – the shrieks of children playing in the sand, a dog barking at the water's edge – she looks around at the familiar scene she has witnessed a thousand times and wonders how the world can look and sound the same when for her it has shifted irrevocably on its axis.

Dan called around this morning, suggested taking her and Gracie to the beach, and now here they are. Gracie and Sean are playing with some kids by the shore, making what looks like a sand fortress, while she and Dan are sitting by the rocks. She has told him everything about the surreal scene yesterday, all about her half-brother, and he listened, nodded, prompted her occasionally, and seems not in the least surprised by any of it. He's possibly the most non-judgemental person she's ever met.

'Believe me,' he smiles ruefully, 'you don't have a monopoly on family drama. But from all you say, it sounds like the worst is over. The problems are out there now and at least they've been confronted, if not dealt with. That'll take time, but the main thing is no more secrets, no more denial. That's all good.'

'But she knew!' Annie shakes her head. 'Mum knew all along. I just can't get my head around it.'

'But your father didn't know she knew?'

Annie shakes her head. 'No. I thought he was going to collapse from the shock, not that I'd have cared.'

'You don't really mean that.'

'Don't I?'

'If you think about it,' Dan looks at her, 'your mom was only doing what you were doing, just for a lot longer.'

'What do you mean?' she says, frowning.

'You were both keeping the same secret and for the same reasons. You were doing it to protect your mom, and she was doing it to protect her family. That . . .' he nudges her gently, seeing her frown,

'. . . is an observation, not an accusation. But when you think of it, it's kind of ironic. Guess you and your mom are pretty much alike.'

Annie hasn't thought of it quite like that. She has been too shocked, too angry, feeling too duped. But now that she considers it, she sees that Dan is right. She and her mother have been doing exactly the same thing, in a manner of speaking.

'What about Dee?' Dan asks. 'How is she doing?'

'She had her stomach pumped and they kept her in overnight for observation. She's agreed to go straight to a rehab centre Doctor Mike recommended. I packed some things for her and Doctor Mike drove her there. He has been so unbelievably kind, that man.'

'You need to talk to your mom,' Dan says.

Annie sighs. 'I know I do . . . just . . . not today. I couldn't face it. I need a break from family drama.'

Thinking of drama, an image of Ed inexplicably pops into her mind. But for once, thinking of him is not accompanied by the usual sense of betrayal. Instead, Annie realises how his life was ruled by drama, as was hers, by association. Initially she had found it exciting, exhilarating, but as time wore on it became exhausting. Barbara was right, men like Ed were children at heart, and unruly ones at that. Annie had never shared her concerns with Ed because he didn't like dealing with other people's problems. He just wanted excitement and adrenalin rushes. She had never told him, either, about finding out about her half-brother, although as her partner at the time he should have been her most natural and obvious choice of confidant. And yet something had made her hold back from telling him. At the time she told herself it was too new, too raw, too private. Now she's able to acknowledge that she wouldn't have trusted him with the information. Not just because he might have been indiscreet with it, but because he would have turned it into even more of a drama than it already was.

'Let's go get some ice cream.' Dan pulls her to her feet. 'Things always look better after an ice cream.'

As they stroll to the old-fashioned van parked in the harbour, Annie is suddenly very grateful Dan has come into her life, for however brief a time. He has been there when she needed someone real, someone who could understand the curveballs life can throw at you and deal with them calmly and wisely, one by one. An unfamiliar feeling steals over her, that it's nice to feel someone is looking out for her, caring about her. Usually it is Annie taking care of everyone else.

When Dan reaches for her hand and smiles at her, Annie feels happier than she has in a long time, in spite of everything.

Pat

Gracie's mom has had to go to hospital. I'm not sure what's wrong with her, but I think she's going to be there for quite a while, a month, even, someone said, maybe longer. Gracie's dad has gone back to wherever he lives. I've heard people saying they're getting divorced.

It's tough for Gracie, so everybody's being really nice to her. Dad and Annie took her and Sean to the beach yesterday, and today Dad has to do some stuff so Declan has offered to take her and Sean water-skiing. They have a powerboat that belongs to the hotel, and although it's seen better days, it's still a good old workhorse, Declan says. Gracie's grandmother thinks it's a great idea, mainly because she wants to go see Gracie's mom in the hospital. So she'll be free to go, and she says the water-skiing will take Gracie's mind off things. So we're all driving over to a different beach for a picnic, and Declan is towing the boat. I'm going to tag along. I used to love water-skiing. I was way better than Sean.

When we get there, we drive over to the harbour side so we can get the boat into the water. Some of the other kids hanging around ask can they go along for the ride, and Declan says just two at a time, because he only has four life jackets.

Sean gets to ski first, because he's a guest, Declan says. So me, Gracie and the other two kids get in the boat.

After a lot of messing about, Declan is finally good to go, and Sean is in the water, holding on to the rope with his skis in position. Declan gives him the thumbs-up sign and guns the engine, and although he's a little shaky, Sean gets up first go. We do a few laps of the harbour, then head out into the bay, and Sean gets a good ten minutes before Gracie has her turn.

When she gets in, she's making a lot of fuss about jellyfish, but no one can see any, and she's got a dry suit on so I don't know what she's worried about, but she says they're always there lurking beneath the surface, just waiting to pounce.

It takes her three goes to get up, but finally she does, and she's concentrating really hard, like she's about to bust a gut. We're on our second lap around the harbour when Declan signals he's going to drive out into the bay again and gives Gracie the thumbs-up sign. She's looking nervous, but nods okay. I can tell she's scared, though, but doesn't want to act it in front of Sean, who waves at her.

We're heading east around the bay when it happens. The boat veers crazily, first to the right, then left, then flips over, throwing everyone out.

Gracie's okay, because she's behind skiing, so she just lets go. But she's spluttering and screaming because she's out there on her own, way back from us. The other two kids are okay, too, just shocked, but they come up hollering, and start swimming for shore. Declan is in trouble, though. He's dazed and waving weakly, but he's struggling, looking around him, trying to call for help but no one can hear him. Then he sees Sean and tries to get to him, but there's no way he's going to make it. Sean has his life jacket on, but he's not moving, and nobody's realised that yet except me, because I saw how his head clipped the side of the boat before he hit the water. He's unconscious. That's when I know I have to do something.

* * *

'Hey!' Dan looks up from his laptop and smiles as Annie comes in. 'Is it that time already?' He asked her to drop by the cable station so he could take her to lunch in Smuggler's.

'I'm early, but only just.' She wanders over to the shelves and pulls down a book.

'I'm almost done, just a couple more minutes, if you don't mind waiting?'

'Take your time, there's no rush.' She sits down, kicks off her flip-flops, puts her feet up on an old table and leafs through the book.

He finds his eyes straying from the screen in front of him to watch her, unobserved. She has filled out since he first met her, and it suits her. She looks healthy and rested and has developed a honey-coloured tan, which makes her eyes seem even greener. Her hair has grown out more and she wears it long and mostly loose, pushing it off her face regularly, or holding it back at the nape of her neck, as she does now, with one hand, as she turns the pages of the book on her lap. She looks . . . beautiful.

Damn! Why here? Why now? Why has he had to travel to the other side of a very large ocean . . . to another continent . . . to find the perfect woman? Because that's what Annie is to him. He suspected it, right from the first moment he set eyes on her, sitting on that rock looking out to sea, looking as if she belonged in another world, and in a way she does.

He thought, after everything he had been through, he would never feel this way again about a woman. Sure, he has needs, like any guy, but he was just too spent emotionally. It wasn't just the accident and the unbearable loss of his boy. The years of relentless worry and responsibility he'd accumulated with Mary had taken their toll. Constantly watching her, wondering if this week or next, or in a month's time, would be the day she changed. If she would stop taking her meds, or if they would simply stop working for her. At which point his beautiful, clever, loving wife would start slipping into the person who could turn their lives upside-down, who could do the unthinkable and not even be aware of it.

Being around Annie was like floating in a calm sea. He could lie back, relax, feel safe and supported. Dan didn't crave excitement or adventure, he'd had enough of that for several lifetimes. But he did long for calm, stability and humour. He had forgotten the last time he had laughed before he met Annie. Lately, despite his ongoing difficulties, he had been walking around with a goofy smile on his face, or that's how it felt anyway.

'What?'

Dan has been staring into space, out the window, out to the sea.

'Huh?'

'You're miles away.' She smiles, gets up and walks over to the window. 'You finished yet? I'm hungry.'

'Oh, sure.' He goes through the motions of shutting down his computer.

'It's a really good place to work here, isn't it? It's so peaceful.'

'I come here most days, just to write, for that exact reason.'

'You know, I've been thinking . . .' Annie says.

'Mmhm?'

'Well, it's just an idea, but it won't go away.'

'That usually means it's a good one.'

'It struck me that day we were out at the Skellig.' She leans on the table and pushes her hair behind her ear. 'Since they used it as a location for *Star Wars*, I believe there's been a lot of interest from production companies searching for locations in these parts.'

'I can see why,' Dan says, nodding. 'What are you thinking?'

'Well, there aren't any facilities, post-production facilities I mean, in the area.' She turns to look at him. 'My parents will more than likely be putting the hotel on the market at some point. And I was just thinking, it could be an interesting project.'

'It certainly makes sense,' Dan says, thinking it over. 'You know, you've got a lot of space there. You could maybe combine it with an upmarket creative retreat. The accommodation's already there, although you'd have to rework it, of course.'

'Yes! I could hire experts, give creative workshops, writing, screenplays, music, art . . .'

'The demand for that sort of thing is huge in the US at any rate. I have a lot of contacts in the field, maybe I could help, you know, put you in touch with some people. Your location is perfect, but it would be a big commitment, though.'

He walks to the window and looks out. He feels her hand on his arm as she comes to stand beside him.

'But it would be good, wouldn't it? Right time, right place, right gap in the market?'

'Yes, it would be good.' He looks down at the gleam in her eyes, the determined tilt of her chin, the animated expression. Then, very gently, he takes her face in his hands and bends to kiss her.

He pulls back, searching her face. 'I've been wanting to do that for a long time.'

She doesn't seem horrified or, worse, disappointed. It's just surprise that flickers briefly across her face. So he does it again, before either of them can think too much about it, and this time he pulls her close, and her arms wind around his neck, and the kiss goes on for quite a while . . . long enough for him to know that he would like to kiss her again, and often, enough to . . . *what was that damned noise?*

They're roused from their embrace by a sound both insistent and eerie.

'What *is* that?' Annie is puzzled, breathless.

Dan looks over her shoulder to the antique Morse key, which is now motoring away of its own accord, without any prompting. He feels the hairs on his arms standing up in cold dread. Not because of the unseen hand or force that is activating the old machine, but because of the message it is transmitting: three dots . . . three dashes . . . and three dots again, over and over . . .

'What the–?' Annie twists to look behind her in the direction of the sound.

'Shhh,' Dan says, overcome with a feeling of foreboding. 'That's an SOS code.'

At that exact moment, Annie's phone rings.

Sean

I don't feel it when I'm thrown from the boat, not physically. It happens so fast I don't have time to think. My last memory is Gracie yelling and waving from her skis . . . watching the wake spread out in a V of white foam behind her . . . and wondering why she's looking so panicked. Then the boat flips. I'm flung overboard, my head hits something, and everything goes dark.

The shock of the water makes me gasp. I come to, and I don't know which way is up, I don't know how I got here. The water is choking me and I'm going down, sinking. I've sucked in so much water I can't yell, but I remember I'm wearing my life jacket, so I thrash and kick, and reach for the surface. My head hurts and I can't think straight, but I don't want this to be the end. That's all I'm thinking: please, don't let me die.

But something is dragging me down, there's a heavy weight . . . something . . . it's Pat! He's come to help me. He's holding on to me, and he won't let go. He's looking into my eyes, like he's trying to tell me something, but I don't understand. My chest hurts. It feels like it's going to explode. The weight of the water is pressing down on me, harder and harder . . .

Please, don't let me die.

Pat

It feels so right. Finally, we're together again, just like we were from the start. Mom always told us that we were one egg in her tummy that split in two, and we stayed like that, together, holding on to one another, floating, just like we are now. It feels like home.

I can feel Sean's heartbeat, just like I could then, and it's like my heart is beating too. I remember everything now, right from the very beginning, how it was meant to be, Sean and me . . . forever. Except we got separated that day, when my neck broke, when Mom swam back down to get me out of the car and she tried and she tried, but she couldn't. When she realised she couldn't save me, she held on to me, held me close as could be to her as the dark water filled us up. That was love. And now I can give that love back to Sean. I can hold onto him. We're supposed to be together, anyway. He's so unhappy without me. It's all going to be okay if I can just hold on to him . . . if I can just hold on . . .

Sean

The water's so cold and I feel so weak. Pat is pulling me down, holding tight, not letting go, and I can't make him. I am going to die. My chest hurts so bad I just want it to be over. But then I think of Dad, and I have to try one more time. I have to make Pat let me go.

I wrench away from him, pulling against him, but we're locked in this – it might look like we're hugging, but it's a death struggle. He's pulling me down, I'm trying to pull away from him. I'm so tired, but I have to try. Dad! And inside I'm begging for help. *Anyone! My guardian angel! Help me! I don't want to die! I don't!*

I kick my legs as hard as I can and I push towards the surface, to the tiny slice of light I can see above my head. But Pat's caught hold of me again, and now he's going to win. There's nothing left. I have no breath.

The light changes. It shimmers, blurs, then suddenly sharpens, takes shape. And then I see her. It's Mom. I'm looking right at her. She's smiling, and she looks so beautiful. She reaches out to me, and then I understand, and I don't mind anymore, not as long as I can see her. I reach out to her and she takes my hands. I close my eyes. I let go . . .

But suddenly, I'm pulled upwards. My eyes fly open, and Mom's pulling me, up, up, towards the light. And now I understand I have to choose. Mom wants me to live, Pat wants me to go with him. Mom is holding my hands, willing me to be brave. And oh Pat, Pat, I'm so sorry. I'm so sorry, bro . . .

I find the strength to kick and I push away again. Mom keeps her hold on me and the light is getting closer. Closer. Then I'm free. My head breaks the surface, and although I can't see, the last thing I feel is sunlight on my face.

* * *

Barry is alone in the church, deep in prayer. Here more than anywhere, he can see his whole life flash before him. He remembers walking five long miles here as a child, to serve at mass, when the place was filled to capacity, a colourful collection of women in their Sunday best, anxious to show off a new winter coat, a handbag and matching shoes. Children were freshly scrubbed and fidgeting, and brand new babies gurgled in carrycots. The men were there too, straining against their too-tight collars, complete with ties and overcoats. And throughout the mass, if it was Sunday, the liturgy was accompanied by the muted drone from the back of the church where the oul' fellas gathered to chew the fat. But at least they had been there. Nowadays, during the week at any rate, the place was mostly empty, not even one votive candle flickered in the racks. Back then, the baptisms, communions, confirmations, weddings and funerals seemed to be constant – the sacramental rituals marking a person's path through life, from cradle to grave.

He had done his best, done all he could do, and now his own time was drawing to a close. He was at peace with that. The blood tests and his recent visit with Doctor Mike had confirmed what he already knew. The cancer had spread and there was nothing they could do for him now. He was ready to go. There was only one reason he was holding on, and he prayed he'd be given the grace to last a little longer, just to help the little fellow who was so lost and struggling. As if in answer to that very prayer, Barry closed his eyes and let the vision overtake him. He felt the struggle, the unforgiving prison of the water closing in, and then, miraculously, the breaking apart, the bid for freedom, then the light, blessed sunlight. Thank God! He breathed over and over. It was done. Over. But Pat would need him now more than ever. *I'm here,* he sent out, *I'm here, Pat, waiting for you, come to me, let me help you . . .*

* * *

Things can happen with surprising speed in a sleepy Irish village when the occasion warrants, and when word of the accident spreads, no stone is left unturned to help Dan.

Sean, they learn, has been picked up by the coastguard helicopter and taken to Kerry General, which by car is an hour and a half away. But thanks to Annie's quick thinking and calling the golf club, a helicopter has been made available – and within minutes they are landing at the hospital, Dan half crazed with terror.

Inside the hospital, the staff go about their business, unfazed by this latest episode in life or death, and Annie asks the questions Dan cannot even think to formulate. *The coastguard helicopter has just landed, yes,* they tell her, *there has been a boating incident . . . that's all we can say right now.*

Through a fog of terror, Dan is dimly aware of a choreography of seamless urgency unfolding before them. Medical personnel rush to the scene, jogging alongside a trolley, neck and neck with paramedics barking stats, who then retreat, their part in the fragile prolonging of life completed, the handover executed as smoothly and efficiently as a baton exchange.

And then he is hurtling down the corridor after them, shouting, frantic, pushing through personnel trying to restrain him.

'That's my boy!' he is shouting. 'You don't understand! That's my boy!'

Two men in scrubs hold him as he struggles to free himself. 'Please, sir!' they say. 'You need to be calm. We've got this. You have to let go now. You have to let us do our job.'

'We'll take good care of him,' a white-coated medic assures him.

Then the doors to the ER slam in his face.

A kind nurse brings them to the Family Room, where Dan sinks onto a chair and puts his head in his hands. He is aware of Annie sitting down beside him, he hears her concern, her quiet support, but is unable to respond. He is somewhere else, suspended between hell and unknowing. Sean's life hangs in the balance, and he is powerless to influence the outcome. Though he would willingly offer his own in exchange, either way, loss wins: a boy who lives but has lost his parents and twin brother; or a father who lives but walks in the shadow of the two boys he has loved more than life itself. He cannot think, he cannot pray, he cannot even bargain, cannot begin to contemplate the abyss of despair that yawns. He tries to hope but despairs, can only think how pitiful, how cruel it would be – given how much of a struggle Sean's last year has been – for it all to come to this . . .

An administrator joins them, sits, asks more questions – Sean's date of birth, blood type, known allergens. Dan is offered and refuses coffee. The clock keeps ticking on the wall above his head, but Dan is somewhere beyond time, waiting, dreading.

Sean

I'm in a really beautiful place, like nowhere I've ever been before. It's like a tropical island, except nicer, and there's a crystal waterfall pouring into a river of diamonds, and fish like I've never seen before swimming and jumping, like they're doing it just for fun. The trees and flowers are crazy, shapes and colours way better than home, like some awesome movie scene. I'm sitting on the grass, except it's not like ordinary grass, this grass sparkles and shimmers and moves beneath you. It feels like a really soft blanket. If you lay back on it, you could sleep forever. I'm touching it, trying to work out what it is, when I hear her voice and look up.

'Mom!' I yell.

And she's right beside me, laughing! Just like a dream, except I know I'm not dreaming. I know this is more real than anything I've ever felt before. She sits down, pulling me into her, folding herself around me, wrapping her arms tight and resting her chin on my head, and we rock back and forth, just like we used to. I want to stay like this forever. The strangest thing is, I know I can.

We talk a lot, I know that, although I can't remember exactly what we say, but that doesn't matter, nothing matters here. We both know everything we need to know and everything is perfect and nothing bad can happen ever again. Then I hear him . . .

'Sean! *Sean!* Come back, bro! You gotta come back!' It's Pat and he's yelling at me with all his might. 'You *have* to! We can't both leave him. You have to come back for Dad. Come on, bro, please. I'm sorry. I was wrong. I shouldn't have . . .' And now he's crying, and Pat never cries. I can't see him, but I can hear him, loud and clear. I look at Mom, and she smiles. She looks off over my shoulder, and I understand then that she's looking at Pat. She can see him. She looks at him like she's real proud of him. I see her lips move. 'My boys.' And in that moment, it's all clear. I made the choice. And it's the right choice. It's what Mom wants, and now it's what Pat wants too.

'Two, three, four . . .'

'Stand clear!'

'Again!'

'I'm calling it.'

'Wait, give it one more go . . .'

'It's been almost twenty minutes.'

'We *can't* lose him.'

'Time of death—'

'Wait! Wait! He's back! We've got him!'

I'm choking. There's a tube down my throat, and an elephant on my chest. I feel like I've been beaten up from head to toe. Bright lights blind me, faces hover over me and something's pricking my hand. My head hurts. But I'm here, and there's only one person I need.

'Get the father!' one of the faces says, breaking into a grin. 'He can come in now.'

A kind face smiles down at me. 'Welcome back, young man. That was a close call.'

* * *

Dan is pacing the floor of the small room, unable to sit still. Annie watches him until she feels dizzy herself. His face is a mask of pain, it hurts to even look at him.

The door opens and a nurse comes in, and Annie's throat constricts.

Dear God, she prays, *Please, please, don't take Sean too. It'll kill him. Sean deserves to live. Please.*

'Mr O'Connell?'

Dan's head snaps up. 'Yes?' his voice is hoarse.

'You can come in now. Follow me, please.'

Dan walks after him obediently, and Annie follows behind. It's like the walk to the gallows. The nurse leads them to the dedicated Resus Room, where the machinations of life-saving bleep and whirr. And there lies Sean, still and unmoving.

A doctor looks up. He has a kind face, like Doctor Mike. Dan tries to speak, but no words come out. Annie steps forward, slips her hand in his and speaks for him.

'Is Sean . . . is he going to be alright, Doctor?'

It feels like an eternity passes between them before the doctor speaks.

'Yes. He's stable now. It was a close call, but he's going to be fine.'

As if on cue, Sean's eyes flicker open, and a groggy smile spreads across his face. Dan looks down at him with a love that seems too big for the room. 'Hey, buddy,' he says, brushing away tears, 'you gave us quite a fright there.'

She is barely aware of the tears of relief spilling down her own face as she squeezes Dan's arm and whispers she has to get back home. He nods, and thanks her for everything – but he can hardly tear his eyes away from Sean. She gives him the name of a nearby hotel in the area if he needs to stay over, then she leaves father and son to their reunion.

Sean

Dad's talking and crying at the same time. I don't think he even knows it. He's beside me, holding my hand. He's babbling, saying over and over again, 'Oh, Sean, oh baby, oh Sean, thank God. Thank God you're okay. I don't know what I would have done . . .' His face is wet with tears. I want to reach out to wipe them away, but I can't move my arms yet.

I try to talk, but I can't. It just comes out as a croak, and it hurts.

'Don't try to say anything, buddy. I'm right here. You don't need to say anything. I'm not going anywhere. I'll never leave you, I promise . . .' and he's talking and talking.

Pat's on the other side of me, standing by the bed. He's saying, 'I'm sorry . . . I'm sorry . . . I'm so sorry, bro,' over and over again. 'I just wanted us to be together again. I thought I could . . . we could . . . I'm sorry . . . I'm so sorry . . .'

I want to tell Pat it's okay, that I understand, but everything's fading now . . . and I'm so tired . . . I just want to sleep.

* * *

When Annie checks her phone, there are five missed calls from Breda. She listens to her voicemail, to her mother's frantic voice.

The accident is the talk of the village. Gracie is with Breda and they are desperate for news.

Annie is so drained, so emotionally wrung out, so relieved that Sean is alright, that previous family events seem like a half-forgotten dream – and certainly unimportant. She rings her mother before she begins the drive back to the hotel.

'He's alright,' she says. 'He's going to be alright, but it was close.'

'Oh thank God! Thanks be to God! Gracie!' She hears Breda call out to her granddaughter. 'Sean is alright, he's going to be okay.'

'Are you staying there, or—'

'Dan's staying overnight, but I'm driving home now. They need some time alone after all that.'

'Will you come up to me, Annie?' Breda asks. 'There's only me and Gracie here, and I need to talk to you.'

'Mum, I'm exhausted.'

'I know you must be, but you'll need to eat. I'll make dinner. I know you're angry with me, but we need to talk, sweetheart. I won't keep you long, I promise. Just, please, come straight here. We'll be waiting.'

'Now, lovey,' Breda says to Gracie when she puts down her phone. 'I know you're dying to see Annie and to hear all the news about Sean, and you will, but I need to talk to Annie about something very important . . . something we won't get the chance to talk about if we don't do it now. Do you understand?'

'So you want me out of the way?'

'Not immediately, but yes. I won't lie to you, Gracie, I have to talk to Annie and it's very, very important and I may not get this chance to explain things to her the way I need to if I don't catch her now. So if you don't mind, I'd like you to watch a movie in my bedroom after we have dinner, then I can talk to Annie in private. Would that be alright?'

Gracie considers this. 'Sure. I'm glad you're not bullshitting me.'

'Gracie! I wish you wouldn't use that word . . . it's . . . it's . . .'

'Rude?'

'Unbecoming.'

'What does *unbecoming* mean?'

'It means it's not worthy of you, of the lovely young lady you're going to become. And it's an Americanism, which I know you hear all the time on television and everywhere, but it's good to cultivate a proper vocabulary to express yourself.'

'Like what?' Gracie asks, her head to one side.

'Well, you could say, *I'm glad you're telling me the truth*, which is exactly what I am doing. Gracie, I wish I didn't have to talk about things you can't listen to, but you're still a young girl, love. And while you are clever and wise and lots of other things I wish I had been at your age, there are still discussions adults need to have in private, and this is one of them.'

'Are you going to be talking about Mum?'

'No, I'm not, although she might crop up during it. I'm going to be talking about Annie, about her life, about where she's going with it and why, and about . . .' Here Breda takes a breath. 'And about what wrong things Granddad and I might have done without realising it that are making Annie make some wrong choices of her own.'

'So you're saying stuff so she can start making better choices?'

'Exactly.'

'I think that's a nice thing for you to do.'

'I don't know how nice it is, Gracie darling, but it is long overdue. And did I ever tell you I thank God every day for sending me an angel like you as a granddaughter?'

'No,' Gracie says with a giggle. 'But as you say yourself, now's as good a time as any to start.'

* * *

Annie does look exhausted when she comes up to the apartment, but there is also a stillness about her Breda knows has more to do with an emotional shift in her daughter's perspective, whether or not Annie realises this herself.

They have dinner, talk about the accident, and the blessing that no one was seriously hurt.

'It was the cable that went,' Breda says. 'They know that now. The boat was gone over with a fine-tooth comb. They could all have been killed. Declan's very cut up about it, blames himself, but no one could have known in advance, the boat engineers confirmed that.'

'I saw a speed boat accident on TV,' Gracie says, 'where everyone fell out of the boat and no one was at the wheel so it locked, and the boat turned around and drove back through the people in the water and they were all sliced up in the propellers and stuff. One boy got his leg cut off, and his mum and his dad were killed. That's what I was thinking about when I was skiing and saw it all happen.'

'Well thank God nothing like that *did* happen, and you're all safe and sound,' Breda says. 'Now, ahem, Gracie . . .'

'Right. I'm off to Gran's room to watch a movie because she wants to talk to *you* in private.' Gracie makes it sound as if Annie is in for a stern telling-off as she slips from her chair. 'See you later, alligator!'

'Actually,' Breda begins, once Gracie has left the room, 'I need you to listen to me, Annie. You can ask all the questions you want afterwards, but just let me have my say for the moment. I need to try to explain, and for myself as much as you.'

Annie sits back in her chair. 'Go on.'

'I learned about your half-brother when he was born, or shortly after. His mother, Lydia, that was her name, she wrote to me because she felt she had a duty to tell me that Conor had fathered a child. I'll never forget that day as long as I live, and I'm not saying that for effect, or sympathy.

'As I saw it, I had two choices. I could confront your father and end our marriage, which would have been explosive, or I could ignore this letter and the information it contained. I could put it as far from my mind as possible and hope it would go away.

'Two years later, this Lydia rang me. She said she was getting married, to a man who would cherish her and her son. After that, I never heard any more, and to be honest, I prayed I never would.

'Now before you judge me, Annie, and yes, you have every right to, remember that I had two little girls of my own to think of. Dee was three, just a toddler, really, and you were barely a year old when he was born . . . Conor, I believe his name is.' Breda smiles. 'She said she was going to name him after his father. That hurt.

'I remembered her, of course. I remembered all of them. I believe you always do if you are married to a man who plays around, that's what we called it in our day. She was a pretty little thing, dark, flighty, spoilt, her parents used to come to the hotel . . . they were wealthy . . . involved in horses as far as I recall . . .

'Anyway, the thing is, the reason I didn't leave him was that I felt partially responsible.' She holds up her hand as Annie leans forward to speak. 'Please, let me finish. These things are never black and white, Annie.

'When I married your father, I was on the rebound myself. I had been very much in love with a man who . . . who . . . well, who didn't want to marry me. I was heartbroken, not because he'd misled me or deceived me in any way, but because he was The One. I knew that then and I know it still now.' Breda takes a deep breath and tries to keep the tremor from her voice. 'I thought I'd never get over him . . . and then one summer, your father came along. I know it's hard to believe, but he was gorgeous then, and he could be terrific fun. Gregarious is the word people used about him. He'd studied at the same school of hotel management on Lake Lucerne as I did, although not at the same time because he was a few years ahead of me, but we had a lot in common. And he made me feel as if I was the only woman in the world, let alone the room. That sort of thing can turn a girl's head, you know. I was lonely, and I wanted to get married and have a family of my own. Your father was the first person to make me laugh since my break-up. He made me feel as if another door was opening for me. And don't forget I had a hotel to run. It's a tough enough business at the best of times, without attempting it on your own.

'You remember Granny Lou, Annie? Well, she hated him. For a while she said nothing. I suppose she just hoped it might fizzle out. When it didn't show any signs of doing that, she told me in no uncertain terms that I would be making a grave mistake if I chose to marry him.'

Annie is listening intently. 'Why?' she asks now.

'She saw it all, I suppose. I think her exact words were that your father was "a good-looking big lout with a roving eye, one that has settled on you, Breda, because you come with a hotel". She also pointed out his fondness for knocking back the whiskey and said that he had laziness written all over him. Not one to mince her words, my mother.' Breda smiles. 'You have a lot of her in you, Annie. And that's a compliment. Granny Lou was a woman far ahead of her time – but I'm digressing . . .

'I'm sure she had my best intentions at heart, but at the time it was too soon, still all too raw after my former romance. I was furious with her, probably because deep down I knew there was a kernel of truth in what she was saying. But I wasn't ready to hear it. I wanted to prove her wrong. Sometimes I wonder if that's all I've been doing ever since, and it has cost me dearly, I can tell you. And now I'm afraid it has cost you and Dee, too.

'What I did may not have been the right thing to do, Annie,

but as far as I was concerned it was my only option. And I knew the child was safe, with a family of his own. It wasn't as if he had being given away or anything, and that made a difference, I suppose.'

'Oh, Mum.' Annie shakes her head.

'So you see, I have to take responsibility for my own part in the marriage. Maybe on some level your father knew I could never love him as I should, maybe I never gave one hundred percent to the marriage, even if I told myself that I did. I put my energies into you girls, and the hotel of course, but part of my heart was always elsewhere . . .'

'Where's Dad now?' Annie has been wondering that since she arrived.

'I'm not sure. I suspect he's with your Aunty May in Dublin, that's where I advised him to go. I told him I was leaving him, that I should have done so long ago, but I was doing it now.'

Annie looks at her, taken aback. 'Are you sure about that?'

'To be honest, I don't know what to think about anything just now. But I do know I want time on my own. There are some big decisions to make, and I need quiet and calm to make them in. And I want to be in a good place when Dee comes out, so I can be strong for her too. I haven't said anything about your father and me to Gracie. God knows she has enough on her plate with her own parents. I just told her Granddad had to go and do some hotel business in Dublin and he might be staying there for a while.'

'How long is Dee going to be in for?'

'Six weeks, Doctor Mike said. That's the usual stay for these . . . rehab places. But this isn't about Dee, Annie. I'll be talking to her separately, when she's stronger. I want to apologise to you, for you ever having to be in that dreadful position, for having to carry that awful secret on your own for these four years. You had no part or responsibility in what transpired and that was a terrible load for you to bear, unforgivable. Annie, I'm so, so sorry.'

'It was my decision too, Mum,' Annie says quietly.

'I know. But one you shouldn't have had to make. And I'm sorry for that. And I'm concerned about you now Annie, worried this has all had a bad effect on you, on how you think of men and marriage . . . please, try not to let it.'

Annie nods. That would be the hard part. But that's not important just now. She thinks instead about the similarities Dan pointed out to her about her own behaviour and Breda's, and as she looks at her mother's face, etched with concern and worry, a flood of sympathy rushes over her. This is her mother. The woman who has been there for her always. It's wrong to be angry with her. They need each other now more than ever.

Annie reaches out and takes Breda's hand. 'I'm sorry too, Mum, for what I said that day. I didn't mean it. I was just frantic for Gracie and . . . and . . . well, you know the rest.'

'We've all had a hard few days,' Breda says, smiling at her. 'Let's just let things settle for a while, and hopefully we can all move forward then. Oh, but there is one other thing . . .'

'What?'

'I'm going to put the hotel on the market. If your father and I are parting ways, we might as well get on with it. And it's a good time, the market is picking up again, I'm told. Apart from anything else, I badly need a fresh start.'

'You're right. It makes sense to do it now. I'm sorry you both have to go through this, but I'll help you any way I can. Now, that's quite enough emotional drama for both of us. I'm done in, Mum. Do you mind if I head off now?'

'Not at all. Go get some sleep.'

Annie gets up to gather her bag and coat.

'And Annie,' Breda says as she heads for the door, 'thank you for giving me a chance to explain.'

* * *

Dan wakes up in a strange bed, and for a moment has no idea where he is. Then he remembers . . . and relief courses through him. Sean is in the hospital, Kerry General, and he is alive. They kept him in overnight, for observation, but after defibrillation his rhythms had returned to normal and he was moved to a regular ward. All going well, they had told Dan, Sean would be able to go home with him this lunchtime.

After Annie left to go back home, Dan had booked into the hotel she suggested for the night, then went back to sit beside a sleeping Sean until the nursing staff told him to go and get some rest himself, that they would make sure Sean got a good night's sleep. The doctors had assured him Sean was over the trauma, that his vitals were stable and that, apart from a bump on his head and mild concussion, he was just as healthy as he had been before the accident.

Now, over breakfast and some much-needed coffee, Dan thinks about the events of yesterday, how close he came to losing Sean, and gives thanks that he's been spared. He would never get Pat and Mary back, but he will cherish Sean for all his days and help him to become whoever he is meant to be, just as Mary would have done.

He settles his bill and makes his way back to the hospital, feeling like it's the first day of a new life for him and Sean.

He walks through the hospital corridors, marvelling at how life can change in a heartbeat. He should know that better than anyone. Yesterday he was crazed with terror; today, he's just anxious to see his boy and take him home. As he heads to the ward where Sean has been moved to, there is a flurry of movement at the nurses' station and he is called over by Bridget, one of the nurses who had been so kind to him last night.

'I'm glad I caught you, Dan,' she says. 'Dr Hanrahan needs to have a word with you before you go in to Sean. Just hold on for a moment, will you, while I call him down.'

She goes over to make the call, and Dan is suddenly overcome with fear again, dread settling like a boulder in the pit of his stomach. What has happened with Sean? Dan has to sit down because his legs are about to buckle.

'Dan.' Dr Hanrahan is brisk as he ushers Dan into a small room. 'We need to talk. Just pop in here for a minute, will you.'

Dan gets up with difficulty, and follows the doctor into a tiny administrator's office.

'There's been a development that I need to advise you of before you go in there.' His expression is kind, but Dan immediately assumes the worst. He's been here before, he knows they always try to cushion the blow in advance. He can hardly force himself to listen, he is struggling to maintain his composure and failing miserably. 'Dan, are you alright?' Dr Hanrahan is concerned.

'I'm sorry ... it's just ... Sean's mother and twin brother died in an auto crash last year. I couldn't bear if ... I couldn't ...'

Dr Hanrahan shakes his head. 'I'm so sorry, Dan. That's just terrible. What a tragedy.'

Dan nods, unable to go on.

'Please don't upset yourself, Dan,' Dr Hanrahan continues quickly. 'I have some good news. When Sean woke up this morning, he asked for you.'

Dan stares at him. 'What?'

'Sean *asked* for you. He said, "Where's Dad?" I didn't want to let you walk in there without telling you first ...'

Dan is staring at him in shock, his mind slowly reaching the obvious. 'You're saying Sean . . . spoke?'

Dr Hanrahan smiles at him. 'He certainly did, and last I heard, he's still talking.'

Dan keeps staring at him, struggling to process this startling information. 'I have to see him . . . can I?' He yanks open the door, nearly taking it off the hinges.

'Go,' says Dr Hanrahan. 'He can't wait to see you.'

Dan sprints down the corridor, skidding to a stop at Ward Seven. He bursts through the door. There on the bed sits Sean, fully dressed. He laughs when he sees Dan come into the room like a bolt of lightning.

'Hey, Dad!'

Dan walks towards the bed in shell-shocked daze. He reaches out to touch his son, make sure he's really there, really real. 'Say that again,' he breathes.

Sean grins at him. 'Hey, Dad.'

'My God,' says Dan, and he sits on the bed, holding Sean so tightly he might break. 'Oh dear God, I don't believe it.'

'I'm sure glad to see you, Dad,' Sean says into his shoulder. 'There's so much I have to tell you.' The voice is weak, but unmistakable, and for a moment Dan is afraid of speaking himself, afraid of breaking the spell, of doing anything to jeopardise this miracle. The last fifteen months fall away, and here is his son again, whole and alive. It's almost too much to take in.

The doctors let them have some time together, but then the registrar, Paul, comes in.

'Well, now, Dad, what do you make of this chatterbox?'

Dan shakes his head. 'I'm still pinching myself.'

'I'm glad, for both of you,' Paul says, smiling at them. 'And I'm sorry to break up the party, but I'm afraid we need this bed and Doctor Hanrahan has discharged Sean, so he's good to go.'

'I can't thank you enough, all of you,' Dan says, shaking Paul's hand. 'I'm so grateful for the care he's received.'

'Not at all, our pleasure . . . all part of the service. Take it easy for a while with the old head, Sean, no bungee jumping, that sort of thing,' Paul says. 'But apart from that, it's business as usual.'

Sean grins at him. 'Sure, Paul. And thank you. You guys are awesome.'

'Well, I don't get called that very often,' Paul says, holding up his hand for a high-five.

'Let's go, Dad. See ya, Paul!'

As they walk to the car hire shop, Dan texts the good news to Annie. He hires a small car, thinking he can have someone drop it back tomorrow, and they set off.

Sean keeps up a steady stream of chatter for most of the ride. From time to time Dan sneaks a look at him, and each time he shakes his head and smiles. He cannot wait to Skype Dr Shriver and tell her what's happened. She'll be over the moon.

'Dad, can I tell you something?'

'Anything,' Dan says, smiling. 'I never want you to stop talking.'

Sean looks unsure. 'Okay, I know you might not believe this, but . . . I saw Mom.'

Dan glances at him. 'What do you mean?'

'Under the water. When I was going down, Mom was there, she pulled me up. She helped me.'

Dan swallows a lump in his throat. 'I'm very glad she did,' he says lightly. He's read about near-death experiences, and he knows it's very common to see a deceased loved one. Sean must have been really close to the edge, he thinks, which makes him shiver.

'And after she helped me, she took me to this other place that was really beautiful,' Sean goes on. 'I just want you to know that she's really happy there, she wants you to know that.'

Dan nods. 'I'm happy to hear that,' he says. He waits a beat, then asks, 'And when you saw Mom, was Pat there too?'

Sean shakes his head. 'But I wouldn't have expected to see him there.'

'Why not?'

'Because Pat's here with us, that's what he chose.'

Dan grips the wheel a little tighter and wonders if he should try to talk Sean out of this ghost stuff. Now that he's talking again, shouldn't he be letting go of these notions? But now is not the time. Sean is alive and talking again, nothing else matters.

'Dad?'

'Yes, son?'

'Can I go see Gracie when we get back? She's going to be so psyched that I'm talking again.' Sean grins.

Dan smiles. 'I don't see why not – she's not going to be the only one.'

Pat

How do you spend your last day on earth?

That's a no-brainer. I just want to hang with the people I love, which in this case is Sean and Dad.

It's a really nice day, and Dad and Annie are driving out to Derrynane with Sean and Gracie. We're going to have a picnic and swim and stuff, just what we usually do. We're early enough to get a good parking space, and set up camp at our favourite big rock on the beach, but it's not long before the place gets pretty busy.

Sean can still see me, but since he can talk again, he's got a lot to share with people, especially Dad and Gracie. So although he knows I'm here, he doesn't pay that much attention to me anymore. Barry told me not to be upset about that, because it didn't mean he loved me any less, just that he was re-engaging with life again, and that was healthy for him. I know he's right, but that doesn't make it any easier for me. If I'm honest, it hurts. So I sit with Dad, who's stretched out beside Annie. They're both reading books, leaning back against the rock, and I try not to notice when they hold hands.

The day goes by really quickly, but it's pretty perfect, one of those days kids remember and look back on, even when they're old. We swim, have lunch, swim some more, race up and down the beach to get dry, and before we know it, it's time to pack up and go home.

I need to tell Sean that I have to go, that I won't be coming back, but I can't seem to find the right time or opportunity. Now that it's come down to it, I'm not sure I can do it. But I have to. The thing is, I could fall apart, and I really don't want to do that – to either of us.

After everything that's happened, I have to find Barry. He's the only one who'll understand. I need to tell him what I did, and what happened with Mom. I follow the path through the trees and come out at the cottage. Millie raises her head, barks, then runs straight over to me. I love that dog.

The top half of the door is open, and a woman with grey hair pops her head out and smiles at me.

'Barry,' she calls over her shoulder. 'Someone to see you.'

He comes to the door then and they exchange a look. Then he opens the bottom part and steps outside.

'I'm glad to see you, Pat,' he says, coming over to me. 'Let's go for a little walk.'

We turn and walk towards the lake, Millie keeping close to our heels.

I tell him all about yesterday, everything, even the horrible part when I nearly took Sean with me. He just listens and nods. He looks tired today.

'I tried so hard to hold on,' I tell him, 'but I couldn't.'

He shakes his head. 'That was rough, lad. But it's over now, and you know you've done the right thing.'

'I didn't understand before, but now I do.'

'Do you?' We sit down on the old wooden bench.

I nod. 'I'm not supposed to be here anymore.' I look up at him. 'Yesterday . . . when I . . . uh, was in the water with Sean . . . I saw her . . .'

'Who, Pat? Your mother?'

'Uh-huh. She helped Sean, then she smiled at me as if she loved me more than anything. I have to be with her now. I've made her wait ages. But it's time for me to go. That's why I came to tell you.'

'That's good, Pat, that's all good.'

We look out at the water for a minute.

'The thing is, I need to tell Sean that I have to go, that I won't be coming back. I don't think he understands that yet. But I'm not sure I can do it. What if I fall apart? Upset him?'

'You do have to tell him.' Barry nods. 'As much for yourself as for Sean. Maybe you could tell him while he's sleeping?'

'Yeah.' I say, feeling better about it. 'That's what I'll do.' I turn to him. 'Thanks, Barry, for everything.'

'I'm very happy I was here to help, Pat,' he says. 'You go on now, and I'll be here for you, waiting, when you're ready.'

* * *

It has been a perfect day, although to anyone unaware of recent events, Annie supposes she, Dan, Sean and Gracie must seem just like any other group having fun at the beach. If she finds it extraordinary to hear Sean talking, she cannot imagine what it must be like for Dan, who cannot take his eyes off his boy.

Watching Sean playing with Gracie and the other kids they have been running around with all day, Annie marvels at the simple acceptance of children, how they have seamlessly moved on, unquestioning, as if nothing were out of the ordinary. As if it were not a small miracle that Sean is talking again.

Gracie's only concern, when she had heard that he had recovered his speech, was whether or not Sean would still be interested in being friends with her.

'Of course he will,' Annie had reassured her. 'Why ever wouldn't he?'

'Dunno.' Gracie shrugged. 'Maybe he was only friends with me because he couldn't talk, now that he can he might be bored with me. I wouldn't mind, I mean, I'd understand . . .'

Annie shook her head. 'I think it will be just the opposite. I think he's going to have lots he wants to tell you.'

Thankfully, this had been the case. And when Dan had brought Sean to the hotel, Gracie's first instruction to Sean was, 'Say something, quick! I want to hear your accent!' That had made everyone laugh. But Gracie's insecurity was a painful reminder to Annie of her niece's lack of self-esteem, despite the bubbly personality she hid behind.

'Come back for dinner?' Dan says, rousing Annie from her thoughts.

They are packing up, gathering their belongings into beach bags, but already Annie feels reluctant to leave this perfect spot, this golden summer afternoon she wants to freeze-frame moment by moment.

'Please do.' Dan smiles, but his tone is serious. 'I need to talk to you.'

Annie nods. Suddenly she feels she has to be very careful of what she says from here on out. The carefree feeling that has lingered throughout the day seeps away, replaced with something more measured, considered. She does not want the wrong words, so easily uttered, to spoil things.

'I'd like that,' she says. 'About seven?'

'Perfect.'

Back in her cottage, she showers and washes her hair, all the while reminding herself that it is perfectly normal to feel emotional after all that has happened. She has watched her sister narrowly evade the clutches of denial and addiction, for the present at any rate, thanks to Dee finally asking for and finding the help she so clearly needs. From now on, Dee will have to find the strength to cope and go forward on her own, for Gracie, and herself. She has watched her mother face her own demons, and although Breda is still shaken since that awful day of the confrontation, she seems resolute about planning for her future, whatever that may be.

But one thing is very clear to Annie, since all this has transpired, and that is that she will not go back to London. In a way, the decision has been made for her, and it is a relief. It is not just all that has happened, although certainly that has contributed. But more than that, Annie simply feels she is not the same person she was such a short time ago. And whoever she has become, or is in the process of becoming, she cannot go back to her old life in London. It is only fair to inform Theo of her decision, so she makes the call now.

'I was afraid of this, Annie,' Theo groans. 'Are you sure?' He sounds more sad than surprised.

'I'm positive. I've given it a great deal of thought.'

She shares her idea of setting up a post-production facility and creative retreat in the hotel site with the money she will get from the agency buyout, and says this is what she is considering. Theo is enthusiastic.

'I think that's a great idea. If you need any help once you're set up, I know just the guy to head it up. He's married to an Irish girl and he's looking to relocate to Ireland, he's just waiting for the right opportunity.'

'Thanks, Theo, but it's not even at the conceptual stage yet.'

'Well, call me any time you like to discuss this new venture of yours. Or even better, come over and see us. I might be interested in investing myself. We could be partners.' He chuckled. 'Even if it costs me, I'm determined to work with you again!'

Annie smiles at her end of the phone. 'I'll keep you posted.'

She feels better when she finishes the call, as if she has finally admitted something to herself, although she still feels tearful. But that's hardly surprising, it is the end of an era in her life and that is always scary, unsettling. It has nothing at all to do with the fact that she suspects dinner tonight with Dan will be goodbye. After Sean's lucky escape, and now that he is talking and Dan's work is all but finished, it is only natural Dan will want to get his boy home as soon as possible. And that's what always *was* going to happen, he was going back, she just never imagined the prospect would be so awfully upsetting. But possibly, a little voice in her head says, that is because she has never allowed herself to contemplate the matter. Now she finds she can think of little else.

The evening is still warm, so she lets her hair dry naturally, and pulls on a pretty white sun dress she bought in Greece years ago and sets off on foot for Cable Lodge. When she gets there, Dan brings her outside, where he has set up a small table, and pours her a glass of wine while he barbecues a couple of steaks.

'Where's Sean?'

'Upstairs on the computer, Skyping some friends. He's eaten already.'

'I still find it hard to believe he's talking again. It's so amazing.'

Dan smiles and Annie notices he looks younger, more relaxed than she's ever seen him.

'I don't even have words for how relieved I'm feeling. No pun intended.' He grins.

'I can imagine.'

'It's been a rough few days, for both of us.'

'You can say that again.'

'How are things with you? With your family?'

'Dad's been banished to his sister in Dublin for the foreseeable. Mum says she told him she was leaving him, and I think she probably will . . . but she wants to think about it all, not rush into anything, you know.'

'These things are never easy.'

'But she's definitely selling the hotel. And there's Gracie to think of, too.' Annie shakes her head. 'Bad enough for her parents to be divorcing, but her grandparents too. It's all such a mess.'

Dan plates up and joins Annie at the table. 'How's Dee doing?'

She's going to be in rehab for six weeks, then she's coming back here for a bit until she decides what to do with herself, I guess.'

'Have you told them about your idea for the hotel?'

'No, not yet. I think I might keep it to myself for a while. I need to do some research first, but it's funny, now that it's come to it, I just don't feel it's right to let the place go. It's been in our family for four generations. My great-grandfather won the original house in a card game, then turned it into an inn when the cable station was set up. I thought I was ready to let it go, but now I'm not so sure.' She takes a sip of her wine.

'So it looks like you're going to be staying around to see how things work out for a while.' Dan is thoughtful.

'It looks like it, wasn't part of the plan, but . . .'

'I can't say I had a concrete one either. We were always just visiting, but now that Sean's talking again and I've got everything I need for the documentary script, I'm anxious to get Sean back home as soon as possible. His grandparents are beside themselves to see him.'

'Of course.' Annie bites her lip. 'That's understandable.'

'Thing is . . . I would have liked to stay for a while longer . . . you and I . . . well, we're only just getting to know each other . . .'

Annie looks away. 'It – it's been a crazy time, Dan.'

'Time enough for me to discover you're an incredible person, though.'

She smiles and shakes her head. 'Believe me, I'm far from it.'

'Look, Sean and I are flying back Wednesday . . .'

Annie swallows. 'That's the day after tomorrow.'

'Would you consider coming out for a while . . . you know, just to visit . . . a vacation . . . but we could—'

Annie shakes her head. 'I don't see that happening, Dan. Not the way things are right now. We both have responsibilities. I couldn't possibly leave Gracie and Mum while . . .'

'But later maybe? When things have settled down?' Dan presses.

'I think we both know that once you get back—'

He takes her hand in his. 'I'm not going to forget you, Annie.'

'I won't forget you either,' she says softly.

Just then Sean runs out. 'Hey Dad, Grandma wants to talk to you on Skype.'

'Excuse me for a minute.' Dan gets up to go inside.

'Hey, Annie,' Sean says, grinning.

'Hey, yourself. Look at you.' Annie ruffles his hair. 'You're a regular chatterbox these days.'

'We're going home day after tomorrow, so tomorrow's our last day here.'

'I know.' Annie forces a smile. 'Your dad told me.'

'Will Gracie be around tomorrow?'

'I'm sure she will.'

'Good. I'll see her then.' He is about to go inside, then turns back to her. 'In case I forget . . . I just wanted to thank you – and Gracie – for being so nice to me and Dad while we've been here. I've had a really cool time, even when I wasn't talking.' He smiles, looking suddenly heartbreakingly like his father. 'If we never came here, I'm not sure I'd ever have been able to talk again.'

'Oh, I'm sure you would, Sean . . . sooner or later.'

'I probably shouldn't say this.' He chews the side of his mouth. 'But since I'm talking and all . . . well . . . I think my dad really likes you. Do you like him too?'

The question takes Annie aback, but she smiles and says, 'Yes. I like him a lot. He's a very—' But she doesn't get to say any more, because Sean interjects.

'Then you should probably tell him. I think he'd like that.' He hesitates for just a second, then . . . 'I really like you too, so does Pat. We, I mean, I just wanted to tell you that.'

Annie's eyes fill at this unexpected declaration. 'I like you an awful lot too, Sean. I think you're the best and I'm sure if I, um, met Pat—'

'It's okay.' He grins, turning to go back into the house. 'He knows you'd like him. He's cool with that.'

'Okay, Sean,' Dan calls from the house. 'Time for bed, young man.'

For the rest of the evening they sit outside at the table on the overgrown lawn, surrounded by rhododendron and hydrangea bushes grown wild, as the shadows fall and the old house watches them. And because they can't talk about Dan leaving, they talk about anything and everything else until night falls and the candle flickers on the table between them.

'There's so much more I want to know about you.' Dan shakes his head. 'I could talk to you for—'

'I . . . it's been lovely . . . but I should probably go.' Annie gets up. 'Let me help you clear this away.'

'It's fine, leave it, really.' Dan puts a restraining hand on her arm as he stands and turns her to face him. 'I don't want you to leave.' He pulls her to him and bends to kiss her, slowly, tenderly. When she finally pulls away, he looks into her eyes. 'Stay? Please.'

'I—'

'Don't overthink it, Annie, please . . . just stay.'

And maybe because she suddenly finds it impossible to speak, or maybe because she knows it may be the only chance they ever have, or maybe because she won't have to worry about what it all means or where it will lead afterwards because there would be no afterwards, Annie stays.

Afterwards, she will not remember Dan leading her upstairs, or him checking on Sean, who was out for the count, but she will remember Dan coming back into the bedroom, softly closing the door, the moonlight pouring through the big picture windows bathing the room in silver light. She will remember him pushing her dress gently off her shoulders, bending to kiss her neck, trace her collarbone. She will remember slipping into bed between cool sheets, the warmth of his body as he held her, and loved her, the heat building between them. She will remember feeling wonder, surprise that someone she hardly knew could read her with every touch, make her body feel as if she were discovering it anew. How his instinctive caress could feel like forever. And most of all, she will remember the moment, without even realising it, when she falls deeply, unhesitatingly, in love with him.

That would all come later . . . but just at this time, Annie is completely, utterly alive in the moment. She is not thinking about what will happen tomorrow, or the day after, only now, as they lie together, as Dan cradles her face, as she listens to him whisper words in a voice she has longed, somewhere deep inside of her, to hear. His breathing, the scent of his skin, the way they anticipate each other wordlessly, as familiar to her now as if greeting and claiming a long-absent lover. Until finally he sleeps, and she fights to stay awake, to watch him, to feel his heartbeat, to savour his arms about her, to remember the moonlight falling on his sculpted body, to memorise his handsome features, relaxed, defenceless in sleep, until she cannot stay awake a second longer.

Pat

I'm sitting on Sean's bed, watching him while he sleeps. He's sprawled on his stomach, with one arm hanging over the edge of his bed. His covers are thrown off and he's lying in his shorts and t-shirt. He's still pretty skinny, but at least now he's tanned. He looks a whole lot better than the sickly kid he was when he got here first. This is tough, but I have to be strong now. Stronger than ever.

So I whisper in his ear. 'I have to go now, bro. I really don't want to leave you, but it's time. Besides, you're okay now you can talk again and all. And I won't ever be far away. Just think of me and I'll be with you, somehow, even if you can't see me.' I was getting a really big lump in my throat, but I had to say it. 'I love you, bro, you're the best brother anyone could ever have, you know? I just want you to know that. And I want you to have a great life, for both of us.'

I had to go then, because if I stayed any longer, I wouldn't be able to leave at all, and that wouldn't be good for either of us.

* * *

At first, he thinks he is dreaming. The voice, for so long silent, now so panicked, rouses him instantly from a deep sleep.

'Dad! Da-aa-ad! Da-aa-ad!'

Dan hurls himself out of bed, blindly, uncomprehendingly, groping for lights, robe, handles, doors, knowing only his son is calling him, wailing for him.

He hurtles into Sean's room, to find him sitting up in bed in darkness, head in hands, sobbing. Dan flicks on the bedside light, wraps his son in his arms and lets him cry, rocking him, soothing him, until only one phrase becomes intelligible.

'Oh, Dad,' Sean wails over and over, 'he's gone . . . he's gone . . . Pat's gone . . . what am I going to do? He's gone . . .'

'It's okay, Sean, it's okay, baby, I promise you. It's okay, we're going to be okay . . . hush now . . . hush, I'm here . . . Daddy's here . . . I've got you . . . it's alright . . .'

He is not aware of Annie, who witnesses the heartbreaking scene from the doorway. She steps back from the intensely intimate moment between Dan and his son. She slips back into Dan's room to gather her clothes and dress, then she leaves quietly.

Pat

Barry is right there waiting for me, just like he promised, even though it's almost getting light.

'I did it,' I tell him. 'I said goodbye. It was really hard, but I did it.'

'I know it was hard.' He smiles at me. 'But I'm so proud of you, Pat.'

'I guess now I have to say goodbye to you too, and ask you to help me to . . . *you* know . . .'

'It's not really goodbye, Pat, it never is,' Barry says. 'And I'll let you in on a little secret. I'll be catching up with you very soon myself.'

'Seriously?'

'Oh, yes. I'm being very serious.'

'In that case, I'll be there for you, Barry – just like you've been here for me. I won't forget you.'

'You have no idea how much that means to me, son. Thank you.'

We look out over the water. The sun's coming up, and the sky is all pinks and purples, the birds are beginning to sing and four swans swim right by us. It's really pretty.

'I guess this is it, then?' I say, and suddenly I'm nervous. 'Do I – do I have to, like, do anything?'

'Not a thing, lad. You leave that to me. You just sit there and relax.'

Barry kneels down and bows his head, and begins talking. I guess he's praying, but it's in a language I don't understand. But I'm not scared anymore, just the opposite. I feel safe and peaceful, a little bit sleepy. I try to stay awake to watch him, and I can see the light in his heart grow bigger and brighter until it seems to shine right through him. Millie stays right by my feet and I close my eyes.

I'm not sure how long it takes, it could be minutes, it could be hours, but somehow time doesn't exist anymore. Then suddenly my eyes fly open. I'm more awake than I've ever been! The light over the water is moving, changing, then it drops away, like a curtain falling. And I see her. Mom! She's holding out her arms, waiting, laughing. And if I thought the morning here looked beautiful, it's nothing compared to this place! I jump up then, and I run and I run, and I never look back.

Sean

After I woke up crying, when Pat had left, Dad brought me down to the kitchen and he made me some warm milk with cinnamon and honey, and he got out a plate of chocolate chip cookies that we both ate. We sat on the old couch there and Dad put on some nice music and tucked some blankets around us and we just snuggled up together.

'I wish we could do this every night,' I said.

'Make the most of it, kiddo.' He grinned down at me. 'You've got school soon, remember?'

Like I could forget.

'Dad?'

'Mmhm?'

'I've been thinking about the day of the car accident, when Pat and Mom, you know . . .'

Dad looked worried then, and I could feel him tense up. 'Try not to think about it, Sean, I know it's hard.'

'But I have to tell you, Dad, I have to explain. It was all my fault. I had a meltdown at Mom's house that day and I wanted to go back to your house. That's why she was taking us back to you.'

Dad sat up more and pulled me close. 'Sean, none of it was your fault, or anyone's fault. It was just . . . just . . . destiny. It was awfully,

awfully sad, but we have to accept it was Mom and Pat's time to leave, and we all have to leave sometime. I promise you, buddy, it was *not* your fault, okay?'

'But—'

'No buts.'

'I keep wondering, though, what happened to her. Mom was so good in the water. I don't understand how she didn't make it out. I mean I *saw* her, she was right behind me, pushing me up.'

Dad gave a really big sigh then. 'There was no one better than your mom in the water, Sean, I know that.' He dropped a kiss on my head. 'The reason she didn't make it is because she went back down to get Pat. She was trying to get him out of the car, Sean. She wasn't to know he was already dead, that his neck was broken.' Dad's voice caught. 'She would never have left either of you, not while there was a breath left in her body. Your mom was the bravest person I knew, and she loved you two boys more than anyone. She died with Pat in her arms.' Dad held me even tighter then.

I thought about that and it made sense, even though it was really sad. 'Do you miss her, Dad?'

'Sure I do. I know you do too, buddy, but we'll be okay. We've got each other. We'll make her proud of us, right?'

I nodded. 'She loved you too, Dad. That's what she wanted to tell you that day in the car, that she'd made a mistake and that she loved you and wanted us to get back together as a family again. She told me that, right before we left, but she never got the chance to tell you.'

Dad was quiet for a moment, then he looked at me. 'We'll always be a family, Sean. You, me, Pat and Mom . . . wherever we are, that will never change.'

I hadn't thought of it like that before, and it made me feel much better because it was true. We would always be a family, no matter what.

* * *

Dan sits on Sean's bed, watching over his son until he falls back to sleep, which takes all of about ninety seconds. When he is sure he is fully asleep, he climbs wearily back into his own bed, where Annie's scent lingers on the pillow. He didn't hear her leaving, but he will call her tomorrow, or rather later today . . . they need to talk.

How many secrets make up a person, Dan wonders, as he looks out at the night. How many stories twist and turn within a family unit? It is astonishing, he thinks, how a single piece of withheld information can have so many repercussions. For fifteen whole months Sean couldn't speak, because he had something too painful to say. It breaks Dan's heart to think of Sean blaming himself in any way for the accident, but he would make sure that notion was well and truly demolished in any and every way possible, and Dr Shriver would be the one to help with that. But right now Dan is just so grateful that Sean is whole and healthy . . . and talking again. Even if what he says is heartbreakingly hard to hear.

He and his boy have been torn apart by loss, each forced to go on and put one foot in front of the other and stumble through the debris of their lives – but now they have turned the corner, he is sure of it. Now he just wants to get Sean home.

He looks out over the water, where dawn is breaking, the sky bruised with purples and pinks, then he opens the bedside drawer and takes out the photograph he keeps with him.

It is a family shot, taken on the twins' seventh birthday at SeaWorld, when the boys had just come from swimming with dolphins. He and Mary smile out happily from the frame, arms entwined, the boys wriggling between them. Only four short years ago . . . before his life was changed forever. But tonight, it doesn't hurt as much as usual to look at it.

'I sure hope you've found peace, Mary,' he says to his smiling wife. 'Don't you worry about Sean. I'll take good care of him. He's doing fine. And I know you and Pat are together . . . wherever that is.'

He kisses the photo, then puts it back in the drawer. When he falls asleep, it is deep and dreamless, just like his son in the next room.

* * *

'What are you doing up so early?' Jerry turns from the sink as her brother comes in to sit at the kitchen table.

'It's half past ten. What's early about that?'

'You only came in after six. I heard you . . . you should have slept on.'

'Sure, I don't need much sleep these days.'

'So he's gone?'

'He is. He's at peace now.'

'Well, thanks be to God for that.' She puts a pot of tea on the table and sits down. 'And you, Barry? Are you at peace?'

'I am, Jerry.' He smiles. 'As much as I'll ever be.'

'You need to take it easy now, Barry, conserve your energy, don't be wearing yourself out. We don't have much time left.'

'I've done what I needed to, Jerry. I'm all yours now.'

'Have you told Breda?'

He gives her a look. 'She has enough on her plate without me adding to her worries.'

'Oh, Barry, you'll have to tell her, she'll have to hear it from you . . . otherwise . . . she'll be so hurt.'

Just as the words leave her mouth there is a knock at the door and Millie goes to it, whining, wagging her tail.

'Well, look who it is!' Jerry says, pulling Breda in. 'We were just talking about you!'

'I hope I'm not interrupting, Jerry?'

'On the contrary, your timing couldn't be better, Breda.' Jerry grabs her satchel and slings it over her shoulder. 'I've just made a pot of tea, but I have to dash out on a mercy mission.'

Breda is startled. 'Will I—'

'Not at all! Sit down there and Barry will look after you. I'll be back as quickly as I can.' And with that she is out the door and into her pickup truck.

'How are you, Breda?' Barry pours a cup of tea for her. 'That's just what we were wondering.'

'Oh, I'm alright.' She smiles. 'What doesn't kill you makes you stronger and all that. But seriously, I came to thank you, both of you, for listening to me that day, when I was half out of my mind. I don't know how I would have got through it without you.'

'Any developments?'

'Yes, yes, good news, I'm happy to report. Annie and I had a long talk, and I – I think she understands everything now; more importantly, I think she's forgiven me.'

'That's wonderful, Breda. I'm delighted for you. Actually,' Barry is casual, 'I have my own bit of news.'

'Oh, what's that?' Breda's cup pauses on its way to her mouth.

'I'm not going to be around for much longer.'

'You're going back?'

'No, Breda.' He meets her eyes, his voice is gentle. 'I have cancer, and it's terminal.'

The cup clatters to the saucer then, and Breda gasps. 'H-How long – I mean, when – oh, dear God, no!'

'They're reluctant to be specific, but we're talking weeks, not months. But I'm not in pain, Breda, a bit of discomfort now and then, but as you can imagine, Doctor Mike and Jerry are taking the best care of me.'

'Oh, Barry!' Tears begin to fall down her face.

'Now don't get all upset on me, Breda. I was counting on you not to.' He's smiling at her. 'We both know this isn't really goodbye. You had great faith, as I remember, I'm hoping you still do, and if you have, then it won't fail you now, and we'll be alright.' He lets her cry until she composes herself.

'In that case, Barry, there's something I have to tell you.' She sounds suddenly decisive. 'I just have to, especially after what you've just told me.'

'What is it, Breda?' He looks concerned. 'Not another confrontation I hope?'

'No, no,' she sniffs, 'nothing like that. It is another confession though, and I have to make it now.'

'I'm listening.'

'Oh, Barry, I love you! I never stopped loving you, not once, it was always you. I never loved anyone the way I love you.'

She sees the shock flicker across his face. And then his beautiful smile breaking, kindness itself.

'Breda, please, don't upset yourself.' He takes her hands in his own.

'I'm not,' she says. 'As mad as it might sound, I'm glad I said it. I'm glad I got the chance to tell you. Can I ask you something?'

'Of course, anything.'

'If it hadn't been the Church . . . I mean, I know it was always a vocation for you . . . but if it wasn't . . .' She is unable to go on.

'Breda, how can you ask? Of course it would have been you. I was torn about it, for quite a while . . . ask Jerry, if you don't believe me. But just because I chose to serve God doesn't mean I ever stopped loving you. I carried you in my heart and prayed for you by name every day of my life.'

'Oh, Barry . . . really? You're not just saying that?'

'I think you know I'm not the type to just say something I don't mean.'

She takes a deep breath then, and says, 'You have no idea how much that means to me. That's the loveliest gift you could have given me, Barry. I – I'll live on it for the rest of my life.' She's smiling then, and in spite of herself, begins to laugh softly.'

'What?' Barry is perplexed now. 'What's so funny?'

'Oh, don't mind me. I'm just remembering something my mother said to me after we broke up.'

'What was that? I was very fond of your mother.'

'She said I was behaving like Scarlett O'Hara, pining over an unavailable Ashley, and to get a grip and pull myself together!'

And then they both begin to laugh, for no particular reason at all, until tears of a different kind are running down their faces.

In her pickup truck parked by the lake, Jerry tilts her head and gives a great sigh of relief, ruffling Millie's head on the seat beside her. 'I think it's safe for us to go back inside now, Millie. I don't know about you, but I'm about done with all this emotional drama.'

Millie pushes a cold nose into her hand in agreement.

* * *

Luke was finishing his current draft of the parish bulletin on the new computer in the study when he heard Father Martin come in after another long day on the road. The older man called out, *Hello the house!*, which meant he was in good form. When Luke heard the clink of glasses being taken from the kitchen press, he thought he might join him and suggest a pre-dinner drink. He had a nice Thai chicken curry simmering on the hob and on impulse had picked up a crisp Orvieto to accompany it. Besides, he was dying to tell Martin about what had transpired on his early-morning run the other day, but he had to choose his moment.

'Whatever's in that pot smells delicious, Luke.' Martin lifts the lid and inhales. 'Remind me again where you learned to cook like that.'

'Oh, I picked it up on my travels, my gap year.'

'Well, your travels were well worth it for that alone.'

'Speaking of travels.' Luke puts on the rice. 'I saw something very peculiar on my run the other morning. You never mentioned Barry McLaughlin has Alzheimer's or dementia, but he's well on in the stages of one or the other.'

'What are you talking about, Luke? Barry McLaughlin is as sharp as a tack.'

'Not when I saw him, he wasn't. I was out on my run, it was early, about five-thirty in the morning, and I was down by the lake when a movement caught my eye. I got closer and I realised it was Barry, out there all on his own. At first I thought I was mistaken, because he was talking away to someone, only there wasn't another soul there, only the black-and-white sheepdog, collie, whatever.'

'That's Millie, Jerry's dog.' Martin frowns.

'Yes, well, as I was saying, at first I thought he was talking to someone, but there was no one there. Then he got up, and I thought maybe he was doing some tai chi, or something . . . but then he knelt down, true as God, and started spouting Latin. I couldn't make out what, exactly, and after a while he got up and began to wave at someone or something out on the water. I was very worried about him. I was going to go over and see was he alright, but the dog saw me and came over and snarled at me, so I left them to it. Anyway, he was seen later in the village, so I knew he had found his way back home, but all the same, he shouldn't be let out on his own like that. It's not safe.' Luke waits for a suitable reaction from his superior.

'Well, I'm very glad you didn't go over, Luke. Poor Barry has had to let go of a lot of things during his life, but his mind isn't one of them. I can assure you of that.' Martin is firm.

Luke is taken aback. This wasn't what he was expecting at all. 'Well, what explanation would you give for that behaviour, then?'

But Martin just smiles at him and shakes his head. 'There are more things in heaven and earth, Horatio, than are dreamt of in your philosophy.'

Luke hated it when Martin did that. The quote was familiar, of course, but he couldn't remember if it was the Old or New Testament. He would look it up later. He might have known Martin would be defensive about the Alzheimer's theory, he was pushing on a bit himself, they were all sensitive about it the older they got. But all the same, it explained a lot. It could account for all the incidents in the village that started when Barry came back. Luke had seen programmes where people did all manner of crazy things, like going back to their childhood homes and undressing and getting into the bed. Sure turning on a few taps or televisions was nothing! And, he was happy to say, things seemed to have settled down on that front now. Things finally seemed to be getting back to normal in Ballyanna.

* * *

'I'm going to miss you.' Gracie is sitting on the wall outside the cable station, kicking her legs.

'I'll miss you too,' Sean says. 'I've never had a friend like you before.'

'Do you think you'll ever come back?'

'Dunno.' Sean shrugs. 'I'd like to.'

'I hope you do, although I suppose it's nice to be going back home.'

'It's kind of strange, but yeah, I'm glad we're going home now.'

'Even without Pat?'

Sean nods. He has told Gracie all about Pat leaving.

'How's your mom doing?' he asks her. 'Will she be back soon?'

'Oh, she's much better, Granny says. We're going to visit her at the weekend. I can't wait. And then when she comes home, we're going to do lots of counselling together, and some on my own. I've met the counsellor woman already and she's really nice. I really like her.'

'That's good, Gracie. Counselling really helps.'

'Will you, you know, write to me? Stay in touch?'

'Sure. We can email.'

'I'd love to see photos of where you live and stuff. But I'm not allowed on Facebook.'

'Me neither. I'll send you photos though.'

'Cool.'

'What do you think they're talking about?' Gracie nods towards the cable station, where Dan and Annie are deep in conversation.

'No clue.'

'What time is your flight tomorrow?'

'Dad says we have to leave at the crack of dawn. We're flying to Dublin, then connecting for the long flight to LA. I think my grandparents are picking us up at the other end. I can't wait to see them. They are going to be so psyched.' He grins.

'I'd love to go to America. I'm going to go as soon as I've got enough money and I'm allowed.'

'When you do, we can meet up.'

'Even if you've a girlfriend by then?'

'Sure. You might have a boyfriend by then.'

Gracie giggles at the thought.

'Anyway,' Sean is serious, 'a real friend is more important than anything. And I'll always be your friend, Gracie, okay?'

'Cool,' says Gracie, looking much happier about the prospect. 'I'm going to start saving from today.'

* * *

'We need to talk.'

'There's nothing to say, Dan.'

'Are you for real?'

'You know what I mean.' Annie is struggling to remain composed. 'We're both grown-ups and we always knew that this is what it was, that you'd be leaving and I'd be staying. So what's the point talking about it?'

'Come back with me,' Dan says urgently, taking her hand. 'Look, I know the timing sucks, but I know better than anyone that you can't plan these things. You meet the right person, on the wrong side of the world, but what the hell does that matter? We have to give this thing a chance.'

Annie bites her lip. 'Dan, it would never work. And even if it did, I can't leave Gracie now, not while her life is so destabilised ... and Mum ... and the hotel. I have to be here to provide some sort of stability and—'

'That's a cop-out,' Dan says, his face darkening. 'I'd have more respect for you if you just said you're not interested.'

'But that's *not* what I'm saying,' Annie protests. 'I can't believe you'd think that!'

'Because it's obviously the truth, that's why. And I've never been afraid to face it. I've had plenty of practice, believe me, and after last night, if you can talk about nieces and mothers and hotels ... instead of thinking about a chance that could change your own life ... well, that means you're *really* not interested.'

'It's my family we're talking about here. I can't just walk out on them, not when they need me more than ever.'

'What if Sean and I need you too?'

'Oh, Dan, please, that's not fair. You must understand . . .' Annie is getting upset now, she can't help it.

'I *do* understand, and more than you know, Annie. I understand how incredibly special it is to find someone who makes me laugh again, who makes me feel that life is worth living again. Someone who makes me feel that finally I can put the past behind me and look forward to waking up each day with the woman I love by my side. But it's a little inconvenient if that woman doesn't feel the same way.'

Annie looks at him, astonished, shaking her head, as if she can't quite believe what she's hearing. Where has all this unexpected emotion come from? She struggles to find the right words, but they turn to dust on her lips.

'I've fallen for you, Annie. I'm not sure exactly when it happened, maybe it was when I first saw you that day on the beach, sitting on a rock looking out to sea.' He smiles ruefully. 'I thought you looked like a mermaid. I even took a few shots of you, because you looked so . . . so . . . I don't know . . . different. Or maybe it happened when I saw how you took care of your sister that night at the pub, or when I saw you standing on Skellig Michael with your hair blowing wild around you like some mythical warrior queen, or how great you are with Gracie. Or maybe it was last night, which confirmed everything I'd ever hoped for us. What does it matter? It appears the very values I love about you are the ones that are going to keep you from me, and there's not a lot I can do about that.'

'Dan . . . I'm so sorry. I—'

'Don't apologise. Whatever else, do *not* apologise. You're an exceptionally bright woman, Annie, but if you can't see what we have together, what we *could* have together, if you don't see how incredibly special that is, I think you're a fool. Worse than that, I think you're lying to yourself. And I don't know why you would do that. But whatever the reason, it's obviously important to you. And that's a real shame, Annie, because in my experience, connections like this don't happen too often. So, I guess this is it, then. This is goodbye.'

'I wish things could be different, Dan,' Annie says, her throat constricting. 'I really do . . . whatever you may think.'

'Sometimes, Annie,' he says quietly, 'you have to make that happen. You have to believe enough to take a chance.'

They fall silent. Annie's mind is spinning, but she can't see any other way. She has no choice.

'We leave really early in the morning, and we've a lot of packing to do, so I'll say goodbye now, okay?'

She nods miserably.

'I'd like to kiss you, but if I did, I'd never let you go.' He smiles, shakes his head again, as if he cannot quite believe it has come to this. 'So goodbye, Annie Sullivan, my life is going to be a much lonelier place without you.'

He turns from her, calls Sean to follow him, then heads for the steps up to the Lodge. He doesn't look back. Sean and Gracie run over to her. Sean throws his arms around her.

'Bye, Annie. It was really great meeting you.'

'I'm going to miss you, Sean,' she manages to say.

Sean turns and hugs Gracie, and Gracie blushes and laughs.

Then he's gone too, haring off up the steps, back to the Lodge, to Dan, and then to LA. Gone.

They take the long way back to the hotel, by the beach, Gracie talking animatedly and Annie mindlessly agreeing every now and then. Annie's head is throbbing, her eyes stinging with unshed tears. Gracie chatters about what Sean has told her, about how she is planning her trip to America. In between handstands and cartwheels, Gracie tells her she wants to see Disneyland, Universal

Studios, SeaWorld, Hollywood, and take a helicopter ride through the Grand Canyon.

'Sean says we can meet up whenever I go over. Even if it's years from now, even if he has a girlfriend and I have a boyfriend and . . . Annie?'

'Hmmm?'

'Are you even listening to me?'

Six weeks later . . .

A lot of thought has gone into the choice of location. After considering the implications for everyone involved, they have decided that neutral surroundings will work best. Somewhere they will feel at ease, yet have sufficient privacy to talk about things confidentially. So Dee suggested they book rooms in the smart hotel in Kenmare with the beautiful spa attached. That way, she said, they could all escape to their respective rooms, or hide in a cubicle with cotton pads on their eyes, or have their frustrations soothed away by the firm hands of a masseuse, which should all ensure that they don't resort to killing each other. They all agree this is a very sensible idea.

They arrived at lunchtime and spent a very relaxing afternoon having various treatments, or in Annie's case, swimming repetitive lengths in the pool, and are now gathered together for an early dinner.

Annie cannot get over the change in her sister. Dee looks healthy, has put on weight, and seems calmer and happier than Annie could ever have imagined, particularly given their last encounter. Breda is overjoyed at the change in her daughter, and trying very hard to behave as if everything is absolutely normal. As if they haven't, as a family, been through a seismic shift.

Barbara is her usual unflappable self, prostrate with relief, she says, to escape her husband and small children for a night.

The dining room is fairly empty at this time, and their table is secluded, partially obscured by a large pillar, and looks out through walls of glass to what might be a rain forest of ferns and greenery. The lighting both inside and out is muted, calming, with scattered tea lights flickering between them. It is very peaceful, rather otherworldly.

They are nursing their coffees when Dee finally says what she's been planning to say all along.

'Annie, I've already had a long talk with Mum, but there's something I need to say to you too.'

Annie nods. 'Okay.'

Dee takes a breath. 'I want to apologise, I *need* to apologise for my horrible behaviour.'

'Dee, you don't have to say a—'

'Yes, I do, Annie, and I really need you to listen to me. If you hadn't come to the house that day, I don't know what could have happened. And all those times you tried to help me, look out for me, and I wouldn't listen, wouldn't let you. It was all stupid, *stupid* pride. I've learned so much already in therapy, but I didn't need it to tell me that I was always envious of you, Annie . . . no, make that downright jealous.'

Annie's mouth drops open. Barbara and Breda smile in sympathy.

'No please, just listen. I really need to say this. It's very hard, but it's very healing for me, and for you too, I hope. I've been jealous of you for as long as I can remember. It probably started out as simple sibling rivalry when you came along, but you were always so clever, and it was so obvious that Dad adored you.'

'Dad adores *you*, he always has,' Annie says.

'Yes, I know, but it's you he looks up to, respects. And I understand why. I was jealous of your courage to leave Ireland, to make a new, exciting life for yourself, your business success . . . everything really. You have to understand . . .' she goes on, 'the thing about alcohol, or any drug really, is that it stunts your emotional development from the time you begin relying on it. So for most of my adult life I've been stuck in adolescence, emotionally speaking. That should explain a lot.' She gives a wry smile. 'It means the choices I made were not good ones and my behaviour was juvenile, at best. And I'm so, *so* sorry I haven't been the sister you deserved, or needed. But from here on in, all that's going to change, I promise. I'm going to be the best sister I can be. Just as I'm determined to be the real mother Gracie needs.'

'Oh, Dee.' Annie shakes her head. 'You have what I'd trade everything in the world for. If you knew how I always envied you having Gracie. What on earth does any of the other stuff matter?'

'I know, Annie. I know that now, but I just needed to explain it to you.'

'I'm so pleased you can be open about all this.' Annie is astonished by this new version of her sister. 'It's so brave of you. I had no idea. I only wish I had, then maybe I could have helped.'

'There's something else, Annie.' Dee glances at Breda and Barbara, who have been listening intently to every word. 'Something else I need to say to you.'

Annie looks anxiously at Breda and Barbara, but they are calm and attentive.

'Dee, please don't tell me you're not my real sister, or that we're both adopted or something. I'm not sure I could take any more family revelations.' She laughs nervously.

'No, Annie, this is about you. Because I mean what I say about being the best sister I can be to you, so I'm going to speak to you very honestly now and I want you to take on board what I'm going to say.'

Annie's eyes widen, she feels suddenly uncomfortable, claustrophobic. She glances over at the door, but as if reading her mind, Barbara gently lays her hand over hers. Annie looks at her, and she smiles reassuringly. Dee is looking at her, and Breda. Annie feels like a rabbit caught in the headlights, about to be mowed down by a truck

'One of the things I've learned in rehab is that when children grow up in an alcoholic household, they adopt certain characteristics, personality types, call it what you will . . . In my case, I repeated Dad's pattern – the alcohol, the chaos, the avoidance. You, on the other hand, are the classic Rescuer. I always joked about you being a control freak when we were younger, but it's much more invidious than that. You're the one who constantly tries to fix things, to right the wrongs, rewrite history, that's your way of coping with it all. But Annie, this is disastrous in relationships.'

She puts up a hand as Annie tries to speak. 'Please, bear with me, just hear me out. We are worried about you, concerned for you. Your professional life has been a huge success, but your personal life isn't. And now, at least, I understand why. And you really need to understand why as well. None of us can ever control another person in a relationship – we may try to, but it inevitably fails – and that idea of an intimate, uncontrollable relationship is terrifying to someone like you. No, please, don't interrupt. You don't even realise you're a commitment-phobe. And none of this would matter if you were twenty-one, but you're not, you're thirty-six and time is going by. Think about it, Annie. You had Philip, who adored you and was the perfect boyfriend. You were happy with him for years, yet just two weeks before the wedding you called the whole thing off.'

Annie sits back in her chair and laughs. 'I don't believe this! Yes, I called it off. I fell in love with someone else! Remember? It was the only honourable thing *to* do!'

But Dee persists. 'You call it falling in love. I call it a subconscious choice to choose someone who was notoriously commitment-shy himself. It's what Ed was best known for, Annie. He left every woman he'd ever been with . . . and eventually that included you. But forget Ed, he doesn't matter now. But here's the thing, we think Dan does matter.'

'What the—'

'She's right, love,' Breda interjects. 'Just listen, Annie, we all have your best interests at heart here. Go on, Dee.'

'It's obvious you're in love with the guy. We all saw it, long before it probably dawned on you, Annie! I was even jealous of that. And we know he's asked you to go back with him . . .'

'How the hell do you know that?' Annie is furious. 'Not that it's any business of yours!'

'He came to see me, love.' Breda's eyes are bright. 'He told me how he felt about you, told me he'd asked you and that you turned him down.'

'So you see why we're concerned, Annie.'

'I think you're stark raving mad! The lot of you! Remember, for just a minute, will you, everything we've been through these last few weeks. You've been in rehab, Dee, and are in the process of leaving John. Mum's selling the hotel and leaving Dad. And . . . and you . . .' She looks helplessly at Barbara. 'You're my best friend! You know me better than anyone. What? You all expect me to just up sticks and follow a man I've just met and leave you, Mum, and you, Dee . . . and the hotel . . . and . . . and *Gracie*? I can't believe you'd—'

'Gracie has *me*, Annie. I'm her mother. I may not have been a very good one, but I'm going to be a great one. She has her grandmother too, and the hotel will sell or not sell, Mum may leave Dad . . . but none of those things are your concern. They're not your problems to solve. They're ours.'

Barbara squeezes her hand. 'Annie, you're my dearest friend and you always will be. I owe every bit of happiness I've found in life to you. If it wasn't for you introducing me to Mike, I don't like to think what my life would have become. So, please, listen to us, listen to your sister. Dee is right. You *have* to stop rescuing people. It's time for you to rescue yourself, to rescue your own life. Don't abandon yourself, Annie. You're the one who needs help and support now, don't be too proud to take it.' She looks over at Dee, who picks up the thread again.

'Annie, maybe Dan won't be the one for you, but we think he's a great guy. And Sean loves you, Gracie told me as much. This is a wonderful opportunity, but you're sitting back and letting it pass you by. At least give him a chance. You have to find and create your *own* family, and you can't let the past get in the way of that.'

Annie looks at them, incredulous, speechless, wondering why on earth tears are running down their faces. Dee is holding one of her hands and Barbara has grabbed the other. Breda is dabbing a tissue to her eyes. They can't possibly be right . . . they *couldn't* be. But if they are so wrong, why have their words touched something deep inside her, something that is slowly, painfully shattering?

And then she is sobbing, her head in her hands. She can't bat away Dee's words, she can't fight them, because they have spoken to the heart of her. She cries and cries, but she is enveloped by the love, kindness and understanding of these women. And even though she feels she might break apart, something loosens and opens in her heart. It takes her a moment to recognise it as hope, unfurling as surely and delicately as a bud.

* * *

Almost 5,000 miles separate Ballyanna, County Kerry, from the great state of California, USA, and of those many miles, about 3,067 of them consist of the Atlantic Ocean. Annie Sullivan cannot help being reminded of this fact as she looks out at that very ocean, from the sand on which she is sitting. Today, the Atlantic appears calm and serene, unlike her own feelings, which are considerably more turbulent.

An awful lot has happened to Annie in the relatively short space of time since she has come home to Ireland, almost all of it unintentional. She has left a career, met an extraordinary man, confronted her family's demons, and her own, and now, she has bought a hotel. She hasn't told anyone about that just yet. That can wait.

But the most important of these events is the fact that Annie has fallen in love. She has tried to ignore this fact, deny it, evade it, rename it, but all to no avail. This frightens her, because Annie is terrified of love. She knows from experience that it can entice you, delight you, seduce you, consume you, and then betray and abandon you in a million different ways. So she is nervous, sitting on her rock, looking out to sea. She feels vulnerable, a little raw, a little too exposed. But she knows she has to do this, or she will forever wonder, *what if?*

She has thought about the words she will use over and over, and no amount of rearranging makes them look appropriate.

I've been stupid and I'm miserable, and if your offer still stands, then I'd really love to come and stay with you and Sean for a while.

She signs it *Annie,* with an *x,* and then she takes a deep breath and presses Send. She wings a little prayer with the words, because second chances are not granted to everyone. And although she has had much good fortune in other areas of her life, she has now accepted that she possesses quite a talent for sabotaging her personal life. She will be devastated if she realises she has done this again, finds out that it is too late.

So she waits, although she knows she may not hear back for some time. There is the time difference, and any number of reasons why he wouldn't be checking his phone just now.

The plaque that marks the location where the submarine Atlantic cable came ashore is behind her, with Cable Lodge sitting on the cliff above it. She thinks of all the messages that have made their way back and forth across that same ocean, wonders at the lives they changed, the people they affected, the drama of life played out beneath these waves. Even now, from this very spot, her simple, heartfelt message will travel underneath the sea, by cable, all the way to America, just as the very first ones did all those decades ago.

It's ironic, it occurs to her now, that although the manner in which we can say the things we say is constantly changing, that no matter how sophisticated technology becomes, the things we say remain very much the same. She is not the first person to wait anxiously for a reply to a message, and she certainly won't be the last.

She climbs up the steps from the beach, her phone in the pocket of her jeans, and reminds herself that life goes on, one way or another. She has done what she can, now she must be patient. She is just at the top of the steps when her phone vibrates and she hears the distinctive *ping*. When she takes it out, her hands are shaking.

Barry has died. I'm with Jerry now. Funeral on Wednesday at 11am. Mum. X

Annie's heart plummets. Poor Breda. And poor Jerry. They'll be heartbroken. She sends up a little prayer for Barry. 'Safe journey,' she whispers. 'Rest in peace.'

When her phone starts ringing in her hand, she almost drops it in shock.

'Hello?'

She hears the smile in his voice, groggy with sleep, when he says, as if he were beside her and not 5,000 miles away, 'So, when are you coming over?'

And she is laughing, and crying, and it takes her a moment to catch her breath and reply, 'Soon, very soon.'

Acknowledgements

As always, grateful thanks to the terrific Ciara Doorley, Editorial Director, and the wonderful team at Hachette Books Ireland. Thanks in particular to editor Rachel Pierce, whose structural insights made this a far better book.

To my wonderful agent, Felicity Blunt, of Curtis Brown UK, who believed in *The Summer Visitors* throughout various incarnations (and titles!), and whose crucial early insights and thoughtful comments proved utterly invaluable.

Grateful thanks also to Dorothy Rudd of Waterville, Co. Kerry who gave so generously of her time and information on the early workings of the Waterville cable station.

Thank you to my Writer Girls (you know who you are!) who make me laugh, and believe in me when I can't believe in myself.

Thank you to my family and friends for putting up with me when I am incoherent with stress and approaching deadlines! Especially Carole and Lucy Shubotham, for support, laughter and unparalleled dog walking!

To Freddie, my beloved four-legged companion, who reads me like a book and knows just when to be good and quiet, or when to insist on dragging me out for our walk.

Heartfelt thanks to my dear friend Sister Mary Carmel,

and her Poor Clare Sisters in St Damian's, www.pccdamians.ie, and to my friends in the Merci Prayer Group, and to everyone who lit candles or said even the tiniest prayer for me . . . I am convinced none of this would be possible without your pleadings on my behalf! 'More things are wrought by prayer than this world dreams of' (Alfred Lord Tennyson).

Thank you to my local, in Sandymount, www.booksonthegreen.com and booksellers throughout the country, who do such a wonderful job, and of course thanks to you, dear reader, you make the long, often frustrating, hours at the laptop worthwhile, and none of this would happen without you. I really hope you enjoy *The Summer Visitors*, do let me know, I love hearing from you.

www.fionaobrien.com

Twitter: fionaobrienbks

Facebook: www.facebook.com/Fiona O'Brien

The inspiration for *The Summer Visitors*

For as long as I can remember, holidays have meant one place for me, and that is Waterville, Co. Kerry. I arrived in a pram, and never left, well, not in my heart, at any rate. I can't remember why we began going there, there were no family connections, my mother was from Donegal, and my father from Dublin, but somewhere along the line, we switched to the Kingdom, and Waterville and I never looked back.

It never rained, either, or so it seemed back in those heady bucket and spade days of the '60's. I made firm friends with the little girl whose parents owned the hotel we stayed in (or occasionally we would rent one of the cable station houses), and the few weeks passed in a happy blur of horse riding, galloping bareback along a local beach, sand yachting, along Reenroe, fishing outings on Lough Currane and Derriana, and trips to Skellig Michael and of course long days spent at Derrynane, and still it wasn't raining . . .

I had the privilege of meeting Charlie Chaplin on several occasions, who at the time seemed like just another nice old man. He and his wife Oona visited that same hotel, with various of their eight children, accompanied by their two governesses (now *that* we did find intriguing!). Two of his girls were our age, a year older and a year younger respectively, and they became part of the gang. We knew their father had something to do with funny movies, and sure, the name rang a bell, but the quiet, smiling old man who took afternoon tea outside on the hotel veranda – accompanied by his younger wife in headscarf and dark glasses, who seemed to be constantly knitting – and raved about the local 'air' bore no resemblance to the Little Tramp of TV fame that I associated the name with. We pestered his kids (who were endlessly patient with us) to know if he ever did anything funny at home . . . and they said apart from the occasional trick at the dinner table, that no, he didn't. However, I do remember a certain amount of mirth on one occasion in this hotel favoured by keen anglers. Every evening, as was the custom, the best of the day's catch would be laid out on trays in the front hall for all to admire, in descending degrees of impressiveness, from the largest salmon to some reasonably sized trout. One evening, before dinner, there was a larger than usual crowd gathered around the display, all laughing heartily, the reason becoming clear on closer inspection – added to the catch was one tiny sardine, strategically placed last. Charlie had gone out and bought a tin for that very purpose.

So it was only natural to me that I would want to set a book in the vicinity. I had always been fascinated by the local cable station, by the idea of this community within a community, so to speak, and its groundbreaking effect on global communications. Originally, this story had an historical aspect, featuring the station in its heyday, in the 1890s, but as so often happens with novels, the book took a different turn.

The theme of *The Summer Visitors* is communication, and the metaphor is the cable station – the submarine Atlantic cable being the first direct means of communication between Europe and America. And so my visiting American, Daniel O'Connell (yes, I named him after the Great Liberator, deliberately! Because communication is what liberates my characters) arrives in Ballyanna, to carry out his research for a documentary on the history of communications. With him are his twin boys, one of whom doesn't speak . . . then we meet the Sullivan family, who have communication issues of their own . . . the rest unfolds as you've no doubt learned by now if you've reached this point! But just in case you're peeking ahead – no spoilers . . .

I must point out, yet again, that Ballyanna as I have described it, and all its characters bear no resemblance to anyone living or dead in Waterville or surrounding areas. But writing this book has brought back a lot of happy memories just the same. I have travelled far and wide in the intervening years but my heart remains in Waterville, and I still think Derrynane, with its lovely sixth-century ruins and graveyard on Abbey Island, is the prettiest beach in the world, and if I can't be there all the time, at least I can look at it as it is my laptop screensaver! I do hope you've enjoyed reading *The Summer Visitors* as much as I enjoyed writing it, and if you should find yourself on the wonderful Ring of Kerry, then do drop in to Waterville, and say hello from me.

Previously by Fiona O'Brien

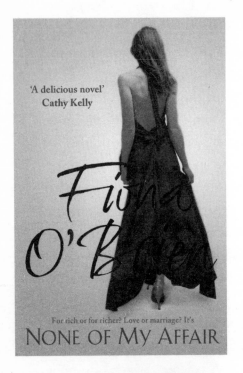

'A delicious novel'
Cathy Kelly

For rich or for richer? Love or marriage? It's
NONE OF MY AFFAIR

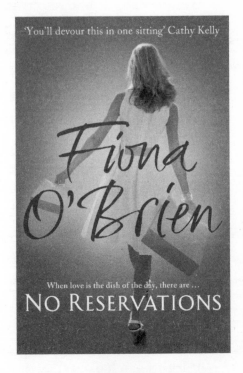

'You'll devour this in one sitting' Cathy Kelly

When love is the dish of the day, there are ...
NO RESERVATIONS

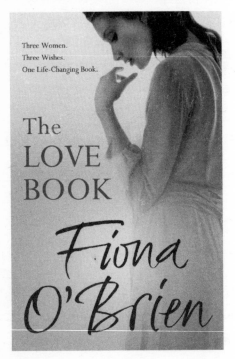

Three Women.
Three Wishes.
One Life-Changing Book.

The LOVE BOOK

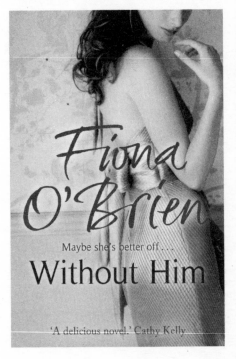

Maybe she's better off ...
Without Him

'A delicious novel.' Cathy Kelly

Also available as ebooks